“Feel-good author” (*Nestled in a Book*) **Jennifer Probst** began her “sexy, satisfying” (*Kirkus Reviews*) Kinnections matchmakers series with these acclaimed novels!

SEARCHING FOR PERFECT

“Entertaining and engaging and real. . . . Jennifer Probst is a romance writing superstar. . . . [A] fantastic series.”

—*Bookish Bella*

“A wonderfully moving, deeply emotional, steamy, sexy, fantastic story of hope, healing, and love. 5 huge loving stars!”

—*Sizzling Book Club*

SEARCHING FOR SOMEDAY

“A sophisticated, sexy romance . . . witty, passionate.”

—*RT Book Reviews*

“Refreshing.”

—*Publishers Weekly*

“Full of emotion and heart. . . . 5 stars!”

—*Sizzling Book Club*

“Delightfully romantic and fun. . . . One of the best contemporary authors!”

—*Under the Covers*

“Offers both he

—*Booklist Online*

ALSO BY JENNIFER PROBST

The Searching For Series

Searching for Someday

Searching for Perfect

"Searching for You" in *Baby, It's Cold Outside*

Searching for Beautiful

The Marriage to a Billionaire Series

The Marriage Bargain

The Marriage Trap

The Marriage Mistake

The Marriage Merger

searching for always

a novel

JENNIFER PROBST

POCKET BOOKS

New York London Toronto Sydney New Delhi

Pocket Books
An Imprint of Simon & Schuster, Inc.
1230 Avenue of the Americas
New York, NY 10020

First Pocket Books paperback edition July 2015

Manufactured in the United States of America

10 9 8 7 6 5 4 3 2 1

ISBN 978-1-4767-8012-2
ISBN 978-1-4767-8013-9 (ebook)

"It takes great courage to see the world in
all its tainted glory, and still to love it."
—*An Ideal Husband*

This book is dedicated to my dog Lester, who is waiting for me at Rainbow Bridge. Thank you for being my faithful writing companion and friend. Your beautiful old soul made my world a better place. Mommy loves you.

prologue

OFFICER STONE PETTY was having a shit day.

It started with some type of brownout that killed his alarm and made him late. He despised tardiness in all forms and enjoyed a morning routine that set him up for the day. Hot, black coffee. Toast with butter, and real bacon. None of that turkey junk. Reading the paper, a quick shower, and taking his damn time.

Instead, he raced to get cleaned up and dressed, forced to skip everything and stuck with the horror that was called coffee in the station. Not even officially on duty, he'd been forced to stop a teenager speeding, dealing with his general mouthiness and hormonal idiocy that hadn't taught him yet not to talk back to people in authority.

After a few hours on his beat, a foul smell in his squad car drove him crazy. He finally pulled over, trying not to gag, and discovered a pile of dog crap buried in a paper bag in the trunk. Sons of bitches. It must've been a boring night at the station, since one of his coworkers had decided to liven things up by pulling the literal tiger's tail. He loved his job, but sometimes he wanted to beat the hell out of them all. Boredom was the worst crime in the police station, and drove the guys to entertain themselves. On a slow fall night in Verily, guess he'd been the victim.

Plotting his revenge, he got rid of the poop, decided to skip lunch, and proceeded to roll over a busted glass bottle and pierce his tire.

Stone realized the Fates were against him today. He was desperately trying to quit smoking, but the thought of the sweet smoke filling his lungs killed him. He dragged in a breath and tried to concentrate on the nicotine patch on his arm, working overtime. He didn't need it. He was strong. He could beat the nasty habit, even though he loved it so hard, he'd pick smoking over anything else.

Finally, the awful craving eased. Good. His best bet was just to clock in enough time to get the day done, lay low, and try again tomorrow. He changed the tire, tearing a small hole in the knee of his uniform, and sweating profusely. It was one of those weird Indian summer days in October, and he'd worn his long sleeves today. Sweat trickled down his brow and under his arms, making him crave another shower. His temper frayed, but he held tight and swore to have patience. Anger got him in trouble every time. Like some kind of downhill roller coaster ride, it descended him into disaster. He was on a tight leash to begin with and needed to chill and ride out the rest of the day.

Calmly.

His partner had taken the morning off and should be hooking up with him within the hour. Devine always settled him with his easy humor. They worked well together, and long enough to call him his friend.

When he got back in the squad car, his speaker beeped.

"Car forty-three. Possible domestic abuse on Two Sycamore Street."

Stone reached for the radio. "Car forty-three en route."

"Backup is needed. Officer Devine on the way."

"Copy."

He eased onto the road and headed toward the house. Any type of domestic abuse required two officers on the scene, which he respected. Hell, it had always been his hot spot anyway, and they did very well with bad cop/good cop. With Devine's movie star looks, and his own rough appearance, everything balanced.

He drove past Main Street in Verily, enjoying the small-town charm and sprawling river views. A bit eclectic and weird for him, with the crazy artists, cafés, and mass of organic food, clothing, and wellness centers, but Verily called to him in some strange way. He always wondered what it would feel like to be one of those people. Centered. Calm. Happy.

He dealt with such intense emotions, and a dark, brooding anger inside of him, that living in Verily was like stepping near the light.

Stone frowned at his sudden poetic thoughts and refocused. He'd reached Sycamore.

He pulled to the curb a few feet away and studied the scene. No nosy neighbors out, but it didn't mean people weren't watching from their windows. He checked his watch. Devine should arrive in a minute. Climbing out of the car, he strolled around the house, scanning for clues and straining his ears to catch any type of noise.

The white Victorian seemed a bit shambled. Peeling paint. Broken step. Porch sagged. The windows were dirty, but he noted a small vegetable garden on the side that was neat and weed-free. Someone had cared and maintained it well. A pink tricycle with streamers that had seen better days lay abandoned in the driveway. Was that crying? His muscles tensed.

"No!"

The female scream turned his blood cold. A crash echoed through one of the half-open windows, and a child joined in with the screaming.

"Bitch!"

Stone shot to the door. Knocked. "Police, open up."

Another crash. Stone grabbed his radio. "Officer entering premises at Two Sycamore. Still awaiting backup." No time to wait for Devine. Enough suspicion of bodily harm to break in.

He did.

The door was open so he shot through.

The scene before him was out of his worst nightmare.

A big, meaty guy dressed in jeans and bare chested beating the crap out of the woman, probably his wife. She was trapped in the corner, hands over her face to protect it while he punched her. Her screams punctured the air, but that wasn't what made him lose it.

It was the child.

A pretty girl, probably around five, sobbed and clutched her father's leg, begging him to stop hurting Mommy. Stone had almost reached him, ready to scoop up the girl so she was safe and get the asshole off, but he was too late.

The guy paused in bashing his wife's face, turned, and picked up the child.

Then threw her across the room.

The girl hit the wall with a bang. Slumped to the floor in a crumpled pile of delicate bones. Her soft blond hair covered her face. She didn't move.

Things happened in slow motion. Stone had been through enough shit to know he needed to keep calm, get the medics, handle the situation, protect the unprotected. His training usually kicked in with no pause.

Instead, he was ripped to another time and place, and the haze of red swarmed his vision and his logic.

Stone grabbed the man in one fast motion. He got an impression of surprised bloodshot eyes, fingers clawing and trying to pry him off, and shrieks peppering the air.

He hit. And hit. And hit.

The man slumped to the ground, but Stone didn't stop. He punched with all his might, all his emotion and locked-up rage that came through to punish a monster who hurt defenseless women and liked it.

He didn't know how much time had passed before he was dragged off the guy. Ambulance alarms sounded in the air, and Devine was shaking him by the shoulders, saying his name over and over, trying to get him to focus and get back to the light. Medics rushed in, cries rang out, and when Stone Petty came to, he realized it was too late.

The damage had already been done.

Yeah. All in all, it was a shit day.

one

ARILYN MEADOWS LOOKED around the cheery bungalow that was now her new home. Boxes lay half-opened, clothes were stacked in piles, and her foster dogs, Lenny and Mike, were battling over her only pair of expensive shoes. Scarlet red. High heels. Strappy. She'd bought them last month to surprise her lover.

He'd been surprised all right. So had she when she caught him banging one of his yoga students.

The black-and-white rat terrier mixes tumbled over the floor in a challenge to see who'd make the first bite. With their floppy ears and white stripes dividing their faces, her new fosters were a bit too cute to live. They also got away with way too much because of their looks. She opened her mouth to discipline, then shut it. Yes, it was bad for the puppies' training, but it felt kind of good to see them tear those heels apart. She'd never wear them again without that memory clocking her like a sucker punch. At least Lenny and Mike could have some rebellious fun.

The low hum of anger buzzing inside surprised her. She'd spent most of her days searching for peace, kindness, and harmony within the world. Last week, she would've announced to anyone she'd found that quiet place inside and had never been happier.

Not this week.

Arilyn held back a sigh and began hanging her clothes up. Organic cottons and linens wrinkled too easily, especially with no dryer. She smoothed her hand down the soft fabrics and lined them up neatly in the closet. At least her new place was sound. After discovering mold at her last rental, and weeks of dealing with bad electric and burst pipes, her friend Genevieve MacKenzie offered to let her rent the quirky bungalow. Thank goodness, Gen had found the love of her life and was now moving in with her soul mate, Wolfe. Even better, she had left an empty cottage to rent. It was situated close to her job, and two doors down from her other friend Kate, who she worked with at Kinnections matchmaking agency.

She tried to concentrate on the positive spin of finding a great place, especially one that allowed her to take in foster dogs on a regular basis, but her usual attitude had taken a hit. Besides anger, depression threatened like a nasty rumble of thunder before a storm. Dammit, she was supposed to be in Cape May on a romantic getaway. She was supposed to be making love and finally working through the kinks in their relationship. She was supposed to hear those magic words after five years of an on-again, off-again affair.

You're the one.

Marriage. Maybe a family. Both of them teaching yoga together in his studio, on a quest for higher peace and satisfaction while they loved each other with open hearts and souls.

Her fingers clenched around the gauzy cream blouse. Instead, she'd walked into that studio and watched her life crumble before her.

The woman bent over, hands on the floor, naked ass in the air. Her lover pounded her from behind, his long gorgeous dark hair streaming down his back, fingers gripped around her hips, driving in and out of her while she moaned and groaned, and he gave tiny grunts of satisfaction.

The woman screamed. He laughed darkly, lifted his hand, and smacked her naked ass. She yelped. Then he did it again, and again, until her rear turned red and she was coming and screaming . . .

Arilyn turned from the closet and pushed her clenched fists against her eyes. The image burned like acid.

He'd never made love to her that way, with a violent, dirty need combined with lust. He practiced tantric sex, a slow-moving, spiritual, gentle swell of need that climbed gradually. Their lovemaking took place in many locations, but it was always completely controlled, quiet, deeply satisfying. He worshipped her body with his. Never bent it to his will or ripped crazy orgasms from her.

She'd never forget his face. So deeply satisfied, like he was surrendering in a way he never could with her. Was this what he'd wanted the whole time? Had he believed she couldn't handle his sexual desires? The almost violent, possessive, hungry primal instincts inside him?

Fighting a shudder, she began to unpack her crystals and meditation supplies. How long had she made excuses for his inability to truly commit to her? Yes, he revered his privacy and followed a spiritual path without conventions, societal role plays, and sexual expectations. That was what she'd loved about him.

They viewed the world similarly and wanted to make a difference. He was a workaholic, but in a good way. Always driven to help others in their journey. Another reason he was afraid to commit to a long-term relationship. He feared she'd become demanding and force him to quit his beloved career.

But after years of being hidden in the background, while he refused to meet her friends or family, and conducted their affair after hours and in secret like a torrid affair, she'd finally given him the ultimatum. The idea that no one ever uttered his first name faded from being a thrilling secret to a quiet humiliation.

Thirty approached. She craved permanence and a chance to have a family. Was that too much to ask? She didn't want to pigeonhole him, only to grow and change by his side. After his first indiscretion, she forced herself to trust him again. After all, he apologized, confessing his fear that love would overpower his spiritual path. He promised never to cheat again. As the in-house counselor at Kinnections matchmaking agency, Arilyn advised clients many times that a relationship couldn't work halfway, so she forgave.

Things finally changed. They'd been happy for a few months, and he even agreed to meet her family.

Humiliation cut through her. The fire crystal shook in her hands. She breathed deep and tried to absorb the healing powers meant to relieve sharp anxiety and induce calm. Stupid. His face when she opened the door haunted her.

Those gorgeous dark eyes widened with shock. Her gaze swept over his beloved face, taking in the high brow bone, long, sharp nose, square jaw. He stared at her, not moving, not speaking, while the silence beat around them in angry waves of energy.

"Arilyn."

Her name on his lips made her shudder. The musical, lilting quality of his timbre usually hypnotized her, whether in yoga class or the bedroom. The hurt rolled over her in waves, and she longed to curl up in a ball in her bed and try to make sense of it. Instead, she just stood there like an idiot, waiting for him to say something.

"I'm sorry, Arilyn." His voice deepened with grief and regret. His eyes filled with sadness. "I broke my promise. My body is weak, but my heart still beats for you. It always will. You must find a way to forgive me."

No. For the rest of her life, she'd remember him grunting and coming in another woman's body. And for the first time in five years, the box deep inside of her finally locked. She'd never let him back into her heart or life again. She'd closed the box many, many times before, but never locked it.

A tiny click echoed in her ears like a gunshot.

It was finally over.

Her heart withered in her chest, drying up any tears that she might have shed. All that was left was a shell and a burning emptiness she'd never get over.

Arilyn studied the man she'd loved for the last time. Her voice came out like a winter's storm. Cold. Brutal. Dead.

"It's over. Don't call, text, or contact me ever again."

Arilyn placed an amethyst stone next to the fire and began setting up her meditation corner. Lenny and Mike collapsed on the wooden floor, temporarily exhausted and exhilarated. Pieces of red straps and a chewed heel lay around them in destructive glory. She envied them. Her emotions bubbled beneath the surface worse than a witches' brew. Maybe a grueling session of ashtanga yoga would help her sweat out some of the mess. Arilyn studied the crystals before her and plucked the dark red stone from its perch. Definitely garnet. Used for balancing overemotional stakes and stuck anger.

She twisted it onto a cord and slipped it over her neck. Maybe work was the key. Keep busy. Two weeks had passed for a solid grieving period, and now it was time to focus. She needed to get the cottage in order, plant her herb garden, run the dog shelter fund-raiser, and work on the new computer program for Kinnections. Since she quit her ex-lover's yoga studio, students had been asking her when she'd be teaching on her own. Maybe she'd rent the firehouse and give classes there. No reason for her own students to suffer just because she refused to set foot in the Chakras yoga studio.

She placed the fat purple cushion in the center of the woven mat and set up the variety of candles around her spot. Two wide bamboo screens kept it private from onlookers and the pups. The incense sticks went up on the circular table, since Lenny seemed to like them better than the organic treats she regularly purchased. Nothing like pooping out incense. That had been a fun vet visit.

Finally, her sacred spot was complete. Her stack of meditation CDs lay next to her ancient stereo, but she disliked wearing pods or headphones when she meditated. Arilyn rolled to her feet and grabbed some matches and the bunch of dried sage she'd brought with her. Final task before making dinner. Each time she set up residence in a new place, she cleared all the old energy to start fresh.

God knows she needed a new slate.

Her throat tightened as she began to light the sage. All of her best friends were now in strong, healthy relationships leading to marriage. As the final single of the bunch, her heart squeezed with envy. When was it her turn? She'd worked so hard in all aspects of her life to be a good person, to open herself to love, to become spiritually sound to engage in a relationship that would bring her joy. Dammit, while others squandered their time partying, being selfish, and giving in to their ids, she did the hard work trying to transform herself. She did everything . . . right.

Right?

Guess not. She'd wasted the best years of her life stuck with a man who consistently lied and manipulated in the name of soul-searching. How could she have been so far off with her instincts? Was she just a chump after all? Was she even worthy of the kind of love she dreamed of, the kind that her friends had found?

She blinked furiously to clear her vision. Stop. She was being whiny and ridiculous. She had a great, satisfying life filled with goals and surrounded by plenty of people who loved her. Arilyn lifted the bunch of sage in the air, closed her eyes, and envisioned a home filled with love, peace, and light. The smoke trickled in thin wisps as she moved from room to room, including the closet and bathroom, paying particular attention to the bedroom and kitchen where most intense emotions were expressed.

Finally, the cottage was properly cleansed. She blew out the flame, moved the small pots containing her herbs to the windowsill for proper light, and grabbed the bottle of celebratory wine in the refrigerator. She deserved alcohol tonight. It would go nicely with her veggie burger and steamed edamame. First, she'd complete her asanas, do some pranayama, and then eat. Tomorrow, things would look better and she'd feel stronger. Peaceful. Back in control.

Arilyn was sure of it.

two

"WE'VE GOT A problem, Petty."

Stone sat in the battered chair and tried to look unconcerned. When the chief called him in and shut the door, he knew he was screwed. The question was simple. How screwed was he?

Since the incident, he'd been whispered about, endlessly questioned, and judged from his past. Devine backed him up and denied he beat up the husband, citing self-defense. Of course, the blood, bruises, and almost concussion were pretty good evidence. Seemed no charges were filed, though, due to the domestic abuse problem and the child who ended up in the hospital close to having brain trauma.

Thank God, she'd finally been discharged, and she and her mother had disappeared into a women's shelter.

Basically, the whole incident was a clusterfuck of mega proportions. All because he didn't wait for Devine and lost his infamous temper.

Chief Will Williams, aka the Dick, stared hard at him from behind a mess of paperwork, pizza plates, and empty Big Gulp Dr Peppers. He despised paperwork, investigations, and anything that brought any tarnish to the small Verily police force. Till now, Stone had been clean, especially with Devine backing him up. The Dick looked upon Devine as the golden boy on the force. As Devine's partner, Stone had crept up on the chief's approval ladder.

"I'm sorry, sir." He kept his voice low and respectful. "I screwed up, I know I did. But he almost killed his daughter, and I had to move fast."

"Oh, you moved all right, you son of a bitch. Do you know what would have happened if the jerk had sued the force? I'm talking newspaper headlines. Page one. We'd be done. Understand?"

"Yes. It won't happen again."

"I can't risk it happening again." Williams rubbed his forehead, and Stone got a bad feeling in his gut. He'd figured on a tongue-lashing, maybe probation, but this looked more serious. What would he do if he got fired? Panic flared, but he fought it back down. No way. He'd do anything needed to stay. "Look, Petty, you're a good cop. Thorough, badass, and I still think a good addition here. The guys like you. But this anger scares the crap out of me. It's the reason you left your last precinct, and I don't need baggage following you here."

"I've been here a year already, sir, without incident."

"All you need is one incident to banish all the good. If you want to stay, I have some new terms."

Relief hit. Okay, this he could deal with. A few sessions with the shrink, maybe. A slap on the wrist. Forced vacay. Whatever he got hit with, he'd do it with a smile and show his boss he could be trusted.

"Of course. Whatever you think is best, I'll do it."

Williams choked out a laugh. "Let's hope. You'll be enrolled in a six-week anger management class."

He pulled out some papers from a thick manila folder and threw them on the desk. "Suspension for two weeks. Devine has already been briefed. He'll remain your partner when you return, but he's lead and you follow."

Stone winced. He hated playing second when they'd been equals, but, hell, he'd swallow it. Two weeks with no work was scary, but he'd swallow it, too, since he had no choice. But anger management? Yikes, that was a new one. He grabbed the paper and began scanning the document.

"And don't think you're gonna show up at these classes and breeze through. From what I've heard, she's hard-core and incorporates an array of unorthodox treatments. In other words, it's gonna be hell."

Private counseling sessions. Yoga? No way. What did yoga have to do with anger management? Charity and community service? Meditation? His heart pounded and sweat pricked his skin. Holy crap, would she force him to sit on the floor cross-legged and chant to Buddha? This wasn't a few hours of lying on a couch and sharing feelings. This was sleepaway camp where the serial killer came in and offed everyone in his path.

Yeah. He could only hope.

Williams stared at him as if expecting a temper explosion or strong denials. Stone choked back his righteous refusal to be a trained pony, because his damn job was his life.

He had nothing else left to give.

"Fine. I'll do it."

"You need to sign."

Stone glared but grabbed the pen and scrawled his

name on the line. Like he had a choice. Williams actually looked a bit surprised at his easy acceptance.

"You start Monday. Take the weekend off and get your head together."

"Who's running the classes?" Stone asked.

"Meadows. Arilyn Meadows. I guess she's part owner of that matchmaking agency, Kinnections, but she also does classes on the side in anger management, counseling, and yoga."

Great. That's where the crazy stuff came from. The name rang a bell in his head, and a faint memory tried to grab hold. How did he know that name? So familiar . . .

"Anyway, do your time, and don't let me see this trouble again. Now get outta here."

"Yes, sir."

He left the office and stopped to talk with some of the other guys who wanted to find out about his punishment. He took some ribbing, but generally everyone had his back. Good thing. He'd just reached his desk when he froze, his brain finally making the connection.

Arilyn Meadows.

He'd met her over the summer during a domestic abuse case with one of her best friends. A long, lithe body. Hip-length strawberry hair and grass-green eyes.

Also the biggest pain in the ass he'd ever met.

She was prickly, mouthy, and superior. She razzed him about smoking, accused him of slacking on the job, and had the balls to call him on the endless cliché that he ate donuts in his spare time. She drove him crazy, yet he'd responded to her physically in an instant. A strange, burning chemistry slammed through him when her gaze caught his, and he had the weird instinct to do things to her.

Sexual things.

There was something in those vivid green eyes that called to him. Secrets hidden he wanted to unearth. A demand to make her surrender.

Nuts.

He was certifiably nuts to get a hard-on by a hippie with a God complex. The thought of being tortured for six weeks in a room with her almost made him go back to his chief and tell him no.

Almost.

But he had no choice. The nicotine patch on his arm itched. Oh, he wanted a sweet smoke more than anything else. Would give up his last dime of savings for a puff. Instead, he gritted his teeth and drew out the one crumpled pack of Marlboros he'd left himself as a reminder. Sticking his nose against the pack, he took a deep breath. The faint scent of tobacco calmed him a bit. Ignoring his coworkers' jibes and laughter, he got himself back together and stuck the pack back in his pocket till the next time. He may miss the habit, but he was nearing forty, loved carbs, red meat, and sugar, and was a walking symbol for an early heart attack. He also despised weakness, and a vice that strong needed to go.

He grabbed his keys and walked out of the station. Now he had to deal with a do-gooder who had no idea what cops went through. Still, he had no choice. Best thing to do was accept it, shore up his defenses, and get through it. A physical reaction meant nothing, and a few hours in a room with her would probably cure any type of attraction. He'd agree to her ridiculous terms, pass the course, and get back to his job and his life.

No. Problem.

"I'M GOING TO SUE you."

Arilyn held her smile. The guy across her desk was a difficult client, full of macho attitude, fear of intimacy, and a bad attitude. Still, she believed in counseling her clients to their full potential in order to be able to pursue a healthy relationship. Since she was also teaching an anger management course, she knew well how to solve difficult issues.

"I'm sorry, Ben. Why don't you tell me what the problem is?"

His eyes narrowed and he leaned forward. "You told me I needed to be a bit softer and approachable around women. You said being a bastard doesn't necessarily get the girl. Does any of this sound familiar?"

She kept smiling and nodded. "Yes, that's correct. Instead of treating women with ego and attitude, letting yourself be a bit more vulnerable and nice to a woman isn't a bad thing. That's the way to find and stay in a solid relationship."

"Bullshit." He had a basset hound kind of a face, with saggy cheeks and a droopy-type mouth. His stocky body was buff, since he worked weights like crazy, and his thick blond waves of hair formed a prideful lion's mane, but Arilyn found his crude mannerisms a definite turnoff. They'd been working with his attitude adjustment for a while.

"Why is it bullshit?" she asked calmly. She dug her fingers into the cushioned arms of her chair and began dragging in long, slow breaths. He was pissing her off, and it wasn't a good sign that she'd rather yell than help him work through his problems. Keep breathing.

"Because I tried it. Met a girl at the bar this weekend and approached. Instead of my usual lines, I gave her my name. Listened to her. Hell, I bought her way too many drinks. When I asked her out, she said no. Said she was more attracted to the dominant kind of man and that we wouldn't fit. Left me at the bar humiliated and broke. Because of you and your stupid advice."

Her smile slipped. Stupid, huh? Maybe he was stupid to think any intelligent woman wouldn't be attracted to a complete macho idiot. "She probably wasn't meant for you, Ben. Perhaps she just wanted one night and not a relationship."

"That's what I wanted, too! I'm over this. Over your counseling and computer surveys just to get a mixer where I may not even connect with anyone. Your agency sucks, and I want my money back or I'll sue."

She'd been well trained. When people dealt with emotions like love and vulnerability, many acted out. The contract was ironclad regarding legal liabilities; Ben would never be able to sue Kinnections. As many happy endings as she had helped with, there were also heartbreakers when a couple just didn't make it. The scenario had occurred many times before, and usually she was able to calm them down, get back on track, and move on.

She opened her mouth.

"Maybe the problem isn't Kinnections but your

lousy attitude problem regarding women," she snapped. "Maybe I haven't set up a mixer yet because I feel sorry for every woman who has to meet you!"

His eyes bugged out. "You can't talk to me like that!"

She leaned forward over her desk to meet him halfway, lowering her voice. "Watch me. You're terminated from Kinnections. Your refund check will be in the mail."

He sat up. "Wait. Maybe we should try again. I saw some of the pics on the website and your clients are hot."

"Good-bye, Ben."

"I'm going to sue you for wrongful termination!"

Arilyn got up from the desk, stormed to the door, and yanked it open. "I'll look forward to the legal papers. Have a good day and thanks for using Kinnections."

He stared at her for a few minutes before slowly getting up and trudging out the door. The other thing she had learned about Ben was that he was a bit of a bully. Stand up to him first, and he backed down immediately. The little bell over the entrance jingled merrily, confirming his exit.

Muttering under her breath, she slammed the counseling room door and marched to her own office. Idiot. A waste of time even trying to get him to see what his real issue was or to treat women as anything other than a bodily ornament for his arm. Better to cut him now and give him his refund. She was sure Kate would understand.

She got back to her desk, moved her mouse, and tried to concentrate on the endless load of work that had piled up. The new computer program had some glitches that needed to be worked out, and she needed to step up her training with Lenny and Mike before she brought them back to the shelter for the adoption process. This morning, she'd found her slippers chewed up, so the little incident with the red shoes hadn't been smart. Parenting a puppy was like raising a toddler, and routine and discipline were key. Of course, their fur ball faces and adorable wide eyes killed her every time.

She reached for her water bottle and chugged the last drop. Proper hydration was the key to good health. Another step she always followed in her endless pursuit of doing the right thing.

The lightbulb crackled and lit.

She did everything right. Always. She listened to authority figures. Treated her body like a temple. Completed karmic service to help others. Kept her mind calm with meditation. Helped others, whether they be human or canine. She gave her full heart and soul to every task, knowing it meant a big difference to do things lovingly rather than grudgingly.

But she ached for more. Something bigger that came to taunt her in the deep night, until she twisted under the sheets and tears stung her eyes with frustration. A yearning for . . .

More.

The familiar anger washed over her. She'd meditated for a full hour last night with a garnet around her neck and the cottage cleared of all negative energy. So why did she still feel pissed off, depressed, and generally miserable? Why was she suddenly thinking a Big Mac, a beer, and a big-assed ice-cream cone would put her in a better mood than chanting in the goal for peace and harmony?

Yep. It was official.

She was losing her mind.

A knock sounded. Kate popped her head in with a big smile. "Got a minute?"

Arilyn forced a smile back at her friend. "Of course."

Kate strode in, clad in her usual black pants and lace top, her blond hair a halo around her face, highlighting her ocean-blue eyes and pale pink mouth. The driving force behind Kinnections, Kate was the main CEO and handler, making sure the business thrived and bringing her own special touch to love matches.

A real touch.

Gifted with the ability to sense a true soul connection between two people, Kate experienced a burst of electricity when she touched a couple meant to be. She'd lost many of her own dates to others until Slade Montgomery came on the scene, determined to prove Kinnections a fraud. Their relationship was rocky, passionate, and ended up with a true happy ever after.

Her friend slid into the purple chair opposite her desk and cocked her head. That assessing blue gaze traveled over her with frank concern. Uh-oh. There was nothing scarier than when her friends decided she needed an intervention. They were ruthless. Arilyn straightened up in her chair, determined to show no weakness.

"How are you doing?"

"Great." The lift of Kate's brow made her change the answer. "I mean, it's hard, of course, but I'm doing much better. How are the wedding plans? Do you need any help?"

Kate was scheduled to marry Slade in a few weeks, and crunch time was upon her. Arilyn had always wondered why she counseled so many women planning weddings, and now realized why. It was a bitch. If a couple actually made it intact and still in love to the ceremony, they had a 50 percent shot for success.

"I'm taking your advice and letting it go. The details are complete. And I'm tired of getting caught up in ridiculousness. I almost had a breakdown when the Asiatic lilies weren't available and they suggested calla lilies. I mean, am I nuts or what? Slade will dump me before I even get to the ceremony. You were right, A. It's not the wedding that's important, it's the marriage. I refuse to stress any longer."

"Good for you. Concentrate on the reward. St. Lucia, right?"

Kate sighed. "Yeah. Sun, sand, and sex. The perfect trifecta."

Arilyn laughed. "Honeymoons are worth the craziness of the wedding."

"Yeah, but we both wish we could bring Robert. We can't put him on a plane, though, so he'll have to stay. Thanks so much for taking care of him."

"He's going to be fine, Kate. He's stayed with me before, and you know how much I love him." Kate's dog, Robert, was paraplegic, and used a scooter to move around. Kate had rescued him years ago, and they were a tight team. Now Slade was just as madly in love with him, and they became a true family. "I'll spoil him so bad he won't want to go back."

Kate chuckled. "Slade would fight you to the

death. He yelled at me the other day for taking up too much room in the bed. I mean, are you kidding me? He literally chose the dog over me."

"And you love it."

"Yeah, I do." Her face became misty, and once again Arilyn struggled to fight the punch in her gut. The need for what Kate experienced. God, she'd never been a jealous person before, and not that she wasn't happy for her friend, she just wanted it for herself, too. "But I'm worried about leaving Kinnections for such a long time. We've doubled our workload, and since we lost Gen as our assistant, I haven't been able to get anyone good."

Arilyn tapped her finger against her lips. "I know the last temp was a bit undependable."

Kate rolled her eyes. "She came in late, and every other day she had her period. Nightmare."

"We'll work it out."

"Let's talk about it. Can you ring in Kennedy?"

"Sure." Arilyn buzzed her friend. "Can you come in here? Kate's in my office."

A few moments later, Kennedy Ashe strolled in. Looking perfect as usual, her caramel-colored hair falling in thick waves over her shoulders, the third in their crew handled all the social events and makeovers for Kinnections. Her red Jimmy Choos clicked on the floor, and she slid into the final seat, legs crossed, looking smart and polished in her Jones red suit with matching polish on her toes and nails. She was a complete dynamo in her job and personal life, until her newest client, Nate Dunkle, nerd extraordinaire and rocket scientist, burst into her life. His awkward social behavior and disastrous physical appearance called to her sense of challenge, until she decided to transform him and find him love. Then proceeded to fall for him herself.

It was a long time before Kennedy was able to admit her love for Nate and accept she was worthy for him to love her back. Since then, they'd moved in together and Nate was working on the next step: getting her to marry him. Arilyn would bet her money on Nate any day. Kennedy was still refusing, not wanting to ruin what they had, but slowly the rest of her walls were coming down.

"What's up, ladies? We're not drinking?" Kennedy asked.

Kate laughed and held up her own water bottle. "It's ten a.m. I think we should hold off on the hotel liquor bottles till at least noon."

Kennedy pursed her lips in a famous pout. "As Buffett says, it's five o'clock somewhere."

"But not here," Arilyn pointed out.

"Semantics. You didn't drag me in here to discuss the pros and cons of truffles versus photo frames for favors, did you? Because I'm on your mom's side. Mini vibrators with *Kate & Slade Forever* imprints are the bomb."

Kate choked on her water. "Never gonna happen, dude. And screw you. Whatever happened to your reassurances that you'll help in whatever capacity for the wedding?"

"I got burnt out. If I ever agree to marry Nate, we are so going to Vegas. Just us, you guys, and Elvis. Heaven."

Arilyn grinned. The numbness melted a bit as she savored the warmth of female friendship. "We'll be there. In the meantime, Kate is worried about leaving Kinnections behind during the honeymoon. I think we're here to reassure her."

Kate and Kennedy exchanged a meaningful look. *Not good.* This whole encounter stank of a setup. "Well, yes, I'm worried. But it's more directed at you, A."

Arilyn blinked. "Me? I'm perfectly capable of handling my job while you're away. I'm fine."

"Umm, did you just throw out a client and tell him to sue us?"

Arilyn winced. Oops. Of course they'd heard her temper tantrum. Not good, since she was the one who had taught them to deal with difficult clients by *not* giving in to anger. "I had a weak moment. He was hopeless."

Kate raised a brow. "You always told me there's no such thing as a hopeless client."

Irritation prickled. Another strange emotion. "I lied. Can we move on?"

"No," Kate said. "You've been a complete mess. Slamming doors. Throwing out a client. Gen said she stopped by and overheard you yelling at Mike."

Shoot. She never raised her voice, but honestly, chewing her expensive basket was way past her normal patience. She apologized later, and they'd made up with a cuddle. "There was a good reason. I'm fine."

"Bullshit," Kennedy tossed out, and leaned forward. "You're a mess over the breakup with asshat. Usually a good cry, a weekend in bed, and a tub of Ben & Jerry's helps, but you're not getting better. Instead, you keep burying yourself in projects and slipping further away."

She stiffened. She was a counselor, dammit, and knew everything about healing. "I have everything under control. Work helps distract me, and time heals all wounds. Forgive me if I can't be all lightness and fun lately, but I'll handle it."

Kate sighed. "Sweetie, we're not saying you need to spring back. You're misunderstanding. There's a distance and sadness around you we've never seen before. Like you're going through the steps but aren't really here. We think you're taking on too much, too soon. Besides offering private yoga lessons, you took on the anger management course, the shelter fundraiser, plus all your duties here. Now you're watching Robert, and with me gone for two weeks, well, I'm afraid."

Pain sliced through her at the thought that her friends believed she couldn't handle her job. "I'd never fail Kinnections."

Kate glared. "Are you kidding me right now? I don't give a damn about Kinnections or the computer system or the matches. I care about you. I don't want to be away in St. Lucia and find out you needed me and I wasn't here! Or that you got sick because you're overworked and won't come to us for help. A, you don't realize this, but out of all three of us, you're the one who never opens up."

She gasped. Her fingers flew to her throat. "What? How could you say that?"

Kennedy nodded. "I agree. You isolated yourself in this relationship, just like Genevieve did with her ex-fiancé. We knew you were unhappy, but you refused to talk about it."

Genevieve MacKenzie was best friends with Kate,

and they had all gotten close over the summer. Engaged to a successful surgeon, she ran out the day of her wedding, right into her best friend Wolfe's arms.

"Gen was being emotionally abused by David. It was completely different," Arilyn said.

"Was it?" Kate asked. "He refused to meet your friends. Insisted you keep your affair a secret. Snuck you around like he was a married man, hiding you from the public. Why didn't you ever call him by his name?"

She jerked back. Why? Because it would make it too real. This way, she was able to engage in the fantasy of a secret love affair with her teacher. She was able to deny the reality of their relationship and the fact that he never really wanted her. At least, not full-time. He'd enjoyed taking her off the shelf to play with but always returned her to his holding place. Shame choked her. God, even her friends had seen the truth. And they were right. She'd never opened up to them the way she insisted they did with their own relationships.

She was a hypocrite.

"I'm sorry." Misery leaked into her voice. "I think I knew if I let you in, it would prove our relationship wasn't real. And I so wanted it to be real."

Kate blinked furiously, the wet sheen of tears in her eyes. "I'm sorry you got hurt, sweetie. Out of all the people in the world, you deserve this the least. But from now on, you need to let us in. No more secrets. You also need to learn to ask for help. Hell, Ken and I have put the call out a dozen times, and you always answered. Gen, too. Now it's your turn, and we want to help."

Kennedy cleared her throat. "We love you, you idiot. Watching you isolate yourself is killing us. Understood?"

She swallowed and nodded. "Understood." She paused, trying to find the words to describe why she'd been avoiding her friends. "I'm just so mad," she whispered. "I mean, really, really mad."

There was a short moment of silence. "Well, duh," Kennedy finally said. "The man you loved was screwing someone else. You have every right to be pissed off, A. Why are you so afraid of a little righteous anger?"

Because it didn't help. Because she'd watched her mother die raging at God and the universe the entire time. Because her dad took that same anger of losing his spouse and spewed it out at himself, until he let himself die just to be with her. Because it wouldn't bring back the man she loved or change the situation. Instead, she tried to take those messy emotions and transform them. Transcend them into something good so she didn't destroy herself as her parents and so many people she counseled had done.

But she swallowed the words back and nodded. "You're right. Maybe I need to get in touch with my angry female side."

"I have a list of great songs on my iPod to give you," Kate said with a grin. "Now, what can we do to make sure you don't work yourself into the ground? Can you get out of any of your jobs for a bit?"

She sighed. "Not really. I can back off on the fundraiser for a bit, since there are other volunteers who can take the reins. I rented out the firehouse for private yoga classes, but when you're away, I won't schedule any."

"Speaking of anger issues, how about that anger management class?" Kennedy asked. "Sounds like a nightmare to me."

Arilyn grinned. "Maybe because you can use a class or two yourself?"

"Funny."

This time she laughed out loud. "Just kidding. No, I have a small group of three this time. It runs for six weeks, for a few hours in the afternoon. I enjoy it, actually. Many of the people have good hearts. They just haven't learned how to control their emotions."

"Well, if anyone can keep them in line, you can. Nate and I will give you any extra help you need for the fund-raiser. We've been doing so well, there's no reason we can't back off on any new matches for a bit. Just until we get our full team back and hire a new assistant."

She fought her instinct to reject the offer, hating to depend on anyone but herself. Instead, she forced herself to go along. "Agreed."

"Done. I feel better," Kate said. Her friends stood up. "Mugs this Friday night?"

Arilyn hesitated. She'd missed the last girls' night out. "I'm in."

"I'll call Gen and check on her schedule," Kate said.

"I'm good, too," Kennedy said. She paused at the door. "Oh, just a quick BTW. If anyone contacts either of you regarding my whereabouts last night, can you just confirm we were hanging out at your house, Kate? You were, too, A."

Arilyn frowned. "What happened? Why do you need an alibi? Why do I?"

Kennedy grinned without a shred of guilt. "I had these rotten eggs in the refrigerator I needed to get rid of. Imagine my surprise when I drove past the house of *he who shall not be named*? Let's just say I got rid of them."

Kate burst out laughing. Arilyn stared at her friend. "You threw eggs at his house? How did you even know where he lived?"

Kennedy wagged a finger at her. "Darling, you underestimate me. We all know where he lives. The stench followed me all the way down the road. It was quite poetic. See you ladies later."

She sashayed out of the office with Kate following, still laughing.

Arilyn buried her face in her hands, wondering what he thought of the childish gesture. Probably took it with a stoic grimness, admitting his fault. Ready to be punished like some martyr.

Asshat.

The image of moldy, runny eggs all over his neat white stucco house hit her vision. Suddenly, she began to laugh, and a hint of lightness flowed through her body.

Breakfast, and justice, had been served.

Arilyn got back to work. She sifted through the papers on the three clients who were attending anger management. One cited by the court. One from the Verily police station. Another volunteer in an attempt to woo back his spouse.

Time to sift through the background information on each man and draft up a plan. Every personality was different, and she respected how unique reactions came from a wellspring of emotion, usually based in the past. The first two were easy. Road rage was more common now than ever, and probably revolved around a type-A personality with control issues. Eli White. Her mind clicked on various paths in order to give him tools to use on the road and in other social situations.

The second man, Luther Jones. Lost his temper too many times with his wife and now was paying the price. She gave him credit for wanting to change, for loving someone enough to sign up for such a class. He seemed to own some triggers within his personality that they'd need to work on, but again, a basic case with a high chance of success.

She picked up the chart for the third man.

Her fingers dropped it immediately, and it floated back down to the desk. Her breath constricted in her chest. Not. Possible.

Officer Stone Petty.

A shiver raced down her spine and goose bumps prickled on her skin. The image of his face floated before her. Staggering height. Massive muscles. A nose that had obviously been broken, craggy rough features, a cruel perpetual sneer to his full lips. The goatee only added to his dark presence, that of a man you'd never want to meet alone. In an alley or anywhere.

From the moment they met, she had taken an instant dislike to the man. He was too big. Too confident. Too masculine.

Too everything.

He sucked the air out of the room and commanded

everyone's attention without a word. Besides the odd crackle of electricity between them, she had an odd urge to bend to his will, do what he said, surrender to anything he asked of her.

Nuts. She was certifiably nuts.

So she'd gone on the offensive immediately, refusing to cower under his dominant stare and deep, gravelly voice, which did bad things to her tummy.

They'd met when he and his partner stepped into a violent scene between Genevieve and her ex-fiancé. Then he responded to another case of vandalism on Gen's house. Both times, Arilyn had called the police, and been met with a stubborn, pain-in-the-butt Stone Petty.

How could this work? How could she possibly counsel him when he'd refused from the very first second to take directions from her? She knew his type well. The know-it-all, superior, "I am God" complex many cops had. Of course, she understood the motivations behind it. Dealing with the underside of human nature eventually takes a toll. She'd counseled cops before, but never one with so much burning energy and . . . darkness.

Arilyn dragged in a breath and picked the paper up again. This was ridiculous. She couldn't pull out now. She'd study his chart, his past, and try to find a route that would work.

After scanning the details of the scene that had forced him into anger management class, her heart softened. He'd tried to protect a child. Yes, his career may be taking pieces from his sanity without him realizing it. She'd need to dig deep into his past and his brain to try to help.

The image of his dark brown gaze boring into hers ripped another shiver from her body.

He was a walking disaster. Smoker. Drinker. A murky past. He'd been involved in another domestic abuse episode in the Bronx. Left a year ago. For peace and quiet? Perhaps. But one thing she had learned was that even Verily had its darkness.

She tapped a finger against the manila folder. She'd need to tread carefully with this one. Make sure he knew from the outset who was in charge.

Arilyn hoped she could pull it off.

three

STONE KNEW WITHIN two minutes he'd rather have gone to an Alcoholics Anonymous meeting. Or passed a kidney stone. Hell, he would've even agreed to be tortured by a drug lord for hours rather than deal with this nightmare.

Anger management sucked.

He tried not to sneer at the other two participants as they sat in their cushioned folding chairs and focused their attention on Arilyn Meadows like two kiss-ass students looking for an A from the teacher. Dude one seemed like an intimidating kind of guy who had a serious case of road rage. Good-looking, with spiky brown hair, blinding white teeth, a nice build, and an obvious horn dog. He seemed way too eager to please Arilyn. His gaze stripped her, his smile seemed too smug, and he tried to keep her questions directed at him. He was too physically eager. Like, maybe if he tried seducing her, he'd get out of class early.

Like that was ever gonna happen under Stone's watch.

Dude two was an African American guy with glasses who seemed the intellectual type, enthusiastic about overcoming his societal issues to restore and heal the gaps in the relationship with his spouse. Yeah, big words, convoluted speaking, definitely some type of teacher. Stone wondered what he looked like when he lost his temper. Could be fun to find out.

"Officer Stone Petty?"

He shook his head and focused on her face. He'd been hoping to walk in and realize that strange connection between them was gone. Counted on putting his time in with no distractions by a pretty hippie with an enchanting scowl and a rocking body.

Yeah. Scratch that.

It had actually gotten worse. The zing of energy in the air practically sizzled like greasy bacon in a hot pan. She knew it, too, just chose to ignore it. The slight widening of those green eyes and the tiny catch of breath in her throat confirmed her own reaction. The pure rush of satisfaction that wracked his body screamed of trouble. This was no woman he could tumble quickly and walk away from in the morning. Unfortunately, his cop instincts burned to figure her out. Craved to know if her surface matched up with the depths of the woman beneath.

He didn't think it would.

In his gut, Stone Petty thought she was a big liar. Push past her sweet, serene, flowing do-gooder façade and who knew what type of woman he'd find? Why did he suspect a wild streak buried somewhere? The moment he began baiting her, she rose to the occasion. She pretended to be all calm and centered, but an angry energy radiated around her and damned if he didn't recognize it well. Maybe because he lived it. Was it possible Arilyn Meadows was a complete fake? Did she own an actual temper and backbone?

It would be damn fun trying to find out. Anything

had to be better than her boring Buddha-like attitude.

She waited for him to answer, seemingly calm and patient. "Officer?"

"Yeah?"

Arilyn gestured to the other men. He'd forgotten their names already. "Eli and Luther have shared the circumstances that brought them to this class. Would you like to elaborate a bit on your own story?"

No. God, he hated sharing, especially in circles with strangers. Why did women always want to talk about their feelings? Didn't actions speak louder than words anyway?

"I was called into a situation. It got out of hand. I lost my temper."

She tilted her head. Long, silky strands of rich strawberry gold slid over her shoulders and wrapped around her waist. He wondered what she'd look like naked, with all that glorious hair spread out over white sheets. Did she think her casual clothes hid her body? The Lycra pants clung like second skin and caressed like a lover, emphasizing every subtle curve. The hard tips of her small breasts pushed against her tank top in a lovely game of peekaboo. Her skin was fair, with a nice array of freckles he'd love to explore. A slight frown marred her brow at his obvious perusal.

"What happened when you lost your temper, Officer?"

"Stone."

"Excuse me."

His gaze bored into hers. "My name is Stone."

Dude A—Eli?—laughed and tried to get back her attention by launching into an explanation. "I think

Arilyn is trying to get you to open up more. This is a safe place. If you don't share, she won't be able to help you." The guy beamed, as if he deserved a medal for being teacher's assistant.

"How about you share your way and I share mine, buddy?"

Arilyn cleared her throat. "Umm, thank you for helping, Eli, but everyone here is entitled to commit completely to this process or fight it. What you take from this class is up to you. We'll be doing daily group therapy, but I'll also be working with each of you privately."

Eli looked way too satisfied. Stone wondered how an anger management class was already pissing him off. Dude B spoke up. "I agree with Eli. There's a layer of trust within group therapy that needs to be carefully built. For instance, I trigger over jealousy. The idea that my wife can be looking at another male short-circuits my brain."

"I hate traffic," Eli said. "Wasted hours trapped amidst stupid people who can't drive."

Both men nodded at each other, congratulating themselves on their accomplishment. On their sharing abilities. Stone was tired. Cranky. He wanted a smoke, a steak, a good night's sleep, and to stop being aroused by a woman who had no place in his life. He put his hands on his knees and leaned forward.

"I get pissed off when drunk assholes beat the hell out of their wives and children."

Eli and Luther jerked back in surprise.

"Guess I win. Is it lunchtime yet?"

He felt better already.

ARILYN REALIZED THE MOMENT he walked in the door she was in trouble.

He was as intimidating as she remembered. The man had to literally duck to get through the doorway when entering the small room they'd rented from the town. Dressed in worn jeans, a washed-out Yankees jersey, and a backward baseball cap, his casual attire did nothing to soften the raw sexual energy that radiated around him. He moved with purpose, each motion economical, his gaze pinned so tight and hot on hers, she fought an answering tremble. What was wrong with her? Sure, she had a weakness for authority figures, but she was attracted to the starving-artist type—long hair, graceful features, charming smile, lean body. She adored men who created, stared softly into space with a dreamy look in their eyes, caught up in their muses and the magic of the world. Gentle souls who needed support and unconditional love.

She wondered if Stone Petty had ever had a dreamy thought in his life.

He was way out of her league. All hard muscle and primitive male, those sulky lips curled up in a bit of a sneer when he reached her. With his midnight hair, thick and a bit unruly, charcoal eyes, and rough goatee, he looked like he'd jumped out of a *Sons of Anarchy* episode. He cocked a hip, meaty fists clenched by his side, and spoke in a gravelly voice that shimmered with command.

"So we meet again, Arilyn Meadows."

She hated the way her heart sped up a bit from the use of her name. He was the one mandated to attend these sessions, and already she sensed his mockery. Jerk. Did he believe he was above the other men here and her teaching methods? Wait till she got done with him. He would not only be a convert, but maybe after forcing him to get real with himself using her creative methods, he wouldn't wear that smirk so often.

Maybe.

"Yes. Welcome. I'd like to do an introduction with all three of you and then give you a summary of what to expect."

That lower lip kicked up a tiny bit. "I'm a nice Catholic boy. Not too keen on chanting to Buddha to channel my inner saint. Against the rules."

Ah, his sarcastic sense of humor was another element she remembered well. Arilyn rose to the occasion. "Funny, I thought nice Catholic boys were taught not to judge others and to turn the other cheek. No worries, Officer. You can always attend confession."

He moved an inch, but she already felt crowded. His massive body blocked out everything else. The light. The shadows. The air. "Maybe. But the first lesson they teach you is being truly sorry for your sins."

She arched a brow. "And are you?"

He had a crisscross scar on his brow. His jaw was a complete square, and his nose had definitely been broken. A few times. He smelled like everything primal. Sweat. Coffee. Earth. No wimpy over-the-counter scent for him. Just all the delicious musky fragrances combined to spell out M-A-N. "Sometimes." He dropped his voice. "Other sins no one should be sorry for. Those are the best kind. Don't you agree?"

Oh, Lord, he was flirting. Wasn't he? How dare he flirt with her? She was in charge. If he thought he'd charm her into letting him off easy, he was smoking more than cigarettes. She chilled her voice. "No," she said. "Much easier to avoid those types of sins completely."

Her skin tingled under his burning gaze. "Pity." He paused. "Maybe you just haven't encountered the right temptation."

Oh, yeah, he was flirting. Or just screwing with her mind—he was too damn smart for his own good. She snapped off her comment with one goal in mind. Total eradication of any future come-ons. "Been there. Done that." Arilyn made sure to rake his figure with a dismissive gaze. "Not tempted to do it again. Take a seat."

He didn't move for a moment, as if reminding her that he did things on his own terms. He finally obeyed, but his mocking grin told her he had allowed her to win this round. Another shiver shook her from the thought of him controlling all aspects of a relationship. Total nightmare.

Arilyn cleared her throat, dragging herself back to the present. The three men listened as she outlined the rough syllabus and goals for the full six weeks. She preferred to keep some of her field trips a surprise until the day of so no one worried or had too much time to weasel out of them. After Stone's last statement, Arilyn decided it was a good time to break for lunch and regroup in the afternoon. Her head throbbed slightly, reminding her that she had forgotten her herbal supplements and had eaten only a Greek yogurt with fruit this morning. Maybe she'd have time to stop for a veggie wrap before she headed home to let Lenny and Mike out. Since the breakup, she'd been extremely unorganized and felt like her head was stuffed with cotton. Time to refocus. The three men in the room deserved it. Kinnections deserved it. And the shelter needed her sharp, considering the current crisis going on with funding. This was the time when she truly wished she was rich and able to funnel tons of money to them so there were no worries.

She hurried out of the firehouse and down the sidewalk, then stopped short.

Officer Stone Petty stood under the bright green-and-yellow awning of Stella's Beauty Shop, transfixed on the object in his hands.

A crumpled pack of Marlboros.

The sudden spurt of rage surprised her. She may disapprove and try to help, but Arilyn understood the power of free choice and being ready to quit any vice. But for some reason, the sight of this powerful man slowly killing himself made her vision blur. Since her car was parked right by him, she forced herself to walk past, yank open the door, and mind her own business.

It didn't happen.

"Enjoying yourself, Officer?"

He turned his head. "Huh?"

She clenched her hand around the handle and shook with temper. "Enjoying your cigarettes?" she sneered. "Having fun destroying the body God gave you so you can wake up one day gasping for breath and talking through a tube?"

He raked his gaze over her in a lazy, assessing way that only made her madder. "This is the second time you threatened me with hospitals and tubes. I take it you don't agree with smoking?"

She fumed. How was he so calm when she wanted to jump across the street and throttle him? The image of her mother slowly dying of lung cancer still haunted her, but she managed to live with it. Watching her dad die after her of a broken heart, not caring that he left his only daughter alone, had been even harder. Mom had fought to live. Dad had fought to die.

Stone obviously cared about people, especially since he was a cop. Why couldn't he care about himself, too? Was that so hard to do? Arilyn swallowed back the words and managed a shrug. "I don't agree with waste," she said. "Or suicide. But it's your choice. Enjoy your smoke."

She turned her back, ready to get in her car, but his words sliced through the air.

"I quit."

She slowly cranked her head back around. "Yeah. That's why you're holding a pack."

He held up the package. "It's empty. I'm on the damn patch, but sometimes I go nuts for a craving and need to smell it." He let out an aggravated breath. "Stupid, I know, but it helps. I've been clean for a month now."

Relief cut through her, but she didn't dare analyze it. "Oh. Well, good for you. I know it's hard. Do you have someone you can call?"

His rough laugh made her tummy dip. He was so . . . virile. "Nah, no smoking sponsor for me. In fact, no one's pretty much given a damn if I quit or not. Until you."

Heat coursed through her, and it had nothing to do with the sun. She cleared her throat. "I care about everyone," she said. The prim tone made her want to wince, but she owned it. "Aren't we all worth more than we think?"

Like a falcon sighting prey, he remained still and silent. Those inky eyes refused to release her. Yet. "Sure. If that's your party line."

The annoyance snapped back. "You don't believe everyone deserves not to be judged?"

"Nope. Criminals deserve shit."

"What if they committed a crime with a higher purpose?" she challenged. "There's plenty of gray areas. Not everything is black-and-white."

"I don't care what someone's lofty ambition is if they break the law. Or are you one of those touchy-feely types who believe the garbage on death row should be forgiven? Released back into society for a second chance?" The already familiar sneer touched his lips. "Easy to forgive when you're not the one who was affected by the crime, huh?"

"I think people make mistakes," she shot back. "Like you did. Now you're trying to correct your behavior."

Why did he set her off just by opening his mouth? He wasn't worth the energy of losing her temper. She'd just breathe, smile politely, and walk away.

"Yeah, you're right. I'm the real criminal here. Too bad the punishment sometimes doesn't fit the crime, huh? I mean, this anger management junk should be saved for serial killers."

Oh, she really, really didn't like this man.

Arilyn turned her back before he baited her further. "Be back at two. Don't be late."

His voice mocked her departure. "Yes, ma'am."

Arilyn got in her car and drove away, refusing to look back.

four

STONE STUDIED HER while he filled out more ridiculous forms with the goal of targeting his "true" anger issues. At least it was a break from Luther's ramblings and Dude A's lame attempt at flirting. They'd been warned that the first day was a full eight hours, and then they would move to three-hour sessions for the rest of the prison term.

Faint lines settled into the crease above her nose, and she seemed distracted. Probably running around saving the world, one criminal at a time. Still, he'd been right about his instincts. She was cute when she got pissed. Trying to hide it by being all Zen and above the regular humans only made her losing it more amusing. He'd try to up his game to distract himself from this daily nightmare. Much better than being stuck with the two bozos beside him discussing *feelings*.

She stood up, collected the papers, and gestured to the four purple mats laid out on the floor. "Thank you for taking the time to fill these out. Honesty is everything in this course. Besides working on your triggers and digging a bit into what makes us angry, we need to learn coping techniques. I'll be focusing on how our bodies feed our responses, so make sure for the rest of the week you come in comfortable clothing."

Great. Here we go with the yogi crap. Stone tamped down a groan. Maybe she'd demonstrate the poses first and he'd focus on her hot body. "If we can shift to our mats, and sit cross-legged, we'll tackle the first element of control: the breath."

Stone got up from his chair, settled on the mat, and barely managed to cross his long legs. His back gave a bit of a spasm and reminded him his gym routine consisted of weights but little else. The smoking had killed his running and endurance, which he was trying to build back up. But stretching? He couldn't remember the last time he had had to sit on the floor like a toddler.

Arilyn took her position in front, easily twisting her legs up on each knee, back ramrod straight, fingers curled and resting on her knees. She practically glowed with a warm energy radiating around her, making the men take a deep sigh. Her presence alone touched something inside of him he rarely made note of. Too bad he couldn't put a name to it yet. He had no idea what it was.

"Anger sprouts from a variety of places, but there's one simple mantra I want everyone to remember. Leave with this one thing from the course, and your entire life will change for the better."

The men leaned slightly forward.

"Control your breath, control your life."

Oh, yeah, he remembered what she touched in him now.

Aggravation.

Dude A and Luther nodded, hanging on to her Buddha-like advice with an openness that made him want to roll his eyes. Puh-leeze. If it were that simple, no one would ever lose their temper. Did she really think they were that stupid?

His face must've shown his doubt, because those meadow-green eyes focused on him. "Officer Petty? You seem skeptical."

He shrugged. Damned if even his shoulders hurt from this ridiculous position. "Not for nothing, but it's a bit disappointing as the big secret to all anger. We breathe every day."

A tiny smile curved her lips. "Correct. All roads lead from the breath. It is our biggest connection to our body, mind, and emotions. When we experience anger, our muscles tighten, adrenaline rushes through, and we stop breathing. The oxygen flow is stopped up, and this is the key turning point where we may lose control."

Damn, her teacher voice was hot. "So, next time I'm in a situation with some dickhead criminal, I should stop what I'm doing to breathe first?"

Her smile never wavered. "Correct."

He wondered if she breathed to ward off a climax. If he had her in his bed, he'd make sure to push every button she owned to make her lose that almighty control and see if she was able to breathe then. Holy crap, where had that thought come from? She'd probably kill his arousal the moment she opened her mouth to speak anyway. Stone decided to push. "And this works for everything?" he prodded. "No matter what the circumstance?"

"Yes. By the end of this course, I'll show you how it can be done."

Oh, no, she wasn't getting off the hook that easy. "Let's take this scenario. Some jacked-up druggie starts his freak-out attack and goes for a gun. Instead of reacting with normal human emotions such as, oh, I don't know, irritation, general crankiness, and *rage*, instead I'm supposed to go all Zen and concentrate on breathing before going with my general gut reaction of self-protection and male testosterone. Does this sound right to you?"

Her jaw tightened, but she remained stubbornly tranquil. "You would experience and feel those basic emotions, Officer, but with this practice you'd be able to transition them by connecting with the breath. You will be taught to move past them. Not attach yourself to the up-and-down roller coaster our emotions put us through on a constant basis. This is the way you avoid making bad decisions."

Dudes A and B looked even more enchanted. Stone scratched his head. It was a good excuse to move his hips and wiggle out of the excruciating position for a moment. "Huh. Sounds a little bit like a magic pill to me. Or like drinking the fruit punch."

Those green eyes flashed. He tried not to chuckle.

"Since I tend to avoid both pills and sugary drinks, why don't we allow actions to make up our minds?" Her smile was forced and not directed at him. "Let's begin. Close your eyes. Breathe slowly in and out, and follow your breath. Thoughts will interrupt the flow, but try to let them flicker past your closed eyes like a movie; you're not attached to them. When you find yourself wandering, bring your mind back to the breath. We'll sit quietly for ten minutes. Feel the air rush in and out of your lungs and let yourself go."

Stone closed his eyes and succumbed to ten minutes of ridiculousness. He intended to do exactly what she said, though, so at the end of this workshop he'd be able to tell her honestly that these methods didn't work.

He listened to his breath. He wished for a cigarette. He thought about what he'd have for dinner. He cursed the growing cramps in his leg but didn't hear the other two wiggle around, so damned if he'd move first. Was it over yet? How long was ten minutes? How would she know the time was up? He craved to open his eyes and peek at her but refused in case she caught him and used him as an example of bad behavior.

He'd rather be bad with her in other ways.

Huh. There was that thought again. All sexual. He must be pretty hard up. How long since his last affair? He ticked down the days, then realized he was going on weeks. Yep. Way too long.

Stone clenched his fists, remembered to relax his fingers, and went back to the breath. Who would've thought he breathed so much in ten minutes? He needed to go to a chiropractor. It had been on his to-do list, but he'd gotten too busy at work and forgotten. Oh, he had to pick up beer on his way home, too—he was all out and yesterday he'd craved an IPA and had nothing in the fridge. Back to the breath. Was ten minutes over yet?

Her rich, smooth voice caressed his ears and immediately calmed him.

"Begin to bring yourself back. Deepen your breath, feeling your chest expand and release. Let your body sink into the mat, feeling the earth support you, and slowly open your eyes."

Oh, thank God it was over.

He heard movement, so he stretched out his legs,

trying not to wince at the wimpy charley horse in his calf. Okay, he was definitely stretching more. She'd proven his body needed something other than manly weights.

"We'll be using that simple exercise regularly. Would anyone like to share how they felt?"

Dude A rushed to answer. "I felt that if I'd known about that technique before, I would've used it in traffic jams. My head got clearer."

She beamed. "Excellent. Luther? Any thoughts?"

Luther looked thoughtful. "It was an interesting technique. Hard to focus but has intriguing possibilities to integrate in the future to avoid emotional reactions due to my wife's male clients. That's usually a hot spot for me."

"Wonderful. Officer Petty?"

"Stone."

He enjoyed the slight flush to her cheeks, but she remained professional. "Stone, did you have any physical difficulty? Usually men have the most trouble sitting in this position for a while."

"Nope. Piece of cake."

"Wonderful. We'll be increasing our time increments until we sit for half an hour regularly."

Well, fuck. Won't that be a barrel of laughs!

"Did any strange thoughts or emotional issues crop up?"

He met her gaze head-on and grinned. "Actually, I kind of had a lightbulb moment. If I hadn't remembered, it could've been a disaster."

She leaned in, intrigued. "Really? Would you like to share?"

"Sure." He never released her from his stare. "I ran

out of IPA. In my house, that's cause for a full temper tantrum."

Luther frowned. "What's IPA? Some kind of file code?"

"It's beer. Good beer."

Luther looked just as disappointed in him as his instructor did, and damned if he didn't feel even better at the dual reactions. Yeah, he was twisted.

Her lips tightened, but she never let the obvious annoyance seep into her tone. "I'm thrilled this session helped, Officer Petty." She emphasized his title so subtly it was like a graceful sweep behind the knees. Quiet but deadly. "I'm looking forward to hearing more on your lightbulb moments in the future. For now, that's it, gentlemen. I'll see you tomorrow afternoon."

She rolled to her feet in one graceful motion, turned her back, and began gathering her things.

Stone gritted his teeth and stood, refusing to show he felt stiff and achy. The bastards next to him seemed fine. Maybe they had kids they sat on the floor with regularly. He needed to get a nephew or a niece or something.

He watched her hurry out the door, enjoying the swing of her tight rear. Her license said five eight, but he pegged her as being a bit taller. Those legs could wrap tight around a man's hips and squeeze so hard he'd probably pass out in pleasure. Of course, once her mouth opened he'd be resuscitated and dragged into hell.

Too bad.

Maybe he'd shoot some pool with Devine tonight. If he was gonna be suspended, he sure as hell wasn't staying at home, bored out of his mind. Since he couldn't have a smoke, he'd stop at Dunkin' on the way and get his favorite chocolate Munchkins. He'd bring some for the guys at the station and see if he could sniff out a good crime someone needed help on. Like who purposefully mixed the recyclables up with the trash.

Stone headed out.

"POPPY, WHAT ARE YOU doing here?"

The bungalow was filled with the scents of onion, grease, and comfort. She laughed at the doggy attack of squirming fur and crazy tongues, then dropped to the floor in surrender while she hugged her fur babies. The stress of the day eased from her shoulders. Dorothy was so right. There was nothing quite like home.

Her grandfather walked over, spatula in hand, and shook his head. "You got your hands full with these monkeys, honey," he said. "Decided to walk them and surprise you with dinner. Unfortunately, I think Mike got hungry early and raided the kitchen. The garbage was torn up and scattered everywhere."

Arilyn groaned. "I thought I locked it up! I was running late and forgot. I need to get one of those big cans with the lid. Hey, how'd you know it was Mike?"

"Because Lenny was already chewing on your sneaker."

Great. She always shut the closet, but Lenny had become smart enough to use his paw to drag it open to find the treasure. Damn, she'd loved those new Skechers. She wagged her finger at both puppies. "You two are in big trouble. No Frosty Paws ice cream to-night."

Lenny scampered up her legs and licked her ear in a sloppy apology. She giggled and scooped him back to the floor. "Sorry you had to clean up, Poppy." She rose to her feet and gave him a hug. The familiar scents of Irish Spring soap and Old Spice surrounded her. After her parents passed, Poppy had become her rock. The only stability left in her life, he gave her structure, shelter, and love. He made her laugh with his wild streak, penchant for fun and gambling, and advice to live large or go home trying. So like her mother, until cancer had eaten everything decent and good within and spat it back out.

He was dressed in his usual uniform of brown pants, white shirt, and sturdy leather shoes polished to perfection. The black tattoos of the memories of his fallen comrades in Vietnam climbed down each arm. A cross and a name. Eight of them. She used to sit in his lap and study the tats for hours, fascinated by the detail and boldness. Though painful for him, he used to tell the story of the war to keep the memory alive. So no military member or person fighting for his or her country would ever be forgotten again.

He lived in a cozy brick house filled with interesting antiques, old movie posters, and an attic bursting with trunks full of old clothes and photos. She'd get lost up there for hours when she needed a connection with her parents, poring over her family heritage ripped away from her too soon. Poppy was tough and smart. He aged with a grizzly endurance that taught her to appreciate life in all forms and stages, good and bad, old and new, giving her hope that each morning would bring a surprise. He'd owned a small auto repair station for years, content to spend his days under the hood, where the memories of war and what he'd left behind faded under the turn of a greasy wrench. He'd taught her a bit about cars and how to take care of herself. Arilyn used a lot of his techniques and turned it toward computers. In some ways, mechanics were the same: there was a larger picture where everything finally fit. The journey was half the fun.

He'd been a handsome man, with piercing green eyes and a full head of silver hair that competed with thirty-year-olds'. Sure, his face reflected a map of deep wrinkles, his teeth were no longer his own, and his hands had been gnarled by a touch of arthritis, but Poppy was still her rock.

When they diagnosed him with type 2 diabetes, she realized he couldn't be alone any longer. He needed to be monitored, and living two hours away wouldn't work. He was the one who agreed to give up his house and move closer to her. The Best Friends Center in Verily was the perfect fit. The center boasted a lively crowd, with bus trips, group activities, and a certain amount of independence. Besides spending more time with him, he'd be able to keep up his social calendar.

Unfortunately, he was having a hard time fitting in.

"Hey, it's Tuesday night. Why aren't you at bingo?"

Those bright green eyes shimmered with outrage. "They won't let us gamble. Tried to get a pool going, and Elmer Fudd ratted me out. What good is a game if you can't bet money?"

"Who's Elmer Fudd?"

"You know that fat guy with the bald head and pudgy cheeks? I always think he's gonna tell me he's been hunting wabbits."

Arilyn pressed her lips together. "It's not nice to call people fat, Poppy."

"Everything's so PC nowadays."

"How about trying to concentrate on the thrill of winning without money?"

"Boring. Bingo is lame anyway. Hey, is there a way to hook up an iPod in my room? If I have to listen to Dean Martin or Frank Sinatra play on the speakers for one more minute, I'm gonna puke."

This time she did laugh. "I can't trust you with an iPod. We've already gone through three cell phones before I cut you off."

He shot her an innocent look. "How was I supposed to know the HOTGIRLS party line cost a dollar a minute?"

"You're incorrigible. What are we having?"

"I made a stew. Potatoes, onions, and the veggies you love. Mine has meat, yours doesn't."

"Hmm, smells delicious." She lifted the Crock-Pot lid and took a sniff. "Did you go to the organic butcher shop for the meat? They're grass fed and use humane techniques with their animals."

"Yes, honey. But I think if you took half the amount of effort to find men as you do food, you'd be married already." The touch of sympathy on his face made her squirm. She'd done a complete turnaround of her life after her mother died. Death suddenly became real, and Arilyn decided not to become a drain on the world with a large carbon print and nothing to show. Dedicating herself to finding true inner peace and quality health, she sought a path her Poppy never understood but had learned to accept. He didn't know about her latest breakup with her lover, because he'd never met him or heard her speak of him. No wonder he was worried. Probably thought she hadn't dated in years.

She shook off the thought and spotted the bottle. "Poppy, alcohol isn't good for you." She pointed to the Guinness on the counter, but he waved her off.

"Beer is. Just heard it on the news. Something about the fermentation or wheat. Just one, A. I had a hard day."

Her heart softened. He was so full of life. The idea of not having him around for another twenty years terrified her, so she always tried to balance her mothering instincts with the knowledge that he also needed some vices. She danced around the pups tumbling at her ankles and took out a full bottle of white wine. Guess she had her own vice.

Arilyn began setting the table. "I had a bad day, too," she confided. "Started an anger management course."

"Another job? Can you handle all this?" Poppy spooned out the stew into two bowls and settled at the counter. "What about Kinnections?"

"My shifts are flexible. I usually enjoy running these classes, but there's a cop in my class who's a bit challenging."

"You mean he's a jerk?"

She nodded. "Yeah, he's a jerk. He's so arrogant! And he has this sneer-smirk thing he probably thinks is sexy, but it's really annoying."

"You'll keep him in line. After all, he's in the class

for instruction on managing his temper, right? By the time you get done with him, he'll be a changed man."

His confidence in her abilities soothed her nerves. She picked up the spoon and took a bite. Heaven. Her family had pure Irish roots and besides making a mean soda bread, Poppy was great at stews, soups, and his famous corned beef and cabbage. He'd almost cried when she became vegetarian. "Yeah, I guess."

"I know. Cops are a funny bunch. I respect the hell out of them, but their job makes them a bit hard-core. Imagine the type of circumstances they run into on a daily basis. Would probably piss me off, too."

She fell quiet, thinking over her grandfather's words. He was right. Stone had his own issues to work out. He may be difficult to deal with, but if she was able to help him perform his job in a more peaceful manner, it would be worth it. He may mock her, but she believed in the tactics she taught. She'd just have to prove it.

"Thanks, Poppy."

"Welcome, sweetie. I'll walk the dogs for you until you finish up class. No need to rush home when I can help out."

She held her tongue, knowing he needed to be busy just as much as she did. "That would be wonderful."

"Good. Now finish your stew and tomorrow give that cop a little hell."

Lenny and Mike howled in agreement, or maybe it was because they smelled meat in a house that never had any.

Arilyn laughed and listened to her grandfather.

five

WHEN SHE WOKE up, Arilyn swore to have a better attitude.

It lasted all the way up till the moment Stone Petty strolled into her class.

He was late. A full fifteen minutes. The worst part? He strolled into the firehouse with a lazy grace that confirmed he didn't give a crap. Luther and Eli glared at him. Dammit, arriving late to her class set the wrong tone. A large coffee cradled in his big hands, he shoved some sort of greasy biscuit with bacon hanging from it into his mouth, rubbing his hands down the front of his jeans. Today he wore a Jets T-shirt, a battered ball cap from Key West, and sneakers with a tiny hole in the big toe. His five-o'clock shadow only added to the dark menace of his goatee, and he nodded to the other men before plopping into a chair.

"Whassup?" he grunted, crumpling the wrapper into the brown bag, and shooting it across the room at the wastebasket in the corner. He made the shot and gave a half grin of male pride before sliding his gaze back to her.

Oh, she was going to kill him.

He was a heathen with no manners. Her nose crinkled with disgust. How on earth did his body look in decent shape? His diet probably consisted of crap. And he may have tried to hide his discomfort during their time in a seated position, but she knew he had difficulty keeping still and pain-free.

Wait till she finished with him today.

"Officer, perhaps you'd like to explain why you're late?"

He glanced around as if surprised that anyone cared. "Had to stop at the station first."

"I see." She dropped her voice to arctic chill mode and narrowed her gaze. "I'm sure your superior informed you that you must sign in to these classes at the appropriate time. Being late disturbs the class and disrespects all of us."

"Yeah, well, I'm sure solving a crime trumps being late."

Her brow lifted. "Remind me again, Officer: Are you currently on suspension?"

Gotcha.

He jerked in his seat, and anger flickered over his features. Those inky eyes slammed her with male irritation. "For two weeks only. How did you know about that?"

"So, solving crimes on suspension would be against the rules, wouldn't it?"

He refused to surrender. Just stretched out his legs like a relaxed predator and sipped from his coffee. "How would you feel if I stepped back and watched a theft happen 'cause I'm on vacay? Is that a great use of the taxpayers' money? 'Cause it seems you've always been concerned with how I spend my day."

She remembered their very first conversation in the summer, when she accused him of being a liability on the taxpayers. Hmm, still sore about that, huh? She tried not to crow in glee. "Oh, I apologize, you were helping with an arrest? Maybe I'll call and thank your boss. Explain to him in this particular case it's fine to be late."

His jaw clenched. She refused to let her gaze waver, knowing if she backed down here, it would be all over. Stone Petty would eat her alive and then ask what was for dessert. "I had to consult on a case," he finally ground out. Waves of heat and crankiness swarmed from his aura. He paused, and his next words seemed strangled, as if he was forcing them out. "I apologize."

She treated him to a brilliant smile, mostly fake. "Apology accepted. Please don't let it happen again. Oh, and you'll need to stay additional time after class. The rules, of course. Each minute must be accounted for. Now, let's start the subject of the day, shall we?"

Eli and Luther looked satisfied by his punishment, and she was back in control.

For now.

She ignored the shiver that raced down her spine and concentrated on her class.

STONE PICKED AT HIS thumbnail and wondered what Devine was up to. Maybe he had been chasing a speeder, and when he got to the driver's window, the driver looked off. Maybe Devine asked him to get out of the car, and the driver refused, and his partner got to slam him up against the hood, cuff him, and do a vehicle search. Maybe he found something incriminating like a weapon or drugs. He'd get a medal and Chief Dick would boast about him in the department, and the whole time Stone was stuck here in anger management class learning how to eat well to decrease anger and stress.

Bastard.

"Officer Petty?"

He looked up from his battered thumb. He was getting sick and tired of her prim and proper tone. His title sounded like a mockery and irritated the hell out of him. "Stone," he reminded her again. "You call that dude Eli and the other dude Luther. How about calling me Stone?"

She smiled again, but it wasn't real and they both knew it. "Achieving the status of a policeman deserves respect. You earned the title and deserve to be called 'Officer.'"

Bullshit. How did she manage to get away with such behavior? She wrapped up insults in phony attempts to be nice. Of course, she'd backed him into a wall on that one. Who would've thought his being a bit late and eating fast food could make her so damn snarky?

Stone smothered a humorless laugh. At least temper made her more real. If he had to hear one sugarcoated statement about avoiding bad foods, soda, alcohol, cigs, and anything else fun in life, he was gonna seriously fake some kind of illness. Maybe food poisoning from his bacon biscuit. Yeah, that was good. Was she calling him again?

"Yeah?"

"Luther and Eli have shared some of their concerns with their diets. Do you have any?"

He began to roll his eyes but caught himself just

in time. He didn't want to have to stay any later in psycho zen detention. "Nope."

She was sitting cross-legged again on the mat. Head rising high above her slender shoulders. Red-gold hair caught in a thick braid that hung down her back. Long, graceful limbs tangled up in a dance of grace and balance he'd never really seen in another woman. Too bad she was so dull and boring. "Wonderful. Why don't you take us through typical meals during a workday?"

Why weren't Luther and Eli normal dudes? If they'd band together and make some serious trouble, the day would go a lot faster. "I get up and have my coffee, toast, and bacon."

"Turkey bacon?" she asked.

He snorted. "Hell, no. Nothing wrong with eating pig. That's why God put 'em on earth for us. To eat."

She literally paled. Stone's mood picked up. Yep, she was a vegetarian all right. Too funny. He warmed up to his topic. "I go to work, and have a midmorning snack of Cheetos or Oreos. Then for lunch I usually swing by Micky D's or Arby's, depending on my mood. Wash it down with a Big Gulp soda. Then, for my midafternoon snack, I hit the vending machine. Dinner is pretty healthy."

She swallowed. "Chicken?"

He scratched his head. "Sometimes. Kentucky does a good job of it. Sometimes steak, nice and rare and bloody. A few IPAs and maybe a shot of Irish whiskey later on. Oh, I eat veggies, too. Like you've been saying, they're important for balance and stuff. I like corn."

"Of course you do." A fine sheen of sweat had broken out on her forehead. He tamped down on a laugh. Damn, she was a do-gooder. Wanted everyone to eat from the earth, probably, and die of starvation and boredom. She cleared her throat. "Umm, do you feel any of these habits need to change after our session? Luther wants to try drinking more water. Eli would like to stop snacking in the evening. What would you like to change?"

Stone pretended to think. "Well, I did quit smoking, so that was a big change."

"Yes, a wonderful decision we all applaud."

"I'd say I'd like to change my choices with fast food." She looked so relieved and happy, he almost felt bad for her. Almost. Her smile seemed much closer to real. His gut clenched. Funny, he had an urge to make her do it again. For him. Her eyes sparkled, and her lips relaxed, and that amazing energy shimmered around her, setting off something deep inside.

Whatever. He was probably hungry again.

"I'm thrilled you want to make those changes. Gentlemen, let's break for lunch and try to use some of our newfound knowledge. Again, the power of our choices affects all aspects in our life. Even anger."

Luther and Eli agreed with way too much eagerness, but Stone was already leaping from the chair and to the door. One hour of freedom. He'd pop back into the station and see what was up. It was also time to get the bastards back for the poop in his trunk incident. Devine had identified the two main culprits—McCoy and Make It Work Dunn. He'd keep this round simple and classic.

All he needed was a trip to the grocery store.

ARILYN FINISHED EATING HER bulgur salad with edamame, bought some doggy treats from the Barking Dog Bakery, and headed back to the firehouse. Now that she'd gotten some fresh air and protein, she was back in good spirits. Yes, the morning had started as a challenge, but at least it ended on a high note. Just having Stone admit he was trying to change some of his bad habits eased her stress. He'd spent most of the morning zoning out, rolling his eyes, and being generally surly.

Usually she worked well with clients who hated the process and even ended up winning them over. She'd never been annoyed or lost her temper before. The only explanation was her crazy schedule paired with trying to heal from a broken relationship. Yes, the man was clueless, but it wasn't his fault. Her job was to enlighten him so that he could come away from the course with some tactics to make a better life.

She couldn't lose her focus.

Humming under her breath, she took a deep breath of the crisp fall air. She loved this time of year, with apple picking, pumpkin harvests, and the gorgeous golden light that bathed the earth. The river nestled between a wall of bright red and burnt orange climbing high to the massive mountains that made the Hudson Valley home. Verily was filled with the lunch crowd grabbing an espresso or wrap or strolling past the gift stores for a bit of window-shopping. Who could be unhappy on such a day?

Her step lightened and she turned the corner. Then stopped cold.

Stone Petty sat on the curb outside the firehouse. He held a Dr Pepper in one hand and a huge sandwich in the other. As he shoved the awful fried mess into his mouth, he barked into a cell phone propped between his ear and shoulder. Instead of backward, his hat now perched to the side like some sort of gangster. He alternated between bites and screaming.

"I don't give a crap what the dickhead said! I clocked him going thirty miles over the speed limit and then the little shit called me names, practically challenging me to make that ticket stick. Who cares if he got a pretty-ass lawyer? I'm going to court, and I won't be changing it to a faulty headlight no matter who his father is. You got it? Good. Nah, I'll be there. Yeah, forced vacay is a bitch, you know? See ya, Sam."

In horror, she watched as he gobbled the rest up, slurped some soda, and this time used a napkin to wipe his face. Her shadow fell over him. He looked up.

"Oh, hey. I'm on time. Just finishing lunch."

Arilyn blinked. A hazy red fog swarmed her vision. Breathe. She just needed to breathe. "I thought you wanted to change your fast-food habits?" she asked. Her voice sounded high and pitched. Definitely not normal.

He squinted in the sunlight and unrolled himself from the curb. Stretching a bit, he studied her with those intense eyes that probed under her clothes and beyond. "I do," he said. "I got a fish fillet. Eating Nemo instead of Elsie the Cow's better, right?" He took a loud, obnoxious sip of soda. "Or do you have a problem with that, too?"

And she knew right then and there he was screwing with her.

He'd set her up for a fall. He thought her methods were stupid, and he wasn't about to try any of them. This was war in all its bloody forms. He'd fight her for every inch, every class, and try to drive her insane.

Did she expect him to embrace her philosophy on the second day? No. But he was deliberately baiting her. He enjoyed pissing her off and making a mockery of everything she passionately believed in. He wasn't even going to be polite about it.

The Arilyn she'd made herself into with all that work would've swallowed it. Bowed her head to his ignorance, prayed for his health, and moved on. She'd take his ribbing with a smile and a peaceful serenity because she was the better person.

Well, forget that.

No. She had one even better.

Fuck that.

He wanted her miserable for the remaining six weeks? Done.

But she'd spend her last waking moments making sure he felt the same.

He stepped back, cocked his head, and studied her as if he realized she'd come to an amazing lightbulb moment that would affect him. "You look funny. A little aggravated. Am I not able to eat what I want, or does this class limit my freedom of choice on that, too?"

She almost laughed. Almost. Instead, she pasted on her false, cheerful smile. Arilyn would die before he figured out he knew how to push all of her buttons. "You can eat anything you like, Officer. I can only offer you other options. I can only remind you that after forty, your statistics for heart attack, cancer, and diabetes rise, especially with a diet high in fat, salt, and sugar. I'm sure it doesn't matter that soda can also be used to burn off corrosion in a car battery and is probably dooming you to ulcers and all sorts of interesting digestive problems." She winked. "But that's America for you. Land of the free, home of the brave, and all that. Enjoy the rest of your lunch, and I'll see you in a few minutes."

"Hey. I'm not forty yet."

She widened her eyes in a total innocent expression. "Oh. Gee, sorry. My bad."

The uneasy expression on his face brightened her mood. *Take that, Officer.* She made her way inside, greeted her other two students, and began setting up for the afternoon session. Her cell pinged and she quickly answered, noting she had two minutes before the official start.

"Hello?"

"Arilyn? It's Anthony from Animals Alive shelter. How are you?"

She smiled. As the director of Animals Alive, Anthony Pearson was the driving force behind the not-for-profit shelter, which rescued animals, spayed, neutered, and did behavioral therapy for problem animals. They struggled every month to pay the bills, and fostering the animals helped tremendously, since the shelter was always overcrowded. Many people were afraid to foster in case they got too attached and couldn't keep the animals, but Arilyn thought of the higher good and tried to take them in groups. The shelter volunteers were all friends and worked overtime to try to make up for the lack of funding.

"Hi, Anthony. Checking up on Lenny and Mike?"

He laughed. "All animals thrive with you, so I'm not worried. Still trying to place them in the right home. Do you mind keeping them a bit longer? I don't want to break them up."

Usually puppies were separated to be adopted, but Mike and Lenny were an extreme case. They were so attached to each other that when Anthony had tried to separate them, both had gone a bit batty. Finding a family to take two puppies was a task. "No problem, you know I love them. If I can teach them not to eat all my shoes."

"I'll buy you new ones. I have a quick favor if you have a minute."

Arilyn glanced up and watched Stone walk in and take his usual seat. He gave a grudging nod to the other men. "Sure, I have two."

"I got a call from a lady on Bluebird Avenue. Complaining about a dog being chained twenty-four/seven in the yard. She thinks he's starving and may be abused."

"Did you call the ASPCA?"

"Yeah. Told me I needed more evidence before they'd come out and investigate. The lady said she doesn't want to get involved because she suspects drug ties in the neighborhood."

Arilyn sighed. "I wish we had more options with these cases. Who else could help? Police?"

"Most people don't want to get entangled with animal problems. I suspect it's a pit bull, so it could be protection or maybe even an underground fighting network. Not sure. Already called the police; they can't do much either."

She tamped down on the flash of temper and glared at Stone. Of course not. More things to do in Verily, such as speeding tickets to make more money for the town. She tried to imagine him risking time and effort on an animal case and couldn't. He was more for the hard-core cases.

"What are our options?"

"I wondered if you could take a quick drive out there. Look around. The house is on a dead-end road with a gate. If you see something that can be used as evidence, we may be able to send someone out."

The idea took root and bloomed. Yes. She'd just figured out a task for Officer Petty to complete while in her anger management course. And it would help not only him but also the shelter.

"No problem. I'll check back with you after I make my run."

His sigh of relief echoed through the phone. "Thanks. It's a load off my mind. I'm kind of slammed with the Fur Ball event going on, and we lost two volunteers last week when they moved away."

"Hang in. I'll talk to you later."

They hung up. Time to use a bit of force from the force to help save an animal.

Arilyn threw her phone in her satchel and took a seat at the front.

"Let's begin."

HE NEVER SHOULD'VE EATEN the damn fish fillet.

Stone lay on the mat with his feet straight out in front of him. The object, besides breathing of course, was to touch his toes with his hands. The two bastards beside him seemed to have little trouble with this task also. As his teacher from hell praised them for their "surrender" to their bodies, he did everything in his power, including praying to God, to just touch one end of his finger anywhere close to his ankles.

Not gonna happen.

Was that look of sympathy she shot him on purpose? Damned if it wasn't. Instead of support, she directed her words to him in her chilly, professional voice with no warmth: "Don't fight your body, Officer. Relax into the stretch and accept your limitations. Not everyone can touch their toes the first time."

He could bench-press an elephant and run two miles without breaking a sweat. But his ridiculous hamstrings were bunched up like cords, and his back wanted to spasm in shock. That was it. He was hitting some kind of Pilates class and screw whoever thought he wasn't manly. This was humiliation in public. Stone glanced over to the other dudes and caught Eli's triumphant look. Then the bastard leaned even deeper, going past his stupid toes.

Show-off.

She chattered nonstop in that lilting musical voice and got him even more twisted up. Stuff about release and the body-mind and the root of disease lying in anger. Had he ever noticed her ass was spectacular? Sure, he knew she was in shape, but when she turned and the perfect, tight, heart-shaped rear was right in front of him, he got all kinds of distracted.

He tried not to pant and curse, pretending to close his eyes and surrender. Instead, he peeked from under his lids and watched her float across the room.

The fish fillet seemed like a good idea at the time.

He only meant to confirm his choice of food and show her not everyone was so perfect. How happy could one possibly be eating wheat and fruit all day? Instead, she'd gotten that scary look on her face, all focused and tight, like she was about to make him pay. As if she actually cared he may die before he hit forty. And that smart-assed remark about his age? Priceless.

Not very yogic. But a hell of a lot more intriguing than her usual. In fact, the way she put him solidly in his place the entire session kind of turned him on in a perverted way. At least she had a spine. A quite gorgeous one, he bet, from that tempting peek of unblemished white skin at the nape of her neck. She'd taken her long hair, twisted it up, and knotted it without even looking in a mirror. Like she didn't give a crap how she looked. Also obvious in the lack of makeup on her face.

Imagine that. A woman who didn't spend hours on her appearance. It was like the yeti—an intriguing but never-before-seen legend.

"Let's breathe in, hold, and release from the position. Excellent work, gentlemen."

His body creaked and cried, but he made sure to look like it was easy. The glint of laughter in those grassy-green eyes called him an outright liar.

"Later this week we'll break from group, and I'll be meeting with everyone on an individual basis. Have a good night."

He pretended to be all Zenlike so he'd get a few extra moments to get himself up. Trying not to hobble, he made a note to check out the gym calendar for Pilates or something, and headed for the door. Thank

God. He was gonna shoot some damn pool and put his supplies to use to gain his revenge. Then he'd—

"Officer? Are you forgetting our additional fifteen-minute session?"

He wanted to close his eyes and groan. Instead, he turned and pasted a confident grin on his face. "Nope, been looking forward to it all day."

"I'm sure you have. Would you like a quick break to smell a cigarette pack? Drink a Coke? Gobble down some chips?"

He chuckled. "No, thanks. But I understand if you're in a bad mood. Did you hear too much fiber backs you up?" He shook his head. "Quite uncomfortable, I bet. Me? I don't have problems like that."

She jerked back and pressed her uncolored, lush pink lips together. Her nose crinkled as if she smelled something bad. "Good for you. Of course, the other issues must be difficult to deal with."

He cocked his head. "What issues?"

"Impotence. One of the major causes is a high-sugar and high-fat diet. Better think before that next Twinkie, Officer."

For God's sake, the little brat caused a hoot of laughter to escape. Damned if she didn't know how to word rumble with the best of them. "Never been a problem before," he drawled. Took a step closer. The clean smell of peaches and soap hit his nostrils. The sheer purity of her scent turned him on. Who would've thought? "Wanna see?"

"No, thanks. Let's get to work. Please take a spot on the mat."

Ah, crap. No more mat work. Stone swaggered to

the dreaded instrument of torture. "Haven't we done enough breath and pretzel work for the day?" he muttered under his breath.

"Agreed. I thought we'd go over another important element we deal with. Frustration. Failure. How the mind can slip and judge us, affecting our anger and how we express it."

She looked way too satisfied, so he knew something bad was coming his way. He could do anything for fifteen minutes. Right? He was a cop, for God's sake, and been put through both physical and mental torture in order to succeed at the academy and his job. "Sounds like a real party," he offered. "So, tell me the big secret."

"No secret. Just practice. We'll begin simply with some balancing asanas."

"Ass what?"

She moved to the front of the room. Her face smoothed out and reflected a calmness he only wanted to shake up. "Asanas. Postures to help open different parts of the body. Balancing techniques are important to learn and explore on the mat."

Yeah. This was going to be bad. "You mean standing on one foot will help anger?"

Arilyn smiled like a female Buddha. "Yes. Let's begin."

Maybe five minutes needling her had already passed. Then he'd only have ten minutes left.

"Our time will start from now."

He really disliked her. A lot.

"Taking in a breath, fix your gaze loosely on a spot on the floor. Lift your right leg and place the bottom of your foot against your inner calf. Once you can hold the position, remain breathing, and lift the leg higher. Watch me first."

In one smooth, continuous motion, she lifted her hands like a ballerina, seemingly rising taller from the earth, her swanlike neck lengthening. Her foot pointed out, rose in the air, and pressed against the inner flesh of her thigh. She looked like a tree rising from the mist, strong in the trunk and graceful in the branches.

"As you gaze at your spot, empty your mind and concentrate on the breath. Let your body lead. You're solid in the legs, unbreakable as the root of a tree. Bendable and open to the wind with your hands and upper body. Now go ahead and try when you're ready."

Stone studied the gorgeous curves of her breasts, her nipples pressing against her tank top, her face open and reflective. He had a quick image of him pinning her to the bed while she welcomed him deep inside, but it freaked him out, so he quickly pushed the image away. Whoa. Who would've thought he'd get turned on by a tree pose?

Shaking his head, Stone mimicked her movements, thinking this wasn't as bad as he thought.

He fell over.

She remained in position, neither swaying nor moving. "If you fall out of a position, recenter yourself and begin again."

Okay, no problem. He got this now. He took a breath, resettled, and did it again.

Then fell over.

A dark cloud of irritation swept over him. This was so stupid, but simple enough he refused to be beaten.

He boxed in the gym, and his trainer told him his balance was spot-on. He'd get this.

Over and over, he tumbled out of position, his crankiness growing by leaps and bounds. When she instructed him to start on the other foot, he found the same problem. The minutes ticked by in growing horror, and Stone finally came to the realization she'd beaten him. He couldn't stand on one fucking foot for more than a second.

He sucked.

Unfolding from her tree stance, she offered him one of those sympathetic smiles that burned in his gut. "Do you feel angry?" she asked, gaze probing his.

Stone clenched his fist. "For being stuck imitating a damn tree when I could be at work catching real criminals? Nah, I'm good. I'm peachy."

Her smile widened. "Good. Let's move on to the next asana."

His mouth dropped open. "It's been way over fifteen minutes."

"No, that was five. And let's begin."

The torture was long and deep and mean. By the time she finally called an end to the session, Stone decided to go to the pool hall and start a fight. Yeah, a nasty, testosterone-ridden, stupid fight with fists and blood and that wonderful feeling of release afterward. So much better than this. Completely manly and dudelike.

"How are you feeling now, Officer?"

And then he kinda exploded.

"We're alone now. My name is Stone. I'd like you to say my real name once instead of jerking me around for fun. Here, I'll even start the conversation.

Did you enjoy our session today, *Arilyn*? Are you finally satisfied with my conduct in your anger management class, *Arilyn*? Will you sleep better tonight knowing you won this round, *Arilyn*?"

An odd expression skittered over her face. Those green eyes darkened, as if his saying her name aloud affected her on some level. He panted for breath, challenging her with his direct stare, and that crackle of electricity went berserk between them. She caught the vibe, because her mouth did a little O and she took a tiny step back in complete denial.

Sexual attraction. Well, damned if that wasn't a kick in the ass. She felt it just as strongly as he did.

The question was what to do about it.

Her tongue dragged over her lower lip in a complete nervous gesture. "Umm, sorry. Stone. You did well."

He ached to make her say it again, but it was already way too weird between them. "Good. Can I go?"

"Not yet. I need you to do me a favor."

He laughed. "Somehow, I'm not feeling too charitable." He turned away to dismiss her, but her voice cracked like a whip in the air, making him freeze.

"I'm not asking."

His brow shot up. Was she serious? Her jaw tightened in that stubborn gesture he was beginning to spot, and she crossed her arms in front of her chest. "Are you blackmailing me?" he asked in a dark tone.

"Of course not! I need you to take a ride with me out to a property. I suspect a dog is being abused and I want to get an overview of the situation."

He didn't respond. Just studied her. Definitely

defensive. Almost like she didn't like pushing him but was forced to, due to the circumstances. No way. She wasn't getting away with bullying him to do something in the name of his job. "As you like to point out, I'm suspended. I can't do anything in an official capacity."

She practically snarled. "Since we already called the police, who refused to do anything to help, that won't be a problem."

"That's what the animal protection groups are for," he shot back. "Unless we witness a crime being committed, we're not allowed to prowl through people's backyards 'cause we want to. We have what's called the Constitution and all."

"Right. So we're supposed to sit around while we know an animal is being abused, waiting for the proper paperwork."

He shrugged. She wasn't saying anything he hadn't seen and fought with on his own. "Some departments have an animal advocate they can call in, but the town can't afford it. Bureaucracy is a bitch. Sorry it's not like in the movies and all. Call the dog rescue people or something. Good luck."

"You're still going with me." She grabbed the giant cloth thing she called a purse and yanked it over one arm. "It's on Bluebird Avenue on the dead end. Do you know where that is?"

He spoke slowly. "I. Am. Not. Going. It's a crappy part of town, I'm not on duty, and I don't care about any animal not getting the luxury-hotel treatment you probably demand. What if the dog likes being outside? It's good for them."

Aww, great, now she looked like he had admitted

to being a child molester. Pure horror carved out her features. "You can't mean that," she whispered. "You cannot be that cruel and . . . and . . . heartless!"

He wasn't about to tell her the real truth. He hated dogs. Stone rarely admitted his fear, but the image from his past had never left him. He still heard the snarling and remembered the sharp teeth rip into his flesh, drawing blood. He'd only been about eight, walking down the street, and the guy had sicced his pit bull on him as a twisted joke. Stone came home with a bad bite and even worse memory. His father, of course, had called him a pussy.

He made sure to hide his weakness from the other cops by pretending he was too cool for an animal, especially one to feed, care for, and clean up after. So far it had worked like a charm, and he wasn't about to let Arilyn Meadows screw up his ruse.

"Sorry to disappoint you, sweetness, but dogs are like rats. The world would be better off without them."

She lifted her nose up in the air, her eyes growing cold. "I should've known you'd be no help. Still, you're driving me out there to be my witness. We'll snap some pictures for documentation. I'm not expecting the police to do anything, but this may speed up the response time from the Humane Society or ASPCA. Plus, being a witness in law enforcement will hold up my story. Let's go."

She marched out the door and didn't even look back, ignoring his refusal. Did she ever give up? Stone had a gut instinct she'd be hell to deal with once she focused on saving something. Or someone. What a pain in the rear.

He followed her out. "You already kept me past

my time. I have a date at the pool hall and I'm not gonna be late."

"My condolences to your date, Officer. But you *are* going with me. I control the sign-in sheets for the course. What a shame if I marked you down as absent one day. Or told your boss you've been uncooperative and I can't advise passing you. Why, you may need to repeat the entire session all over again!"

His mouth fell open. Her look of satisfaction steamrolled over him. "You *are* blackmailing me! Dammit, that's a crime!"

"Prove it. Where's your car?"

He cursed viciously, pulled out his keys, and marched down the street. "You're a hypocrite. The worst kind. Pretending to be all good and wholesome and kind, when underneath you're completely spiteful."

"You're delusional. I'm doing this for the good of a higher power."

"And you're a liar. Isn't that bad karma or something?"

She hummed something maddening under her breath, easily keeping up with his stride with those long legs. "You worry about your karma, and I'll worry about mine." He stopped at the curb and went to pull open the door. "Please tell me this is not your car."

He shoved his anger aside for a moment to puff up with male pride. His sweet baby was his pride and joy, and he didn't get to drive it half as much as he craved. "It is. A 1965 Pontiac GTO Tempest, 335 horsepower, 389-cubic-inch engine. Montero red." He waited for her long sigh, but she curled her lip in disdain, hitting him with one of those arctic gazes.

"This car should be a crime," she said primly. "We're on a mission to save the earth, and you're destroying it with this hunk of metal and dirt. Besides being a gas guzzler, it's completely inefficient. The emissions alone should be criminal."

Now she'd gone over the line. Mess with his job or his friends, but no one insulted his car. He lowered his voice to a warning. "Dirt? Careful. I restored this car and rebuilt it piece by piece. She's a classic you can't appreciate."

"A classic nightmare," she muttered. "Do you know they actually make cars that help the environment instead of harm it?"

"And you couldn't get up a hill. This one goes zero to sixty in record time. Bet you have one of those ridiculous Fusions or something." Her startled look made him laugh. "So predictable. Now get in."

She shivered with distaste and carefully slid onto the black leather seat. He sucked in a breath filled with that old car/new car smell and revved the engine. The loud growl still got him excited. He revved the engine, the loud noise a symphony to his ears, while she made all sorts of faces and talked to herself under her breath. Stone pulled onto the road and headed toward the far edge of town. The sheer dimensions of the car reminded him of a bully in school, taking up the entire hallway while the other kids shrunk away. Total badass.

She did not look as impressed.

"It's huge," she complained. "Almost indecent."

"Aww, now you're flattering me."

She stiffened her shoulders in that puritanical way of hers and gave him another look. His body roared to life, completely contradicting his mental state. She'd be smokin' if she had those librarian glasses she could peer over. With a Britney Spears Catholic school outfit. Oh, yeah, he so needed to get laid. He was losing it. Arilyn Meadows probably had sex with the lights off, in a proper bed, with her eyes closed. She didn't look like the wild screaming type.

"Very funny," she sniffed. "Again, I feel bad for your date."

"Trust me, I'd feel worse for yours." She glowered, and they were off and running again. If she was gonna force him to help with her ridiculous plan, he'd at least control the conversation. "Honestly, I'm curious. What type of men do you date?"

Her body language told him he'd hit a hot spot. She shut down, gazing out the window. "Men with morals," she finally said. "Men with ideals of what they want to give to the world. Men who serve a higher purpose."

Stone rolled his eyes. "No wonder you're so backed up. There's no such thing. Men like that simply don't exist."

She jerked in her seat and swiveled her gaze around. Her tone warmed to a molten lava heat of general pissiness. "That's ridiculous, of course they do. I've dated them!"

"They lied to you. Men are simple creatures. We're controlled by our id. Food, sex, work. More sex, and we're pretty damn happy. We're simple."

The shocked expression made him feel a bit bad for her. Did she really believe there were men who followed their higher morality over their dicks? Well, he was sure many tried but few succeeded. She needed a wake-up call or she'd spend the rest of her life chasing a dream that didn't exist.

"I disagree. The last man I dated focused on his spiritual work and craved to be a better man. He was sweet, giving, a great listener and supporter. He transcended the physical."

Stone groaned. "If he's so great, how come you're still not together?"

"It's none of your business," she snapped. "This is a stupid conversation anyway. I bet you think jumping into bed with anyone just to scratch an itch is acceptable."

"It's definitely fun. When was the last time you had real fun?"

"I have fun all the time. I go out with my friends on the weekends. I volunteer with charities I'm passionate about. I practice yoga, and take care of dogs, and spend time with my grandfather."

He laughed. "Yeah, I bet Grandpa is a barrel of laughs."

"He's more fun than you'd ever be. At least I have a ton of outside interests. What do you do when you're not buried in your all-important job?"

"Tons."

Her mocking laugh scraped his nerve endings. "Hmm, let me take a wild stab at this. You drink beer with some cops. Shoot a bit of pool. Maybe lift a few weights at the gym. But basically you're a workaholic who spends most of his time alone. Even your dating probably is wrapped up in your inane ideas about women and sex. Keep it to the physical so no one figures out you're not cool. God forbid a woman messes with your career, or Friday nights at the pool hall. You, Stone Petty, are just as big a hypocrite."

She lapsed into a simmering silence, deliberately tuning him out. He opened his mouth to tell her a few hard truths, realized he didn't have any, and shut up. Sure, he loved his job. That's why he worked all the time, but he had plenty of outside interests. A lot. She had no idea what she was talking about, and he wasn't about to waste his precious time arguing with her. This past relationship of hers had probably blown up in her face, and she was still sore. He'd bet his balls the guy had done something scummy. Maybe cheating. His cop instincts flared to life from her guarded expression and what he suspected was the real reason they'd broken up.

Transcendent, his ass.

He made a right onto Bluebird and scanned the area. Not much going on. The dead-end street held neglect and the stink of something illegal. Drugs? Teens? Or just people who'd fallen on hard times?

"The house at the end of the street. There." She pointed toward a run-down ranch in puke brown. Weeds choked the yard, and empty bottles littered the ground. There was a large area in the back, behind the rusty metal gate, but he couldn't see much from the curb. Stone parked, cut the engine, and studied the property. Lots of garbage cans. A charred fire pit. Seemed to be deserted, but he bet the place came alive at night. He may need to do a drive-by with Devine and make sure there wasn't some kind of weed fest going on in his town.

"Let's go." She reached for the handle. His hand

shot across the seat and circled her wrist before she could escape.

The feel of her soft skin sliding under his made him jerk, but he kept his grip firm. Holy hell, what was it about touching this woman that put all his senses on high alert? "Where do you think you're going?"

That cute little frown marred her brow. "To check it out, of course. That's why we're here. Got your phone?"

He shook his head. "This isn't some vice squad drama. We're not allowed to go traipsing around on private property and snap pictures. Let's walk to the end of the street and get close. Maybe we can see the backyard better."

"Fine. Great plan, Officer." This time he let her go, but he cursed under his breath and jumped out of the car. Her insulting tone made him want to prove what he could do to her as an officer of the law. Some good things. Some bad.

Very, very bad.

He made sure to look casual while he took in his surroundings. Yeah, they were definitely doing something back there. The yard contained a pile of rusty car parts, large paint-type cans scattered around, and a beaten-up doghouse. The wood was rotted, and the roof sagged. He stayed back, taking note of the tin bowl, a few leashes, and mud pits. A nasty smell radiated from the yard, like a rodent trapped under the porch. Ugh. Not a good situation. Bet there were rats running around.

Stone shuddered more from the thought of encountering a dog than a rat. Rodents he could handle—he'd seen and lived with his fair share. Dogs? Not so much.

"See, there's the doghouse. There *are* dogs. Who knows how many? We have to get closer."

Again she went to march onto the side lawn in plain view of any asshole checking them out. If there were drugs or dog fighting involved, things got complicated. Best to go back with Devine and poke around at night.

He stepped in front of her, lowering his voice to his famous cop growl everyone obeyed. "No. You can take a picture from here, noting the gate and the doghouse. But there's no animals evident around, and we can't go further."

"I'm not leaving a helpless animal trapped inside without proof. Cover me."

Moving in a blur, she jogged toward the side lawn, her iPhone held out in front of her for any Tom, Dick, or Harry to see. Cover her? What the hell did she watch on television? He muttered a vicious curse and took off. If he were on duty, he'd be tempted to lock her ass in jail for a night for disobeying a police officer. Instead, he looked like some poor chump racing after her with a helpless look on his face.

She reached the gate and flashed a few pictures. His instincts told him they were alone, but he didn't want to take a chance. Arilyn pressed her face against the creaky metal and lowered her voice to a soothing pitch. "Are you in there, sweetie? Come on out, we won't hurt you."

Stone thanked God he was on the other side of the gate. She was nuts. He braced himself for a snarling, angry pit bull to race out and try to attack, but the doghouse was silent. She snapped another photo.

"Enough. There's no dog here, and we're trespassing. Let's go."

"But—"

"Now." This time he grabbed her wrist firmly and led her away, not bothering to pause to let her catch up. Her Amazon legs were almost as long as his. "You don't have to be so pushy. I know there's a dog in there, Stone. I'm telling you, something is going on."

The sound of his name on her lips by her own accord made a funny thing happen to his gut. Probably indigestion. "I know, but there's nothing to do right now. Listen, I'll come check out the situation, okay? I'll bring my partner and we'll look into it."

"When?"

He let out a breath. "When I'm back on official duty."

She got that mulish look on her face again. "Too late. We need to check it out now."

"Oh, for God's sake, get in the car. Fine. I'll tell Devine to do a drive-by this week. Will you get off my case now?"

"Yes. I'm sending these photos to Anthony. If I need you as a witness, I'm giving them your number."

"Who's Anthony?" The question popped out of his mouth before he had time to think. It was the familiarity in her tone that made him curious. Maybe she'd moved on from her other perfect relationship after all. "New boyfriend? Ex?" He couldn't seem to stop himself, which was frickin' embarrassing.

She didn't seem to notice his question was out of bounds, satisfied she'd gotten what she could from him. "The director of Animals Alive. We work closely together."

"Oh. Is he spiritually enlightened, too?"

She rolled her eyes. "We're not dating. Though he's perfect for me. Just more in the friend camp."

He relaxed and got in the car. Yeah. Friends. That was good. Not that he cared. "Let me guess. He loves dogs, helps out with charity, wants to grow as a better person, doesn't hunt, and is super nice."

Her gaze narrowed. "Are you making fun of me?"

"Nope. Just running down the requirements of the men you condescend to date."

She buckled her seat belt, looking at both him and his muscle car with pure distaste, and stuck her nose in the air. "At least I date more than a body. Bet your requirements are as simple as you are. Big boobs, small brain, undemanding, and a seeker of fun."

He drove, refusing to tell her how close she was to the mark. Not that he enjoyed women of little intelligence. He loved a sharp, witty female who didn't let him get away with his normal stuff. It was just easier to date someone he'd never have a long attachment to. That way, he didn't have to deal with the slow eroding of a relationship that was doomed from the start. Cops were among the highest casualties in marriage, and now he knew why. He wasn't gonna make that mistake again.

"You're wrong." He paused. "Boobs can be any shape and size. I never discriminate."

She shuddered with distaste. "Please drop me off at the firehouse."

"Fine." They drove in silence back into Verily. "Where's your car?"

"There."

He pulled up to a shiny, tiny Ford Fusion in an awful sea-green color. Just as he thought. The car was just horrible. "Have fun saving the environment. Oh, and thanks for the blackmail trip. Let's do it again sometime."

She yanked open the door, spun around, and shot him a glare. "I don't like you, Officer Petty."

"Good. Don't like you much either. Night, Arilyn."

She gasped, slammed the door, and turned. He grinned, roared away, and turned on the radio. Yeah, that was almost worth the trip. Something about getting her all irritated satisfied him on a deeper scale. He sang aloud to some pop music and headed to Ray's Billiards. It may be a long six weeks, but at least he'd manage to keep himself entertained.

six

ARILYN SLOWLY OPENED her eyes and eased out of her pranayama practice, going back to regular breathing. The soft sounds of a flute whispered past her ears.

With slow motions, she stretched out her legs in front, raising her arms to the ceiling and stretching straight out and dropping her head to her calves. The delicious stretch loosened the last of her stress. Rising back up, she pressed her palms together, bowed her head, and said a quick prayer of gratitude.

Finally. Her emotions were back under control. A lightness flowed through her body, her mind was crystal clear, and she was ready to face the day.

No more thinking of Stone Petty and his aggravating ways.

Arilyn parted the Chinese painted screens that blocked off her meditation center. The scratch of paws on the floor echoed in the air, and she braced herself as the two piles of fluff threw themselves at her, wiggling and slurping at her in ecstasy. It had taken a while to get them past whimpering and crying behind the screens. Dogs had no sense of time, and to Lenny and Mike, it was hours that she had isolated herself from them in a maddening game. They heard her breathing but couldn't get to her. Now, thank goodness, they slept behind the screen as close as possible and waited for her to come back.

She laughed and gave them snuggles, refilled their water bowl, and began making a cup of ginger tea. Piling fresh berries in a ceramic bowl, she added organic granola and Greek yogurt. Today was going to be great. She'd focus better, be more balanced, and complete the multitude of tasks needed. The big bachelorette party for Kate was coming up fast, and she needed her strength. Kennedy was scaring the hell out of her about the strippers. Or exotic male dancers, as she corrected. She was insistent on hiring a cop to arrest Kate, but Arilyn hoped she went with her suggestion and got a fireman instead.

She couldn't take any more sexy cops.

Arilyn gobbled the rest of her breakfast and made a plan of attack for the day. She meditated, ingested protein and antioxidants, and owned a clean, pure aura. For good measure, she grabbed some crystals from her meditation corner. Definitely some turquoise to advance healing, communication skills, and prana, the essential life energy. She'd tackle the anger management course with tranquillity. No more losing her temper over Stone's sarcastic comments or deep drawls or confident male grins.

Arilyn washed the bowl and spoon, dried her hands, and grabbed her purse.

The doorbell rang.

She frowned. What now? She peeked out the window, then held back a groan. No. Not now. But she had no other choice, so she pasted on a smile and opened the door.

Mrs. Blackfire stood on the porch. Her new next-door neighbor, dubbed the Wicked Witch of Verily by Genevieve, and the Spawn of the Devil by Kate, glared from behind her thick-framed glasses. She was a short, petite woman but made up for it in crankiness. Gray tufts of hair sprouted from her head. Her face was a road map of wrinkles that couldn't have been laugh lines. She wore a faded pink housedress with snaps down the front, support stockings that sagged around her ankles, and thick-soled old-lady shoes. She held on to a walker in her brown-spotted hands, but Arilyn suspected she didn't need it and only used it for a prop or weapon.

Genevieve and Kate had warned her before she moved in about their problem neighbor. Seems she counted the wine bottles in their recycling bins, used a telescope to spy on people in the neighborhood, and had been previously kicked out of visiting the Best Friends Senior Home for calling the food inspector in to check out the Jell-O. She despised animals, including Kate's beautiful dog, Robert. And now she stood on her doorstep when Arilyn was already running late.

"Mrs. Blackfire," she greeted politely. "How are you? It's a lovely fall day, don't you think?"

"Not when you have to rake up all the leaves," her neighbor spat out. "I wanted to talk to you about your property."

She held back a sigh. "Well, you'd need to speak with Genevieve, since I only rent. Is there a problem?"

"Besides that tree ready to fall on my house?" Her bony finger jabbed at the towering pine tree in the front lawn leaning gently to the right. Genevieve called it the Tree of Spite, since they'd gone to the mats regarding its condition and right to stay.

"Gen said it was a healthy tree," she said. "I'm sorry, but there's nothing I can do."

Suddenly, her lemon face smoothed out. Her lips curved a bit upward. Was that an attempt at a smile? "I have an idea," Mrs. Blackfire said quite nicely. "My landscaping service is coming, and they'll be happy to trim it. No charge, of course. I just need your permission."

Warning bells clanged in her ear. She glanced at her watch, knowing she had to leave now. "Well, if it's just a trim, I'm sure Gen won't mind."

Her neighbor smiled. Arilyn almost fell back at the flash of straight white, fake teeth. She'd never seen her smile before. Arilyn wondered why her tummy clenched and her skin prickled with danger. Unfortunately, she had no time to decipher why Mrs. Blackfire was that happy over a tree trim.

"I'm sure she'll be surprised at the finished product," Mrs. Blackfire said. "Now, you look like you're in a hurry, dear. I'll see you later."

Dear?

The bells clanged louder, but she'd run out of time. Arilyn watched her neighbor disappear down the path with her walker, grabbed her keys, and hopped in the car. No reason to worry, she reminded herself. If a trim made her back off, it was for the best. She'd call Gen later and let her know.

Arilyn sped off down the road. She'd spend a few hours at Kinnections, hit anger management, then conference with Anthony about the dog. She'd already sent the photos over and hoped it would be enough to gain some help.

Her cell pinged on her Bluetooth. Poppy? Arilyn hurriedly pushed the button. "Hello?"

"Arilyn! Thank God you answered. Can you hear me? Hello?"

"Poppy, it's me. Yes, I can hear you. Are you on a cell?"

"I borrowed Emma's when she was getting pudding."

"Are you okay?"

"Bastards! They said I can't leave. I told Ralph I'd meet him on Main Street in the billiards room for a beer, but they said it's too far for me to walk and they won't put me in a cab without your permission. So then I told them I was walking to your house to take care of the dogs, but now they don't believe me and said they were going to call you to confirm. I won't let them keep me a prisoner. I'm sneaking out. Doing the Great Escape. But I'll do the window instead of dig a trench."

"It's ten a.m.! You can't drink a beer and play pool this early."

"Bah. It's close to lunchtime. Besides, Ray likes when I help him set up for the day."

"Did you check your insulin level today?"

"Yes, I'm good. Ray keeps a close eye on me, I swear."

She squeezed her eyes shut and recalculated her agenda. It was hard to get used to letting others know when he wanted to do something, especially with restrictions. She'd been hoping the trips and packed daily calendar would help, but Poppy was stubborn about what he liked and didn't. Shoot. "No sneaking out," she said firmly. "You'll get in trouble. Give me twenty minutes and I'll pick you up. You can spend the afternoon with Ray, and I'll pick you up after my class and we'll do dinner. No pipe smoking. I mean it, Poppy. Ellen from the center said you were sneaking it in the janitor's closet and almost set off the smoke alarm."

"Big tattletale. She needs a man in her life under seventy."

Arilyn held back a laugh. "She's just doing her job."

"I guess. Thanks, sweetheart. I knew you'd understand. You're the only one who ever did."

Her chest tightened. "I always will, Poppy. See you in a few."

She disconnected the call. Okay, she'd get Poppy, hit Kinnections, go to anger management, then go back to pick him up.

No problem.

The morning flew by, and Kate promised to go walk Lenny and Mike at lunchtime. By the time she got to anger management, her morning meditation had become watered down and she lost her temper twice.

Both times with *him*, of course.

She went over specific techniques to gauge various emotional triggers. Luther and Eli offered honest responses, shared some of their journal writing, and seemed to get a bit closer in their achievement of controlling anger.

Stone took four phone calls during class, citing work, and shared his own creative cartoon he drew in place of journaling.

She was thrilled until she saw it. It consisted of a series of drawings with a criminal running from a cop, turning around, and trying to shoot said officer. Then it showed the officer pausing in the chase, taking a long, deep breath, and chanting "Om." The final picture showed the cop dead, the criminal free, and a big balloon over the heading *Can Breathing Stop Anger or a Criminal?*

She'd gotten so angry she made him do endless rounds of Salutation to the Sun and told him he needed to stay another fifteen minutes after class because he had mocked the journaling exercise. His smug grin told her his goal of annoying the hell out of her was working well. She was a teacher who succumbed to anger in an anger management class. If she didn't calm down, she'd eventually lose Luther's and Eli's confidence.

After making him hop on one foot for a long time in the goal of balance, Arilyn checked her watch. Darn. She was late picking Poppy up, and he'd already been at Ray's way too long.

"That's enough, Officer," she said, grabbing her satchel. "I'll see you tomorrow at Kinnections for our one-on-one evaluation."

Sweat gleamed on his brow. He wore his usual outfit of jeans, old sneakers, and a worn T-shirt. Today he sported a navy blue NYPD shirt that stretched over a mass of indecent muscles and hard abs. Swaggering off the mat, refusing to show any weakness, though Arilyn knew she'd worked him hard today, he perched his ball cap back on his head and smirked. From under the hat, strands of silky black hair stuck to his forehead. She wondered briefly what his hair would feel like under her fingers. That delicious scent of sweat, soap, and man swarmed around her. How could she be even the tiniest bit attracted to someone who made her nuts?

"Better watch out." His hot gaze swept over her body. "All this keeping me after school will make me think you got a crush on me."

Damned if her belly didn't slide down to her toes at that probing stare, but she crossed her arms in front of her chest and gave a humph. "Yeah, it's a real funfest with you, Officer."

He laughed then, a deep, dark sound that caressed her ears. "G'night, Arilyn."

She ignored him, turning around and racing out the door. His laugh followed her out. Damn him. Every time she tried to take him down a notch, he found a way to twist it around to his benefit. Completely maddening. Her feet flew over the pavement, hoping Ray had checked Poppy's insulin and didn't sneak him any tobacco. She finally reached her Fusion, grabbed for the door handle, and stopped short.

Her front windshield was shattered.

Damn. Damn, damn, damn.

A rock had hit it a week ago and caused a tiny hole, but she hadn't had time to call the insurance company to get it fixed. So stupid. No way she could drive with the spiderweb of glass blocking her view. A slight buzz of panic hit, along with the now-familiar pang of anger at having her careful plans screwed up. Why now? Wasn't she doing the right thing by helping out Poppy? Did everything have to go consistently wrong on a regular basis?

She had the urge to kick the tire, so she did what she'd just taught her students. Dragged in a breath. Let it out slowly. Did it again.

Her heartbeat slowed and her mind cleared. Good, back in control. She'd walk to the billiards room. It was a long walk but doable, and a crisp fall afternoon. Of course, she'd be super late and hoped Poppy wouldn't worry.

Run. She'd run. Good exercise, and it'd cut her time in half.

She quickly stripped off her long-sleeved T-shirt until only a tight black Lycra top molded her small breasts. Catching her long hair and twisting it up in a hair band, she secured it to the top of her head, then turned.

"If I had known I'd miss out on a free striptease, I would've gotten here sooner."

She jumped back. "You scared me! What are you doing here?"

Officer Petty took a long, measured glance at her windshield. "Doing my civic duty and responding to a call. Vandalism?"

Arilyn took a casual step backward. In class, she was able to keep reminding herself of the distance between them. Here on the street, having him invading her personal space was a bit disturbing. Already she had to tip her head back just to look at him, and she was pretty tall. "Sorry, no crime to uncover here. Just a rock that hit last week and I never got it fixed."

He studied her face. To assess if she was lying? His sharp observation skills fascinated her. When under his stare, a woman felt stripped to the bone, and a tiny flare of vulnerability caught her off guard. What would it be like to be Officer Petty's lover? Did he bring that fierce brutality to the bedroom and all that intense observation to give his lover pleasure?

The memory of her ex-boyfriend's face as he pounded into another woman's body made her wince and want to rub her eyes. Another bleachable moment in her life. Would she always be thinking of him and his betrayal? Had he ruined her for future relationships and sex by not only breaking her heart but also her trust? And why the hell was she thinking of this stuff in the middle of the road with her windshield cracked and a man she didn't like screwing with her head?

His voice softened, as if he'd spotted something in those few moments of her weakness. "Hmm, driving with a shattered windshield is a crime."

"Yeah, and wouldn't that break your heart to ticket me," she shot back. "No worries, Officer. I'll get my car towed. I have to go."

"Where are you going?"

"Is that your business?"

He arched a brow. "Besides helping tow your car, I can offer you a ride. You seem to be in a hurry."

Arilyn hesitated. Her pride begged her to decline and run away with her head held high. Somehow, she had an instinct it would end up being a favor he'd want to cash in. She didn't want to owe him a thing. But Poppy had been waiting awhile, and he was more important. Besides, she could handle Stone.

Her mind said his first name with a breathy sigh and a shiver.

God, maybe Kennedy was right and she just needed plain, good old-fashioned sex. Her hormones were beginning to do a number on her.

"Thank you," she said stiffly. "I need to go to Ray's Billiards."

"Interesting choice. My chariot awaits."

He escorted her to his souped-up, overpowering

muscle car. She might hate it, but it was hard not to smile at his obvious adoration for the vehicle. He actually stroked the steering wheel as he pulled out. Those long, tapered fingers were extra large but seemed tender. Would he treat a woman with a combination of roughness and care? Somehow, the idea of him being gentle shattered her composure.

Oh, my goodness. What was she thinking?

Arilyn cleared her throat and dove into a neutral topic. "Did you always want to become a cop?"

He eased the car out to the main road. "Seemed like a good way to stop the criminals. No one else was doing anything about it."

"Did you grow up in a rough neighborhood?"

"The average Bronx apartment in Woodlawn."

"What was it like?"

He shot her another glance. "Poking around in my head again?"

"Just making conversation. You don't have to answer if it's too painful."

He laughed, deep and long, and Arilyn studied his profile. Carved from granite, the roughness of his features pieced together a simple brutality that warned her this man could be dangerous. "I may be a disappointment to you, little one. I hide no secrets, and made peace with my crap a long time ago."

The distracted endearment made her tummy free fall. Maybe it was the dark, sensual melody of his voice as he said it. He'd called her that once before over the summer when they first met, and she had never forgotten it. It was so . . . intimate. Her body sprung to life, surprising her with its sudden demand for his lips over hers. Odd. She rarely had a reaction to men on such a primal, physical scale. Her poetry professor from NYU. The artist from that watercolor class she took. Her yoga teacher. And now Stone Petty.

All had ended badly. But at least she had *liked* the others.

If her past was any indication of luck, she'd better pass right over Stone Petty. Arilyn refocused on their conversation. "Most people have a difficult time accepting the truth of the past and who they are."

"I learned it's much easier to deal with facts and truth than with pretty lies and denials," he said. "Tell you what. I'll give you the short version of my bio and you do the same."

A warning bell clanged in her head. "I'll be sifting through your past during our individual sessions anyway."

"Thought this was a conversation," he shot back. "What's the matter? Too above the rest of us to share?"

"I'm not above anyone," she said calmly. "I don't think it's necessary."

"I do. Tell you what. I'll keep it simple. Just answer one question from me, and I'll give you all my dirty laundry. Fair?"

The idea was tempting, but she squirmed in her seat. "This is stupid, we don't have to make a deal. Let's just keep our relationship strictly to the anger management classes and how they pertain to your treatment."

"Chicken? I bet you're so used to having everyone open up, no one ever demands the same of you. When was the last time anyone asked you questions about your past? About who you are? About what you want?"

He murmured the last question, and the heat in his seething gaze made her press hard against the door. Her heart thundered in her chest, making it difficult to take a cleansing breath. A strange surge of emotion rocked her normal calm and seeped out. "You don't know anything about me or my needs," she hissed out. "I have no trouble opening up."

"Good, then it's a deal. I'll give you the short version. Grew up in a tough Irish neighborhood where boys ended up being cops or firemen. I got jumped at the school bus when I was seven and put in the hospital. My father told me it would teach me a lesson to be either tougher or faster. I made sure I was both, and my training intensified when he began beating the crap out of me and my mother with a baseball bat. I learned how to steal, how to hide in the parks, how to survive, but I never got to save my mother. She died from a nasty fall deemed an accident. I left and dedicated myself to catching bad guys and working out my past karma with my asshole father. Thoughts?"

His speech was thorough and honest, and it broke her heart. Because beyond all that analysis was a little boy who'd never forgiven himself for not being enough. Her intrigue deepened when she realized how much more lurked beneath the surface.

What really freaked her out was how she suddenly wanted to find out.

"You nailed your anger issues and current occupation choice," she finally answered. "And though my heart breaks for the little boy you were, I've heard a bunch of horror stories that ended up far worse than yours. But it's not your mother you're still mourning, is it?"

His fingers clenched around the wheel. A dangerous cloud settled over him, holding a tinge of violence Arilyn bet would always be a part of who he was. "What are you talking about?"

Her instincts screamed for her to back off. He wasn't ready for a bigger truth. And, dear God, neither was she. "Nothing," she said lightly. They were almost there, and she had a sudden urge to jump out of the car before anything more passed between them. Arilyn had learned that a physical connection was difficult to fight, but an emotional one would destroy them both. "Oh, there's a spot."

He remained silent, maybe sifting through her odd answer to his speech. She regretted diving in when neither of them was ready. He pulled into the parking space and turned to face her.

"Thanks so much for the lift, I appreciate it," she said. "See you tomorrow."

Her hand never reached the latch.

He moved so deadly fast, she didn't even sense his movement. His fingers closed around her wrist, holding firm. The controlled grip did something weird to her belly, as if she was helpless under his command.

"Not yet."

She refused to look at him, keeping her head down. "Umm, I'll take a rain check, I really have to go."

"I'll be quick. Look at me."

His voice deepened, slowed. An explosion of heat

and want slithered in her blood. She turned and met his gaze.

Lust.

No. Not possible.

She caught her breath at the naked desire on his face, in his eyes, as he looked at her. For a second she was caught up in a tidal wave of pure feeling, her usual logic and calm, serene thoughts like a crystal lake suddenly turning into a tsunami of choppy waves and tidal flooding. Her body shook in response to the primitive male need in his eyes. This was nothing but pure hunger at its elemental level.

"You promised an answer to one question."

Arilyn managed a nod. The words were stuck at the back of her throat, trapped there under his blistering male power.

"What's his name?"

She blinked. Her voice came out rusty. "Whose?"

"The man who fucked you up. The man who broke your heart. The man who pretended to transcend the physical and lied. Give me a name."

She opened her mouth to tell him to go to hell. He'd tricked her with his own Jedi mind tricks, forcing her to give up the most private, vulnerable part of her soul. Her friends and family barely knew his name. How he knew a man had done something to her was beyond her understanding, but somehow she realized he had the same type of instinct that she did, and she had walked right into his trap.

She almost jerked herself out of his grip and left without another word. Until his voice softened and he spoke so gently, she felt wrapped up in a cocoon of protection and warmth. "Tell me, little one."

His endearment touched something deep inside, a yearning of such vastness she fought the trembling that wracked her body. If he had kept pushing, she could've fought him. But his tenderness broke her resolve.

"Jacob."

She didn't wait for a response. She yanked free of his grip, dove for the handle, and stumbled out of the car.

Arilyn refused to look back, but she already knew it was too late. Like a wizard casting a spell and obtaining a lock of hair, Stone now held her rare secret. With information came great power. The only way out was to make sure she obtained more on him to balance the scales. She ignored the flicker of guilt about violating her ethical responsibility as a counselor and reminded herself it was a good thing to probe Stone's past. For his own good.

Not hers.

She headed past the Swan Pastry shop, walked into Ray's Billiards, and found Poppy waiting for her. The place had stained, worn carpet, four pool tables, a full bar, and wood-paneled walls filled with weird mirrors and classic art like dogs playing cards. Straight from the seventies, Ray's catered to the hard-core crowd that came to gamble, downed shots of whiskey, and smelled of smoke and must. Cigars? They'd gotten busted for not adhering to the no-smoking laws, and her neighbor Mrs. Blackfire called the cops on them weekly. The fines must be in the double digits now, yet Ray stayed open every day.

He slid off the stool, called a good-bye to Ray, and gave her a hug. "How was your day, sweetheart?"

She hugged him back and craved to tell him the truth. Her pain-in-the-butt police officer was not only driving her crazy but starting to turn her on. Horror. Instead, she sighed. "Fine. How about you?"

"Won twenty bucks. Helped Ray with the lunch crowd. Did you talk to the center about trying to jail me?"

"I will, Poppy, promise. I'll set it up so they allow you to walk to Ray's when you want. You just have to make sure someone calls or texts me so I know where you are. Deal?

"Deal."

"Let's go home for dinner."

"'Kay. Listen, can you also tell them to do something about their chef? He sucks. Yesterday I wanted a cheeseburger with a Coke. They gave me grilled chicken with an Ensure. Do they think I have one foot in the grave? Ensure tastes like powdered chalk."

"If you have a burger craving, I'll bring you one. You can call."

"You're not my babysitter, Arilyn. You also try to sneak me a veggie burger, and there is a difference, kiddo." His voice softened with a twinge of sadness. "You already spend too much time with me. You need a man to settle down with and marry, not an old coot who keeps you running back and forth."

"I like your company, so stop. If you really hate it there, move in with me."

He shook his head. "No way. I'll never get any babies from you if you can't even date. Maybe I'll sign up for the bus trip to the city. They're going to see a play on Broadway."

Guilt coursed through her, but she swore to make

the situation work. She knew the center was the best place for him. If only he could make a friend. Maybe with more time. "That sounds like fun. What play?"

Gray bushy brows snapped down. "*Mamma Mia!* Ugh, I hate Abba. I voted for *Chicago*. Hot women in prison. They shot it down. But I'll try."

Her lips twitched. "Come on. I'll let you have a real burger tonight after I make sure your insulin is okay."

"No Ensure?"

"Not tonight."

"And fries."

"I'll roast some sweet potatoes instead."

"I love you, A."

Damned if those ridiculous tears didn't sting again. "Love you, too, Poppy."

She linked arms and led him down the street. She'd just need to work harder and be more organized to get everything done. When she returned to the house with Poppy, she realized things weren't getting any easier.

The neighbor from hell had struck.

A large truck parked next to her house proudly claimed *Rusty's Tree Service*. Two bulky men wrapped up in ropes were hoisted on some type of contraption, calling orders back and forth to each other. A large buzz saw lay by their feet. Pine needles exploded everywhere, and the tree shook as if calling out to her in a plea for help. Mrs. Blackfire stood at her porch, arms crossed in front of her, watching the scene with a mad glee.

"Oh my God," Arilyn whispered. "She *is* evil."

"Who?" Poppy asked. "You cutting down that tree, sweetie?"

She launched herself toward the men. The loud buzzing screamed in her ears, and she waved her hands frantically, jumping up and down. The blond spotted her and turned off the machinery. "Hey, lady, you gotta get back. This is dangerous."

"No!" she yelled. "It's a mistake! You cannot cut down this tree!"

The other guy strolled over with a frown. "We already got paid. Now move aside."

And once again her temper snapped. The beautiful peace and harmony of her morning drifted away in a trail of smoke, leaving a mess of writhing emotions that flooded out. "This is my house, and I demand you back away from this tree!"

The two men shared a glance. "You live here?"

"Of course I live here! You took a job from a neighbor who has no right to cut down this tree. If you touch one more pine needle, I'll sue you!"

Mrs. Blackfire shouted from next door. "Don't listen to her! She's crazy. She believes in auras and crystals and refuses to even use a dryer!" She made motions toward the clothesline, which held all of Arilyn's linens and organic cottons to air-dry naturally.

"I'm trying to save the environment," she shot back. "Now back off or I'll call the police!"

"I paid you already to do this job," her neighbor called out. "Ignore her and cut down that tree."

"If you move any closer, I'll sue both of you," Arilyn warned.

Mrs. Blackfire snapped her mouth closed and glared.

"Please pack up your stuff and leave," she told the men.

They nodded. "Sorry lady. It won't happen again."

They gathered their equipment, got back in the truck, and pulled away. Shaking with fury, Arilyn tried to breathe, couldn't, then gave up altogether. She marched next door and stopped at the bottom step. "You lied to me," she said.

"I'm afraid for my life," she hissed. "When that tree falls on my roof and crushes me in my sleep, it will be too late."

Arilyn tried not to roll her eyes. "It's not even close to your roof," she pointed out. "You would've gotten me in big trouble with Genevieve."

"I need to protect myself. Besides, what are you doing in there?" She squinted over her glasses with suspicion. "I see that strange altar. Do you sacrifice things? Are you into witchcraft?"

Her body trembled with pent-up frustration. She had no time for this. "No, Mrs. Blackfire, I meditate. And you shouldn't be spying."

"I'm looking out for the neighborhood. I'm the one who caught the vandalizer over the summer. You should be grateful."

"I'm sure Gen is. I have to go." She turned and almost bumped into Poppy. "Ready, Poppy?"

Her grandfather didn't move. Just stared at her neighbor. "Who are you?" he finally asked.

"Joan Blackfire." She peered over her glasses. "Who are you?"

Poppy smiled and held out his hand as if he were asking the queen to dance. "Patrick Flynn. Arilyn's grandfather. Why are you cutting down her tree?"

Her neighbor muttered something under her breath, staring at his outstretched hand as though it were a bomb. She slowly took it and gave it a short shake. "Because it's diseased. Are you living here now?"

"Tree looks fine to me. Does bend to the right a bit, though. I'm visiting. I live at the Best Friends Senior Citizen Center. Do you know it?"

She gave a grunt. "Place makes poisonous Jell-O and serves Ensure with every meal. Plus, their road trips are stupid."

Arilyn's grandfather beamed. "I totally agree. Hey, want to come over for dinner? I'm a great cook and promise no Jell-O. Or fake shakes. We're having burgers and sweet potatoes. Arilyn doesn't eat meat, so there's veggie burgers there if you want."

Arilyn blinked. Huh?

Mrs. Blackfire snapped her gaze around. "What's wrong with meat? God put animals on the earth so we'd eat them."

Arilyn bristled. "We've evolved since then. No reason to ingest bad animal karma into the body."

"Ridiculous. The body needs protein to function. What do you eat?"

"I eat from the earth," Arilyn said stiffly. "I also use soy protein as a substitute."

Poppy shook his head sorrowfully. "It tastes really bad, but she's free to make her own choices."

"What about sugar?" Mrs. Blackfire frowned. "Everyone needs sugar."

It was confirmed. She'd stepped into the Syfy Zone and would soon be involved in the zombie apocalypse. Her neighbor from hell was questioning her food choices after trying to cut down her tree illegally. "I avoid refined sugar and keep to natural ingredients.

Dried and fresh fruit. Dark chocolate. Whole grains in cereals."

"So who drinks all the wine you take out to the curb?" Mrs. Blackfire asked. "You don't drink alcohol?"

Her grandfather spoke up. "Oh, no, she drinks plenty of alcohol."

Arilyn fought off a blush. "Red wine helps the heart," she said.

Poppy tilted her head. "You like those cosmos and martinis," he pointed out. "And lots of white wine, too."

Mrs. Blackfire gave a knowing humph. "Knew it. The recyclables never lie."

Okay, she'd had enough. She tugged at her grandfather's arm. "Umm, we'd better go in."

"Are you joining us for dinner, then?" he directed toward her neighbor. "Maybe we can sort out this tree problem. Neighbors should get along." Arilyn held her breath, heart beating madly, praying for just one tiny, itty-bitty break in her crappy week. Of course, Mrs. Blackfire would never agree. Her neighbor hated her, and Kate, and her whole crew. Lenny and Mike would probably howl as if they'd seen a ghost, sensing her dark, innate evilness.

"Yes, I'll be over in a minute. Just need to lock up."

"We have dogs!" Arilyn burst out. "Lenny and Mike are very misbehaved. Puppies. They're still learning, and I know how you dislike dogs."

"Why wouldn't Joan like dogs?" Poppy asked with confusion.

"I never said I hate dogs," her neighbor snapped. "I don't like them doing their business on my property and ruining my roses. I'm fine with dogs."

No. No, no, no, no . . .

Poppy lit up, looking ten years younger. "Wonderful. Looking forward to getting to know each other better. Let's go, Arilyn."

Arilyn's mouth fell open.

He walked away, and she followed in a fog. Then he patted her arm. "I'm quite disappointed in you. Not inviting your next-door neighbor over is horribly rude. Why don't we open that bottle of champagne you've been saving? It's a special occasion." With a light step, he walked inside, humming under his breath.

A shudder broke through her. She gripped the turquoise crystal around her neck and tried to absorb some of its healthy, clearing energy. Why was this happening to her? What had she possibly done in her previous life to deserve a neighbor from hell, a broken relationship, and an annoying, sexy cop?

Arilyn sighed and prepped herself for the long night ahead.

STONE CAREFULLY SCREWED THE caps back on the two Coke bottles and breathed a sigh of relief. Perfect. It had been way too long since he last attempted such a classic practical joke with soda and Mentos, and even had to YouTube the steps, but now he was in business. He headed over to McCoy's desk first, placing the bottle on the right-hand side and quickly tossing out the half-empty one.

"Whatcha up to, Petty? Aren't you still on suspension?"

He turned around. Sergeant Tim Dunn was nicknamed Make It Work Dunn, in honor of *Project Runway*'s host. Of course, this drove him apeshit because the host's name was really Gunn. To Stone and the others, it was close enough. Dunn gave him a suspicious look. And well he should. Stone slouched and sneered. "Just looking for McCoy. Wanted him to check on a speeder. He's going to court in my place. Here, want this? I'm ready to piss like a racehorse, I've had so much Coke."

He shoved it in Tim's hand like he didn't give a crap. Tim took it. "I'm a Pepsi man, but sure. Thanks. Hey, we're having some problems with the rookie."

Stone lifted a brow. "Patterson? What's up?"

Tim rolled his eyes. With his cropped blond hair and Irish red cheeks, he was the scrappy sort, with a mean hook that could knock a guy on his ass in two seconds flat. "He's got a stick up his ass. OCD sort. Organizes his locker, paperwork, desk. Don't care if he keeps it to himself, but he's starting to piss everyone off. Trying to get Jessica to alphabetize the call-ins by last name and shit. Then told McCoy his paperwork wasn't up to snuff."

The dispatcher, Jessica, didn't like anyone to tell her how to run her desk. When she got pissed, the department felt the heat. And criticizing a higher-ranking officer was just not done. Stone shook his head. "Bad news. What do you want to do?"

Tim grunted. "He likes his locker so damn much, let's move it where he can see it easier. Like outside."

A juvenile glee zipped through Stone. There might be only about seven people working in the department, but they were tight. Newbies needed to learn when they went off course, and the right practical joke put them in their place and made the point crystal clear. "Let's do it. He's on night shift, right?"

"Yep."

"Good. We'll put it by his car. Upside down, of course."

"Of course."

They both chuckled. "I'll stop back. Heading to the gym. See ya."

"Later, dude."

His hand had just pushed open the door when the sound of Dunn shouting and cursing hit his ears. Guess he had opened up his bottle early to a total explosion. Grinning, Stone walked faster. Yeah, the classic jokes were the best.

He was in a good mood the whole way to the gym. Changing into his shorts and tank, Stone headed toward the weight room and started with the bench press. When his shoulders revolted a bit as he pushed up, he was reminded of the hellish Salutation to the Whatever routine Arilyn was always putting him through. Unbelievable. Who would've thought yoga could be such a workout? He made a note to see when the next Pilates class was. Time to stretch out so he could stop embarrassing himself in front of her. She seemed wickedly satisfied every time she caught him trying to hide a wince.

Stone settled into reps, working each core muscle until it ached. He'd learned when he was a skinny, too-tall delinquent that knowing how to fight and defend himself was key to survival. From both the streets and his father. He'd kept up a strict routine of lifting and running, so he'd always be able to either flee first or do damage to his opponents. When he'd met Ellen, that part of his past fascinated her in a dark, shocking way. She used to shiver and tell him a bit of violence was sexy.

Yeah, real sexy. Sure, the testosterone was a rush, but waking up in a blur of pain and blood just wasn't that hot. Even if you were the one putting the other guy there.

Stone gritted his teeth and began on squats. If he was honest with himself, he'd admit Ellen's background was also a turn-on. She was so different from him, all classic elegance begging to be messed up, and boasted an easy childhood with no ghosts. Since she worked as an executive assistant to a banker, she wore conservative suits and high heels and perfect makeup. She was gorgeous and confident. Attracted to her flirtatious manner and fun sense of humor, he'd dived headlong into an affair, and on impulse, he asked her to marry him. Surprisingly, she said yes. Had they even exchanged deep "I love yous"? Talked about the future and children? No. They'd both figured everything would work out, because neither of them was a planner or too interested in analyzing tomorrow. In a way, they were too alike ever to make it.

Maybe that's why they ended up married and engaged so fast. The first hit of something new and fresh probably turned them both on. Of course, after the fun ended and his work ate him up and spit him back out, she wasn't as turned on by that side of him.

His work schedule blasted them back to reality. Hard reality. Endless shifts, sleepless nights, and little entertainment caused a tear. Soon they were fighting, insulting, taking potshots that left shallow cuts and little time to heal. She wanted to travel and be fabulous. He wanted to slay the demons and catch the bad guys. Suddenly, it wasn't so much fun anymore, and Stone finally figured out he wasn't a man worth fighting for.

The incident confirmed the end. After he shot his gun and got dragged into an investigation that put the spotlight on him, she distanced herself. All the intense energy he exuded that used to intrigue her became distasteful. Like turning over a big, smooth rock and spotting a bunch of slugs beneath. They'd been on the literal rocks before the incident, but afterward? There was nothing left to save. Her affair only confirmed how far they'd sunk.

It hardly stung anymore. Stone wondered how long their marriage would have lasted if he hadn't walked in on her. Had he ever loved her on a bone-deep, emotional level? Or had he just been lonely and lost after the shooting, looking for a connection to save him?

When his request for a transfer to Verily went through, he couldn't wait to get out of the Bronx and away from all the damn memories. Even his partner hadn't cared, but their relationship hadn't been tight like his with Devine. He bet Devine would've backed him up and fought for him to stay.

Bet he wouldn't have slept with his wife either.

Sweat ran down his body. He clenched his teeth and pushed past the strain, his muscles working overtime, the exertion clearing his mind. He spotted the pretty blonde staring at him, her blue eyes wide with appreciation of his form. He was a realist when it came to his body. He put a lot of crap into it, but he balanced that with steady workouts and training to help sculpt the physical traits needed to succeed as a cop. His Black Irish blood had also been a gift. Women seemed to like that type of heritage, something about the dark hair and eyes with fairer skin. The tall, skinny youth had finally grown up until he towered over all the other punks in the neighborhood and gained respect. Growing the goatee just added to the rough appeal.

Whatever. He wasn't the type to stare in a mirror. As long as he was clean and had some type of clothes on, he was good to go. Getting women had never been a problem for him. Stone finished his squats, wiped his face with a towel, and grabbed the hand weights for biceps curls. The blonde inched closer, an open smile curving her lips. Definitely an invite. He hadn't seen her before, but she was cute. Seemed as if she'd be open to grabbing a shake at the juice bar and accompanying him home.

The image of Arilyn's face drifted past him.

Ah, crap. He grunted and rolled out a few sets. Fingers gripping the hand weights, his veins bulged, the warmth of adrenaline flooded his blood, and he became half-aroused. He hoped it was the pretty blonde making him semi-erect, but the damn image of his long-limbed teacher who owned her body with a pride he rarely spotted in females was starting to kill him. Worse? He was imagining her doing the Salutation thing naked. With him.

He clanged the weights back on the shelf and cursed. Grabbed his water bottle and drained it dry in one long gulp. He wiped his mouth with the back of his hand, tossed the towel over his shoulder, and headed out.

The blonde stared. Her eyes begged him to stop

and converse. Flirt. Do the dance that would eventually lead him to a satisfying bout of sweaty, fulfilling sex. He paused, getting closer, ready to open his mouth. Waited for the subtle spark of attraction that told him they'd have a good time tonight.

Instead, he walked past.

The sharp flash of disappointment on her face pissed him off. What was wrong with him? Why not have a quick tumble? Why was he suddenly obsessed with the one woman he really, really didn't like? Sure, they had some kind of crazy spark, but damned if he was interested in getting electrocuted. And that woman would surely kill him if they ever got involved. Hell, electrocution would probably be less painful.

He muttered to himself the whole drive home, swearing to get his head on straight. When he walked into his small brick ranch, he shoved a frozen pizza in the oven to cook while he took a quick shower, then settled in front of his television. Maybe *American Ninja Warrior* was on. The quiet settled around him, and Stone looked around, wondering what Arilyn Meadows would say about his home.

He was neat but not ruthlessly so. His house screamed bachelor, but not in a seedy way. Besides the latest electronics, including wireless sound stereo, a sixty-inch flat-screen TV, and two Macs, the surroundings were simple. He'd gone with wine and black colors. Leather couches, burgundy throw rugs, and dark-wood tables. A ton of bookshelves and a battered desk in the corner piled high with folders and work stuff. Black-and-white photographs accented the walls, mostly views of Yankee Stadium, both new and old. The kitchen was big enough to hold a table and chairs, but he mostly ate at the breakfast bar. The gray and blue granite hadn't needed updating, nor had the new stainless steel appliances, though he never cooked. His one bedroom had a thick chocolate rug, mahogany furniture, and a sleigh bed he'd grabbed on clearance. He wasn't big into knickknacks, but he had a tendency to buy blankets in various patterns and colors, so they were tossed all over the furniture.

Grabbing his pizza, he cracked open an IPA and settled onto the sofa in his boxers. Stone clicked through the channels, paused on a boxing match, and stretched his feet out. This was nice. Just another night at home, on his own terms, in the peace and quiet.

Arilyn's melodic voice whispered in his ear.

You drink beer with some cops. Shoot a bit of pool. Maybe lift a few weights at the gym. But basically you're a workaholic who spends most of his time alone.

He froze. *Get out of my head,* he ordered. *I'm damn happy. Content.*

You, Stone Petty, are a hypocrite.

He groaned, squeezing his eyes shut. He refused to think about her. He'd finish his pizza, watch the rest of the match, and go jerk off to the mental image of the pretty blonde in the gym. Then he'd get his shit together tomorrow and find someone to actually have sex with.

Stone cranked up the volume and shoved the cardboard-like pizza into his mouth with false gusto.

Take that, Arilyn Meadows.

I don't hear you.

He had a great life.

Really, really great.

seven

STONE LOOKED AROUND. The purple room was filled with soothing blends of sights and sounds that made him itchy. Water trickled from a fountain with glossy river rocks. Classical music streamed through hidden speakers. Instead of sitting behind the large oak desk, Arilyn perched on a velvet cushion across from him, notepad on lap, a slight frown marring her ginger brows. The room was essentially female—Goddess of Fertility or Venus or shit like that. Plants sprung from the corners, silver sparkly pillows accessorized the endless violet, and the carpet was thick beneath his feet.

Did she always sit so still? She reminded him of an exotic bird, watchful of every situation and ready to either dive in to save a buddy or fly off into the wild blue yonder.

And why was he suddenly composing weird analogies to animals when he thought of this woman?

He took in her black Lycra yoga pants, low-heeled boots he bet weren't real leather, and a snug T-shirt with the Kinnections logo in bright purple and gray. No makeup marred the lines of her graceful features or hid her creamy white skin. So different from all the women he knew, who obsessed on beauty, channeling their inner peacocks in order to compete in the world.

He'd been surprised when she said she wanted to have his one-to-one counseling in her Kinnections office, but thought it would be a great opportunity to analyze her further. The endless spreadsheets and three computer systems impressed him. Also intimidated him. He wasn't such a program expert, so that seemed pretty cool, though he had no idea how such an extensive computer setup could possibly help in connecting couples or doing whatever Kinnections promised people it did. Make matches. Find love. Whatever.

She seemed to have something on her mind. It showed in the slight tenseness of her shoulders and the assessing gleam in her sea-glass-green eyes. He kept his face impassive, interested in finding out what she wanted.

"Nice office."

She glanced around as if viewing it for the first time and nodded. "Thank you. My partners, Kate and Kennedy, helped decorate."

"Very girly."

That brought an annoyed snap of the brow. "It's generic," she offered politely. "Purple is the color of the highest chakra, opening up the mind center."

He scratched his head, hooked one ankle over his leg, and slouched in the chair. "Thought the heart was more important in your business."

"A clear mind and connection with your highest inner power is key to all. The rest follows."

He made a noncommittal snort, and her lips tightened. Stone tamped down on a chuckle. She was so much damn fun to spar with and piss off. It was becoming his favorite hobby. "Why do you need computers? Thought love was a magical mystery thing."

"Love is magical but also scientific. It takes a lot to find your match. Personality, beliefs, upbringings—all are brought to the table when we meet someone new. Ignoring those pieces of a person and waiting for an invisible chemistry connection to make everything okay wouldn't be reasonable. It would also put us out of business."

Her sharp intelligence intrigued him. A mix of new age hippie crap and nerd scientist. Fascinating. "Do you work the computer side of the business?"

"Yes, I also do the counseling. Which we should get to."

"In a minute. Did you study computers in school?"

She shifted in the chair. "I graduated with a double master's in psychology and computer science."

"How'd you end up working here?"

"My friends and I discussed the benefits of opening up our own business and using each of our strengths to create a unique spot in the market."

Huh. She was lying. Her gaze dropped down to the floor when she spoke. Now he was dying to know how this matchmaking business got started. "I'm impressed. Most businesses fail, especially ones started with friends."

Her voice dripped with sarcasm. "I'm so glad. Now I can sleep at night."

"I know better ways to make you sleep." He paused. "Or not."

She sucked in a breath, and that weird zing burst between them. He'd only meant to tease her and get her irritated. Instead, the joke was on him. He was suddenly hard and aching to trap her against that chair and kiss her. Long. Deep. Find out if she tasted as sweet as sugar cookies warm from the oven. See if she melted all soft and gooey once he pushed his tongue past her lips and his hands past her clothing. And now he'd moved from comparing her to animals to food. He was losing it.

"Don't."

The word shot in the room like a bullet. He'd made her uncomfortable. A surge of adrenaline and satisfaction mingled. He grinned real slow. "Why not?"

"Because as I told you the other night, I don't like you."

"I don't like you either. Does it matter?"

She crossed her arms in front of her chest. The thin material of her shirt stretched across perfectly small, perfectly formed breasts. Her nipples were already hard. "To me it does. Unlike you, Officer Petty, I don't jump into bed to scratch an itch. I need a connection beyond the physical."

"Is that what you had with your last lover? A connection?"

He regretted the sudden pain that flickered over her face and cursed beneath his breath. Damn. He didn't want to hurt her. He was curious as to what type of man had claimed her heart and stomped all over it. She'd defended him regarding his good-guy intentions, but he sensed the truth was quite different. When she'd finally given his name, something had flared in those green eyes. A hot anger rolled up with raw pain. It was the real stuff buried beneath all that meditation junk she always threw in his face. Stone opened his mouth to apologize, but she was already answering.

"Yes. At least I followed my heart. When I die, I intend to have little to regret. Not taking a chance on love would be one of them."

He'd never met a woman so deep and ready to get real. When he proposed to Ellen, he figured he was following his heart. Now he realized he'd only been in lust and too lazy to wait. Too lazy to figure things out. Too lazy to make it work when the relationship got hard. And though he'd never forgive or forget, part of the relationship failure was solidly on him. A trickle of shame raced through him. Something told him Arilyn Meadows wouldn't shrink from difficulty. She'd flourish.

He shifted in the chair. When had his complete dislike turned to sexual interest? In only a few days, she'd begun to intrigue him on a whole new level. Physical, of course. Nothing more. "What about passion? Isn't that the foundation for love? Wouldn't you regret being too focused on the future and missing an opportunity to experience great sex?"

Her lips were pale peach. He wondered if her nipples matched. The bottom of that lush lower lip curled up a bit. "No."

The simple answer bugged him. Another lie. It was in the tilt of her stubborn chin, and the challenge sizzling in those emerald eyes. Damn, she'd be fun to try and push around. Ripping the truth from her in breathy little gasps while he pushed between her thighs may be worth the trouble.

Maybe.

"Then you've never experienced true passion," he said.

That got her. Annoyance carved out her graceful features. She wasn't as calm as she made people believe. "Yes, I have. You have no idea how great the passion was between us."

Defensive. Cheater? The image of his wife, naked, on top of another man, still panged. He despised cheaters and their cowardice. Hated not being able to fight fairly and being made a chump. He could've forgiven Ellen for a multitude of sins but not that one.

"I'm not talking about good sex. A few orgasms. A cuddle. I'm talking about the down-and-dirty lust that wipes everything else from your mind except how your body feels against your lover. Over him. Under him. The feel of naked skin. The sweat, and the smells, and the excruciating, sweet agony of need for him to take you completely, over and over, until there's nothing left of both of you."

Her mouth formed a little O, and sweat broke out on her upper lip. Her fingers clenched in her lap, and Stone knew she was completely turned on. Her nipples beaded against her top. The pulse beat madly at the base of her swanlike neck. And he knew if he walked over to her right now, tipped her chair back, and hooked his fingers under those tight Lycra pants, she'd be soaking wet.

Playing with her affected him just as much, and he tried not to shift again in his chair as he hardened to full length. Why did he have to experience such chemistry with a woman completely wrong for him? In one week they'd tear each other apart, they were so different. Yet his primitive need to claim her beat through his body like an animal craving to mate.

"That—that was inappropriate." Her voice wobbled. "You know nothing about how we felt for each other. We transcended the physical to an emotional bond you'd be afraid to experience. A man like you believes in a quick roll in the hay, and a quicker retreat in the morning."

He grinned. "Never quick, little one."

She practically spit with fury. "Why do you call me that? Stop. I don't like it."

"Why not? I like it." Arilyn jerked her folder open and dragged in a few of those deep breaths she counseled him on. "You mad?"

"No."

"Good, 'cause I don't think that breathing's workin' too good."

Her dirty look made him want to laugh out loud. "If you're done avoiding the real reason you're here, I'll begin. I know what you're doing. Trying to distract me by talking about sex, so I get so rattled I'll forget this session is about you. I'm not that dumb, Officer."

"Never said you were. It's just a more interesting topic."

"Tell me a bit about the domestic scene you witnessed."

Guess playtime was over. Stone resigned himself to a long, boring session of talking about feelings. Yuck. "I went inside the house when I heard screaming. Found the husband beating up the wife, with the little girl hanging on his leg. He kicked her to the wall and she went unconscious. Guess I snapped. Don't remember much afterward until my partner Devine pulled me off."

She scribbled some notes like a shrink. He imagined her naked and was less bored. "How did you feel when you realized what you did?"

The questions were textbook. He wondered why he felt disappointed in her techniques. "Pissed that I snapped. Happy that I beat the crap out of him."

"Is the little girl okay?"

"Yeah. She's in a shelter now. But who knows if the mother went back. Battered women usually do. They're too afraid to leave sometimes. It's all they know."

She quirked a ginger brow and studied him. He made sure his face remained impassive. "You said your father beat you with a bat. Hurt your mother. How old were you?"

Stone shrugged. "Guess it started around five. Went till I was a teen."

"Did it happen often? Did he beat you and your mother?"

He picked at a cuticle and tried not to groan. Ugh. He'd done the mandated therapy after the first incident, and even checked in on his own for a few sessions. It was too brutally inane to continue. Maybe if he seemed more emotional, she'd hurry things up? Show her he realized his issues and wanted to work on them. "Yeah. He liked to mix things up in the household. I'm sure when I went into that scene it was a trigger for all the times he hurt both of us. I'm more aware of my shortcomings now. I think I can handle incidents better in the future."

Perfect. He sounded apologetic, knew about his own limitations and wanted to work on them. She jotted down more ridiculous notes, probably on his mental state, then looked up.

Her smile stunned him.

Like the sun on crack, she blinded him. His heart

got a bit mushy and weak, and he was unable to talk. Why did he suddenly crave to revel in her warmth? Why did he want to be the man to elicit that smile on a regular basis? And what did she find so funny?

"You're smart, Officer. Wicked smart."

He refocused. "Back to 'Officer' so soon?" he drawled. "Makes me want to force you to say my name in all sorts of interesting ways."

"You think I'm a chump asking these questions. You think I'm easily manipulated."

"I never said any of those things."

"Didn't have to. Who else were you protecting?"

He blinked. "Just told you. Me. My mother."

Her voice softened, deepening to a velvety, soothing pitch, urging him to spill all his secrets. "I think there's someone else. Another person in the house. A foster brother or sister? A friend? You got used to dealing with your father's rage until he went after someone new." She leaned forward, gaze locked on him with a sense of urgency. Within those emerald depths lay a vastness of understanding and gentleness he'd never been on the receiving end of. "Who was it, Stone?"

He jerked back. He'd gotten bashed in the face with a baseball bat and refused to cry. There was so much inside scarred up and dead he was grateful he never had to revisit. But Arilyn's final question stole his breath and drew blood.

He was done.

Stone stood up. "This is bullshit," he stated quietly. "I told you before I'll be straight with you, but don't dick around in my head and think you won't get hurt."

She never flinched. Just studied him for a long

time, their gazes locked in a battle, until she slowly nodded. "I apologize. I went too deep, too fast. Why don't you sit back down and we'll talk about something else."

Who did she think she was? A yoga teacher turned matchmaker playing at being a therapist? She led a charmed life and had no idea of the harsh realities in the world. She controlled her reality while she viewed others through a set of rosy glasses so she could avoid the true mess. Breathing. Meditating. Helping animals. Even with a broken relationship behind her, she pretended to understand and transcend, citing a higher purpose and acceptance she didn't really feel.

It was a bunch of crap.

Maybe it was time she knew what it felt like to have her safe bubble ripped away.

Stone made his decision and slowly stalked across the room.

SHE'D SCREWED UP.

Arilyn watched the bristling, towering male approach her. Why did she push? Usually the first counseling session was easy, a getting-to-know-you phase and an opportunity to build trust. Instead, she'd done the unthinkable and hit on some hard issues way too soon.

Now she was in trouble.

Damn him. It was all his fault. All of that rippling male sexuality squeezed into a tiny office space would make any woman crazy. He practically gobbled up all the oxygen, and his wicked smiles and hot inky eyes roving over her figure should be illegal. Who owned biceps that massive? Her fingers curled with the need to sink her nails into them and test the hardness. She bet he'd be able to lift her high and pin her against the wall without strain, without needing a breath. How hot was that?

He was literally the worst type of man in the world to be attracted to. All that experience training her mind to be stronger than her body faded to nothing when he looked at her as if he planned on ripping off her clothes and ravishing every inch of her body with his tongue and lips and teeth.

Oh my God, what was she doing?

Arilyn fought the treacherous, weak need for his touch and struggled for calm. She needed to be in control of the situation, speak firmly, and get the session back on track.

Before he reached her.

"There's no need to get any closer or prove your point. I made an error, and I apologize again. Why don't we take a break, get some water, and meet back in a few minutes?"

His gaze pinned her to the chair. He took a few more steps.

Her heart exploded in her chest. Arilyn tried to breathe.

"W-We need to make sure we keep our professional distance and don't blur any of the lines. I'm your counselor and teacher. Emotional highs and lows are expected when we're exploring triggers that cause anger."

He didn't break a smile or his stride. He stopped in front of her, forcing her head to tilt way, way back to hold her ground. Showing strength was key. Stay cool and calm. Even though his body heat was blistering in waves around her, and he smelled so damn good, like woods and musk and ocean and soap. With his tight, worn jeans, black T-shirt stretched over meaty biceps, and the deadly focus from those carved features, a shiver raced down her spine. Sexy stubble hugged that square jawline, emphasizing the lush softness to his lips, framed like a gift. He was total male predator, domineering cop, and sexual alpha male wrapped up in one package.

"Let's talk triggers."

She shivered. "Y-Yes. For instance, it seems we hit one now. Why don't we talk and explore it?"

He laughed low. "Do you soothe all your angry male clients this way? Talk them down with that musical voice of yours? Pretend to know what they've gone through? Tell them the world is a big, beautiful place full of rainbows and leprechaun gold?" He dropped his voice. "Is that what you tell yourself?"

She jerked in the chair. Her breath strangled in her throat. He wasn't touching her, yet her skin blistered from his nearness. "I understand more than you think," she said calmly.

"Bullshit. You know nothing about hard times or pain, other than the normal breakup of a relationship. How do you expect to counsel us on anger when you've denied yourself that human emotion?"

His words stung and pummeled. She lifted her arms halfway to cover her face from the attack. Then felt herself snap.

She jumped from the chair and faced him head-on. The look of surprise on his face only urged her forward. "You want to know how I know about pain?

Do you think I was raised in a bubble of goodness and light, dragged from Buddha's mountaintop? I earned my peace by working for it! I sweat blood and tears and opened myself up for something better to climb out of such a deep depression I never thought I'd survive. My mother died of cancer. I watched her disintegrate before my eyes, changing from a laughing, robust woman to a shell. She smoked, drank, partied, had bad food. She was the poster child of extremes in the pursuit of fun. Before I barely buried her, my father died right afterward, committing suicide because he couldn't live without my mother. You think I wasn't angry? Sometimes I'd scream at the top of my lungs just to stay sane. My father killed himself because I wasn't enough. Try living with that one."

"Arilyn—"

"No, I'm not done. I was a complete nerd and geek and had difficulty making friends. I was left alone with no one except my grandfather. Instead of taking a bucket of pills to live or becoming like my mother and trashing my body, I decided to search for more. I studied yoga, meditation, religion, and learned how to live in the light rather than in the darkness. I learned how to treat my body like the temple it is. I forced myself to open up and confess my fears and my pain to a therapist. I decided to help others, but I work on myself every damn day, even though I sometimes don't want to."

The silence was shattering. Her righteous anger drained away and left her with pure horror. What she shared almost crippled her, but she dug deep and owned every last shred of truth. Why not? Why hide any more from him or pretend to be something she wasn't? Maybe it was best he knew all her crappy secrets and that most of the time she had no idea what she was doing. That she'd been broken once, too.

"Feel better now?" she asked. "I believe our session is over. I'll see you tomorrow in class." Wrapping the last shred of her dignity around her, she backed away around the chair and walked to her desk. Lengthening her breath, she reconnected with her center and allowed the rioting emotions to ride through her.

He turned and stopped at the door. "I'm sorry."

"You have nothing to be sorry for."

"Yes, I do." He glanced at her. Those inky eyes pierced into hers and right through to her soul. The energy between them knotted tighter. "I misjudged you. I make mistakes, too, and when I do, I say I'm sorry."

Her tension eased. Slowly, Arilyn nodded, accepting his gesture. "Apology accepted."

"Good." He grasped the doorknob and pulled. "I won't make the same mistake again."

He left. His words echoed in the air, more like a threat mingled with a promise.

One she definitely didn't want to explore.

Her cell phone chirped. Arilyn grabbed it, grateful for the distraction, and collapsed in the chair. "Hi, Anthony. What's up?"

"Two things. Lenny and Mike are ready for their foster parents."

A combination of grief and joy rushed through her. She'd gotten attached to those fur balls and the house wouldn't be the same. "That's great."

Anthony's voice softened. "I know it's hard, A. You gave them a priceless gift. The shelter would be in trouble without you."

She blinked back the sting of tears and fought through. She loved fostering the animals to go into their forever homes, but the good-byes were brutal. Still, the puppies would be together and happy and that was what mattered. "I'll bring them by tomorrow."

"Thanks. I also got those pics you sent me. Place looks like a breeding ground for abuse. I'm waiting on a few organizations to get back to me so we may be able to move on this by late next week."

Arilyn knew she should be happy. Hell, it was great progress, especially with Stone's backup confirmation, but she kept thinking about that empty doghouse. She sensed a presence there, but who knew what type of shape the dog was in? "Any possibility of getting it checked out earlier? I'm worried."

Anthony sighed. "I know. We all are, but this business requires patience. Move too fast or get sloppy and we don't get any results. Right?"

"Yeah, right." That depression was slipping back over her. "Thanks for calling, Anthony."

She hung up and tapped her fingers on the desk. Usually she was the embodiment of patience. Waiting for karma to kick in. Waiting for justice. For happiness. For . . . everything.

She was tired of being passive in so many areas of her life. Opening her heart and hoping for good things.

Maybe some action was needed in order to make

a difference. She didn't want to hang around anymore like a good girl. She wanted results.

Tonight.

When the idea took root and flowered, she refused to doubt herself.

Arilyn made her decision and got back to work.

HOW'S ANGER MANAGEMENT?"

Stone shot his partner and friend a withering look. Taking a long pull of beer, he chalked up his cue stick to buy some time for his next shot. After stalking the station for the past few nights because he had nothing better to do, Chief Dick was pulling him off suspension in two more days. Sure, he might get stuck with the night shift, but it was better than nothing.

"Sucks."

"Is your teacher hot?"

His fingers jerked around the stick. Yes. Unfortunately, Arilyn Meadows was too hot for his taste, and he couldn't afford to get burned any longer. Their conversation at Kinnections had been . . . disturbing. He'd ached to walk over and kiss her, soothe away the sting of pain in her eyes and replace it with want. Dirty, lewd sex was okay.

Not tender, emotional crap. Ugh.

That's when he knew she was big trouble.

Her words haunted him last night. The way she admitted to her past and all its ugliness. He'd assumed she lived some type of enchanted life in an ashram where everyone sang "Kumbaya." Wrong on all counts. Losing both parents so tragically had to take a toll. Yet she'd fought through and not only survived but flourished. She actually gave a crap about others, too. He knew people who led charmed lives and didn't care about making anyone else's better.

Yeah. She was big trouble, all right.

He needed to complete the course, prove to his captain that he had his life together, and return to his normal routine. Normal may be a bit lonely, but it worked. The ups and downs of complicated relationships just wasn't for him. His past marriage had taught him well.

But damned if he still didn't want to have one night of dirty sex with his teacher.

"Yeah, she's hot. But a pain in the ass."

"How so?"

Stone lined up and took the shot. The six ball sank in the corner pocket. "We met her before. Arilyn Meadows. Remember the domestic abuse case with Genevieve MacKenzie and David Riscetti? She called it in."

His partner whistled. "Damn. How's that for karma? She so did not like you. Thought you ate too many donuts. Liked me a lot, though."

Stone glared. "Yeah, what woman doesn't like you, dude? She's everything I'm not."

His partner grinned, those shiny white teeth mocking his own dull ones from years of smoking and too much coffee. "Like what?"

"Vegetarian. Buddha worshipper. Believes breathing staves off criminal intent. Probably refuses to kill ants or spiders, cleanses her colon on a monthly basis, and stalks fur warehouses to vandalize for the greater cause."

Devine nodded his head. The dim lights flickered, highlighting white-blond hair and reminding Stone of a real-life Gabriel. The guy was pure Hollywood and recruited female groupies on a regular basis. He also rarely got embarrassed, backed him up in any situation, and was the best shot Stone had ever seen. When they got a chance to shoot.

Devine gave him the famous smirk that would make Pitt weep. "Maybe you need to change it up a bit. The women you usually date haven't worked out well. Try someone different."

Stone snorted. "Yeah, after one night that one would be sniffing after china patterns and picking baby names. No, thanks. I don't need that type of complication."

"Why not?" He jerked and screwed up the shot. Devine gave a snort of laughter. Bastard.

"I'm just sayin' there's nothing wrong with hooking up more than one night with a good woman. Just because the last one screwed you doesn't mean they're all like that. Maybe she'll surprise you."

"I don't like surprises," Stone said.

His friend shot him a knowing look. "You don't like the bad kind. Like walking in on your wife and finding her screwing another guy. At least this one sounds like she has character."

Yeah. She did. It was evident in every move she made. Character and good intentions. Still didn't mean he wanted to try a woman like Arilyn Meadows. She'd probably lecture him on health issues, want to engage in deep conversations regarding their relationship, be the queen of lost causes, and drive him crazy.

Total disaster.

He watched Devine study the table and crack the stick. Nice shot. "I don't like any type of surprises," Stone finally said. "And maybe this advice shouldn't be coming from a man whose future with women consists of what they want for breakfast. You're a man whore, Devine."

His friend shot him a grin. "I'm ready to settle down the minute I meet the right woman. It's not about quantity, man. It's about quality."

"Whatever. Hey, there's Dunn and McCoy." Stone lifted his beer and slapped his coworkers on the shoulder. Tim Make It Work Dunn was the only sergeant in the department, ambitious, and on track for detective. His ginger hair and pale skin got him a lot of ribbing, but he still drank anyone under the table. Jay McCoy had been on the force a long time and had settled down with the wife and three kids. He managed to balance family life with the workload, and was definitely the most chill in the department. He was also the best practical joker. When the worst pranks came out, everyone knew Jay was behind them.

McCoy bumped his shoulder and grabbed two beers from the bar. "I put this on your tab, dude. That Mentos thing got me in trouble. Spilled the damned soda all over my papers and had to redo them, you asshole. The Dick went nuts."

Stone laughed and lifted his beer in a salute. "The classics are the best. Took me long enough to rig the whole operation. Needed some revenge for the shit you put in my trunk."

Tim cocked his hip against the table and rolled his eyes. "A little soda explosion is hardly revenge. You gotta step it up if you want to play in the big leagues, Petty. Now let's play some pool."

"Fine. Rack 'em up, Devine. I'm getting a refill."

Stone walked to the bar, chatting a bit with Ray, and spotted Patrick at the far end of the bar. The older man was new but had become a regular. Stone enjoyed his conversation and friendly ribbing. He was a veteran who had kicked ass in Nam, played a mean game of pool, and could swig a Guinness like nobody's business. He lived in the senior citizen home, but he seemed fine to Stone.

"Hey, Pat, how's it going?"

The man looked up and grinned. His stately silver hair and bushy eyebrows spoke of good, solid genes. "Stone! I'm good, man. You playing with your crew? What happened to bustin' criminals in Verily?"

Stone laughed and nodded to Ray to put the drinks on his tab. "Not too much going on lately. Maybe you should go stir up some trouble at the center and get me some excitement going."

"Man, do I wish." Patrick rolled his eyes. "I'm trying to fit in there, but for God's sake, it's so lame. No interesting women. All they do is talk about their arthritis or foot problems or gas. Tried to go on that bus trip to see *Mamma Mia!* It was painful. Abba songs and girly stuff the whole time. It's like they're all halfway to the grave."

Stone shook his head. "That's tough. Can you live on your own? Have any family members to help you out?"

"Nah, I had to sell my house because of the diabetes. It was time. Can't drive anymore anyway. My granddaughter already does too much for me. She's a good girl."

Ray set down the beers. Stone nodded his thanks. "Good to have family who cares."

"Maybe I can set you two up? She needs a decent man."

Alarm bells rang. "Sorry, Pat, I seem to do better with the bad girls."

Patrick laughed and raised his Guinness. "I did once, too. Maybe you just need to try a good girl for a change."

"Tell you what. Devine over there knows the right way to treat a woman. Why don't you ask him?"

Patrick nodded. "Seems like a handsome guy. She picks me up here a lot, so we'll see."

"We're playing a game. You want in?"

"How much?"

Stone grinned. "How much you got, old man?"

"More than you'll ever take from me. Might as well empty your pockets now."

"You're on." They walked over to the table and Patrick greeted the other men. "You got a ride tonight from your granddaughter?"

"Nah, don't want to bother her. I'll walk."

Stone looked outside. It was getting dark earlier with the change of season. "I'll drive you later."

Patrick agreed, and they spent the next few hours playing pool and darts and trading war stories. By the time Stone dropped Patrick off at the center, he felt more relaxed. It was nice to make a new friend, especially one who seemed to get his rough sense of humor. He fit right in with the cops, being used to the blue-collar talk from his military past and having been a mechanic. Plus, he'd gone nuts over Stone's muscle car, declaring it one of the finest automobiles he'd ever seen, and the man knew his cars.

Stone turned the car toward home, then decided to stop and get some Munchkins at Dunkin'. He picked up a pumpkin spice coffee, too, and realized he was close to Bluebird. He'd mentioned the property and missing dog to Devine, who promised to do a drive-by, but they'd gotten backed up and it had fallen off the docket. Maybe he'd cruise over and see if there was any suspicious activity.

Munching on his donuts, he turned on the dead-end street and saw a familiar Fusion parked on the corner. Slowing down, he studied the sea-green color. Waited a few beats.

Son of a bitch.

Arilyn Meadows was there.

Cursing, he parked and cut the engine. His body temperature shot up to inferno range. What the hell was she doing? His heartbeat increased as he slid the flashlight from the glove compartment, praying she was okay. Darkness bathed the property. The moon was full and leaked enough light to make out the gate, doghouse, and fire pit.

Stone began foot patrol, straining his ears for any sound. A chain rattled. Holding the flashlight steady, he walked deeper into the shadows and caught a flash of black. Tall, lean. Ski hat. The person perched on top of the dilapidated gate, hunching over as if to protect something in the jacket. Senses pricked, he ducked and stood behind a large tree, waiting.

The person climbed down and jumped to the ground.

Shaking with fury, Stone desperately reached for

the stupid breathing exercises before he killed her. He stepped out from behind the tree.

"Stop right there."

The person froze. Taking a few steps closer to make sure he was right, he confirmed the criminal and whipped his voice like a lash. "Take off the mask, Arilyn."

Slowly, she peeled off the knit material. Her strawberry hair was twisted up in a knot. Even with the darkness, he caught the flash of her grass-green eyes, the stubborn lines of her face. Then his gaze dropped to her prize.

The dog was more like a rat. Hardly any hair except for a few tufts on his head. Open wounds scattered over his tiny body. Batlike ears poked up from his bulletlike face. His eyes were the worst, though. Dead. Like he'd seen too many bad things out there and decided to check out. Uneasiness coursed through him, and Stone jerked his gaze away. "What the hell are you doing?" he gritted out.

She stood up from the ground. "Why are you here?" she whispered. "I didn't make any noise. Who called you?"

Red blurred before his eyes. He was gonna strangle her. "Are you kidding me right now? If I was someone else, I could've shot you! You look like a fucking burglar. You're stealing a dog from someone's house, a serious crime, and you're concerned about who tipped me off?"

Her lower lip trembled. "I had to. I came back just to check again. I swear I was careful! I found her right away, lying in the mud. She's severely traumatized, and if I didn't get her out in time, she'd die."

Stone swallowed. Dragged in another breath. Calm. He needed to be calm. "You could've called me! Or the animal shelter, or the abuse hotline, or something! You broke the law. You cannot go sneaking onto someone else's property and kidnap their dog!"

"Calm down," she hissed. "Lower your voice or someone will hear you. Besides, you're scaring Pinky."

Stone shook his head, sure he heard wrong. "You did not just fucking say that to me. I'm the police. I have to call this in and arrest you for kidnapping. Do you understand how bad this is? And what if someone else had found you? My God, does anyone else know about this crazy plan you concocted?"

"No. I'm the one who decided to take Pinky. No one else."

Pinky? He would've called it Rat Fink, the creature was so ugly. As little as the thing was, Stone still didn't want to get near it in case it broke out from its trance and bit the hell out of him. He'd heard little dogs were just as vicious as the big ones. He fought a shudder.

He would've bet she'd shrink back, apologize, and kiss his ass. Instead, she did what she did best. Annoy the crap out of him and challenge him to the teeth.

"Why are you here? You're suspended! Did you just decide to stroll the neighborhood or are you following me?"

He shot her an amazed look. "You have got to be kidding me right now! Like I have nothing better to do than follow you to your yoga classes and monitor your criminal dog activity? I was getting myself some damn donuts and figured I would do you a favor and check the place out. I told you to wait for Devine."

"Donuts at this hour? More fast food, Stone? Do you know what sugar does to your body late at night?"

"Do you think I'm an idiot? Changing the subject to foods that cause stress is not the way to calm me down right now, woman!"

"Use your breathing exercises like I taught you. Besides, I don't think you're an idiot. I think you're extremely smart."

He groaned and rubbed his face, trying to make sense out of the whole nutty situation. "Yeah, flattery will get you everywhere now." What the hell to do? He better move fast before someone else came. "Put the dog back and get in the car," he finally said. Stone knew it was a stretch, but maybe he could pretend he didn't find anyone on the property. The dog wouldn't tell. Yeah, he'd save her ass and then ream her big-time.

"No. I can't leave her." Uh-oh. Her usually serene face turned fierce, and she had the nerve to jab her finger in the air at him. "If you make me put her back, she'll die. Can you live with that?"

"Yes. Get in the car."

"No." Her jaw set. "You can arrest me, but I'm not leaving Pinky."

A vicious curse escaped his lips. The muscle in his eye ticked with fury. "Okay, now I'm pissed. If I arrest you, you'll have a record. Charges will be brought against you. You'll be written up in the Verily paper, and the dog will be returned anyway. Everyone loses. Do you understand? Now get your ass in the car!"

Then it happened.

His worst nightmare came true.

Her entire body shook and tears filled her eyes. "Please don't do this." Her voice broke. "Please let me save her. I'll do anything. I can't leave her behind."

Fuck. Fuck, fuck, fuck.

Even though he hadn't known her for long, Stone sensed she didn't fake tears. No, this woman didn't cry easily or use emotion for manipulation. Genuine distress and fear was written on her face, but it was for the rat fink dog rather than herself. She probably didn't care if she went to jail and lost her job. She just wanted the dog to be safe.

A headache pounded at his temples. Think. If he decided on his next course of action, it might haunt him forever. Stone believed in rules. He despised dirty cops who used their authority to give out favors or make their lives easier. He served the public for a reason and had never faltered. This next decision would go against every rule he'd ever abided by, on his oath to serve and protect the world against injustice. He might be out of uniform, but what he did next would affect him.

Yeah, he was gonna kill her.

"Don't say another word," he warned. "Not one. Cover up the thing with your jacket quick."

She obeyed quickly and trotted quietly behind him. "What about my car?"

"Leave it. I don't trust you right now. I'll take you home and make a call for someone to get it back to you by morning." He muttered under his breath, berating himself for his own stupidity and weakness against female tears. He cursed her, the rat fink, himself, and the whole damn situation. She got in his car without another word.

He refused to look at her or speak while he drove. She sat beside him, the dog still under her jacket, staring straight ahead through the windshield. She didn't even look sorry. More like resigned to take her punishment. Stone simmered through the drive, examining each angle and hoping he made a clean getaway. Stealing a dog was a crime. As an officer of the law, he'd assisted a criminal. He hadn't even gotten to finish his donuts.

Finally, he pulled up to her house, a small yellow bungalow with a large pine tree in the front yard. He'd been there a few times over the summer when Genevieve had lived there and he'd been called in to a crime scene. Without a sound, he got out of the car, opened her door, and escorted her to the front porch.

"Umm, thank you very much for helping me and—"

"Open the door and get inside."

She jumped a bit but slid the key in the lock and walked in. He followed, kicking the door closed with his heel. She jumped again but took off her coat, holding the dog tight against her. For protection? Oh, she was sorely mistaken if she thought anything would keep him from exacting punishment. He'd risked his career and his reputation.

Stone was gonna take retribution.

And it would be sweet.

ARILYN REFUSED TO SHOW fear. It wasn't the type of fear she'd experience if a stranger threatened her with violence. No, this was the uneasy, sick feeling in her stomach when she realized the man she was really attracted to was severely pissed off. At her.

What surprised her the most was the hard twist of excitement ramping her up. Her skin tingled, and an odd arousal pounded between her thighs. Was his anger turning her on? She'd heard about things like make-up sex, role play, and all sorts of darker kinds of sexual elements that intrigued her but she'd never experienced. Her lovers abhorred rough treatment or bringing negative emotions into the bedroom. She'd thought the same, though the occasional fantasy cropped up.

Now she was living one.

He practically oozed alpha male and sex. Jeans cupped his powerful thighs and rear, and the washed-out cotton of his hunter-green jersey clung to those meaty biceps and pecs. He glared with hot, dark eyes, devouring her with his gaze. Hands propped on hips. His full lips tightened to a thin line. His jaw locked. Stubble roughened his cheeks.

Her nipples rose and begged for attention. Arilyn squeezed the small, frightened dog a bit tighter for security. She needed to be calm and explain why he had made the right decision. He'd saved a dog's life, and Arilyn owed him gratitude. Now she just had to show him the danger was over and ease his temper.

Why, oh why had Stone found her? The plan was supposed to be simple. Arilyn never intended on kidnapping a dog. The intention was to scour the area one last time so she could find proof of an actual animal.

Until she found the Chihuahua.

Definitely abused. The poor thing lay in filth, with

no water or food. She approached cautiously, ready for a giant pit bull or German shepherd to come out, but it seemed the doghouse had only one broken resident. The dog never moved, just stared at her with flat, emotionless eyes. Open sores bled on its starved body. She had no idea what the dog was being used for—it didn't seem like a breeder situation—and the breed was a bit small for a bait dog. But the dog served some purpose for its sick owner.

There was only one thing to do.

She climbed the gate. Blinking back tears, she slowly lifted the dog. A quick check confirmed it was female. When Arilyn cradled her against the warmth of her jacket, a shudder wracked the tiny body.

Arilyn had always felt an affinity for animals, and her parents loved taking care of a wide menagerie before her mom got sick. She'd grown up sharing her bed with dogs, cleaning up cat hair on a regular basis, and playing with reptiles at a young age. Connection with the creatures in God's world made her happy and helped her believe in something bigger. Like with children, an animal's soul was pure. There was a reason dogs were used for therapy and helped children with a variety of issues such as autism spectrum disorders. They reminded people of love, devotion, and the simplicity of giving.

The last Chihuahua she'd met was named Pinky. She had a pink glittery collar, wore pink ribbons in her hair, and walked with a haughty dignity that reminded every other dog she was a queen. Arilyn's heart squeezed at the broken creature in her arms. This dog deserved what Pinky had. Love and security made dogs confident. Maybe with Arilyn's help and the name of a dog who had been well loved to remind her she was worth everything, there'd be a glimmer of hope. Sometimes it started with the basics. Safe shelter. Food. A bath. A name. All the things both animals and humans deserved in this life.

"I'm gonna get you out of here, Pinky," she whispered. Then, tucking her close and zipping up her black jacket, she took her prize and jumped over the gate.

Right into Stone's path.

Arilyn refocused on the scene before her.

"Put down the dog."

He may be hot, and he may be pissed, but there was no way she was giving up Pinky. Besides being her protection, Arilyn wasn't sure how the dog was going to handle being in her home. "She needs some time to transition." The excuse sounded lame to her ears, and Stone didn't buy it either.

"Trust me. *Pinky* will be safer on the ground right now." His low growl reminded her of his intent to throttle her. Maybe this would be a great time to introduce some other skills to control anger management?

"Let me settle her on the dog bed." He didn't answer, so she took her time placing the dog down on a thick fuzzy mattress she kept in the corner. Arilyn grabbed two bowls, filling one with clean water and the other with dry dog food. She lay the bowls close to the bed.

The dog lay listlessly, staring into space. Her heart broke, but her next task was to get Stone Petty calm. She straightened up to full height, breathed from her belly, and reminded herself to radiate serenity. After all, she was his teacher.

"There. Better?" He lifted a brow. "This may be a good time to go over basics of anger management. Control your breath, control your life. Remember?"

He took a step closer. "Oh, I remember."

"Envision yourself bathed in a pool of white light, calming each nerve ending. Envision yourself in peace."

"Oh, I'm envisioning something right now."

Arilyn swallowed. He didn't look peaceful. He looked . . . hungry. She decided to try another tack before he closed the distance between them. If he caught her strange arousal, he'd use it to his advantage. She didn't need weaknesses regarding this particular cop.

"Listen, Stone." Her tongue tumbled over his name, knowing he preferred it to "Officer." She refused to admit how right the sound of his first name felt spilling from her lips. "I know you're upset and I know I broke the law. I never intended to steal Pinky, but in abuse cases, many times the organizations don't have enough time to get the current animals out. I made an impulsive decision."

The eyebrow lifted a bit higher. "You think?" he drawled. Primitive waves of masculine energy beat from his figure.

"Y-Yes. All I can say is thank you for not arresting me and letting me save her."

"Don't thank me just yet, little one. You may not like the price."

A shiver built in her belly and flooded her bloodstream. Heat rushed to her face. She forced a shaky laugh. "What do you mean? What price?"

Stone leaned in and spoke each word slow and deliberate. "Whatever price I choose to exact."

She couldn't have heard right, of course. Sounded like one of those dark romances Kennedy was always trying to make her read. Unease slithered through her. "Well, if you're thinking I'm going to be some kind of sex slave for you, you're crazy."

Her false smile slipped. He studied her with such depth and intensity, she knew right then he was seriously considering it. "Not a bad idea. But you'd need too much training."

Her body sprung to life and wept for him to try. Her brain shut down in pure horror. What was happening to her? It was like some kind of voodoo sex spell came over her when he got near. "Hardy har har. Look, do you want to blackmail me? Fine. I'll sign off on your classes if you force me to, but it's wrong. I'm begging you not to use me in that way. You need to learn the techniques, and I'll never forgive myself for giving in."

"Now you've made me really mad," he said softly. "What I should do is yank down those yoga pants and smack your ass for your insulting view on my character."

Arilyn gasped. She'd never been spoken to like that. Yet she yearned in such a fierce, horrible way she didn't know what to do. He closed the distance, grasped her upper arms, and kept her in his firm grip. He loomed over her with a dark, deadly energy that sucked the rebellion right out of her. God, she wanted his lips on hers. Dreamed of him taking what he wanted, with no endless questions if this was okay or that was okay. Fantasized of being woman enough to satisfy this male creature on every sexual level he chose to show her.

"That's outrageous," she finally managed to respond. "Archaic!"

"And needed for a little brat with a God complex. You think because you meditate and eat from the earth and bend your body like a pretzel, you're the only one with morals? I'd never blackmail you or lie to my boss. I'll finish every one of your ridiculous classes and prove your techniques don't work."

"I don't think like that! And my classes aren't ridiculous. I'll prove they work by the time you finish the course."

"I'm tired of hearing about how beneficial anger management is. I want to talk about a more important subject."

"Pinky?"

"No. I wanna talk about sex."

She shook in his grip. There was nowhere to run, nowhere to hide, and damned if she hadn't lost her ability to tell him to move out of her space.

Because she didn't want to. A strange heat loosened her muscles and made her sluggish. Her belly tightened. Her panties dampened. Oh, she'd been turned on before and was no stranger to arousal, but this was different. With other men, she chose. With him, it was as if her mind disengaged from her body for the very first time and she had no control.

The words shot like a bullet and made her jerk. Those cruel lips tipped downward in a sneer. "Let's talk about this attraction we have for each other and what we're gonna do about it."

Arilyn was way past yoga breathing and now tried

to gulp for air. "Nothing. We do nothing. There is no attraction, and you've proved your point. I bow to your testosterone need to control all situations. "

He leaned in. The crisscross scar hooked into his brow. Even his eyebrows were strong looking. Full and dark like his midnight hair, which was free from his usual ball cap and spilled all messy and sexy around his ears and forehead. Individually, his features weren't remarkable. His nose hooked to the left, a sure sign of past fights. His cheekbones were high. Jaw square. Skin on the fair side. But together? He was devastating—the Black Irish look that made women weak in the knees, on the edge of civilized, yet not. Would his goatee be rough and scratchy, or silky smooth if she touched it? And why did his lips look soft, when his features were chiseled from stone?

"Damn, you're hot. Too bad you're also a pain in the ass and completely wrong for me."

She bared her teeth, more comfortable with the punch of anger that flooded her system. "Good, because it'd be a cold day in hell before I'd pick you as a boyfriend."

"How about a lover?" His breath rushed warm over her lips.

She opened her mouth to tell him this little scene was now over. Instead, the denial tumbled from her lips. "You're my student. We need to keep the boundaries appropriate."

His thumb brushed her lips, as gentle and light as a feather stroke. "That's just an excuse and you know it. You're not my official therapist. There's no hard-and-fast rules about a six-week course."

She stumbled over her next denial. "I don't want

a lover. I need three months to cleanse properly from my last relationship."

"What if I can help?"

She managed to snort. "Oh, I know how you want to help."

Stone chuckled, tracing the outline of her lips. She tried hard not to tremble and show weakness, but the melty sensation in her stomach grew worse, and when she tried to squeeze her thighs for relief, she only managed to tip him off that she was aroused. Sweat pricked her brow. She would not lose this battle. If she kept strong, he'd back off and they'd be able to finish the six-week course in harmony. She needed Officer Stone Petty as a sexual distraction as much as she needed a neighbor like Mrs. Blackfire.

"I have a proposition," he drawled. "One kiss. Let's prove to each other we'd be a disaster together."

"I don't need a kiss to confirm you'd be a nightmare to deal with," she shot back. "You're an ex-smoker, workaholic, anger-ridden, meat eater cynic."

His fingers moved to caress her cheek, the line of her jaw, up to her temple. Little brushes of tenderness, contradicting the raw strength and power in those hands and body. Ready to crush her but choosing gentleness. The lust rolled over her in waves, and she fought back with all her power.

"And you're a tree-hugging, naïve, post-world hippie with a God complex," he retorted. "Vegetarian, to boot. Plus a hardened criminal."

Arilyn growled under her breath and dug her nails into his shoulders with fierceness. "You know nothing about me, Officer! I am not naïve."

"Stone. Now shut up."

His mouth took hers.

She planned to fight back and give him everything she got.

And she did, but not in the way she planned.

The moment those blistering-hot, soft lips met hers, she lost it. Swamped by the delicious scent and taste and feel of him, she arched upward and opened her mouth for more. He muttered something dark and dirty, and slid his tongue past her parted lips and beyond.

Then he showed her who was boss.

Oh, he kissed her with all the hard passion and lust she always dreamed about but never inspired. With her past lovers, she got tender, slow lovemaking, and poetic words murmured in her ear. Moves were coordinated like a beautiful song, and though she was satisfied, and emotionally full, there was an ache deep in her body that never felt completely fulfilled.

She'd thought something was wrong with her and happily ignored that part of herself.

Until now.

Stone Petty owned her. Possessed her. His tongue took what he wanted and demanded it all, with each thrust and complete deflowering of her mouth. He reached around and sunk his fingers into her hair, tugging her head back to expose her throat and keep her helpless beneath him. Her breasts pressed against his hard chest, his erection notched between her open thighs, and he ravished her body and soul, leaving nothing behind but an aching, horrible want for more.

She exploded with her own demands, turning the kiss into something much more. Whimpering, she opened her mouth wider, arched her body up to rock against his hardness, and dug her short nails into his scalp.

"You taste so good," he muttered, biting and sucking on her lower lip. "Like sugar cookies. I want to spread you out, taste you, eat you until you come apart."

His dirty words caused a rush of liquid warmth to trickle between her legs. "Oh, God, this is bad," she gasped, clinging tighter. "Very bad."

"And so good." He ground his erection against her, bumped her clit, and she shuddered, writhing to get closer. "Need more." He ripped his mouth from hers, grabbed the stretchy halter top, and pulled it down to bare her breasts.

She wasn't wearing a bra.

"I just died and went to heaven," he groaned, his hands cupping her breasts and rubbing her tight nipples. She bit down on her lip to keep from crying out, especially when he plucked at her, watching her tortured face as if to see what she liked. "You're like butter and cream, silky smooth. Peach nipples, just like I thought. How do they taste?"

"No, don't, I don't think—oh!"

His lips opened over one aching tip, his tongue swiping over and over, nibbling on her like a feast. She drowned in a tidal wave of sensation, her brain shut down, her body exploding on overload like a bad circuit firing up.

Her past seductions consisted of scented candles, romantic verses read aloud, and the taste of champagne. Silken sheets turned down. Long, endlessly orchestrated scenes that she always dreamed she wanted.

Now she realized how they'd barely scratched the surface of her need. Right now, she wanted to push Stone Petty on the ground, climb on top of him, and sink down until he slid deep inside her. She wanted to get sweaty, be loud, and take pleasure on her terms, with nothing holding her back. With a man who wasn't afraid to be rough, and demanding, and bad.

"I want you. Now. Here." He looked up, his mouth wet, eyes fierce and so filled with hunger she began to shake. "You want it, too."

She did.

But she couldn't.

My God. What was she doing?

Sanity returned. He was all wrong for her! This man irritated her on a constant basis. They'd have crazy sex, and he'd saunter away and torture her with his smug grins for the rest of the anger management class. She was recovering from a broken heart and had no energy to tackle such a sizzling affair. He'd eat her alive. In a good way. In a bad way.

"I can't." Arilyn pushed weakly at his shoulders. Her voice got stronger. "I can't."

She gave him credit. He backed off immediately, hands lifted in the air as he grabbed for his composure. "Okay. Give me a minute." She took the time to yank up her top, straighten her clothes, and get herself together. Stone shook his head hard, rubbed his hands over his face, and let out a breath. "Got carried away."

Satisfaction surged. It was nice to know she wasn't the only one affected by the kiss. Arilyn wondered if she'd ever be able to kiss another man without thinking of Stone. His goatee was a combination of silky and bristly, a delicious contradiction to the softness of his lips. His taste was better than those apple martinis she loved so much. Tart, spicy, with a heat that slid into her bloodstream and exploded in her tummy.

"I did, too," she offered. "I'm sorry."

He scowled. "I'm not. Thought you had more backbone than to apologize for a great kiss."

And just like that, the annoyance was back. "I don't need this type of complication in my life right now," she snapped. "You're a client. We can't blur the lines."

Those lush lips that had bestowed such pleasure now treated her to his famous sneer. "Don't give me that crap. As I just said, I'm not your client, and you're not my real therapist. You counsel me to control my temper, which is getting frayed right now by your sad excuses."

She bristled in fury. "Excuses? I don't need an excuse! We kissed, it was good, I'm over it. Let's move on. The last thing I need is a pushy cop wrecking my life."

He got in her face. "Lady, you wrote the book on pushy. A relationship with you would be a nightmare. But you can't deny we'd steam up the sheets together."

She gave up poetry for this? He was rude, crude, and owned no soft edges. First he kissed her, then he yelled. Even if she wanted a transitional lover, he was all wrong. Arilyn refused to back down, even if she had to tilt her head back to eyeball him. "Classy. You can go ahead and steam them up with someone else."

He shook his head as if disgusted by the thought.

"Can't. Chemistry this good is rare. It may piss me off, but we have to explore it."

She gasped. "In your dreams! It was a complete fluke. I'm not exploring anything with you!"

He studied her with hard eyes, and the man did something so outrageous she didn't see it coming.

He kissed her again. Just manhandled her, pulling her in and planting his lips over hers for a long, deep, thorough kiss that curled her toes and revved her body right up to Ferrari status.

The worst part?

She responded.

He slid her back down to the ground, letting her feel his rock-hard abs and thighs, ran his tongue over his bottom lip as if to taste her one last time, then gave a cocky grin. "Yep. That's what I thought. I'll keep this crime a secret for now, but you owe me big. See you in class."

Stone turned his back on her and walked toward the door.

Arilyn squeaked with outrage, shaking with the urge to belt him and wipe out his satisfaction. Finally, she found her voice. "I still don't like you one bit, Officer Petty!"

He glanced back over his shoulder and winked. "I still don't like you either."

Then he left.

Arilyn turned to look at the dog, who still hadn't moved. Just stared into space, looking at something else.

A premonition washed over her. If she allowed her body to weaken, she'd ask him to take her to bed. And he'd destroy her in ways even her ex hadn't touched.

She couldn't risk her heart being broken a second time so soon.

She might never recover.

Arilyn knelt beside Pinky, gently stroking her head. She didn't respond. She'd clean the wounds, maybe feed her through a dropper to get some water in her system. Anthony would know the best plan to undertake. In the meantime, she'd keep her head down and get to goal.

The end of anger management and the end of seeing Stone Petty.

nine

A FEW DAYS LATER, Stone realized he should've just thrown her in jail.

It would've been a hell of a lot easier.

The motley crew of the anger management class gathered around the outdoor kennels at the Animals Alive shelter. At first, he'd looked forward to a field trip. Spending hours locked in a room with her, trying to do yoga or meditate or talk in the circle, was painful. For his mental state *and* his body. Besides a constant state of blue balls, they'd formed another type of connection.

They shared a secret. Stone knew there was a level of intimacy in sharing something no one knew about. Every time their gazes touched, energy shimmered between them, a reminder of the favor that hung ripe and beat through every undercurrent of conversation.

He figured a little air was good for the soul, and they'd visit some crazy ashram or help children or serve food to the homeless. But this he refused to do.

He hated dogs.

Stone tried to focus on her lecture.

"Animals are statistically proven to help lower stress and ease anger issues in humans," she said. Today she wore jeans, scuffed brown boots, a snug tank, and some sort of crochet cape thing in bright red. Her hair, caught in a high ponytail, was shimmering red-gold under the weak rays of sun. The leaves, which had fully turned in a stunning display of orange, amber, and yellow, crunched beneath their feet. Acres of woods spread out behind them, with a small building as the welcome center, horse stalls, and different types of gates holding various types of animals. "Now, I'm sure you're all wondering how volunteering our time with rescues can possibly help control anger management. First, serving the community helps us get out of our worlds and reminds us of what we do have. Though anger is a trigger and caused by a multitude of stresses, it is also part of ego. It's selfish. Getting in touch with less fortunate creatures, big and small, ground us in the reality of what we do have. If you're driving to work, get caught in horrific traffic, and start to lose it, reminding yourself of the dog who was abused with no home or the child struggling with cancer can actually help ground us in the bigger reality."

Luther and Eli looked fascinated. Stone grudgingly admitted she was a good speaker. Spending years around lies and bullshit and criminals made it harder to be empathetic or believe in something bigger. She did. The pure energy of her spirit practically rolled around her in waves. She drew people in with the urge just to be around her, listen to her speak, maybe touch her. She had a gift, and Stone bet she had no idea how she affected people.

"I'll be handing the training over to Anthony, our director. He's going to show you the procedures, and then we'll spend the next hour working with the animals on a one-to-one basis."

No way.

Stone studied the guy who stepped up and thanked her. He had those moony eyes Stone knew too well. The director had a crush on Arilyn big-time. As he took them through the greeting center and showed them how to put on a leash, how the dogs they walked or spent time with were coded, and how to follow the rules, Stone wondered how Arilyn felt about him. She'd told him in the car he was in the friend zone, but could that change? No. She kissed him like a woman who was starving and not actively dating or interested in another man. Stone was trying to be her transitional. But Anthony seemed to be a better fit for her lifestyle over the long term.

Stone brooded. They were similar. Both shared a passion for animals. He worked for charity. Good-looking guy, too. Looked Italian, so the guy probably knew how to cook. If she were smart, she'd date this guy and stay away from him. Stone couldn't promise her anything but the best night of her life. Oh, and hanging out with a workaholic, anger-ridden divorcé who wanted no children.

Yeah, it was a real win-win.

His mood soured. He trotted behind Anthony, learned the rules, and then was handed back to his teacher. They both smiled so brightly at each other, Stone wondered if he'd be blinded for life. He got a fucking cavity looking at them. Weren't they just perfect together?

Anthony squeezed her hand, leaned down, and whispered in her ear. She laughed, swatted his arm playfully, and turned back to the group. "Okay, guys, we're going to focus on the dogs today. Listen to

Anthony's instructions and go by the color-coded tags. Green is acceptable to take for a walk. Blue is no touch. Yellow is needs social interaction."

She led them to the long, narrow aisle of gates. The smell of earth, rotting leaves, and dog poop rose in the air. The whines and barks grew to a shrieking level as the dogs recognized company and tried to get noticed. He watched Luther and Eli choose their dogs, clipping on the leashes and leading crazy bundles of energy out the squeaky gate door. Luther seemed delighted with the large black Lab rushing toward freedom, and Eli had a small smile with the medium-sized mutt with the long snout.

Stone took in their lolling tongue, sharp eyes, and big snouts. Then he freaked.

Sweat broke out on his skin. A low panic clawed at his stomach. He took a few steps back.

"Stone, are you okay? Just pick one and clip on the leash."

He stared back at her, shaking his head hard. "I'm more of a cat person. I'll go to the cat house instead."

She frowned. "The cat house is being refurbished, so it's off-limits today."

"Then I'll hit the stables."

"Horse training is an entire day."

The image of the pit bull leaping at him, teeth bared, drawing blood while he screamed like a baby and writhed on the ground hit him full force. It was suddenly hard to breathe. He was getting the hell out. "Well, I'll help in the office or something. I'm not doing this. I told you I hate dogs and always have."

He beat a hasty retreat, but she was suddenly in

front of him, placing her hands gently on his arm. "Stone? I'm so sorry, I didn't know."

He gritted his teeth. Wished for a cigarette so bad he figured the patch would explode off him. "Know what?"

"The dogs. Did you get bit?"

The horror of her knowing his one weakness made him snap. "I'm not afraid of the damn dogs, okay? I just don't like them. Is that a fucking crime?"

Instead of yelling back or telling him to breathe, she smiled. Her voice lilted like soothing music, and her fingers interlaced with his. The touch of her skin against his grounded him back to earth. "No, it's not a crime," she said. "Neither is being skittish around an animal you don't know. It's called being smart." She gazed at the kennels, her eyes sad. "Many dogs, especially the pit bulls, are bred for meanness. It's almost like having something good but shaping it into evil. Some can't even be saved, they're too far gone in the darkness and fighting for survival. Others still manage to see the light and the goodness. See, they're just like people. Some good, some bad, some right in the middle."

She faced him again. "It's my fault for not checking with everyone about how they feel about animals. I'm sorry. And if you were bitten, that's a traumatic experience very difficult to get over. Dogs need to earn your trust back, just like we need to earn theirs sometimes."

He suddenly felt stupid being embarrassed over something that wasn't his fault. How did she do that? Make him see things in a different way? He cleared his throat. "Sorry. I was a kid and a pit bull knocked me down, bit the hell out of my leg. The owner just laughed and urged the dog on."

She nodded. "Yeah, I hear those stories a lot. Most dogs don't start off that way, but it's probably too late. We can't save them all. That's why I wanted to rescue Pinky so badly. I thought maybe there'd be a chance."

How often had he uttered condolences to a family member who lost someone? A weak excuse but all he had left to offer. The tightness in his chest eased. In her own way, Arilyn knew the battle he took on every day. So much loss, but you did it for the occasional win.

"Why'd you name that thing Pinky?"

She gave a half shrug. "Knew a Chihuahua with the name. She kicked butt and carried herself like royalty. Thought the poor thing could use a cool namesake."

"It's an awful name."

She grinned, and his heart lightened. Damn this woman and her ability to make him feel good as much as she pissed him off. It was terrible. "Next time you rescue an animal, you can name her," she said.

"Catching criminals is bad enough. I'll pass."

She pursed her lips, and her green eyes sparkled with laughter. His gaze focused on her lush mouth and what he wanted to do with it. She cleared her throat as if she knew. And wanted it, too. "How are you doing with the smoking?" She jerked her head toward his arm.

"Not bad. I'm on the last level, so I'm almost fit for real society now. Still get the cravings, though."

"Maybe I can help." She unzipped her small

satchel, fished around, and drew out a purple stone. It had a brown cord attached to it. "Here. I want you to wear this."

He fingered the rock. Shades of violet and white, it was carved into a type of pendant. "What is it? Heart of the newt?"

She snorted, reached over, and slipped the necklace around his neck. The cord was soft, like a moccasin. It hung low enough to hide in his shirt. When her fingers brushed his chest to tuck it inside his button-down Henley, he sucked in a breath. She paused, and that crackle of electricity struck again.

He tried again for humor instead of tumbling her into the grass. "You didn't put a love spell or anything on me, did you?"

She yanked her hands away as if she'd been scorched and stepped back. "You're a real comedian, Officer. It's a crystal amethyst. Wear it against your skin. It's a very powerful stone and helps smoking cessation."

He fingered the polished stone briefly before letting it drop back against his chest. "Didn't see it in the how-to-quit-smoking aisle."

"You won't. Amethyst is known as the master healing stone. One of its many uses is to transform addiction." He studied the high flush on her cheekbones. "Forget it. I know you think I'm crazy; you don't have to wear it." She spun on her heel to flounce off, but he grabbed her wrist, halting her retreat.

"No," he said softly. "I'll wear it. I need all the help I can get." She lifted her gaze and suddenly they were drowning in each other. He suddenly felt like one of those testosterone-ridden chumps from the teen movies. Completely smitten by a girl's eyes. Ugh. "Thanks." Better. His voice sounded stronger.

"Welcome." They stared some more. If a guy saw them, his man card would be officially pulled. "Can I ask you to do something? I wouldn't ask anyone else, but I trust you."

He tried to ignore the pleasure that raced through him at her comment. "What?"

"Pinky's here. She was deemed unfit to be in the kennel with other dogs. She's completely comatose most of the time, but if she gets close to another dog, she goes berserk. Anthony may not be able to keep her, since they're too short staffed to give her the proper amount of therapy, plus they need to keep her isolated. People don't scare her, so she was probably used for bait."

"You mean bigger dogs attacked her?"

Arilyn nodded. "They try to spur on the bigger dogs. Usually bait dogs are other pit bulls meant to antagonize, but sometimes they'll use a smaller dog and keep them away to taunt the dogs. She was probably never mauled but consistently threatened and frightened on a regular basis. Something may have snapped."

"Sons of bitches," he muttered. "The house is on my radar, you know. I called in a few tips and we've got the place being watched. Any more dogs that go in will be caught immediately."

Her face softened. "Thank you. If you'd just sit with Pinky, it would be a great help. Talk with her. Maybe pet her. Whatever you feel comfortable with. She needs to get used to being back in the real world and feeling unthreatened."

He wanted to refuse. Stone still hated being around any type of dog, especially in a cage, but the way she looked at him made him want to slay all her dragons. And Pinky's.

Oh, yeah, he was a chump who wanted that woman bad. Ridiculous. A few days ago, he only wanted to strangle her.

"Fine. All I have to do is sit?"

"Yes. Just be a steady presence. Sometimes they just don't want to feel so alone."

Stone knew how that felt.

She led him over to a cage in the corner, away from the other dogs. A small bed, various bowls, and some toys lay haphazardly in the cage. Pinky lay on the right side, staring into space, not moving. Didn't look vicious. Even if she freaked out, if he stayed by the door, he could get up. Wasn't like the bigger dogs that could overpower him.

Sweat pricked his brow, but he manned up. Stone opened the gate, dropped down on the rough, damp ground, and propped his back up. Pinky's head turned a bit toward the sound, but she still didn't seem interested. She was still just as ugly as the night he first saw her. A few bandages were wrapped around her body, probably to heal the sores. She looked cleaner, too, even though there was no fur. Weren't dogs supposed to have hair? Her skin was a tan color, with her paws and belly a light pink. Three weird white tufts of fur sprouted from the top of her head in some kind of kooky headdress. Beady black eyes. Pinkish bat ears that sprouted up from the sides of her bullet head. Her black snout stuck out slightly, making her look like she owned a crazy overbite. A simple black collar circled her neck.

Arilyn peered through the gate. "You okay?" she asked.

"Sure. Go ahead, I'll be fine."

He heard her footsteps fade away. The sound of a bird screeched in the air, along with whimpers and other doggy noises down the way. The rat's—umm, Pinky's nose twitched as she caught a scent. Yeah, she was still in there somewhere. Whatever had happened was bad. He knew how that went.

Stone gave a long sigh. "Guess it's just me and you for a while. That acceptable?"

No answer.

Stone settled back for a long, long silence.

ARILYN SLID THE BROCCOLI bake in the oven, sliced some multigrain bread, and poured a glass of wine. It had been a good day. The guys had been great at the shelter, no mini disasters had cropped up, and now she was ready to relax with a good book and a bath. Sure, she couldn't stop thinking about the amazing kiss with Officer Stone Petty. Both of them. The way he touched her and commanded her body, tempting her to do a whole bunch of dirty, delicious things she'd never tried.

But she controlled herself. Repeated the mantra over and over that he was a client and off-limits. Kind of. Definitely a gray area but easier to sketch the boundary lines in bold black-and-white.

At least, that's what she kept telling herself.

Holding back a sigh, Arilyn grabbed her laundry basket and headed outside to get her clothes from the line. She hoped that Mrs. Blackfire wouldn't be out spying. Guilt pricked her at the second empty wine bottle she'd be forced to put out in recycling this week. The evening spent together hadn't gone as bad as she expected, and Poppy had entertained them both with stories. Mrs. Blackfire had actually smiled at one point. Arilyn couldn't stop staring at her, wondering if it was a trick of the light, and then Poppy gave her that sharp look—that she was being rude—and she'd concentrated on eating. At least, Poppy seemed more inclined to try some other activities at the center this week.

She opened the door and rammed right into the man on her doorstep.

When she refocused, her world shook, tilted, and dumped her in a tangle of limbs on the cold ground.

Jacob.

He looked exactly the same. Shoulder-length dark hair tied back, revealing the graceful, etched lines of his face. Long limbed and lean from his many years of yoga. A watchful, reflective aura surrounded him. He'd studied in India under a powerful yogi and dedicated his life to serving others.

Too bad he was also a lying, scheming cheater.

The nasty thought helped her breath return. Her world rebalanced. Her many years of practice and study under his tutelage came roaring back. Once, he'd made her feel as if she was the most important thing in his world. Now he only reminded her of how little she meant to him in the bigger picture.

Arilyn checked the lock on the door inside her heart.

Still tight.

"Arilyn." His voice lilted, carried, stroked, like

poetry whispered in a lover's ear. "I wanted to come sooner, but I realize how angry you must be. I thought a bit of time would be better for us to talk."

He'd come before, of course. Twice. The first time he cheated, he fell to his knees and cried. Begged her forgiveness. Spoke of man's weakness and his mockery of monogamy. Said if she demanded it, she was worth the sacrifice of giving up other women. She forgave him and took him back.

The second time was more delicate. He waited two full days after the righteous, horrid anger passed and she fell into grief mode. He admitted his fault and spoke for hours about how scared he was of being close with her. How she filled him up in ways his meditation and spiritual practices never could. He wanted a chance to show her they could be more together, because he was no longer afraid. Long into the night, they discussed their dreams and ambitions. She laid down the law. No more cheating. She wanted to move forward into the light with a real relationship. She wanted him to tell the students.

He promised it all, and slowly Arilyn believed they'd make it.

Now she looked at the man she'd given five years to and wondered why. Why him? What did he truly give her other than the mirage of communication and connectedness? Even their lovemaking was a lesson in spirituality. He made her study tantric sex in all its forms but never seemed to give himself completely over to her on an emotional level. It was more like the practice itself turned him on rather than her. The idea of giving himself over was better than the actual process.

Arilyn wondered if he'd been lying to himself, too. He seemed more satisfied banging his student without any higher emotional connection than he ever did with her.

"There's nothing more to discuss," she said evenly. "We've done this scene before. Twice. We both need to move on."

Confusion flicked over his features. "You're the one I love. I know I've hurt you, but I think we need to discuss our relationship. Close the cycle."

Ah, yes. Cycles. Jacob was big into honoring the beginning and ending of any type of relationship. Once, she'd thought it was beautiful. Now she had sunk to such a level, she only wanted to bash him in the face.

The hurt and humiliation simmered. Her heart, though, remained beating and whole. "With all the hours we talked and dissected our relationship, I think we've done enough. You need to go. Back to your studio, and your spiritual path, and your many, many female students."

"Please." His voice reached out and begged. "Tracey and I had been spending late nights discussing her path. She'd graduated to the intermediate student pool and felt pressured. She came to me, needful, and I was weak, Arilyn. It's the fault I'm consistently struggling with. My body was weak, but I swear, you're the one I live for. The woman I love. Please give me a chance to talk."

Still holding the laundry basket, Arilyn wondered what would happen if she let him in. Every woman had a certain weakness, and Jacob was hers. He represented a sense of authority and knowledge that always turned her on and played on her mind and emotions like a conductor at the symphony. He'd been her guide on the path of yoga, opening her body and soul to the ancient practice. Textbook stuff. The symbol of the teacher-client relationship and schoolgirl crush.

And he always came back to her.

Arilyn knew that, in his own way, he did love her. But it wasn't the way she could live with anymore, and it wasn't the type of love she wanted. She ached for so much more.

If she let him in to talk, she might forgive him. Be happy for a while. Maybe six months. Maybe a year. When they worked together well, she equated it to being high on drugs twenty-four/seven. He made her feel like the most important woman in the world, the keeper of his heart and happiness, and she drowned herself in those dreams. She'd trick herself into believing in something real, believe his lies about meeting her family and friends, and find herself in the same position.

Stone Petty was more honest than this man was. He was also more passionate.

The odd thought trickled past her, but she pushed it aside and concentrated on her ex-lover.

Her voice strengthened. "No more. I like my life now, Jacob. It's more real than what we had. I'm moving on, and it's time you do, too."

"I love you. We're soul mates. If you give me a chance, I'll prove it."

The final pang from his loss struck deep. "I loved you, too. But not anymore. Good-bye, Jacob. Please don't come here again."

The shock on his face told her more than she ever needed to know. Rarely did a woman turn him down. As she sagged against the closed door, heart pounding, Arilyn realized it was the first time she'd ever stood up to him and told him no. On her terms.

A laugh escaped her lips. Shaking, she dropped the basket and grabbed her wineglass. She felt freer than she ever had. The sadness of a broken relationship would always haunt her. She'd given him so much of herself. But she was stronger now. It was time to figure out what she needed and pursue that path with her eyes wide-open and no more lies clogging her vision.

Arilyn sipped her wine. And thought of Stone.

An affair. The thought of giving in to her body and allowing herself to experiment tempted her like a siren call. Still, she was afraid if she couldn't handle it, she'd break again too soon. Not that she'd be in danger of falling in love with him, of course. But if she got addicted to the sex? Began to cling to him in an unhealthy manner due to her leftover need from Jacob?

Nightmare.

The doorbell rang.

She shook her head, grasping the knob, ready to show Jacob what it felt like to get in touch with real anger.

Kate, Kennedy, and Gen were perched on her doorstep.

"Surprise!"

Arilyn laughed and hugged them. "What are you doing here? I thought the bachelorette party was Friday night."

"Did you start the party without us?" Kennedy

asked, swinging her hips clad in a trendy pencil skirt with a short leather jacket. She opened up the cabinets and took down three more wineglasses. "Oh, goody, I love sauvignon blanc."

Gen slid onto one of the breakfast stools and sighed. A successful resident surgeon in training, she looked tired but happy. Her dark hair was caught in a messy ponytail, and she wore old jeans and a sweatshirt with the Purity Hotel logo. "I miss this place. I'm so glad you live here now, Arilyn. It's the next best thing."

Kate smiled and plucked a half-filled wineglass from the counter. "This is where you and Wolfe fell in love watching HGTV. Maybe it'll bring the same magic to Arilyn."

Arilyn sighed and leaned against the refrigerator. "I wish." In her attempt to be more open, she told them the truth. "Jacob was just here."

The girls all stared. Gen finally whispered. "You mean Yoga Man? Here?"

Kennedy frowned. "I'll show him a new yoga position he won't soon forget. Do I need to get more eggs?"

Arilyn laughed. God, it was so good to have a tight circle of friends who knew all her crappy issues, her choices in bad men, and loved her anyway. "No eggs needed. He wanted me back, of course. I said no, I've moved on. He looked shocked that I knew how to say no to him, and I began to drink buckets of wine. Oh, and there's a healthy broccoli bake for dinner."

Kate pressed her lips together. "He's such a jerk. If he thinks you're gonna transcend two cheating incidents, he's nuts. Are you okay, A?"

Her friends waited for the answer. Slowly, she nodded. "Yeah, I am. It hurt, but I know I made the right decision. I don't want that kind of life for myself."

Gen nodded. "That's why I ran out on my wedding day. It just hit me, and I had to make a choice. You won't regret it. Something better is on the horizon."

She thought of her hot cop ready to do dirty things to her, with her, and felt heat rise to her cheeks.

Kennedy pounced. "Uh-oh. And something already has. Or someone. Spill."

"Nothing. Let me get the casserole out."

Kennedy blocked the oven and crossed her arms in front of her chest. "Hell, no. Who's got you blushing? I know it's not those dogs you love so much. Oh, is it the director from the shelter? He seemed hot."

"Anthony? No, he's great but more of a friend."

Gen tilted her head. "It's not that cop from the summer, is it?"

All the girls turned to look at her. "What cop?" Kate demanded. "How do you know about this and I don't?"

Gen grinned. "When Arilyn called the cops on my ex, we rode in the squad car with him. He had a gorgeous partner—Devine, I think his name was. But it was the other one that held Arilyn's attention."

Arilyn squeezed her eyes shut and groaned. Nightmare. She couldn't lie. She had promised. "He's in my anger management course," she finally said. "Officer Stone Petty."

"That's the one!" Genevieve snapped her fingers. "He was looking at you like he wanted to gobble you up. He reminded me of the big bad wolf. Really tall, dark, and badass."

Yes, on first sight he was a bit scary. Now? He'd saved her and Pinky. He hated children and women getting abused. He'd been through a crappy childhood and didn't whine. He was amazing.

Huh?

When had she actually begun to like him? *Did* she like him?

Kennedy clucked her tongue. "About time you date a hottie. A cop in uniform? Kill me now. I'm hiring one for Kate's stripper Friday night."

Kate groaned. "I don't want a stripper! I have Slade in my bed and have no need to see any other man naked."

"We have to do it. Tradition. It will be tasteful."

"Strippers aren't tasteful."

"Exotic male dancers," Ken corrected.

Kate rolled her eyes. "Back to hot cop. Are you dating?"

Arilyn waved off the question. "No. He's my client. Kind of. And he's completely not my type. We fight, and you know I never fight with people."

"Fighting is a source of releasing sexual tension," Kennedy pointed out. "This could be a good thing. Did you ever fight with Yoga Man?"

"No, never." Arilyn thought over their relationship. Had she ever even argued with him? When she got upset, they sat down and discussed. Made compromises. There was never yelling or anger, even when inside she seethed. Instead of letting the emotion back up and fester, she used her meditation and yoga practices to come to terms and release.

With Stone, she wasn't afraid of snapping back at him. In a way, it was sort of fun. Nothing was left behind to work out, because she always told him exactly what she thought and felt, with no worries about how he'd handle it.

Interesting.

Gen nodded. "Kennedy's right. The two of you exploded together. Why don't you just date him?"

"No, we're too different. It would never work."

"Then just sleep with him." Everyone stared at Kennedy. She lifted her hands up in the air. "What? Why does everything always have to be heavy and relationship centered? Affairs work. Get him out of your system. He's your transitional anyway."

Arilyn sighed and took out the casserole. Grabbing some plates, she began slicing pieces for each of them. "Maybe."

Kate laughed. "Wow, he really did get to you. Normally you'd tell us to mind our own business and you'd never involve yourself with just sex."

"She's opening up to new opportunities," Kennedy said. "Which is a perfect introduction to the real reason we're here."

Arilyn gave out the plates and forks, then dug in for a bite. "Now I'm nervous."

"Don't be. We just brought you an outfit to wear on Friday night."

Suspicion laced her voice. "I already have an outfit."

Kennedy shuddered. "I know. It's unacceptable. Boring. You're gorgeous and need to play up your assets. No yoga pants allowed."

"I'm not wearing leather or fur, and you can't make me."

"Fake leather," Kennedy pointed out. "And you need to show some leg. You never wear skirts."

Gen giggled. "She's right, A. If there's going to be exotic dancers, you need to expose some skin. You're gonna love what Ken picked out."

Arilyn groaned. "I am so not ready for this."

Kate sighed. "Neither am I."

Kennedy smiled. "This bachelorette party is gonna be epic."

They all shared a glance. "That's exactly what I'm afraid of," Arilyn said.

Then they all burst into laughter.

ten

HANDS REACHING HIGH, palms together, and sweep down to the ground. Touch the floor. Deep breath in and right foot back. Lift the heel if you can. Inhale and release left. Hold. Fully exhale aaaand push back to plank pose. Hold for a breath. Lower down, chin touches mat, push back to Downward Dog. Hold. Breathe. Lower back down aaaand right foot all the way to your palms. Walk it forward if you have to. Inhale and left foot steps in. Rise back up, full breath in and out. Beautiful. Let's do it again."

Fuck. Fuck, fuck, fuck.

She was hot as sin and the spawn of the devil. An enchantress of death. Because if he had to do this fucking Salutation to the Moon or whatever the hell it was one more time, he was gonna die of a heart attack.

Dying of smoking was so much more pleasant.

He shot a sidelong glare at his prison mates. Luther embraced the punishment, pushing through the routine with a tiny smile on his face. Seemed he was reading up on yoga and meditation practices and was consistently adding educational side notes to Arilyn's lecture. She seemed to love it, too.

Eli was more manlike, but he liked to mess up to get her hands on him. At least, Arilyn didn't seem interested. Her touch was strictly impersonal, and her chats with him after class were brief. He knew, because he waited for her after class. Insisted on walking her to the car, citing her past broken windshield as the reason. Just in case she had a stalker who liked to vandalize. Maybe a previous anger management client.

She laughed it off, but Stone knew she liked their chats/fights. In those few moments together, they covered a lot of territory.

They didn't agree on much. Politics, hobbies, likes, and dislikes were a mess. She disliked TV and he lived for it. She read self-help, and he preferred horror novels. He hated dogs, and she helped them. He had a sweet tooth, and she preferred fruit for her fix. He was unorganized and loud. She was ruthlessly neat and soft-spoken.

A real mess.

He still wanted her in his bed, though. But if she kept up the physical torture, he might not make it.

Stone did another round, and she blessedly called to sit back on their mats. Trying not to huff and puff, he took in her glowing face, bright eyes, and blinding aura. At least, he thought it was an aura. He'd been daydreaming when she discussed anger as blurring a person's aura and fogging their vision, but it was as if a glow followed her, confirming her goodness. In her yoga pants, bare feet, and tiny tank, her muscles and lithe limbs made his mouth water. She was comfortable in her skin, which tempted him as a lover. How rare to meet a woman who seemingly had no body issues. Who wore no makeup, who used no trappings to hide. It was like she'd come to terms with what she had, her limitations and strengths, and accepted them with an open heart.

Ah, crap, now he was starting to think like her. He needed to get a grip.

"Grab some water and let's come into a circle."

He hated circle time. Trying not to mope, he took a long swig of water and sat on the godforsaken mat. Why, oh why did she hate real seating? What was this thing about being on the floor all the time? He'd learn better in a chair.

She shot him a mischievous grin when he carefully stretched out his legs and tried not to wince. "You okay, Stone?"

He shot her a warning glare. "Just peachy."

Minx. If she gave him the chance, he'd tire her in other ways.

"I'd like to do some sharing before we break for the day."

Oh, goody. His favorite. *Sharing.*

Eli and Luther sat cross-legged, ready to open themselves up and bleed in the name of healing. Stone tried not to gag.

"Have you been writing in the journals I gave out?" she asked. Back ramrod straight, ankles crossed on opposite knees, thumbs and index fingers touching in circles, she radiated everything beautiful about yoga and peace and harmony. But all he could think of was her beaded nipples against her tank, the heat between her thighs, and the way her hair wrapped around her body in a sensual cloak. He grunted and shifted his position, trying to get his erection down.

Luther nodded. "I write in the morning, as you suggested. I read this book once called *The Artist's Way*, and one of the tasks was to keep morning pages. By dumping out all our random thoughts and fears for the day, we're able to get out of our own way."

She beamed. "That's right, Luther. I'm so happy you're finding the book helpful. There's so much junk in our day-to-day routine, we block ourselves from connecting with our true center. When the mind is quiet, and we are sitting in our body, it's like being in church. Or that childhood place you loved so much. It's everything holy and good. Another reason I call the body a temple. Unfortunately, TV, phones, and computers slam us with so much information, we're overloaded. This is a way to clean ourselves out. Make sense?"

It did. Not that he was writing in a stupid journal. He had already gotten in trouble for the cartoon he'd sketched out. She'd gotten so mad he'd waited for her to throw him out. But she made a lot of sense. Even after the dreaded yoga routines, he felt more connected to himself and his aches and pains than before. Stone knew he used drinking, smoking, and harsh exercise to try to wipe out the junk. Hadn't worked half as well as this stuff.

Not that he was an advocate or anything. Still, he'd signed up for that Pilates class even though he was going to take a lot of crap from his coworkers.

"Eli? What do you think?"

The man shrugged. "It was okay. I get a lot of nightmares, so I started writing those down."

"Can you share one of them with us?"

Another shrug. "I'm trapped on a bridge with all this traffic, and the thing collapses. You know, just like in that *Final Destination* movie? I'm trying to get out of the car and run, but everyone's beeping and screaming, and then I wake up."

She wrinkled her nose. The freckles scattered across her nose were so damn cute, he wanted to kiss them. "That nightmare is directly related to your road rage issues. Did something happen to you before on the road? Something you may have forgotten?"

Eli frowned. "Don't think so. I mean, I was caught up in a bad traffic jam when one of my friends got in a motorcycle accident. Tried to get to the hospital but didn't make it in time. That pissed me off. Made me feel guilty."

Stone felt a twinge of sympathy. That sucked.

Arilyn widened her sea-green eyes. "I'm so sorry. Did you ever think that's your primary reason for slipping into anger on the road? You could be dredging up the nightmare of not making it to see your friend in time. That's a very difficult situation to process. Sometimes our emotions and bodies do it for us because the mind can't accept it yet."

Recognition flickered over his face, and his jaw tightened. Raw emotion glimmered in his eyes. Ah, hell. Stone had a crazy urge to pat the guy on the shoulder and tell him it was gonna be okay.

"I never put it together," he said slowly. His hands pushed through his hair. "It makes sense now."

Arilyn spoke in a soothing voice. "I'd like to meet you after class, Eli. Talk a bit more. This is a big breakthrough for you."

Stone suddenly didn't feel sympathetic anymore.

Luther reached over and pounded Eli on the arm. "Really sorry, buddy."

Eli nodded and ducked his head.

Suddenly, Arilyn's gaze swung to him. Challenging. As if she'd thrown down the gauntlet and dared him to be more than he pretended. What did she want from him? He was as honest and open as anyone he knew. He certainly wasn't trying to hide anything.

The scene of the accident flashed before him. He pushed it right back out of his head.

"Stone? How about you? Have you used the journal yet for more than comics?"

He thought of the simple black composition notebook with his name printed neatly on the cover. Just like in school. All those blank lined pages ready for him to spill his thoughts onto.

He decided to keep to the truth. "Not yet."

"Nothing to share? Or not ready to open yourself up?"

He met her gaze head on and pushed right back. "No time."

"Understood. Have you had any realizations or thoughts regarding your anger issues this week? Anything we explored that interested you?"

Like what? Sitting with dogs? Breathing on the floor? Writing in a journal? Circle time?

The emotions deep inside stirred, then slowly settled. "Not really," he finally said.

He refused to deal with the flash of disappointment in her eyes. Who cares? This was a game of chess to get her into bed, not to leave pieces of himself behind.

"Very well. I'm going to ask each of you a question. I want you to respond from the gut. Don't think about it too hard or try to reach for the right answer. Just tell me the first thing that comes to mind."

Stone began to sweat. He wouldn't let her beat him.

"Eli. Give me a memory, any memory, that made you angry."

"What I just told you. Sitting in traffic, waiting to see my best friend. Hoping he wasn't going to die while I was stuck there with a bunch of assholes going to work or lunch or having fun."

"Excellent." She turned. "Luther. Again, give me one quick memory of when you were angry."

Luther didn't hesitate. "When I found out my dad was having an affair with some other woman. I went to the college to visit him, and he was in his office kissing someone else. I wanted to kill him."

"Very good. Stone? Same question. Give me your memory."

He paused.

Her voice caught him like a silken whip. "Now. Don't think. Just talk."

He opened his mouth and damned if something didn't come out. "When I walked into the bedroom and found my wife screwing my partner."

Eli whistled. "Bru-tal, man. Sorry."

Luther shook his head. "That may be worse than my dad."

Arilyn stared. Shock carved out the features of her face. "You were married?" she whispered.

He narrowed his eyes. "Yeah. I was married. Now I'm divorced."

Silence descended. Luther and Eli shared a glance and then looked uneasily at their teacher. Clearing her throat, she seemed to try to shake off some type of mental fog. "W-Well. That's excellent, Officer. Thanks for sharing."

Hmm. Back to "Officer" now, huh?

She rolled to her feet and forced a smile. "That's it for today, gentlemen. Eli, may I speak with you for a few minutes?"

"Sure."

Stone rolled up his mat, stacked it neatly in the corner, and checked his cell phone messages. He grabbed her elbow as she walked past him. "Arilyn?"

"Yes?"

Oh, yeah, she was mad about something. He felt like he'd stepped into Antarctica. "I'll wait for you outside?"

She shook him off as if he were an annoying bug. "No need. I'll be a while with Eli."

"I can wait."

"Not necessary. Have a good day."

She turned her back, smiled at Eli, and began chatting.

Stone cursed under his breath and stormed outside. Well, screw that. Screw her. He had finally given her what she wanted with her damn *sharing*, and now she was pissed at him? He couldn't help the divorce. Yes, he had baggage. Must be nice to have a perfect life. Must be nice to be Arilyn Meadows.

He ignored the strange bite of pain that hit his gut and swore not to think about her again. He was finally back at work and had a few hours to kill before his shift. He was done mooning over a woman who was all wrong for him. Fuming, he got in his car and drove.

He didn't realize until he looked up that he was at the shelter. Getting out of the car, he checked to make sure there were no strays running around. His nerves jangled, but he ignored the slight panic, making himself trudge into the main center. He scrawled his name on the volunteer list and headed toward the back. Trying not to wince at the noise, he strode past the barking dogs, nodding to another volunteer, and went inside Pinky's cage.

The dog sat almost in the same spot as the other day. A twinkle of interest lit her eyes, and her head cranked around a bit. Then she went back to gazing into space.

"You're a hard case," he commented, stretching out his legs and leaning against the gate. "I don't mind. I need some peace and quiet right now. I'm about done vomiting my feelings for everyone to judge. I mean, do you really want to talk about what happened to you? No. You dealt with it, and now you need to move on."

No response.

He sighed. "Listen, you gotta eat. If your body collapses, those assholes win. You survived for a reason, girl. Arilyn got you out, and if you die on her, she'll be heartbroken. I may be pissed at your rescuer, but I can't let you fall apart on my watch."

A tiny head movement.

"How's your food? You need to eat to get stronger. Looks like crap to me, but what do I know? Tomorrow I'll sneak you a hamburger. They'll never know. Bet that's a bunch of organic beans and rice. No wonder you don't eat it."

No response.

Stone didn't mind. His temper calmed, and he kept talking.

THE NEXT DAY, ARILYN kept things strictly business. She escorted her crew to the local soup kitchen so the men could serve food to the homeless and be reminded of gratitude. Arilyn learned that being happy with the simple things of your lot helped to manage anger. When she struggled with her mother's death and was ripped apart by rage, Poppy took her to the veterans hospital and showed her all the men and women who'd had their world ripped from them, too. Seeing the physical and emotional injuries and how they fought to not only survive but to live gave her some peace. It also gave her the strength she needed to begin sorting through her rage.

Screw you, Stone Petty. I won't tell my secrets either.

She couldn't stop thinking about yesterday. His confession stunned her. The proof she knew nothing about him and he'd never voluntarily share anything of himself confirmed how wrong he was for her. Of course, she hadn't dumped her own truth about what had happened with her ex. But a divorce? Couldn't he have given her a hint before, even in the counseling session? She was greedy to know all the details. How badly had he been hurt to find his wife cheating on him? They shared such an intimate, raw experience in two different worlds. Instead of feeling closer to him, he seemed miles away. His confession came out snide and cold, making her feel intrusive. She'd only wanted to help, but he was determined to keep his past and his emotions private. Refused to share.

They'd only shared a kiss. Well, two. Yes, they may have been earth-shattering to her, but it was another reminder that physical contact with Stone meant nothing. He'd never open himself up to more. Arilyn refused to acknowledge the sadness that accompanied the fact. She'd already known they wouldn't work. The fact that she was suddenly despondent over the truth annoyed her.

Stop thinking about him.

Her gaze swiveled in rebellion. He surprised her again. Seems the staff at the Verily Soup Station knew him well. After some manly thumps on the shoulder, high fives, and general caveman talk, Stone took up an apron without any instruction from her and got to it. Watching him engage with the crowds that lined up squeezed her heart in a very bad way.

He seemed like one of them. With his usual cap perched sideways like some gangster, his worn T-shirt stretched over his wide shoulders, and faded jeans clinging to his tight rear, he was completely mouthwatering. She noticed he towered over the other guys, his fingers gripping the large spoon with a masculine grace she usually didn't spot in such musclebound men. Legs braced apart, an easy grin on his face, he greeted them by name, talked sports, and never broke his stride. Luther and Eli kept looking at him with a faint twinge of admiration she'd never spotted before. The black sheep was getting some recognition. Too bad she wasn't happy.

Too bad she was so pissed off.

Arilyn kept her distance and concentrated on helping Luther and Eli, making sure there was plenty of space between them at the table. The three hours whizzed by, and she made sure to stay busy as she wrapped up the session, thanked the director of the kitchen, and transitioned out.

"Do I smell?"

Arilyn jerked around at the deep growl of voice from behind. His brows snapped in a ferocious frown. Arms crossed, hip cocked, he studied her with a mocking judgment that made her temper soar in familiar tempo. "Excuse me?"

He didn't seem to care that they were on a public street. Pedestrians hurried back and forth, heads ducked from the late fall wind. Cars rushed by, and low chattering filled the air with the steady stream of customers entering the soup kitchen. She took a few steps toward the edge of the building for breathing room. He ignored her request, stepping forward and blocking both the wind and her view with his big body. She shivered under his drilling gaze. "I asked if I smell bad. Because you've been avoiding me like the plague since Tuesday, and it's starting to piss me off."

She pressed her lips tightly together. "Maybe you're being paranoid. You're not my only client, Officer. I can't dedicate all my time to you. I'm sorry if you thought differently."

Arilyn tried to push past, but he refused to budge. "I'm not your damn client. And every time you use that snotty tone of voice to call me 'Officer,' I want to kiss you again until you shut up and apologize."

He was crude, and rude, and impossible. Why had she ever thought for a moment something could work with them? Or had she? Maybe her body had just responded and her brain had melted like a Popsicle. So embarrassing.

She clenched her fists and shimmered with outrage. "Don't talk to me like that," she snapped. "I will not have you bullying me on the street. We'll talk in class or not at all, and you'll just have to respect that. Now move."

She didn't wait for his answer. This time she ducked and fled down the street, hurrying into her car. There. Take that. This was better, anyway. They'd be a disaster, and maybe his holding back was a sign for her to stop the crazy train ride before it was too late.

A few blocks in, she noticed the big muscle car bullying her on the road, keeping tight to her bumper. She seethed, maneuvering through the town until she got to her bungalow. Parking quickly, she climbed out and stomped over. He did the same, slamming the door and facing her down.

"How dare you follow me! I should've stopped short and forced you to rear-end me. Don't cops know how to drive, or are you too big and bad to follow your own rules?"

He made a noise deep in his throat and sneered, "If I had followed my rules, I would've had your pretty ass locked up last week in my jail. To say I'm regretting it is the fucking understatement of the year."

"Watch your language," she hissed. "My neighbor likes to spy. I suggest you take your car and your attitude and leave." Turning her back, she marched up the stairs, unlocked the door, and stepped inside.

He was right behind her.

"Hey! I didn't invite you in!"

"Too bad," he said. He shut the door behind him. "I don't feel like yelling at you in the damn street."

"What's your problem? Are you frustrated because I didn't fall all over myself trying to *catch* you over one lousy kiss? Get over it. I'm your teacher, and that's all I'm ever going to be."

He gritted his teeth and hissed, "I'm telling myself to breathe right now, woman. If I don't, I'm gonna lose my shit. And guess what? It's not working, just like I tried to tell you."

"Stop cursing!"

"Stop being a damn hypocrite!"

Arilyn panted for breath and tried to scramble for calm. Dear God, she was supposed to set a good example, but this man drove her to the insane asylum within minutes. "A hypocrite? Oh, this will be interesting. How do you possibly imagine I'm a hypocrite?"

He moved closer. The air between them sizzled and crackled. Her breasts lifted as she tried to draw in air, and his gaze roved over her body, trying to eat her alive. The anger combusted and turned into something dangerous and dark, but Arilyn fought with all her strength not to surrender. His husky growl dragged over her skin like velvet and thorns. "Oh, you are one. Begging us to tell you our secrets, and the moment we do, you judge. You disappoint me."

"What are you talking about?"

"The divorce," he ground out. "You heard I was divorced and judged me. Hell, I didn't even get a trial, just a conviction." He leaned in, his minty breath striking her mouth. "Sorry I don't have a clean, pure past like you do. I made a crapload of mistakes, rolled around in the muck, and moved on. Sorry if I'm not good enough, but you don't have to ignore me and treat me like I'm the Elephant Man. I get it. I won't bother you again."

Each word struck a deliberate blow. Her lungs collapsed, and before he turned, she reached out and grabbed his arm. "It wasn't like that," she said. "I wasn't judging you."

"Yeah. Sure. I saw the look on your face. Must be nice not to have made mistakes."

Arilyn shook, fighting to understand the strong connection between them. Fighting the whole mess that threatened to overwhelm her. Still, he couldn't go without knowing the truth. Her fingers tightened around his arm, refusing to let him walk away. Her voice tore out in ragged fragments. "It wasn't your divorce. I don't care about that, I never did. It's— "

"What?" He leaned back in. His demand vibrated against her skin, almost tangible with its command. "Tell me."

"You never told me." She half closed her eyes, not wanting him to see the depth of her emotions, then forced herself to face it for both of them. "I was hurt. I felt . . . stupid. It was a huge part of your life, and you didn't say anything in counseling. It wasn't in your file. I had no idea, and when you threw it out in class, like it was no big deal, I got hurt." Her cheeks flushed. "I'm sorry, I'm an idiot. But don't think I was judging you. I was judging me, and my reaction to it." Arilyn forced a laugh. God, this was a humiliation he'd never let her live down. One lousy kiss and she wanted a heart-to-heart. "Can we just forget this whole thing? I'm sorry. We can go back to class and maybe, in a strange way, be friends. Or maybe not. I don't know anymore," she muttered. Stop, Arilyn, just stop. It was getting so much worse, and then he closed his eyes as if her confession made things awkward.

Desperate for distance, she let go of his arm and took a step back.

He reached out and yanked her close.

Her breath stopped. Those inky eyes snapped open and suddenly she was gazing into a pit of seething, raw desire. Very deliberately, he slid the pins holding her tight topknot in place out of her hair one by one. She stared, helpless, until the long strands hung down to her waist, masking her face. Never breaking his slow motions, he twisted his fingers into her hair and tugged her head back.

"I don't want to be your friend," he growled.

Arilyn stiffened. Every inch of her body tingled. "Fine, we're not friends. You've never been civil anyway."

"You're right. I'm not civil or even civilized when I get near you. Wanna know what I really want to do?"

"No."

"Tough shit. Gonna tell you anyway." A low moan escaped her lips, because she was burning up for him and hated every minute of it. "I want to strip these organic clothes from your body, lay you out on the bed, and explore every inch. Bite, suck, lick. I want to push inside that wet heat I know is waiting for me and make you come so hard you won't be able to speak for at least five full minutes. I want to do bad things to you, Arilyn. Dirty things. Things that would shock you to the core and cause you to run screaming out the door if you're a nice girl. Are you a nice girl?"

Her skin was on fire. Her ears roared and her thighs clenched in a desperate attempt to stop the rush of warm liquid trickling between them. This type of arousal was insane. Wrong on so many levels. Stone Petty was the type of man who would take his pleasure, be rough, and demand she leave nothing behind. There would be no sweetness or tender words. There would be no gentle care when he finally took her, or slow smiles, or easy climbs to a pleasurable orgasm.

If she surrendered, he'd wreck her completely. He was dangerous.

She was a good girl.

She craved a healthy, satisfying relationship. A deep, abiding friendship with a man on the same spiritual quest. She was searching for always. Forever. He'd give nothing but physical satisfaction and wouldn't look twice when he walked back out the door in the morning.

She was a good girl.

His grip never gentled, but his voice softened. Stone leaned over, his mouth inches from hers. Their breath mingled. She watched, hypnotized, while he ran the tip of his tongue over her bottom lip, bestowing little nips until she began to sag in his arms and moved an inch forward for more.

"You're not sure, are you, little one?" he murmured, pressing that lush, soft mouth to hers in tiny kisses that did nothing but inflame. "You're caught between what you know you should want and what your deepest fantasies torment you to ask for. I warned you that you owed me a favor. I can't be the one to take constantly. You need to walk into this with your eyes wide-open, because I'm a son of a bitch and I know it. Here's my price for saving you and the dog: when you're ready to take the leap with me, you have to ask."

She fought for sanity, but that wicked mouth kept

teasing, caressing her jaw, the sensitive slope of her neck, biting, licking, making her crazy. "Ask for what?" she managed to ground out. Another bite on her earlobe caused a shudder to wrack her body.

"God, you're so responsive. I could devour you whole."

"You smell so good," she muttered. She wanted to savor the deliciousness of woods and musk. Of sweat and man.

His low laugh raked across her ears. His erection notched between her thighs, tempting her to be a very bad, bad girl. "I'm not gonna force you and hear you cry foul in the morning. When you're ready to take the leap, to seize the moment and not think about tomorrow, or what fits in your overall plan, you ask. Ask me to take you."

"I can't." The idea of asking a man to take her to bed, to be so vulnerable before a man who was not her lover or boyfriend, horrified her. Scared her. Paralyzed her.

"You will. Because that's the price." He licked the place where her shoulder connected to her neck and she cried out.

"How do you know I won't lie?"

"Because you're honest. You told me the truth today even though you didn't want to. I trust you. And I'll know from the look on your face."

This was the craziest bargain she'd ever heard of. It wouldn't be a problem. She could just keep a safe distance, bury herself in work, and after the course was over she wouldn't see him again. She'd never allow herself to beg a man to make love to her, knowing he wasn't interested in the person she was inside.

Arilyn didn't do sex just for sex. It'd be empty and unfulfilling.

Wouldn't it?

She opened her mouth to protest, but he sealed it shut with a deep, soul-stirring kiss that took all the fight from her. Arilyn surrendered to the masterful embrace, reaching up on her toes for more, helpless to every stroke of his tongue until he slowly eased his mouth from hers.

They stared at one another for a long time. His thumb pressed against her bottom lip, dragging across the tender flesh before finally pulling back.

"It's hard for me to share. The marriage was good in the beginning, but too easy. When things got hard, we both gave up without a fight. I worked too hard, too much, and didn't care. Then one night I came home to find her with my partner. Something died in me. Don't think it'll come back." She listened hungrily to every word, every expression flickering across his rough features. "I detest lies and cheats. I'm still a workaholic and suck at relationships. But I didn't mean to hurt you. And I want you, Arilyn Meadows. Real bad." He turned and headed for the door. "But next time you have to ask me. See you in class."

He left.

She pressed shaking fingers to her mouth. The rules had changed, and she wasn't sure what she was going to do about it.

eleven

ARILYN LOOKED IN the mirror.

No. Way.

She couldn't go out looking like a—a tramp. A hot tramp, but still. She turned around to check out her behind and admired the snug fit over her curves. Hmm, she had nice assets back there. Too bad no one was ever around to enjoy them.

She bet Stone Petty was a butt man.

No. Not thinking about him. He was completely off-limits on girls' night out.

Arilyn dragged in a breath, thought about changing, then realized Kennedy wouldn't allow it. She'd probably march her right back inside and wait until she chose another outfit. Might as well stand tall and try to pull the look off.

The short black miniskirt barely skimmed the tops of her knees. The boots covered her whole calves and boasted high, chunky heels, making her even taller. The shirt was a button-down silk, but it was defective. The buttons only began halfway down, so what little cleavage she had was on display. The badass fake leather jacket gave the whole outfit a naughty edge.

She squinted at her face. After carefully checking to make sure the makeup Kennedy dropped off had been produced without animal testing, she buckled and used some of it. Mascara darkened her gold lashes, blush highlighted her cheekbones, and red lipstick brought out the paleness of her skin and the green of her eyes. Pretty cool.

Her hair was left loose, but Kennedy made her curl it with the iron. Fat waves rolled over her shoulders and tumbled over one eye. She looked sexy.

Maybe this wasn't so bad after all. If she could walk in the heels, that is.

A loud beeping echoed down the street. Arilyn grabbed her clutch and raced out the door. The white stretch limo pulled to the curb and a bunch of giggly, happy women waved through the tinted windows. Oh, boy, what was she in for?

A tingle of excitement shimmered down her spine. Maybe she'd let go tonight. Kiss a strange boy. Man, she corrected herself. She'd kiss a hot, sexy man in the club, in the dark. Maybe that would get Stone Petty off her mind. She needed this night to get a fresh perspective. Getting involved with him was bad on all levels. If she was attracted to someone else tonight, maybe it would prove that her hormones were overloaded and it had nothing to do with him.

Oh, she hoped.

Arilyn ran to the limo and climbed in. The scents of mingled perfume, alcohol, and feminine excitement simmered in the air. Kate, Kennedy, and Genevieve were dressed to the max, so she suddenly didn't feel awkward. Everyone wore short skirts or dresses, cool jackets, and super-high heels. Kate's sister-in-law, Jane, even sported a flouncy skirt and boots. She was introduced to three other girls Kate had met from Slade's office, and then they were zooming down the Verily streets toward wildness.

Champagne flowed, gossip flew, and bonding began in the primitive way only females knew. After eating and partying at the famous Lucky Cheng's, they piled back in the car and hit a few trendy after-work bars, then a gay strip club where they danced like no one was watching. And no one really was.

By the time they headed back to Mugs in Verily, they were ushered to the back room. Halfway drunk, relaxed, and finally not caring, Arilyn waited for the big event.

The male stripper.

Kate bumped into her, spilling some of her drink and groaning. "A, you gotta help me. I don't want another naked man pawing me, and Kennedy won't listen. As the single one in the group, you need to step up and be my wingman."

Arilyn hiccupped. These cosmos were so good. Extra fruity. Oh, and she felt so light and warm. How long had it been since she'd gotten tipsy? Way too long. "Wing woman. What do I gotta do?"

Kate motioned to the chair in the middle of the room. "I overheard the plan. The cop comes in, pretends we're too rowdy, and then drags me to that chair so he can writhe all over me."

"A solid plan, according to Kennedy."

Her friend glared, but it was ruined by the slurp from her drink. "I need you to take the hit for me. When the guy comes in, you take my place."

Another hiccup. "I don't look like you," she pointed out.

"I know! I'll be hiding in the corner, so you go by the chair and offer yourself up. Everyone's drunk, no one will notice. They just want him to take off his clothes."

"Yeah. How did we end up with more women than we started with?"

Kate squinted. "I think we picked up Janet and Evelyn in the gay bar. I don't know about the others. They want to see a stripper. Will you do it?"

Would she do it? On a normal day her response would be a loud "Heck, no." But tonight she was in the mood to view a hot, naked man who wanted nothing from her but to give some visual pleasure. How bad could it be? It would take her mind off the other man who remained nameless who she really wasn't thinking about. At all.

"Okay, I'll do it."

Kate pressed a noisy kiss to her cheek. "Thanks, babe. Oh, here, you'll need a lot of these." She stuffed a handful of dollar bills into her fist.

Cool. She'd finally get to stick money in a guy's G-string. Arilyn hugged Kate. "I love this party!" she gushed.

Kate hugged her back. "Me, too. And I love us." She raised her glass. "To friends forever!"

"Friends forever!"

Their glasses clinked and tipped over, and half their drinks spilled on the floor. They looked at each other and burst into giggles. "Bartender, we need another one!" Kate yelled.

Arilyn snorted with laughter.

This was gonna be good.

"ANOTHER ROLLICKING EVENING IN Verily. Why are we here again, Devine?"

A few days back from his suspension and he was itching for some action. Not that there was any. Already at the end of his shift, the night was barren of anything interesting. This should be a good thing in Verily, especially since he had never had that problem in the Bronx. Drug raids were routine, gangs were hunted regularly, and crime abounded. He'd craved to take it down a notch, but sometimes on a night cruising the still streets of the small town, he wondered if he'd been nuts to leave.

Not that he'd had a choice. After the shooting and its fallout, the only logical thing was to request a transfer. Stone wondered again how different his life would've turned out if Devine had been on the scene with him a year ago. But he hadn't, and his life had fallen apart. No going back now.

His partner shot him a look. "Good retirement. Great odds we won't be shot at. Excellent karma for our next life."

Stone rolled his eyes. "Now you sound like Arilyn. She gave me an amethyst to help with the smoking cravings. The other day she made us chant 'Om Nemah Shit' something."

"Om Namah Shivaya."

Stone remained silent. "Now I'm worried."

Devine shrugged. "It's a common phrase to reach

your highest center. I read about it in a book. Sounds cool."

"It's crazy."

"Like you're not crazy? Dude, you got more issues than a phone book has pages. At least her stuff tries to make the world better."

Yes. She did want to make things better. He couldn't get their last encounter out of his mind. The way she admitted her feelings. Damned if that didn't take balls. Of course, if they ever did manage to get together to explore an affair, he'd probably become her charity project. "I guess."

"Is the amethyst working?"

"Doubt it. Probably the patch." Sure, he'd begun experiencing fewer cravings since he put the amethyst on, but that was coincidence. Crystals didn't do stuff like that. Still, it was nice of her. Most people couldn't care less if he smoked his whole life. There was no one left to care.

That sad thought pissed him off, so he buried it deep and kept driving.

He felt Devine's hard stare. "You kissed her, didn't you?"

Stone winced. "Yeah. Stupidest thing I ever did in my life."

His partner let out a shout of laughter. "Or the best. Why not see what happens? Why do you have to doom everything from the start?"

"You some kind of in-house therapist now?" he mocked. "We kissed. It was good. But she's a damn grenade ready to go off. I need her to be sure she knows it's just physical between us."

"Why do I think you're the real grenade here, Petty?"

"Shut up, Devine. Go grow a pair."

His friend laughed harder. "You're still wearing the amethyst, aren't you?"

He refused to answer. Bastard.

A voice crackled over the speaker. "Car Forty-one. Fight developing at Mugs Tavern, 120 Main Street."

Devine grabbed the radio. "En route."

"Over."

Stone looked at his partner, then grinned. "Bar fight, dude!"

Devine motioned to him. "Drive faster or we're gonna miss it. Hit the sirens."

Stone hit the lights and they sped to their destination within minutes. Trying to hide their eagerness, they put on their game faces to look like aggravated cops and walked in. Stone looked around, scanning the surroundings for broken glass, shoving, yelling, and overall male good times. He saw nothing. Just the usual battered booths, wooden Irish bar, dartboard, and various tables scattered around. The place was packed, but nothing rowdy caught his gaze.

He went to the bar and held up his hand. The bartender came over. "Got a call on a fight going on?"

The bartender nodded and pointed across the room. "Yeah, those two drunkards. Fighting over some girl. I don't get paid to break up fights, man. We have no bouncers here."

Devine nodded. "We'll take care of it."

They strolled over. A heated argument was taking place with two men who'd seen better days. One had a beer belly, white skin, and paunchy cheeks. The other was whip skinny, had a bony face, wore schoolteacher glasses, and reminded Stone of Ichabod Crane. Their voices rose higher and higher.

"I looked at her first! She was ready to leave with me until you slobbered all over her," Pudgy yelled.

Ichabod leaned in. Saliva sprayed. "I already bought her a drink when you came sniffing around. My night was set until you interrupted and scared her away with your face!"

"Fuck you!" Pudgy roared. "She'd never leave with a skinny-ass punk, four eyes!"

"Four eyes? What are you, twelve? Go drink some more beer, why don't you, fatso?"

Stone and Devine shared a humorous glance. Damn, what a pansy-ass fight. At this point, no one would even make a move. Holding back a sigh, Stone moved toward them. "Gentlemen. I'll need you to lower your voices or leave the establishment."

"Oh, good, the police are here," Pudgy sneered. "Arrest this asshole for being ugly."

Ichabod narrowed his gaze. "Arrest this asshole for being stupid!"

Devine clamped his lips together, probably to stifle a laugh. "Follow me; let's get some air before things get nasty."

Stone watched his partner guide the squabbling men out the front door. Nah. Neither one was gonna take a punch. He turned on his heel to follow them out when screams rang through the bar, making everyone crane their necks to look at the commotion. The back room, usually used for parties, was rocking. Music blared, and he caught a swarm of short skirts, swishing hair, and loud revelry. All women.

Bachelorette party.

A grin tugged at his lips. That was probably rowdier than anything he'd seen in the past month. Should he make the excuse to check it out by asking them to lower their voices? Not that he wanted to be a dick, but it would be fun to see what they were up to.

He reached the door, when a petite brunette stumbled out on teetering heels. Her blue eyes sparkled, and she held a martini of some sort that was a bright green color. "I'll send him in when he comes!" she screeched. Another round of giggles floated past. "Get the music ready! Oh!"

She ran into his chest. Stone caught her. "Officer Stone! It's you!"

He frowned, then realized he held Genevieve MacKenzie in his arms. He'd met her over the summer during the domestic abuse and vandalism cases. He had liked her immediately and was glad she got rid of her asshole ex who was an abuser. Stone smiled. "Dr. MacKenzie. A pleasure." He raised a brow. "Are you involved with these shenanigans?"

She laughed and found her balance. "My friend Kate's bachelorette party. Girls' night out, you know."

"Nice. No drunk driving, right?"

She shook her head. "Limo service." She paused, a calculating light gleaming in her eyes. "Arilyn's inside, you know."

"Arilyn?" His brain stuttered. Stone glanced at the door, then tried to act cool. "That's nice."

Gen smiled real slow. "She mentioned you tonight. Said she had something to tell you? Seemed important. Does this sound familiar?"

His blood turned to lava and his dick hardened. Was she kidding? Was Arilyn ready to ask him to take her to bed—on his terms? Had she told Genevieve the entire story? Knowing how girls gossiped, he tried to remain calm. "I'm surprised she told you such intimate details."

Her grin widened. "Girls talk. I think if you went in there, she'd be real grateful."

Now he was turned on and confused. "Huh. I don't want to break up a women-only party."

"No, she'd *love* to see you. Seriously. Go talk to her."

He shifted his weight. Maybe he should. After all, Gen wouldn't send him in there if Arilyn didn't want to see him. He'd just spend a few minutes. "Sure. Let me tell my partner and I'll be right back."

Stone poked his head out the door. His partner had both bozos in the backseat and a satisfied expression on his face. "What the hell happened?"

"They took swings at each other! Tumbled on the ground like two girls rolling around and punching. It was awesome. I'm gonna book 'em and take them in."

Fuck. He'd missed it. "Listen, I gotta talk to someone. We're off shift anyway, so get 'em to the station and I'll get a ride home."

"Sure? Gonna leave all the fun to me, huh?"

"Yeah, I'll grab a cab. I may stay for a drink."

"Got it. See you tomorrow."

Stone headed to the back of the restaurant. Genevieve grabbed him and nudged him inside. "Go ahead. She's going to be so excited to see you!"

Feeling a bit better on seeing Gen's enthusiasm, Stone stepped into the room. The door slammed behind him. He looked around, expecting to find Arilyn, pull her aside, and have a private conversation.

Instead, he found himself in the snake pit.

Women surrounded him. Lots of women, all staring at him with a scary hunger that made him shudder. The group began to scream and stamp their heels on the floor as if he were the main attraction they'd been waiting for. What the hell was going on?

"He's here!" a tall blonde yelled. "Get ready for an arrest, ladies!"

Huh?

A lone chair stood in the center of the circle. Suddenly, his ears hurt from the music blaring through the speakers. Was that "You Can Leave Your Hat On"? Wasn't that a stripper song?

"Take it off, baby!"

"I'm breaking the law, sweetheart, come on over here!"

A brunette giggled and crooked her finger. "I've been real bad, Officer," she yelled. "And I'm concealing a deadly weapon. Come frisk me!" Holy shit, she began jiggling her breasts at him.

It finally hit him. He was in a room full of very drunk women who thought he was their cop stripper. He didn't know whether to laugh or cry. Stone opened his mouth and tried to tell them, but a pretty woman with caramel-colored hair shook her head as if annoyed by his silence, walked to the center of the room, and grabbed his hand.

Her smile reminded him of a shark's. "I paid good money for you, dude," she whispered. "Don't just stand there. Give us a show; we won't bite."

"I got money, Officer!" a brunette screamed. "Come and get it!"

No way. This wasn't really happening, was it?

"I think there's been a mistake, ma'am," he said firmly. "I'm not a stripper. I'm a cop."

The blonde rolled her eyes. "Sure, sure, you're a cop. Take your shirt off, dance a bit, and arrest someone. I promise I'll tip you extra. Oh, Kate is the bride, she's hiding over there." She pointed a finger at a woman dressed in black with silvery blond hair, squashed behind two of her friends with a scared look on her face.

"She doesn't look real interested," he said. "Maybe getting her a stripper wasn't such a great idea."

The woman glared at him with whiskey eyes. "Everyone needs a stripper. Now, I'm sorry if you're suddenly shy and want to choke, but I promise we'll respect you. Just take some clothes off, shimmy your hips, and make us happy. Deal?" He opened his mouth to tell her no way in hell, he was no damn stripper, but she clapped her hands. "Okay, ladies, our hot policeman is ready! Kate, get your ass in the chair."

The group screamed and whistled and stamped their feet. Dollar bills waved madly in the air. Women swayed to the beat, waiting for him to take his clothes off.

"Arilyn, help me!" Kate screamed.

Then he saw her.

She walked toward him, weaving her way through the screaming women, and positioned herself right in front of the chair.

Holy. Shit.

Miles of long legs. Feet clad in fuck-me knee-high boots. He groaned as the sudden image of those legs wrapping tight around his hips while he drove inside of her swarmed his vision. Her mouth opened in a little shocked O, and her gorgeous meadow-green eyes were slightly blurred and unfocused. Definitely tipsy. On the way to drunk. She held a green fruity drink—probably an apple martini like Genevieve's—and wore the tiniest, hottest outfit he'd ever seen.

His gaze pinned her tight, allowing her no escape. Her top was mostly unbuttoned, showing off a huge amount of smooth cleavage, and a bad-girl leather jacket topped the whole thing off. Even her hair was different, the long strands curled in big waves that tumbled over one eye, spilled over her shoulders, and hit her hips.

With no makeup and casual clothes, the woman was gorgeous. Dressed tonight? She was Eve, Helen of Troy, and Kim Kardashian all rolled up into the hottest bundle he'd ever seen.

Her appearance screamed sex, from her pouty red lips, to her come-hither eyes, to her fuck-me boots. There wasn't a shred of organic cotton in sight, and in that moment, all the blood rushed to his other head and he was toast.

Ignoring the noise and urging of the crowd, he stared helplessly at her, hard as a rock and completely intoxicated.

Her teeth pulled at her lower lip. Her breath made a catchy little moan, and when she finally spoke, her voice came out husky, like she'd spent the night in his bed screaming his name and had nothing left. "What are you doing here?"

"Gen said you wanted to talk to me."

She blinked. "No. I didn't even know you were here."

"I think I was set up. They think I'm a stripper."

A giggle escaped her lips. Fascinated, he wanted to hear the sound again. She hiccupped. "Kennedy hired a cop stripper. Kate freaked and begged me to take her place." Her head tipped up to look at him. "I'm her wing woman," she said proudly.

Damn, she was adorable. "So you're gonna take the stripper on for the sake of your friend?"

Her eyes heated, roving over him like a hungry she-lion. "Yeah. I am."

Stone ached all over. He'd give over a damn appendage just to touch her right now. "You're a good friend. I kinda wish I was the stripper right now."

Her tongue snaked out and wet her bottom lip. Those eyes heated and took in his uniform with more than a hint of lust. His dick wept. "You look like a stripper," she whispered.

He moved closer. "You think?"

"Yeah."

The women roared their frustration, begging him to do something. The blonde looked like she was about to start ripping off his clothes herself for giving her a bad deal. Nothing mattered except the woman in front of him who tortured his body and mind on a daily basis.

"What should I do?"

She reached over, placed her hands on his face, and dragged his head forward. Her breath rushed in his ear.

"Take it off."

He growled low, ready to grab her, toss her on his shoulder, and take her to bed. Oh, she was brave with the alcohol and her friends and wanted to play now, huh? Did she have any idea he was a master?

"Be careful what you wish for," he warned. "Payback is a bitch, little one."

She had the nerve to nip at his earlobe and touch her tongue to the inner shell of his ear. He hissed in agony, and she pulled back a few inches. Smiled. "So you've said before. Unless you're all talk and no action?"

He wasted no more time. She squealed as he tossed her over his shoulder, his hand on the gorgeous curve of her behind, and dumped her right into the chair.

The women screamed with encouragement. He blocked her escape by standing right in front of her, so her gaze was in line with his rapidly growing erection. The music rolled out its sexy rhythm, and Stone decided to teach her a lesson of a lifetime.

He began to take it all off.

ARILYN WAS KIND OF drunk, but not drunk enough to realize he'd called her bluff and raised the stakes.

The man was a walking, talking sex god.

Her body became completely magnetized around him, humming and softening as if she recognized him as her master. Those seething inky eyes demanded deliciously bad things she craved to give him. His black hair was messy and tousled, emphasizing his carved features, sexy goatee, and full lips. His whole aura beat out one mantra. Primitive Male.

But the uniform pushed him past the edge of droolworthy into laminated list territory.

He was wearing a dark navy blue shirt with long sleeves and a padded vest with his name stitched on the upper right side. He was intimidating enough in a baseball jersey and jeans. But with the leather belt slung low on his hips, filled with an array of gadgets that stole her breath, Arilyn was crazed to touch him. Her gaze took in the gun holster, cuffs hanging to the side, and some type of stick in its holder. God, it was like an erotic fantasy come to life. The tight fabric molded to every meaty muscle, his chest stretched to capacity in crisp, clean navy blue, Stone Petty was a package any woman would die to unwrap.

He towered over her, his gaze never leaving hers. As the music pumped, his fingers paused at the top button of his shirt, stroking slow, listening to the screams of the crowd, and then flicked it open lightning quick.

Her belly dropped.

He repeated the motion with the second button. His refusal to dance for them only made everyone crazier. Dollar bills started flying through the air and chants of "Take it off!" vibrated in the air. He ignored the other women, focused intently and only on her.

It was the most erotic thing she'd ever experienced.

In this crowded room, he stripped for her eyes. A line of naked flesh appeared in the gaps. Arilyn caught the hues of light brown skin, and a patch of dark hair swirled over cut, chiseled muscles. Hungrily, her gaze followed the tempting path until his shirt gaped open, giving her a tantalizing peek.

She wondered how he tasted. Wondered how it would feel to run her tongue over that intriguing line of hair and follow it downward.

"Do you want me to open my shirt, Arilyn?" His question burned her ears in more of a command. Even with the deafening noise, she heard him clearly, as if they were alone in a darkened room on a quiet night. Her body began to shake, and she gripped her martini glass tight. Oh, how she wanted. Bad, dirty, wonderful things. She was helpless to fight.

"Yes."

His lower lip lifted. Those dark eyes pinned her to the chair as capably as the handcuffs hanging on his belt. With slow, deliberate motions, he finished unbuttoning his shirt and slowly parted the material.

The women went wild.

"More, more, more!"

Her mouth went dry. Her fingers itched to run over that gorgeous broad chest, tracing every carved muscle. Feeling the strength and power under each flex of movement, the drag of his breath in and out, the sound of his heart beating under her palms. She ached to feel him, stroke him, hear the groans from his lips as she pleasured him. A low whimper fell from her lips.

"They want more," he said. "Do *you* want more?"

She licked her lips. "Yes."

Reaching over, he grabbed her hands and pressed them to his chest. "Then take what you want."

Arilyn realized she was in a packed room where everyone thought he was a paid stripper, and she couldn't care less. It was literally the craziest thing she'd ever done, but she couldn't stop now. Her fingers hit the hard wall of his pecs and she stroked him. He let out a groan through gritted teeth but remained still. The song switched to Prince's "Get Off," and then she heard her name chanted in unison, commanding her to take it all off.

Trembling, she savored the iron wall of his abs, gently tracing the edge of his belt buckle. She paused. Their gazes locked.

"No." Her voice broke. Waves of his body heat radiated and uncoiled around her. "Not here."

"Do you want me for yourself?"

His harsh question demanded truth. Logically, they were all wrong. But her body didn't care, and a raw possessiveness caught her off guard. She wanted him to belong to her. She didn't want a bunch of women watching him strip with greedy eyes and hands.

"I don't want anyone else to touch you."

He muttered a vicious curse. "Good. I don't want anyone else to touch you either."

He quickly refastened the buttons on his shirt. Loud boos filled the air.

Without missing a beat, Stone picked her up easily from the chair, lifted her high, and slammed his mouth on hers.

Arilyn was lost. Not caring that they had an audience, she twined her arms around his neck and kissed him back with a hunger she couldn't hide. The boos turned to catcalls and whistles, and a dollar bill floated down between them.

"Come with me now," he growled against her lips.

"Yes."

Stone took her hand and tugged her out the door. Gen jumped when they went past her, cheeks red and flushed. "Oh! Ugh, guess you guys found each other, huh?"

Stone gave her a look. "You'll pay for that."

She swallowed. "Hey, I was just trying to help."

"I'll deal with you later," he warned. "I'm taking Arilyn home." Gen shot her a look, checking to make sure it was okay. Arilyn nodded, and Gen relaxed.

A young guy dressed in a police uniform, complete with hat, stick, and handcuffs belted to his side, blocked their way. "This is the bachelorette party?" he asked. His brow rose. "Didn't know we were doing a tag team, dude. I'm not splitting the tips."

Stone jerked his thumb toward the door. "I warmed them up. They're all yours now."

He didn't pause. Led her out the door and pushed her into the cab waiting at the corner for drunk patrons to take home. He snapped out her address. They didn't speak during the short drive. Soon he pressed some bills into the driver's hand and escorted her into the bungalow. Arilyn fumbled with the keys but finally got the door unlocked.

Then they were alone.

No foster dogs greeted them. The house was eerily silent and watchful. Arilyn embraced the floaty, warm feeling of being tipsy and allowing her body to win the war. He stood with hips braced, lips in a hard line, studying her with those dark eyes as if looking to unlock her secrets.

Tonight she wanted to fly and be impulsive. Tonight she wanted to be a bad girl.

"Why tonight? Why now?" he asked.

"Why not? You win. I want you for tonight."

His brow arched. "How drunk are you?"

She smiled real slow and took a step closer. "Does it matter? I'm here. I'm ready."

He muttered a curse. "I don't want our first time to be a blur of memory. I also don't want to leave room for regret in the morning."

Annoyance surged. "I'll remember. This is what you wanted. I'm asking. So, are you going to keep talking and questioning me, Officer? Or are you going to take it all off?"

He paused for a beat. His eyes burned. "We'll compromise. I'm no saint, and I can't leave you untouched tonight."

"Should we go into the bedroom?" she asked bravely.

His smug grin caused goose bumps to prickle her flesh. "We don't need a bedroom, little one. Have I told you how gorgeous you look tonight?"

Her tummy slid to her toes. His gaze raked over every inch of her body until her breath strangled in her throat and she was unable to move. She'd never felt so alive. Her nerve endings thrummed until waiting for him to finally touch her became almost painful. Stone dragged off his shirt and dropped it on the floor. Her fingers rolled into fists with the urge to reach out and grab him.

"You're dressed for naughtiness tonight. I think that's what you want, isn't it?" He finally closed the distance and backed her up against the wall. His bare chest pressed lightly against her breasts. His thighs intertwined with hers.

A moan escaped her lips. "I want you to touch me," she said huskily.

"I want that, too." His hands pulled through her hair, dragging the strands forward and draping them over her breasts. "I've dreamed of you naked except for all this hair. Dreamed of you in many positions naked. But first you have to reach under that short skirt and remove your panties."

The dirty command was like a lightning shot straight to her core. She grew wet and achy. "I thought you'd do that for me," she managed to grind out.

He never stopped touching her with light, teasing strokes. Her cheek, her collarbone. Her jaw, her lips. Brushing the hard tips of her breasts pushing against the thin silk. Arilyn fought for sanity. Her experiences were more traditional. She'd never done it against a wall, almost fully dressed. "I may be bossy, but I always leave the choice up to you. Want this to go any further? Remove them. Hike up your skirt and pull them off, then hand them to me."

Oh, he was bad. The command stole her breath, but she wanted to do it, craved to see the lust light up those dark eyes and know she was the one who put it there. He took a tiny step back to give her room, and Arilyn tugged up her minuscule skirt, hooked her fingers around the waistband, and pulled her panties down. Very slowly, she stepped out of them, one leg at a time. Straightened. And pushed the lacy, damp fabric in his hand.

"Oh, yeah, you're a bad girl," he drawled. He brought the lace to his nose and took a deep breath. "And you're very aroused."

A blush tinged her cheeks, but she was too far gone to care. These games made her hotter than Hades, and all she wanted was relief. Her folds were so swollen and wet, Arilyn figured one touch of his fingers would set her off. And oh, how badly she wanted that orgasm.

He watched every catch of her breath with that half smirk tugging at his lips. Moving closer, he dipped down and nudged her legs further apart with his thigh. Cool air rushed over her. She gritted her teeth against the sharp arousal, and he muttered something under his breath.

"So damn responsive. So sexy. I'm never gonna get enough of you."

He lowered his mouth to hers, sipping at her lips like a drink to savor before finally sinking his tongue deep. She sighed, twining her arms around him. Arilyn sank into the kiss and his embrace like she belonged there. Like she found home. His taste swamped her, his skin burned beneath hers, and she twisted for more of him, afraid she'd never get enough of this man.

He possessed her completely, diving in and out, controlling the kiss until she hung on and let him take her. And then his knuckles rubbed against her swollen heat. Like a cat, she writhed, pride and dignity long gone under the tempting siren song of orgasm. Little mewls escaped her lips as his fingers brushed her clit, circled, then rubbed so lightly she thought she'd go mad for more contact.

"Oh, please," she moaned into his mouth.

"You want to come?" he muttered darkly. "How bad?"

"Bad." She dug her short nails into his back and tried to open her legs wider. "Crazy bad."

"You can take more." She let out a little scream as he pushed his fingers deep into her channel. God, the pressure was so good, and he twisted and hit that sweet spot, driving in so hard the climax shimmered before her in all its glory.

"Stone."

"Ride my hand while you say my name again."

Arilyn slipped into a primitive animal state she never knew existed in the world of sex. Her body demanded, and she rolled her hips over his hand swiping her clit with just enough pressure to clench every muscle in her body as she waited. Again and again she rode his hand while he whispered dirty commands in her ear, finally taking her mouth deep and hard and shoving her hard against the wall, lifting her up slightly to get even deeper.

"Stone!" she screamed as she came hard, shattering around him as waves of release gripped tight and threw her around. He never stopped the motions, forcing her to ride out the rest of her climax until pain and pleasure blurred into one, and she fell into another mini orgasm. After endless minutes, she slumped against him, her skin damp with sweat, limp and completely satisfied.

"God, you're fucking magnificent," he said, scooping her up and cradling her in his arms. He walked to the couch and sat down, cuddling her close. "I want to do that so many times you beg me to stop."

She lay her wobbly head against his chest and breathed in his musky scent. What had just happened? She had never done anything close with her previous partners. Sure, she enjoyed sex and the beautiful rise and fall of pleasure, but this type of carnal delight was nothing she had ever experienced. It was sex stripped bare. Animalistic. Brutal pleasure.

She wanted more.

"Now can we go into the bedroom?" she murmured against him.

His muscles stiffened. "No, little one. I can't take you tonight the way I want. You're drunk."

She lifted her head and glared. "Am not. Just a bit tipsy. When did you suddenly become a gentleman anyway?"

He laughed and pressed a hard kiss on her lips. "I haven't. But I don't want our first time to be blurred by alcohol. I intend for us both to be stone-cold sober when we start this affair."

The word stole some of her happiness. That's right. It might be great sex, but to Stone, that was all it ever would be. Could she handle it? Could she accept such amazing pleasure without an emotional connection? Was she strong enough to walk away at the end with her head held high and no regrets?

"Ah, you're quiet. Let me tell you exactly what I want, Arilyn, so we both know where we stand. I want you in my bed. I want to give you multiple orgasms, excruciating pleasure, and sleep with you at night. I refuse to let you belong to anyone else during our time together and vice versa. We can keep the affair out of the public eye if you'd like, but I don't give a crap either way. I'll take you to dinner and the movies and we'll date. And when we're no longer content or happy with the arrangement, we swear to be honest with the other and walk away with no lies. That's what I can offer."

Arilyn studied the man before her. Yes, he was honest to a fault. He was also giving her the choice. She could walk away or accept his terms. The problem?

She wanted him. He'd stirred a hunger she never knew she owned, and Arilyn wouldn't be satisfied until she followed the path to the end. She tried to live her life with some simple rules. One of them was not to make decisions based on regret. If she declined a choice, would she ever regret not trying? The answer helped guide her.

In this case, the answer was simple.

She would always regret not having Stone Petty in her bed.

"I agree."

He arched his brow. "That was quick. No thinking about it? We're very different, you know."

"I know. But this isn't for always. It's only for the moment."

His face tightened, then slowly smoothed out. "Yes. It is."

"I'd like to date. But I don't want Eli or Luther to get a hint we're together. It could make classes more complicated," she said.

"Agreed."

"And don't think I'll go easy on you in class. I'll treat you the same as always."

He chuckled. "I wouldn't have it any other way. Now, I better go. It's late." He kissed her thoroughly and stood. "Would you like to have dinner tomorrow night?"

She grinned at his formality. "Yes. But why don't you come over here? I'll cook."

"Sounds great." He headed toward the door.

"Stone? I need my panties back."

One eyelid dropped in a naughty wink. "Think I'll keep them as a souvenir. Night."

He left with her panties. Arilyn sighed and laid her head on the aqua-blue couch. What an odd night. He had stripped for her, she had had an orgasm, and they had decided to embark on an affair.

Bad girl.

She giggled to herself. About time.

twelve

ARILYN FINISHED TENDING her herb garden. Tilting her head up to the weak rays of sun that streamed down, knees in the dirt, she smiled. Gardening was like meditation and helped ground her mentally. Nature in all its forms reminded her there was a place for everyone in the great, big world.

Humming under her breath, she plucked a few leaves of basil and oregano for dinner. She had enough time to begin cooking, shower, and get ready for her date.

In a way, Stone had been right. She woke up with a headache and a hangover, and wondered if she would've regretted taking him into her bed. Remembering him in his uniform, unbuttoning his shirt in a class-act strip show, her mouth basically watered for him to do it again. The way he'd dared her to take more, though she already knew he wouldn't have gone any further with an audience. No, that was his way of forcing her to take control and take what she wanted.

The man was brilliant.

Wiping the dirt off her jeans, she brought the herbs into the kitchen and began grinding them for the meal. Her famous vegetarian lasagna was hearty, and the soy protein crumbles she used as a substitute for meat would be perfect for Stone. Crushing the organic tomatoes she purchased at the farmers' market, she slipped into the beauty of preparing wholesome food to nourish, sinking into the sounds and smells of the cozy kitchen.

Once the lasagna was in the oven and she'd kneaded the dough for the bread, Arilyn took a quick shower and changed into a long gauzy skirt and a pretty button-up cream peasant blouse. It may not be sexpot, but the loose material floated over her body and gave her a feminine, flirty look. She even put on some of the red lipstick Kennedy had bought her and donned long, jangly silver earrings that made noise when she moved her head. The coconut body oil rubbed into her skin gave off a yummy scent and wet sheen.

She was ready.

The doorbell rang.

Arilyn glanced at her watch. Hmm, he was early. She smiled and flung open the door. "I hope you brought your—Poppy! What are you doing here?"

Her grandfather stood on the porch with a small brown bag in his hand. His silver brows drew together in a fierce frown. "I ran away." He stepped over the threshold and dropped his bag. "What are you cooking? That smells good. I'm starving."

Her mouth fell open.

This was so not happening.

"Are you okay? What happened? Did you tell them you were coming over?"

He went into the kitchen and opened the refrigerator. "A, you need to buy some beer. I'm not really a wine drinker. The center doesn't know 'cause I snuck out the laundry room."

Arilyn groaned. "Poppy! You know you can visit me anytime, but you have to tell them."

He pulled out some cheese sticks and began munching. "Emma told Ted I was a bad influence, 'cause she's mad I got Ted hooked on poker and took his money. Emma's sweet on Ted and jealous he spends more time with me. I set her straight, and then Al got all crazy 'cause he's got a crush on Emma—which I don't understand, because the woman is a real pain in the ass—and then the staff got involved and sent everyone to their rooms. Like I'm five and need to be punished. So I figured screw them. I walked into the laundry room, borrowed one of the uniforms, and walked right out the back with my bag. They need better security. Got any soda?"

"Soda is bad for you and so is beer. I'll get you some water." She rubbed her temple. "Umm, okay, why don't you bunk here tonight? Did you bring your insulin and your shots?"

"Of course."

"I thought things were getting better. Didn't you go on an outing a few days ago?"

He rolled his eyes. "We took a bus to the Poconos, where they had this dance teacher trying to show us how to country line dance. Lame. I found a ride down the road and hit the casinos instead. It was awesome, but I got in trouble again. Was told the program I signed up for was the only thing I could do, and that I wasn't allowed to go off on my own."

Emotion surged. Dammit. Her grandfather wanted to embrace life to the very last minute. Inside, he felt young, and diabetes wasn't about to stop him. What was she going to do?

"Poppy, I want you to move in with me. I'll look for a bigger place and hire a nurse, and we'll make it work." She couldn't stand knowing he was unhappy. He'd taken care of her and supported her, and he deserved a home he loved.

She waited for his excitement, but instead he laughed and took her in his arms for a hug. The smell of Old Spice and Irish Spring soap comforted her. "Sweetheart, don't be silly. I don't want to live with you. I actually like the center for what they offer. I'm just finding my way. Besides, you'd cramp my style."

She sniffed against his shirt. "I love you. I want you to be happy."

He patted her shoulder. "Life isn't about constant happiness, you know. Sometimes it's work, and you need to allow time to do its magic. I'll be fine. I like being able to walk to your house, take care of the dogs, and be a part of your life. But I need to live on my own. Can I stay for dinner?"

"Of course. I'm cooking vegetable lasagna."

"Sounds perfect. You have enough for three, right?"

"Yeah, I forgot to tell you I'm having—where are you going?"

He trudged toward the door. "Going to invite Joan over for dinner."

"No! Absolutely not."

Her grandfather clucked his tongue. "Why not? I had a great time last week. She's alone too long in that house with her binoculars. She needs company."

Arilyn shook her head. "She doesn't have friends

because she's mean, Poppy! And it's a telescope so she can spy on the whole block!"

Poppy laughed. "Smart woman. Now, don't be rude. You're usually the first one to say we need to open our house not to the easy ones but to the more difficult ones who need love. I like her. She's got spunk."

"Ugh. I never said that. Plus, there's another reason."

"What?"

"I'm having a date over for dinner," she finally burst out.

"Really? That's wonderful; no wonder you look so nice. I always said you should wear more makeup. Then it will be a celebration. We'll get to know him a bit better. I'll be right back."

Her voice died out. She watched her grandfather disappear to invite the Wicked Witch of Verily into her house, where she'd probably sneak in a hatchet and cut down the Tree of Spite on her way home. The night was officially ruined. No hot sex. No slipping her panties off under the dinner table. No crazy orgasms.

She'd be lucky if Stone didn't run for the hills now and sign off on the whole thing.

Arilyn reached into the refrigerator and uncorked a new bottle of wine.

She was going to need it.

THE DATE WAS NOT what he expected.

When she opened the door, his breath literally caught. She was gorgeous. Didn't matter if she was in yoga pants, a short skirt, or nothing at all. The woman owned her body, and he loved how each motion held an undercurrent of deliberate grace. Like a dancer, she moved as if music were always playing.

He handed her the bottle of wine and the six-pack of beer, bent to kiss her, and stopped cold.

Seemed his date had become a threesome.

And not in a good way.

Mrs. Blackstone—was that her name?—stood a few feet behind Arilyn, glaring in her usual way. He'd met her only a handful of times, but she was a constant complainer and the cops usually ducked when she called. She'd been the one to catch the vandal in action over the summer, but she kind of scared him with her narrowed eyes peering behind thick frames and a harsh manner. What was she doing here?

Another older gentleman had his back to him. Probably her grandfather. Stone leaned over to whisper, "We have an audience?"

"I'm so sorry. My grandfather surprised me and invited the witch—er, Mrs. Blackfire to dinner. I couldn't stop him."

She looked worried, as if he'd be pissed. Actually, his sense of humor kicked in because it was kinda funny. Stone patted his pocket. "Guess I won't be handing over these babies tonight."

She flushed, but then a chuckle escaped her lips, and Stone couldn't help it. He leaned down and kissed her again, right in front of her audience. He had a feeling Arilyn would always be picking up strays along the way and inviting them to dinner.

"Stone Petty?"

He jerked back at the familiar, booming voice. Lifted his head. "Patrick? What are you doing here?"

Patrick let out a laugh. "I'm Arilyn's grandfather. You're her date?"

Arilyn glanced back and forth. "You two know each other?"

Stone grinned and moved forward. "Are you kidding? We call him 'the Hustler' down at Ray's Billiards. He's always making our wallets lighter on the force. How the hell are you?"

"Good. Guess I'm bustin' in on your date, huh? Hey, wait a minute." His face scrunched up. "Are you the jerk cop in her class giving her trouble?"

Arilyn groaned. "Poppy! That was between us."

Stone laughed. Her skin grew more flushed. He couldn't wait to show her the many ways he intended to make her blush later. "Me? I've been a model student. Besides, aren't you supposed to lead by example? Seems you have a bit of a temper yourself." He tugged at her hair and she gave him the familiar glare he knew and was beginning to like.

"I refuse to allow you to bait me tonight. Stone, this is my neighbor Mrs. Blackfire."

Stone straightened and entered the senior firing squad. He offered his hand. "A pleasure to meet you again, ma'am."

She shook his hand with pure suspicion. "I know who you are. Why aren't you in uniform?"

"I'm off duty now."

"What if something happens and the town needs you? The board said you were short staffed. That's how drug dealers invade small towns, you know. Lack of police supervision."

"That's true. A solid reminder not to bother the police unless it's urgent."

She sniffed. "Are you referring to me personally, Officer?"

Stone grinned. "Were you the one who called three times to make a citizen's arrest on the poor kid who delivers newspapers?"

"I caught him spying through my window. He may have been trying to see me in a compromising position."

A shudder shook him at *that* visual. Patrick looked amused, though, and seemed to be a bit sweet on her. Interesting. "The paper got caught in one of the bushes and Pete knows how you like it centered on the front porch. You almost got him fired."

"If he can't throw, he shouldn't be hired for such a position."

"He's twelve."

"Good, he'll learn early."

Oh, yeah. This was gonna be a fun night.

Patrick eyed the six-pack of IPA and lunged for it. "You brought beer! My kind of guy!"

He caught Arilyn's eye roll and held back a laugh. "Just one, Poppy! I mean it."

"Yeah, yeah, of course. And it's IPA, my fave. Joan, wine?"

Mrs. Blackfire sniffed. "Half of a glass, please. I noticed that tree branch is still overgrown. It's sticking out on my property. If you had let my tree guy cut it, we wouldn't have this problem."

Arilyn sighed. "You wanted to cut it down, not trim it!"

"A good thing they gave me back my money. I can't afford to waste money with Social Security."

Patrick interrupted, his tone firm. "Joan, I thought we discussed the tree. It's not a danger, and Arilyn won't cut it down. But if we're going to have a nice dinner together, we no longer bring up the tree. Agreed?"

Silence descended. Stone held his breath, even though he had no idea what was going on. Somehow, he sensed a shift and didn't know if it was going to be good or bad.

Mrs. Blackfire grunted. "Fine. Make it a full glass of wine, please."

"You got it."

Patrick smiled and winked.

Arilyn looked surprised. There was definite history between her and the neighbor. In Stone's experience, neighbors made for the most dramatic fights in cop history. Stone walked into the small kitchen and began pouring the drinks. "Something smells good."

She pushed her hair over her shoulder, donned oven mitts, and began serving. "Lasagna."

"One of my favorites." His stomach grumbled on cue. "I skipped lunch."

She shot him a glare. "That's not good, Stone. You should keep a granola bar in your car, or some fruit. It's not good for your body to slip into starvation mode. Messes up your metabolism."

"My shifts have been switched around since I got back to work."

"How long have you been a cop?" Patrick asked.

Stone handed Mrs. Blackfire her wine, uncapped an IPA for himself, and checked on Arilyn. She seemed to have everything under control in the kitchen, so he sat down on one of the stools. He sucked at anything domestic anyway. She might as well find that out now. "Enrolled in the academy after graduation. Worked the Bronx for a number of years, then transferred to Verily." He left out all the important parts.

"Tough neighborhood. Needed a break?"

"You could say that." He pictured Arilyn's ears pricking. "Got into a bad situation on a domestic abuse case. Things got ugly. I had to transfer. I picked Verily."

He took a sip of his beer and waited for the twenty questions. Hell, it was the truth, and he had nothing to hide. Patrick swigged his beer, stretched out his feet clad in old-man shoes, and nodded. "Yeah, that's how that stuff works. I kinda lost it in Nam years ago. I was commanded to take out a child for getting too close. Kids back then held grenades like stick candy, but it was my instinct to protect. I couldn't do it." His lively green eyes dulled as he got sucked back into the memory. "Damn war was so dirty. Good guys and bad began to blur. Anyway, I refused, citing my moral obligation to protect, so my officer commanded Bill Evans to listen to his order instead. Bill did. Shot the kid right in front of us. I think about Bill all the time. Remember his name, and think of that big chain-type restaurant. I think of how bad I wished Bill had gotten out clean and opened up a food chain empire."

Patrick stopped talking. Arilyn walked over and gently touched his shoulder. "What happened to him?" she asked softly.

Patrick squeezed her hand. "The child died. Child was clean."

Stone fought through the punch of emotion at the

waste of war. The things people had to live with in the dark of night, when all they wanted was justice for all.

"Things got bad after that. I started with eight guys. Lost five. Bill was one of them. Sometimes I wonder if he didn't fight hard enough after that incident because he couldn't live with himself anymore."

Arilyn pressed a kiss to the top of his head. "I'm sorry, Poppy. You never told me that story."

Patrick stroked his arm, where his tattoos held the memory of the men he'd lost. "Lots I don't tell people, honey. A man needs some secrets. Some need to bleed out to heal. Others you just live with."

With sheer astonishment, Stone watched as Mrs. Blackfire reached across the kitchen table and grabbed Patrick's hand. They both shared a look that Stone didn't understand, and he didn't think he was meant to.

"My husband died at the Tet Offensive," she said. Her voice lacked emotion, but her face screamed otherwise. "We'd only been married a year. I didn't want him to go, and neither did he, but the draft has no mercy. He accepted his fate with pride and a head held high, even though people spit in his face." Rage shimmered in her eyes. "He was a good man. We decided to wait to have children until he returned. I was stupid back then. I thought he'd come back. He didn't, of course. I lost him with thousands of others. Of course, if he had come back, he wouldn't have been the same anyway."

Stone had heard about the Tet Offensive from some vets who'd made it out. It was the biggest surprise launch of attacks by North Vietnam against the United States and South Vietnam. Massive numbers of troops on both sides were lost, until it was a bleeding black hole in history that no one forgot.

Patrick reached out and put his other hand over hers. "I lost many friends during that mess. It was a bloodbath. Took me a long time even to be able to sleep again at night. What was his name?"

"Ryan Blackfire," she said quietly. "He was quite gentle. Loved reading. Wanted to be a history professor and teach kids about their heritage."

"Joan, your face must have been the last thing he saw. You gave him something worth hanging on to, until the last moment. I know this for a fact. The women we loved were the only thing that helped us keep our sanity and humanity. You gave that to him."

Stone held his breath, not wanting to interrupt the poignant scene. Somehow, the silence that descended was full of understanding and mourning.

Arilyn sank into the last chair, dinner forgotten. They all stared at the elderly woman, who recited her story as if she were reading a book. Stone knew better. Her wounds had never healed. Maybe by her own choice. Maybe not.

"How old were you?" Arilyn asked.

Mrs. Blackfire removed her hand from Patrick's and shook herself out of her trance. "Old enough. Twenty-two."

"You were so young," Arilyn said softly. "I'm sorry." Simple words that couldn't heal, but by being spoken, it was a start. Stone stared. Arilyn's natural need to heal carved out the lines of her face. Stone bet she ached to wrap her up in a hug but was too scared her neighbor would strike like a cobra.

Stone couldn't imagine Mrs. Blackfire at twenty-two. Happy. In love. Full of life. The woman across the table emanated a bitter strength that told a different story of how her life turned out.

"I made do." Mrs. Blackfire stiffened her spine and her voice.

Arilyn offered a small smile. "You deserved more than that."

Her neighbor looked startled. Cleared her throat. "Are we going to eat, or are you gonna launch into one of your healing chants?"

Patrick laughed and the spell was broken. Stone moved from the breakfast counter to the sturdy pine table and sat down. Arilyn handed out plates filled with steaming lasagna, fresh bread and butter, and a small side salad. Stone took a big whiff. Damn, it smelled good. When was the last time he had a home-cooked meal?

Too long ago to remember.

He took his fork, dug into a huge portion, and popped the bite in his mouth.

Stone didn't know how long he chewed before the taste hit him. Along with the texture. What the hell kind of lasagna was this? He frowned, trying to figure out why the meat was soggy and tasted like crap. The tomatoes were good, but his teeth caught a carrot and some mushy stuff that mingled in his mouth. And not in a good way.

He managed to swallow. Shot a glance around the table.

Mrs. Blackfire chewed, then spit it out. "What is this?" she shrieked.

Patrick looked resigned, picking around the junk and trying to find a piece of plain pasta.

Arilyn blinked. "Vegetable lasagna. I told you."

Mrs. Blackfire shook her head. "This is no lasagna, girl. And this is no meat."

"It's a soy substitute exactly like meat. Fresh vegetables, tomatoes, herbs. Oh, and the ricotta cheese is tofu based."

Stone pushed his plate away. Nope. Not even for sex could he choke that junk down. If the guys at the station heard that he had even tried tofu, his man card would be yanked for good. "Umm, Arilyn, thanks, but I'm not as hungry as I thought. I'll have bread."

She glared and crossed her arms in front of her chest. "You said you were starving! What's the matter? It took me all afternoon to make this. It's healthy and filling."

"Definitely healthy. And I do appreciate it. I had a late lunch, though." He reached for bread, spread butter on it, and shoved it in his mouth. He'd fill up on carbs and it would be fine. He chewed, but the bread refused to dissolve.

Oh, hell, no. It was as if a field of wheat had been harvested and spread over his tongue. Crunchy seeds snapped under his teeth. Bread wasn't supposed to taste like this! He managed a swallow and surrendered.

So did Mrs. Blackfire. And Poppy. They all stared at Arilyn and their plates in shared misery and guilt.

"You don't like it?" she asked. Confusion flickered in her green eyes. "It's all organic ingredients. I don't understand."

That's when his heart did a strange flip-flop. He should've felt irritated at her for starving him, reminding himself once again why they were terrible together. But when was the last time a woman had cooked for him? Cared about his diet?

He spoke up. "Arilyn, thank you. I know you cooked your ass off for us, and we appreciate it. But we're just not as highly evolved. At least, not yet."

She nodded. "Too many processed foods and sugars in your regular diet? You can't appreciate the flavors of food in a natural environment?"

"Yes!" they all said in unison.

Poppy lit up. "Can we order a pizza?"

"I don't like peppers or anchovies," Mrs. Blackfire stated.

"Pepperoni?" Stone suggested. "And half veggie." Poppy and Mrs. Blackfire stared, obviously not happy with that. "It'll be good for us," he said more firmly. "Okay?"

Poppy nodded. "Okay. I'll get the phone. Garlic knots, too?"

"Definitely."

He snuck a glance over. Prepared for her temper or general crankiness over having her dinner guests rebel after she had spent her day trying to please them. He didn't blame her. He'd probably be bitchy if he tried to do something nice that no one wanted.

Instead, a reluctant smile tugged at those lush lips. "Fine. But I want black olives and eggplant on mine or I'm not eating it."

Stone realized she was even more trouble than he realized. Because she was beginning to touch not only his body but his heart.

ARILYN LOOKED UP as Kate and Kennedy barged into her office, sank down in the matching purple chairs, and waited.

She glanced back and forth between them. "What?" she finally asked.

Kate sighed. "Are you really going to make us beg?"

Kennedy tapped her finger against her lip. "I thought you were better than us, A. I thought you could be trusted to give us all the dirt without having to threaten, blackmail, or assault you. You disappoint me."

Her lip twitched. She leaned back in the chair and gave herself up. "You want to know about my hot cop not stripper?"

"Yes!" Kate screeched, all dignity completely abandoned. "I haven't had any time to get the dirt since he scooped you up all cavemanlike and carried you out the door. Oh my God, I wanted to die. And he stripped for you? Well, his shirt at least. Kind of. I was so hot, poor Slade had to call in late the next morning. I almost killed him."

Kennedy looked quite satisfied. "Nate told me if I was going to come home like that more often, he'd hire a stripper himself. I told him it was the romance between you guys that got me crazy. Oh, and BTW? The stripper I actually hired was so not up to par with Stone Petty. If he ever wanted to quit and make a living taking off a quarter of his clothes, tell him he'd be rich."

Arilyn laughed. It was fun being the one gossiped about for a change. When she was dating Jacob, no one asked her questions because he was off-limits. A dark, private secret no one liked to bring up. They'd gotten so used to her silence that her friends stopped trying to pry. She never got to cry, bitch, or chatter about sex or her relationship. Finally, it was her turn. "I'll be sure to pass on the compliment. Knowing him, it'll make his day."

"Did you have great sex? Glorious, orgasmic, all-night, I-can't-walk-this-morning sex?" Kennedy demanded.

"No."

"What?" Kennedy threw up her hands. "Dudette, if that didn't make you give it up, nothing will!"

Arilyn rolled her eyes. "I wanted to, but he said I was too drunk. Gave me the speech about wanting me to remember it and no regrets in the morning." Every time she thought back on the scene, he edged a notch up in the respect department. It took a strong man in control not to follow his penis, and he'd been as crazy in lust as she had. Yet he wanted her to be sure. How sexy and cool was that?

Kate nodded in understanding. "I like. I'm sure you were pissed at the time. I think Slade did that to me once, but the next morning you realize he's a real man."

"Agreed," Kennedy said. "So when are you guys gonna do it?"

Arilyn groaned. "Is nothing sacred?"

"Hell, no. When?"

"Not sure. Our date this weekend got hijacked by Poppy and Mrs. Blackfire."

Kate choked on a sip of water. "What? You actually saw the Wicked Witch of Verily in a social gathering?"

"Worse. Poppy invited her over for dinner. It was quite cozy."

Kate shuddered. "That woman scares me. Is she still trying to cut down the Tree of Spite?"

"She tried, but I foiled her wicked plan. Poppy likes her, so he keeps inviting her over." She paused, trying to introduce the odd thought delicately. Ever since Mrs. Blackfire talked about her lost husband, she'd become more sympathetic in Arilyn's eyes. "She seemed different. Kind of human."

Kate shot her a look. "It's a guise so she can cut down Gen's tree in the middle of the night. Don't trust her! Even Robert avoids going by her lawn, and he loves everyone."

Arilyn decided it wasn't a good time to list the few assets of her neighbor. "Well, they were the main reason nothing happened. We're keeping the relationship hidden because of the anger management class."

Her friends shared a pointed look. Kate gentled her voice. "Babe, you have to listen to us. Stone is not asshole Yoga Man. You can't begin a relationship trying to hide things. Did you talk about what you both want?"

"Yes. He clearly said it will be an affair for however long we were both happy."

Kennedy frowned. "Did he say he wanted to keep it private? Or is that your idea?"

"No, he said he wanted to date and take me out. I'm the one who doesn't want my two other students from anger management to know. It would be awkward."

Kate beamed. "Good, so he doesn't want to sneak around. I want you to invite him to the wedding."

Her mouth fell open. "What? No, that's impossible; you already have the seating charts and food orders. Absolutely not."

Kate stabbed a finger in the air. "I'm the bride, and I want him there. This will give us an opportunity to meet with him. I won't let you go down that road again, A. No more secretive affairs that only end up hurting you. This guy is gonna have to deal with your friends or he's toast."

Kennedy jumped in. "Agreed. It'll be a good test. A guy who goes to a friend's wedding is brave. Confident. He's not afraid because he has nothing to hide."

A rush of emotions flooded her body. The idea of having a real date to accompany her in public thrilled her. She'd gotten so used to being alone while her friends brought their partners. How would it feel to finally belong? To be happy with the man by her side and show him off?

But they weren't serious. Not like that. They'd have sex, and date, but when things got too complicated, he'd check out. Funny, she'd always believed Jacob was honest about his limitations and that made him a better person. Now she realized it was just a convenient excuse. How much better to claim she had been warned when he eventually hurt her?

Was Stone the same? Was his honesty and up-front deal to her all disguised to make his exit clean and stress free?

Maybe inviting him to the wedding would be a good test. If he declined, she'd know he'd never intended to be anything more than a roll in the hay. If he accepted?

Well, she didn't know.

Arilyn pressed on the energy points on her wrist to open up the chakras. Stress was beginning to block up her channels, and that wouldn't be a good start to her day. "I don't know, Kate. Why is dating so damn confusing?"

"Because we're dating men," Kennedy offered. "Invite him. You're at the bridal table anyway, we'll all have dates, and there's room to squeeze one more in."

"But it's in a few days!"

"Even better. Spring it on him before he has too much time to analyze."

"Please, A," Kate urged. "Just ask him."

Arilyn nibbled on her lip. "Okay. I'll try."

"Good." Kate jumped up from the chair. "I can't believe on Saturday I'll be married. You're all set to take Robert Friday?"

Arilyn nodded. "I have the house all set up for him. Poppy's going to walk him in the afternoon. I have the vet on call, and I promise to text you twice a day with updates. You just need to enjoy St. Lucia."

Kate smiled. "Thanks. You guys are the best." She began to tear up, and Kennedy groaned, tugging her hand toward the door.

"No more crying, I can't take it anymore. We need

to save ourselves for the ultimate breakdown on the wedding day or we'll have nothing left."

Kate sniffed. "You're right. Thanks for being the bitch in the relationship, Ken."

"Welcome."

Arilyn laughed as her friends disappeared. Now all she had to do was take their advice and ask Stone Petty to the wedding.

Her heart beat so hard it almost exploded out of her chest. Half of her prayed he'd just beg off with a polite excuse and they'd never mention it again.

But it was the other half that hoped he'd say yes that disturbed her the most.

LATER THAT DAY, SHE was still trying to get the courage up to ask him after anger management class. Ugh. Like a prom date after the bell rang. She was humiliated.

She walked through Animals Alive and checked on her crew. They came to the shelter for a session once a week to walk and socialize the dogs. Luther and Eli seemed enthusiastic about returning, but Stone seemed stressed. She wondered if he was still leery about being around the dogs, even though he had done well with Pinky last week.

Anthony was giving them a lecture on the horses, so she decided to allow Stone to move to the carriage house. It was hard dealing with a dog bite from childhood and not fair for her to push him. She paused at the door and studied them. They worked hard, and she'd seen some huge leaps with Luther and Eli regarding their anger. With half the course behind them, the next three weeks would consist of drilling in the proper techniques they'd been learning.

Her gaze greedily took in Stone. The familiar Yankees cap was perched on his head. Today, his wardrobe consisted of a long-sleeved blue T-shirt proclaiming I GOT YOUR BACK. The kicker was the stick figure sketched out with no back. Total guy humor. His jeans were so tight and worn, Arilyn wondered if he'd had them for the past decade and refused to get rid of them. His five-o'clock shadow mixed with his goatee and added to that almost dangerous, criminal look he did so well.

Now she knew how his beard scratched against her skin. How soft his lips were, and how his experienced tongue drove into her mouth. She knew the hard strength of his thighs anchoring her to the wall, and the delicious grace of those fingers when he skimmed her bare skin. She knew that his ass, which was perfectly on display right now in those jeans, was as tight and firm as it looked.

She wanted to know so much more.

"Arilyn?"

She refocused. Her students were all gazing at her, waiting for an answer when she hadn't heard Anthony's question. "Sorry?"

Stone gave her a slow, smug smile, as if he knew she'd been caught staring at his ass. She fought a blush. "Everyone's ready. Luther wants to go to the horse stalls today, so I'll oversee him if you'd like."

"Great. Stone, you can follow them. Eli, why don't you go ahead and check which dogs need working."

Anthony motioned Stone and Luther toward the door. "I'll catch up with you two in a minute. Can I talk to you for a minute, A?"

"Sure." She turned her back on Stone's ferocious frown, wondering what had suddenly pissed him off, and grabbed some dog treats. "What's up?"

"Pinky."

Her stomach tightened. She'd been hoping the dog would be better, but it was a slow process. Her breakdowns around the other dogs in the kennel made it difficult to rehabilitate her, especially with so little space. Anthony pushed his fingers through his hair with frustration. "I gotta be honest. I have the word out to other shelters to take her in, but so far, no offers. I lost my behaviorist, and we're looking to rehire. I can't keep her too much longer. Can you foster her until things calm down?"

Arilyn bit her lip. "I can't. I'm watching my friend's dog for the next two weeks and my place is too small to keep them separated. What about the Trumans? Can they take her?"

Anthony shook his head. "Nope, they already took three in. My fosters are filled up, and I'm out of room. I can squeeze a few more days, but then I have to put her somewhere."

She dug her fingers into her neck to try to ease away the muscle ache. What was she going to do? They couldn't advertise too publicly because she'd literally stolen her. She racked her brain for candidates, but not one came up. "Let me work on this. Maybe I can find someone to get her off the grid for a while until we come up with a solution."

"Okay. I'm sorry. I know you took a risk saving her. Look, even if I have to ship her out of state, we'll make sure she stays safe."

Arilyn knew that with dogs this severely traumatized, sometimes the journey didn't go well. Time was ticking, and she needed to learn to trust someone. Her world begged for stabilization and a shred of kindness so she could reset and decide if she wanted to fight.

Arilyn sensed Pinky was a fighter.

Shoulders slumped, she headed out to the horse barn with Anthony to help. Luther was checking out the two horses in the stall, one blindfolded from eye surgery, the other sporting a bum leg because his owner had thrown him out after proclaiming him a useless racehorse. "Where's Stone?"

Luther shrugged. "He took off. Said he was heading somewhere else."

Anthony cocked his head. "Probably with Pinky. He's been showing up here on a daily basis—his name is always on the sign-in sheet."

Shock cut through her. "What? He's been coming on his own?"

"Yep. Our volunteer, Natalie, saw him in Pinky's cage. It's too bad he couldn't foster her—he seems to be the only one making progress with her."

"Yeah, too bad. I'll be back."

Her boots crunched on the gravel. She walked down the path, past the woods, and headed down the private road where Pinky's kennel was located. Sure enough, Stone was in the same position as last week. On the ground, back against the cage. She heard a low murmur as he spoke. Holding her breath, she moved silently over the grass until she got close.

The scene slammed in her vision.

Pinky sat in the middle of her kennel. Head cocked. There was a safe distance still between them, but she was definitely listening to his ramblings. Those dark, soulful eyes held a spark of interest, fighting to blossom.

"I told you the hamburger was better. I'll keep bringing them if you keep eating them. But you can't tell anyone or I'll get in trouble. I was supposed to be with the horses today, but I knew you'd be pissed if I missed my visit. Trust me, a female with a temper is nothing I want to deal with. I already got your mistress to handle, and she's enough for anyone."

He paused. Pinky waited. Her ears pricked.

"Oh, I forgot to tell you yesterday Devine and I finally saw some action. Sweet heaven. Found a hijacked car and got to go on a real car chase. Reminded me of the good old days in the Bronx. Man, some of that shit was fun. Ended up being some teen who stole it for a joyride, nothing serious, but damned if that didn't liven up a weeknight. Feel bad for the kid, though—he's going through a rough time, and he's got no one to look out for him. No parents, and in foster care. Like you. I know a shelter isn't the best place, but at least you're warm, safe, and fed, right? No one's gonna hurt you anymore. But it's not gonna be easy. You gotta fight. I can't do it for you. Up to you. Just hope you make the right decision. Hope the kid does the same."

Arilyn eased back, not making a sound, and turned the corner. Her body shook. Her throat seized up with such raw emotion, she didn't know what to do. Stone was a liar. She may have rescued Pinky, but Stone was the one who could save her. He took his precious time to come and visit. He pretended not to care about anyone or anything other than his job, but it was a façade. He cared, deeply, but he hated to show or admit it.

The possibility he could grow to care about *her* shook her foundation.

What was happening to her? When had their relationship turned from dislike, to passion, to a powerful liking with the hope of more?

Arilyn made her plan and waited.

STONE CHECKED TO MAKE sure the coast was clear and then snuck out of Pinky's cage. She was getting better, but like any girl, she was stubborn. Wasn't gonna come around easy. Still, he didn't mind hanging out talking for an hour. It was even better than seeing a shrink, because he was able to say whatever he wanted without judgment or being given a plan to fix him.

Pinky didn't give a shit.

He muttered under his breath about the stupid name she'd been stuck with, but at least Arilyn had had good intentions. He'd head to the horse barn, pick up a few tips, and go home for his shift.

He turned the corner and almost bumped into her.

Stone stopped short. God, she was beautiful. With her hair snagged in a casual ponytail, she wore jeans, boots, a loose jersey, and a purple scarf wrapped around her neck. Ever since their dinner that turned into pizza and a rousing game of Pictionary, he couldn't stop thinking about her. He should be obsessed with the prospect of sex, which he was, no doubt, but the fact that he had actually enjoyed himself on a date with her grandfather and senior neighbor bothered him. It screamed of an intimacy he hadn't experienced in years.

"Hi," he finally said, keeping cool. Better off to twist the truth with fiction. "Just wanted to check on Pinky. How's she doing?"

Her brow lifted. "That's nice of you. Actually, we have a big problem. I don't know what we're going to do."

"About what?"

"She can't stay here much longer. They lost the behaviorist and ran out of foster homes. She's not good with other dogs, so most other shelters are out because of the overcrowding issue."

"You can take her in, right? You said you always foster dogs."

"Usually I could, but I'm watching my friend Kate's dog for the next two weeks. She's going on her honeymoon and she needs me. His back legs are paralyzed, so he needs careful watching."

Concern hit him. "So, what happens?"

"Anthony may need to send Pinky away to a shelter out of state. It could be traumatic, but we may not have any choice. Maybe you can ask around? See if there's someone you know who could take her in?" Her voice softened and she moved closer. Her body heat shimmered and pulled him in like a wicked spell. "I can take her back after Kate returns. I need your help, Stone. Pinky deserves a shot, but she won't have it unless someone amazing steps up and helps her."

It took him a while, since his dick was in play and his response was purely physical. He opened his mouth to tell her he'd do anything for her, as long as she kept that pleading siren expression on her face that promised him the moon, the stars, and nirvana on her knees.

Then it hit him.

He was being played.

Stone hadn't graduated from the academy and worked in law enforcement by being stupid. His brain clicked back on, and he realized this whole scenario was to get him to take in Pinky.

No. Fucking. Way.

"You saw me, huh?" he muttered. "You think now I'm a big pussy and I'll take a damn dog into my house because we're into each other?"

The sexy look was wiped off her face. Besides the cute sulk on her lips, her green eyes spat fire and smoke. He fought back a grin. Damn, he liked her spunk. "Why do you have to be so crude?" she hissed. "Why do you have to do something nice and then wipe it away with a smart remark?"

"Oh, you're good. Trying to turn this one around on me so I look like the asshole. I helped cover your crime, and my role is done. It's up to you to find the rat fink a proper home."

"Don't call her that! I'm asking you to take her for just two weeks. Two lousy weeks to give her a chance at survival. Why can't you be reasonable?"

"Me? Reasonable? Woman, you didn't even ask me. Just tried to do your female mind tricks on me so I offered to help."

She huffed out a breath, shuffled her feet, and gave him the words. "Will you watch Pinky for two weeks?"

"No." She clenched her fists and squeaked. "Don't forget to breathe."

"Forget it; I was an idiot to think this could work. I'm outta here."

She turned, but he jumped in front of her, lowering his voice so no one could eavesdrop. "*This* works just fine. Me and you. Not me and Pinky cozied up night after night. I don't like dogs. I don't do dogs."

Her brows snapped together. "Oh, I know what you don't do, Officer. You don't do commitments. You don't do future or long-term. You don't do anything that's not easy. Forget this."

Her words stung like pebbles hitting his naked body. Is that how she saw him? Was she right? And if so, was it so wrong? He was only trying to be honest and protect them both. "Listen, I'll help you find someone. I'll ask around at the station. There are plenty of wives and girlfriends who may want to help. I just can't be the one to take her in."

"I only have two days left."

Ah, shit. Her voice did that wobbly thing that left him vulnerable. He cursed under his breath. "I'll find someone. I promise." He regretted the words the moment they left his lips, but relief flickered in her eyes, and Stone realized she trusted him. Somehow, someway, she believed him. Most didn't. Only Devine. There was no one else, and wasn't that kind of sad and pathetic? He wasn't about to let down that trust. He'd done harder stuff before. How difficult could it be to find a nice, quiet home for a small dog for two weeks?

"Thank you."

"Will you not be pissed off at me now?"

She smiled. "I'm sorry I yelled at you."

"Yeah, you may want to put that on a recording for the future. Just hit Play time and time again."

She did that half-giggle thing and completely charmed him. "I have something else to ask you."

Uh-oh. "What?"

She must have sensed his wariness, because she shifted her weight, looked at the floor, and began to babble. "Actually, it's not a big deal, and you're probably working anyway, and my friends kinda pressured me, so you can just say no."

He grinned. "Might want to tell me what it is first I'm saying no to."

"Oh! Umm . . . so . . . remember the bachelorette party? Kate's getting married this Saturday at Bear Mountain, and everyone has dates, so I figured maybe you'd want to go with me. But you don't have to."

"You want me to go to a wedding with you?" He couldn't help the surprise from leaking out. Weddings were a big deal, meeting friends and family. Getting dressed up. Putting on your best behavior for strangers. Hell, he couldn't remember the last time he attended a formal function. He had one good suit, and it would need to be dry-cleaned.

But the idea that he wasn't her dirty little secret was kind of nice.

"Only if you wanted to go," she volleyed back.

"Do you just need a date? Or do you want me to go?" He only pushed her to clarify because she looked so adorable, hating having to ask him and looking nervous about his answer. Like she gave a crap. Warmth settled in his gut, and a pleasant feeling flowed in his veins.

She gave a frustrated humph. "I wouldn't ask if I didn't want you to go. But I don't want you to go unless you *want* to go."

"You want me to want to go?"

"Yes!"

He couldn't help it. A hearty laugh escaped his lips. "I'd love to go to the wedding with you, little one. Thanks for asking."

She peered at him with suspicion. "You really want to go?"

"Yes."

"Don't you have to work?"

"I can take the day off. What time is the wedding?"

"Two p.m."

"One of the guys will cover for me."

"Oh, okay. Great." She chewed on her lip. "Are you sure you want to go?"

He shook his head. "I knew from the beginning you were high maintenance."

"I'm not! I flow!"

He reached out to tug at her ponytail. "Sure you do."

She growled and stomped around him. "I'm going to the horse farm. Class dismissed."

His laughter echoed in the fall air, drifting down the path after her.

Stone couldn't remember a time in his life he'd had more fun with a woman.

DEVINE, YOU GOTTA take the dog."

His partner snorted and refused to break his stride. He poured some disgusting dregs of what they called coffee into a stained mug, tossed in some sugar, and moved toward his desk. "No fucking way, man. I'm allergic."

Stone rolled his eyes at the outright lie. Propping a hip on the battered metal desk, he blocked the stacks of paperwork they were both battling through. "Bullshit. It's only for two weeks. She's so small, you won't even know she's there."

"Good, so you take her. I don't like foo-foo dogs, anyway."

"Besides her ridiculous name, she's cool. Been abused. Fighting her way back. Isn't that a story you want to star in as the hero?"

"No. Now get off my desk so I can finish this by midnight and not turn into a pumpkin. I hate paperwork. Can you get me a donut and an iced latte?"

"If you take Pinky."

"Forget it. Hey, Dunn! Get me a pumpkin donut and an iced latte, and I'll owe you!"

"You gotta do my police report, too," Tim called back from his own desk of hell.

"Fuck you! I don't know the details."

"Then fuck your pumpkin donut, Devine!"

"Fine. Give it to me. But you gotta buy, too."

Tim smirked, knowing he got the better deal. Dropping more papers on Devine's desk, he headed out the station door.

Rookie Patterson came in from his shift. Features tight with annoyance, he walked stiffly to his desk. Stone took a whiff of the air and recoiled. "What the hell is that smell?"

Patterson glared. "I'm sure you think the locker thing was funny, but I had cologne in there. When you turned it over, the bottle opened and spilled all over my damn spare uniform. I didn't have time to go and change."

"Dude, what the hell you need cologne for anyway?" Devine asked.

"To smell good!"

"Well, you smell like you got drowned in the ocean. Women like manly stuff better. The uniform should be enough to get you dates anyway," Stone pointed out.

"I'm in a dry spell," Patterson muttered, straightening up the folders on his desk in his usual OCD manner. Stone guessed the dry spell was due to the guy's attitude toward cleanliness and organization rather than his looks. The kid was average looking, of decent height and stature, with dark hair and hazel eyes, and should have been seeing more action since he got on the force. Inspiration struck. "Hey, you know what chicks love? Dogs. You need to get a dog."

Patterson shuddered. "I hate dogs. They smell and mess up your house. No way."

"Fuck you, then, rookie. I'm trying to help."

Devine cackled.

Stone let out an aggravated breath. For God's sake, his time was up and he still hadn't managed to find a temporary home for Pinky. Didn't anyone have hearts anymore? What was wrong with the public when no one wanted to help an innocent, battered animal?

Bastards.

"Why are you suddenly worried about a dog?" his partner asked suspiciously. "You hate dogs. Is this because you're trying to get Arilyn into bed?"

Was it? No. He'd bed her anyway, but he couldn't let her down. He'd promised. Stone glared at his friend. "Nah. I told her I'd take care of it."

Devine nodded. Both of them understood the power of a promise. A man's word meant shit in today's society, but they still believed in the dream. Kind of medieval, maybe, but if it was the only thing he brought to this world as his footprint, he'd go to the grave trying. "You're screwed, man. Everyone's busy and broke. No one takes dogs in for a few weeks and gives them up."

Arilyn did. Time and time again. She spent her money and her time and never questioned or whined.

Stop thinking about her.

The wedding was tomorrow. She was babysitting that other dog, and Anthony had run out of options. So had Stone.

On cue, his cell rang.

Cursing, he answered. "Yeah?"

"Did you find a place for Pinky?"

He closed his eyes. With his next words, he'd put himself on a path of regret and inconvenience and aggravation he really didn't need.

Fuck.

"Yeah. I'll take her for the two weeks."

He heard her breath catch. Then her voice—rich, silky, melodic—poured out of the receiver. "Thank you, Stone. I know what it cost you to do this. And I'll never forget it."

Oh, yeah, she was good. Real good. And he was toast. "Yeah. Sure. What do I need to do?"

"I'll bring her over in the morning. I'll have all the stuff you need, and I'll help you, I swear. You won't regret this."

Yeah. He would. He hated dogs, was terrified of them, and now he was sheltering one in his bachelor pad. Ugh.

"Arilyn?"

"Yeah?"

He gave a low growl. "You better make this worth it."

Stone wondered if she'd get pissy with him or hang up. Instead, she drawled her answer in a way that made his dick stiffen and his body go on full alert.

"I will. But you better bring it."

The phone clicked.

Hot damn.

Devine smirked. "Guess you're taking the dog, huh?"

"Guess so. You suck, Devine."

"Have fun at the wedding, Petty."

Stone walked off, grinning.

"KATE? THEY'RE READY."

Her friend turned, a smile lighting up her face. Arilyn forgot to breathe. The vision before her was familiar, yet not.

"How do I look?"

Arilyn shook her head, tears pricking her eyes. "So beautiful I can't even talk." Her silvery hair caught up in an elaborate twist, the veil spilled past her bare shoulders in bridal glory, highlighting the clean, elegant lines of the dress. Like Kate, the gown was classic, with its fitted bodice and a crisscross of shimmering pearls and diamonds cinching the waist, then falling gloriously to the floor in perfect sheer chiffon. The crystal-embedded peekaboo heels added to her graceful stature. She held a small bouquet of cocoa and pink roses.

Kennedy sniffed. "So beautiful that Slade will try to rush you through the reception. But we won't let him." With her rich caramel hair and sleek curves, the chocolate bridesmaid dress with its gorgeous pink sash looked perfect. They'd all been crazy over the dresses from the moment Kate showed them. With a flattering V-neck, the dark brown chiffon held a top layer of gold shimmer to make them look as if they were lit up. Dark pink accessories gave the classic color a unique makeover.

Slade's sister, Jane, fanned her hand in front of her face. "I don't want to ruin my makeup, but I'm so happy you came into our lives. Not only are you now family, but you helped me meet the love of my life."

Jane had signed up for Kinnections to meet her soul mate. In an effort to protect his sister from a broken heart, Slade had stormed in and demanded Kate match him to prove the business wasn't a scam. Kate did. With herself. Sometimes, when Arilyn was lonely at night, she'd think of Kate's story and soothe herself with the possibility that anything can happen.

Kate laughed. "Without you, I'd never have met Slade. I love you, Jane, just like a sister. And no crying or I'll never stop!" She steadied herself and drew in a deep breath. "Mom, tell them I'm ready."

Madeline, Kate's mother, gave a long sigh. "Are you sure you don't want some marijuana just for the walk down the aisle, sweetheart? I don't want you to be tense."

"Thanks for the offer, Mom, but I'll pass."

"If you're sure."

Jane giggled. "I'll check and make sure everyone's in place," she said, following Madeline out.

Arilyn moved next to Kate and took her hand. Kennedy grabbed the other one.

"This is it, ladies," Kate whispered. "Nothing will ever be the same."

Kennedy grinned. "Nope. It'll be even better."

Arilyn squeezed her hand. "Better than better. It'll be epic."

They all smiled at each other. Arilyn realized her friendship with these two women had changed her life and had given her strength, support, and much-needed humor. They'd built a business together, gone through heartbreak together, and were now moving on to pick their lifelong mates together.

Kate looked at them with love. "Let's do this."

They nodded. Then walked out of the room, together.

A FEW HOURS LATER, the reception was in full swing. Bear Mountain was ideal for a late fall wedding. The main lodge spread out over acres of property in rustic splendor, with the mountains in the backdrop. Winding paths encircled the large lake, and the trees were still clothed in colorful foliage. The weather held out and offered a crisp sixty-degree day with the dying sun drenching the woods in golden light and flickering warmth.

Arilyn knew she'd never forget the moment Kate began walking down the aisle. Instead of looking at her beaming friend, Kate found her attention grabbed by the groom. Elegant and handsome in his dark tuxedo, the once cynical lawyer who never believed in happy ever after watched his bride make her way toward him with tears shimmering in his eyes. Never taking his gaze off her, he ignored the faint ribbing of his groomsmen and stepped forward to take her hand from her mother's.

In that moment, Arilyn ached all over as if she had come down with a bad case of the flu. Joy and sheer envy choked her, along with a burning need to one day experience such love and devotion for herself. For always.

And then her gaze swung over to Stone.

He sat in the third aisle, eyes piercing into hers as though he knew her exact thoughts. Arilyn waited for him to look away. Duck his head. Ignore her raw want with a practiced ease.

Instead, he refused to retreat from her gaze, taking it all in, until she was the one who finally broke the spell.

"I like your friends."

She refocused her attention. The lively strains of popular music spilled from the huge speakers, and the DJ held the crowd with an expert ease. The ballroom featured a huge fireplace, gorgeous bay windows with views of the mountains, and rich wood floors. The tables were decorated with endless candles in fall colors, miniature dark pink and chocolate roses, and gaily wrapped boxes of truffles.

"They like you, too. Especially the guys."

He arched a brow. "Why?"

She gave him a good-natured shove. "You called Slade a big crybaby. Guys love that stuff. They think you're funny."

"Do you think I'm funny?" he asked.

"I think you're a smart-ass."

"Takes one to know one, little one."

"What were you talking to Kate and Slade about?"

He gave a half shrug. "A buddy back in the Bronx went through a divorce and used Slade as his lawyer. Slade took good care of him. I appreciated it."

She fiddled with the napkin. "Even Kennedy likes you. She's the toughest, you know."

"Funny, I thought you were." That comment startled her and made her meet his gaze. His face softened, and he reached out to trail a finger down her cheek. "What's wrong?"

"Nothing."

"I find it interesting how you all fit together. Kinnections was a brilliant idea."

"Yeah. Who would've thought a drunken evening would actually churn out a successful business?"

His brow lifted. "Drunken evening, huh? Didn't you tell me it was the result of a rational, long, thought-out discussion between businesswomen?"

She gave a half hiccup. "I lied."

"I should've known." They gazed at each other for a while, the air electric between them. "There's something else bothering you, though. You don't want your friends to like me?" He stared hard, searching for answers. "Ah, I know. Your ex charmed everyone, so now it's hard for you to introduce someone new into the mix. I'm just the transitional guy. Am I on the right track?"

Pain slammed into her chest. She jerked back, trying not to hiss at the raw well of emotions that tried to suck her down into a black pit. God, it still hurt. The way five years had passed and Jacob had known nothing about her real life. Sure, she told him things, but this was so different. So real. Stone engaged in conversation, shared a meal, and experienced her best friend's wedding. Jacob never would've attended. Oh, he probably would've soothed her by trying, then canceled at the last minute as he had done so many times before. She'd never had a real relationship. She'd been mourning something that never really existed.

"Do you not want me here, Arilyn?" he asked directly. "Is it too soon? Are you regretting taking me?"

The glimmer of hurt in his dark eyes helped her make a decision. Swallowing her pride, she took his hands and gave him the truth. "No, just the opposite. I love that you're here with me. That you met my friends, and they like you, and we can have fun and laugh together. I never had this, Stone. My ex-boyfriend, well, he didn't want anything to do with my real life."

Stone frowned. "I don't get it. You didn't go out on dates?"

"No. You see, he was my yoga instructor, and he wanted to keep our relationship private. At first, it was fun. Secret affairs usually are. But eventually, when I asked him to meet my girlfriends and take our relationship public, he refused." Shame heated her cheeks. Why had she never demanded more? She'd been so passive, taking what he could give her and telling herself she was satisfied. Lying was easier than forcing herself to make a hard decision to leave him behind. "He's never met Kate or Kennedy. Never been to Kinnections. Never had dinner with Poppy. He gave me . . . nothing. And I guess it was my fault, because I told him it was enough."

"How long did you date him?"

This was the worst, but she couldn't lie. "Five years."

She tried to look away, but he tipped up her chin. The heat from his hand and the delicious scent of his musky cologne warmed her. Stone Petty was deadly in a suit, confirming she might never look at him the same way again. With his staggering height, the navy blue fabric molded to each bulky muscle, stretched across his broad chest, hugged his massive shoulders. The red tie gave him a distinguished dash of style that made her knees weaken. His goatee was neatly trimmed, and he'd shaved, so his cheeks were silky smooth. It was a miracle she hadn't pulled him by the tie across the table and ravished him right there.

She had high hopes for later.

"Don't apologize for him being an asshole, little one," he said. "It's his loss. You have an amazing support system, and I'm honored you asked me to come with you."

Her heart melted into a gooey puddle; Arilyn wondered if it would ever recover. "Thank you." She paused. "Why are you being so nice to me?"

He laughed, then dropped his head to press a kiss against her lips. "'Cause I'm hoping to get lucky later."

She smiled against his lips. "What if I told you I was a bona fide guarantee?"

"I'd drag you out of this reception right now. Especially before that disco shit comes on, 'cause it always does. Or even worse, one of those 'I am woman, hear me roar' songs like 'I Will Survive.'"

On cue, "Single Ladies" by Beyoncé beat through the speakers. The women roared and began stomping and flailing their arms around, singing loudly to the familiar lyrics. Arilyn giggled at his disgusted expression. "And if I begged you to dance?"

"I'd say no. But I'll catch you when they put on a slow song. It'll give me an opp to get my hands all over you."

The sexy drawl to his gruff voice made shivers dance across her skin. Before she had time to counter, Kennedy, Kate, and Genevieve shrieked and grabbed her.

"Get up now! We're dancing!"

Stone put his hands up and shrank in his chair. "Take her. Just leave me, please. I'll keep your men company."

Kate's veil assaulted her face, Gen's fingers tickled her ribs, and Arilyn laughed uncontrollably as she was pushed and pulled onto the crowded dance floor. She caught sight of all the men with an expression that matched Stone's. Standing by the bar, they motioned her date over and closed in on him with male support, slapping shoulders, ribbing, and doing the classic testosterone dance boys learned when they were young.

Joy skittered through her. It was so very . . . normal. The way having a real boyfriend should be.

Of course, it was mostly about the sex, but she wasn't about to ruin a perfect night reminding herself that Stone belonged to her temporarily. At least, his temporary was more than she'd ever gotten before.

She was going to enjoy every moment.

STONE STOOD IN THE circle of men and watched the women dance. He tried not to shake his head at the awful moves they attempted in public, but their enthusiasm made up for their lack of true R&B talent.

Kennedy's man, Nate, held some kind of odd drink in his hand and seemed to be thinking the same thing. He grinned and jerked his head toward them. "Gotta give them credit for trying."

Stone chuckled. "What are you drinking?"

"Darth Maultini."

Stone raised his brow. "Cool, I love *Star Wars*. Arilyn said you used to work for NASA?"

"Yeah. Then when it disassembled, I focused on private space travel."

"Impressive. I don't know too many aerospace engineers."

Nate's face lit up. "You got the term right."

"Why wouldn't I?"

Wolfe laughed and clapped him on the shoulder. "'Cause everyone calls him a rocket scientist and pisses him off. Good to see you again, Stone, especially off duty."

Stone had met Wolfe over the summer, had the unfortunate task of arresting him once, and admitted he'd always liked the guy. With his serpent tat, badass attitude, and tenderness toward Genevieve, he was someone he could definitely hang with at the billiards room. "Good to see you out of a jail cell," he hit back, which gained him a hearty catcall all around.

The groom himself leaned in. "How's it going with Arilyn?" Slade asked curiously. "She's the most mysterious out of the group, you know. I'm glad she got rid of that Yoga Dude. Kate hated him."

His lips twitched. Something told him this group of men was just as bad at gossiping as the women. Another thing he liked about them. Stone enjoyed dishing the dirt. "Well, it's been a strange ride. Anger management classes aren't the ideal way to build a relationship. But after we decided we weren't mortal enemies, we figured we'd try dating."

Slade grinned. "Cool. She comes off real chill, but inside she's tougher than nails. She ever make you do hot yoga?"

Stone shuddered at the thought. "Hell, no. Even I have my limits."

"It was insane. Cranked the temps to over one hundred degrees and then drilled my ass like an army sergeant. I didn't think I'd survive."

Nate lifted a brow. "Hot yoga, huh? Now, that could be interesting."

Slade shook his head. "Not. My body cut out on me, and I got embarrassed in front of Kate. That shit's hard-core."

"Bet sex after that type of workout would be off the charts," Nate murmured thoughtfully.

They all fell silent. Huh. Stone never thought of it like that.

"Gotta keep Kennedy on her toes, huh?" Wolfe commented. "Maybe she'd finally agree to marry you if you exhaust her."

Nate looked calm and resolute. "She'll say yes. Just a matter of time. I already calculated the odds of how many times she can reject me, so my projections tell me within the next three hundred days I'll secure a yes."

"Or I can just throw her ass in jail until she agreed," Stone suggested.

The guys laughed. "Welcome to the club, dude," Slade said. "It's a bit crazy here, but we take care of our own."

Wolfe nodded. "Damn straight. And them, of course."

They watched as their women swung their hands up in the air off beat, tipsily stamping around the dance floor while Kate's veil whipped around the crowd. And for a little while, Stone realized how badly he wanted to be part of this group of men who knew how to joke and gossip, and loved their women without question or apology.

ARILYN DANCED HER ASS off, making a good-natured fool of herself as the crowd clapped around the bride in happy abandon. After a solid set of oldies but goodies, they limped off the dance floor to recover with cosmos and a quick summary of events.

"Wasn't the ceremony amazing?"

"I'm so glad you picked the goat cheese salad to offer. It was delicious."

"Did you see the way Slade teared up at the ceremony? I swear I almost lost it."

"I thought I was having a heart attack when the little button thing busted off your train, but no one's noticed."

"I'm not taking you to the damn bathroom again, let Arilyn do it next time. Seeing your white ass is not on my bucket list; that's Slade's."

Arilyn rolled her eyes at Kennedy's last statement, and her friend went strolling off to find Nate. She turned to go get Stone but caught sight of the group of females weaving their way across the floor toward her and Kate.

"Oh my God, Kate, you're married!"

Gen's older sister Alexa threw herself over, her inky corkscrew curls bobbing as she hugged Kate tight. She was flanked by her best friend, Maggie Ryan, looking elegant in a floor-length, figure-hugging red dress. Maggie shook her cinnamon hair at Alexa's emotion. She was a famous male underwear photographer, and Arilyn always found her dramatic ways and quick wit a blast to be around. "They were already living together, dude," Maggie drawled. "You're acting like they're having sex for the first time."

The third woman, a curvy, petite brunette with laughing dark eyes, waved her hand in the air. Carina was Maggie's sister-in-law. "Maggie, stop shocking these poor girls. Wedding-night sex is more exciting than any other. Well, not for me, since I was forced to marry Max and was pissed, but later it was the best."

Arilyn leaned forward, hoping to get the full story,

but Alexa was talking. "Puh-*leeze*. I had no wedding-night sex. Just a poker game that got out of control." She grinned cheekily. "But Nick and I made up for it later."

Maggie let out a breath. "Am I the only one who had great wedding-night sex? Damn. And Michael and I were faking a marriage the whole time. Who would've known?"

Kate's blue eyes were wide. Arilyn cleared her throat. "Umm, guys, think you can give us the background on this? You all seem so perfect and happy."

The three women laughed. "Oh, we are!" Alexa said. "But it didn't start off that way for any of us. Anyway, we came to say this is an amazing wedding and we're so happy for you, honey. Thanks for inviting us."

Kate sniffed. "I love you. Gen's been like a sister to me, and you're my family."

That made Alexa's blue eyes fill up, and then she was hugging Kate and Gen and crying. Arilyn felt her own throat tighten. Weddings were such a harvest of emotions.

A masculine voice rang out over the music. "Ah, here we go. My wife will always be the one to lead the charge of happy tears." Alexa's husband, Nick, decked out in a designer charcoal suit, winked at his wife and slipped an arm around her waist. The naked adoration on his face made her want to sigh.

Nick's sister, Maggie, gave him a friendly poke. "Coming from Mr. Sappy himself. Ever since you had those gorgeous girls, you've gone soft."

Arilyn looked up as the elegant Italian man strode over and leaned in to whisper something in Maggie's ear. Maggie's cheeks turned red, which made Carina giggle. "Who's the softie?" Carina teased. "Your hubby owns you, babe. Admit it."

"Never. I just let him think so," Maggie said.

Michael nuzzled his wife's neck and winked. His Italian accent curled like rich smoke and caressed her ears. "Ah, *cara*, don't make me prove to you who's the real boss in the household. We'll be up all night again."

Maggie grinned wickedly. "Promises, promises."

The third man, a tall, elegant James Bond look-alike—Pierce Brosnan, of course—took his place next to Carina. He was deadly sexy, with thick dark hair and piercing blue eyes. The protective way he tucked her by his side told Arilyn they were just as crazy about each other as the other couples were. "Why do we always talk about sex when we're together?" he commented drily, his hand stroking his wife's belly. "What happened to interesting topics like business, politics, and cuisine?"

Maggie rolled her eyes. "Says you, who can't keep your hands off Carina. When is baby number two due, Max?"

Carina patted her small belly, which was just beginning to show. "Spring. Baby Max is just as excited as Daddy to get a little brother or sister." Her brows drew together in a frown. "I have to finish my collection before chaos lets loose again. My show is on Valentine's Day, so you all must come. We'll go to dinner and celebrate afterward."

"I don't want you stressed-out like last time," Max said firmly. "I'll cut back on my work hours so you have more time to paint."

Carina was a well-known artist who brought erotic

art to a whole new generation. Arilyn was amazed at the power couples before them. How did they manage? They had huge careers, thriving businesses, children, and were still madly in love?

She looked at Kate. Slade and Stone, who had joined them, stood behind them listening to the whole conversation.

Kate finally said what they were all probably thinking. "How do you do it?" she burst out.

Alexa cocked her head. "Do what?"

"Everything!" Arilyn said. "How do you stay in love while managing careers and babies and stress and life and family? What's the secret?"

A shocked silence fell over the group. Alexa looked at Nick. Michael rested his chin on Maggie's head. Max placed his hand over his wife's belly.

Then they all burst into hysterical laughter.

"Oh, boy, it's official!" Alexa announced. "We're old."

Maggie groaned. "Yep, getting asked by the younger generation how you handle it all sucks. Should we tell them the super secret to lifetime bliss?"

The group leaned in. Arilyn held her breath.

Maggie snorted out a laugh. "Gotcha! Trust me, there is no super secret. It's a lot of hard work."

Carina giggled. "And fights. Lots and lots of fights. Oh, and making up. And wrong choices."

"And crying, lots of crying," Alexa added.

"But it's all worth it, as Mama Conte would say," Maggie pointed out.

Then the three women linked arms. "You'll figure it out. We did. Let's go dance."

The couples left for the dance floor.

Kate sighed. "Damn them. Why don't they just tell us the real truth?"

Slade leaned over and kissed his new wife. "'Cause we already know, baby. And I'm going to make sure we never forget."

Kate reached up and slid her arms around his neck. For a moment, they were lost in each other, alone. Just a bride and groom with a brand-new life stretching ahead of them.

"I love you, Slade Montgomery."

"And I love you, Kate Montgomery."

They kissed. And when Arilyn turned, Stone was staring at them with a mix of emotions in his eyes, so raw and so real, she wondered if she'd ever figure him out. Because for just a second, it looked like he also wanted what they had.

But that was impossible.

Arilyn reached out and touched his arm. Wanting to belong to him for a sliver in time, she sought connection. He answered the call, drawing her close, his arms wrapped tight around her waist. The music pounded, and guests chattered, and couples whispered.

"I want you."

His words were stark. Stripped bare. No pretty words, or promises, or poetry. Yet Arilyn felt his wanting in her soul, and bones, and heart. She lifted herself up on the toes of her pretty shoes, and whispered the only answer in his ear.

"Take me home."

fifteen

ARILYN IMAGINED A few things on their first night together. Pulling at each other's clothes, slipping into a world of dreamy sensuality with little awkwardness and an all-encompassing, blistering heat. Somehow, in her fantasy, they didn't walk into her bungalow at midnight and deal with a series of fantasy-popping occurrences beginning with Mrs. Blackfire.

They reached the porch and the slam of a door echoed in the quiet. The scrape of the walker warned her before she heard the familiar, hissing voice. "Officer Petty! There's been a break-in at Arilyn's house. I called the police, but they refused to send someone, and I'm going to sue the town."

She heard his quick intake of breath. Hmm, he still wasn't practicing the technique of drawing the air from his belly up to his chest. She'd have to go over that in class again on Monday. "If the police didn't send someone, they didn't think there was a break-in," he pointed out. "What did you see?"

Her face lit with the excitement of a crime. "A young girl. Small, blond, braces. Wearing jeans with one of those shirts that show off her belly button, which is kind of ridiculous in this type of weather, and way too old for her."

Arilyn turned, swinging her high heels from her fingers. She grasped for her own patience. Was it so wrong just to want to go inside and have sex without talking to anyone? "That's Tina, my dog walker, Mrs. Blackfire. She was here to walk Robert. I'm watching him while Kate's on her honeymoon."

"Oh." The brief disappointment quickly disappeared. "But she had something under her arm! She stole something from you! Why didn't Patrick walk the dog? I don't trust these young kids anymore. They don't know the value of honest work."

"Poppy had a field trip today, so I had Tina take over. I let her borrow a few books of mine; that's probably what you saw under her arm."

Her face fell. "Well, you should check anyway." She pointed toward Stone. "I wasn't pleased with the police response. They said that since she had a key, she wasn't a burglar. In my day, it would've held true, but this is a new age. Burglars have keys now! We need to be watching every second!"

Arilyn tried not to groan, forcing a smile and opening her door. "I agree. I'll talk to Stone about it. Good night, Mrs. Blackfire!"

She gave a small humph, then disappeared back inside. Arilyn figured she had a few minutes before the telescope began moving. She motioned toward the windows. "Pull those blinds down so she can't spy," Arilyn hissed.

Stone chuckled, moved forward, and froze.

Robert, Kate's paraplegic pit bull, came racing down the hallway at top speed. Happy and desperate for company, he dragged his back legs behind him with expert ease, his large body hauling his way toward Stone for a classic doggy greeting.

Pure fear carved out the lines of Stone's face. His skin looked clammy in the hall light, and he huddled against the door, watching the dog bound closer, stuck in a memory of horror where he couldn't fight back.

Oh, God, she'd forgotten. Pit bulls. The bite. His fear of dogs.

Robert.

"Robert, stop!" she whipped out, firming her voice and stepping in front of Stone to block the path.

The dog skidded to a halt. Eyes filled with trepidation for doing something wrong, he whimpered low and ducked his head.

"Shhh, sweetheart, it's okay." Arilyn dropped to the ground and hugged him, pressing her forehead to his in a gesture of humbleness. "You're a good boy. But Stone doesn't realize that yet. You need to give him a chance to get used to you before knocking him over for kisses. Understood?"

Robert wriggled, licking her cheek gently. She snuggled, reached out to check his bladder, soothing him with a pat. "You did good tonight. We have to be careful of bladder infections while Mommy and Daddy are away. Let's get you hooked up and bring you outside."

She straightened and walked toward Stone, who watched the whole encounter with wary eyes. "I'm so sorry," she whispered, reaching out to place her hands against his chest. "I forgot to tell you Robert is a pit bull. He doesn't have a mean bone in his body, Stone, I swear. Kate saved him when a car crushed his back legs. I know he looks big, but his back legs are useless. He's a good dog."

Stone let out a breath. Color seeped back into his skin. "I'm sorry for being an ass," he muttered. He wiped his palms down his pants, his gaze stuck on the dog, who was waiting patiently to say hello. "He just looks like—looks like—"

"The dog who bit you," she said softly. "I know. But Robert isn't like that. Can you give him a chance?" He remained silent but nodded. "Thank you. I have to take him out first. I'll be a minute. Why don't you grab a drink and make yourself comfortable?"

Keeping his distance, he skirted around Robert's excitedly shaking body, and put the high counter between them. Arilyn hooked up the dog's scooter, adjusting the straps, and let him go free.

Laughing, she watched him race over the lawn, round and round as the wheels turned. His head thrown back in doggy abandon, he breathed in the cold night air and managed to go to the bathroom under the Tree of Spite. After some of his energy had been spent, she brought him back inside, unhooked the scooter, and grabbed his box of treats from the table.

"Peanut butter or bacon?" she asked.

He barked twice. Stone jerked back, startled.

Arilyn laughed. "Bacon it is." He took the treat gently between his teeth and raced back down the hall to finish the snack in his special orthopedic bed with his favorite purple bunny squeaker toy.

"He knew what you were saying?" Stone asked in disbelief.

"Yep. Kate's had him for years. He's extremely smart."

He walked around and knelt to examine the scooter. "And he's able to move around using this cart?"

"Yes. It was specially made for him. Allows him to run and play like the other dogs."

"So he had a tough life," Stone murmured.

"Some of the most extraordinary animals I know had it tough." She paused. "Some extraordinary people, too."

He turned. Stared. Suddenly, the domestic ease leaked away, replaced with a simmering sexual heat that softened her limbs and made her thighs tremble. Playtime was officially over.

Arilyn couldn't wait.

"Come here," he commanded. She shivered from the dark, sensual tone of his voice and obeyed. Each step closer tightened the knot in her belly, until she stood before him, waiting. Her hair was curled and secured with a dozen bobby pins to cascade from an elaborate knot on top of her head. With infinite patience, he reached over and began pulling out each pin, one by one. Taking his time, he pulled his fingers through the strands, rubbing her scalp, until a low moan caught in her throat. Like a cat, she lifted her head for more, enjoying the luxurious sensation of being taken care of. Finally, when her hair fell loose around her waist, he stroked her cheeks.

"Do you know how beautiful you are?"

A flush heated her cheeks. "I'm glad you think so."

"I know so. Sometimes, I gaze at you demonstrating those yoga poses and lose my breath. You remind me of a dancer. Your body is like an instrument, begging to be played and worshipped. Begging to be fucked."

She shuddered, the dirty words pushing her arousal higher. Her panties were wet between her thighs, and a deep aching made her want to howl. "No one's ever talked to me like that," she admitted, pressing her forehead against his chest.

"No hiding." He pushed her gently away, forcing her head up to meet his gaze. Pupils dilated, she sank into a seething blackness filled with lust and need and a hunger so real she wanted to cry with pleasure. "Not between us. Not ever. I'm not like the men in your past. I won't tell you lies or make love to you with tenderness. I'm rough, and crude, and loud. I like sex in all its messy, raw ways. I want to make you come all night, in ways you never imagined. I want you to say all those dirty things you fantasized about in my ear and make them all come true. Do you understand, little one? I'm not just going to be your lover tonight. I'm going to take every shred of you and demand each last piece of your darkest, secret soul. Are you ready for this? I'm giving you one last chance."

Arilyn couldn't run if the demons of hell were about to seize her soul. Held transfixed to the floor by his delicious body heat, and scent, and words, and touch, the room spun around her and she gave up, gave over, and gave him everything he wanted.

"I want this," she whispered. Every muscle in her body shook like an answering storm. "I want you."

His smile was slow and full of promise.

"Good. Now take off your clothes."

Pushed by the need to experience everything he promised, she reached back and unhooked the clasp on her dress, then drew the zipper down. The sound cut harshly through the thick silence. Without pause, she wiggled the bodice down her body and let the chocolate chiffon pool at her feet. Since the dress was strapless and she wasn't well-endowed, she wore no bra.

His quick indrawn breath told her he appreciated the lack of underwear, and her skin flushed with awareness. Standing before him, the only item keeping her from being fully naked was the scrap of black lacy panties covering the apex between her thighs.

His gaze roved over her like an intimate touch, probing and exploring every part of her with a fierce appreciation that made her feel beautiful. Arilyn knew what he saw. She'd come to terms with her body image and learned to love who she was. Yoga taught her to care for and appreciate the skin she lived in. Yes, she was slim hipped, with a boyish figure and small breasts. She was no hourglass-curved temptress many men lusted after. Her pale skin held a scattering of freckles, and a funny mole on her upper thigh, and her feet were way too big ever to be called delicate. But it was her body, and she lived in it well, so Arilyn tilted her head up, drew her shoulders back, and let him drink his fill.

"I always knew you'd be extraordinary," he murmured. "But still the reality has me weeping."

A smile touched her lips. "I thought you weren't going to offer me poetry."

"I also said I tell the truth. Turn around so I can see your luscious ass." She turned slowly, taking her time, enjoying his frank gaze and the obvious erection that told her she was beautiful to him. When he spoke again, his voice was thick with lust. "Now take off the panties. Slow."

She hooked her fingers under the elastic and dipped down, dragging the skimpy material over her hips, thighs, calves, and kicking them away from her feet. She kept her pussy neatly trimmed but not bare, preferring a more natural state. His low growl told her he liked it.

"Oh, I want to make you do so many bad things, Arilyn," he drawled. "All for me." Still fully clothed, he began walking around her, close but not touching, until he teased her with his scent and body heat trapped beneath a suit of civility. "Later, I'm going to make you touch yourself. I'm going to watch you orgasm by your own fingers, so I can see every move you like to ensure your pleasure. I'm going to feast and devour you whole. But we have plenty of time for that. For now, I want you to walk ahead of me into your bedroom."

Heart tripping madly against her chest, she tried to breathe while she led him down the hall into the bedroom. Knowing her bare ass was on display, she gave an extra swing to her hips, enjoying her role of Eve and temptress. It was as if the secret bad girl inside burst out and refused to be caged again. With Stone, she could be everything she wondered about. She felt safe with him.

"Will Robert be okay alone out there?" he asked.

"Yes, he sleeps in the living room."

"Good." He kicked the door closed with his foot, unknotted his tie, and slid it from around his neck. The fluttering of red silk caught her attention as his tie slipped to the floor. He watched her face and his eyes darkened. "You like that? Maybe I'll bind you with my tie. Keep you open to anything I want to do to you."

Oh, she knew about kink and spanking and secret games played by adventurous couples. She just never thought she was in the same field, but the idea of Stone tying her up turned her on to such an extent, she didn't know what to do. He laughed low as if he knew exactly what she was thinking. "Ah, little one, we're going to have so much fun together." He shrugged out of his jacket, flicked open the buttons on his shirt, and closed the distance. "But not tonight. Right now, I need you to take away this brutal urge I have to mark you in every way." He tugged her close, so her naked breasts pressed against the hair on his chest and her nipples hardened. "Open your mouth and kiss me."

She parted her lips. He ducked his head.

It wasn't a kiss as much as a possession. His tongue drove forth with no teasing foreplay, just a carnal hunger that held no politeness or civility, just as he had warned. She clung to him, taking every swipe of his tongue and demanding more, drinking in the spicy male essence that beat from his core, drunk on everything he could give her. Arilyn moaned and rose up on tiptoe, lost in his kiss, surrendering not only to the embrace but also to the night stretching before them in all its wild glory.

He wasn't gentle. His teeth bruised, nipped. His hand tangled in her long hair and tugged hard, the prickling at her scalp reminding her he owned her for his pleasure. With his other hand, he stroked her breast, plumping, his thumb flicking back and forth over her sensitive nipple until it peaked and lengthened, shooting sparks of arousal to her core. Her body melted in happy confusion, so many sensations building inside, until her clit throbbed for attention and she grew wet and swollen.

As she scissored her thighs to achieve the needed pressure she craved, he broke the kiss, laughing low against her mouth. "My greedy girl, you're so sweet. I've been dreaming of how you'll taste and I refuse to be rushed." He hoisted her up and walked to the bed, laying her down on the mattress. "This is what I dreamed of, you spread out for me, skin flushed, eyes soft and needy. So fucking beautiful."

"Take off your clothes," she demanded, her voice husky.

He obeyed, quickly removing his shirt and pants, shucking off his shoes with expert ease. He stood by the bed, letting her study him the same way he'd studied her. Arilyn propped herself up on her elbows, taking in every last mouthwatering inch of him.

Dear God, she'd never seen a man built quite like Stone Petty. From his rock-hard muscles, to his impressive stature, to the huge erection pulsing between his legs, he was larger-than-life. Larger than any man she'd ever seen. For an instant, worry seized her, wondering how he'd possibly fit with his wide girth, but then he grasped her ankles and she stopped thinking.

Slowly, he pulled her thighs apart. Wide. Wider. The cool air rushed over her pussy and contrasted with the burning heat tearing her apart. He licked his lips and leaned over the bed, his shoulders keeping her legs spread wide, trapping her deep in the mattress. His palms slid up her trembling belly and stroked lightly, peppering her skin with goose bumps. The amazing sensations of cold and hot, hard and soft assailed her. Another moan tore from her lips.

He looked up from her body and slowly smiled. "Now let's see how many times you call me 'Officer.'"

He dipped his head.

Sanity was ripped away from her inch by ragged inch. He was the devil himself, with his wicked tongue and lips and teasing strokes. He settled in and refused to be rushed, even with the urgent lifting of her hips, grinding against his mouth with no shame, only the need for release. Those soft lips sucked at her clit with just enough pressure to turn her on but not get her off. His tongue rubbed and licked down her slit, over her labia, making hungry noises that buzzed vibrations through her body.

Oh, she begged. Every inch of her ached and burned, her muscles straining for what only he could give her.

"Please, Stone, I need to—oh, God, please."

He circled her aching, hard clit with the tip of his tongue, then massaged it with his thumb. Pinpricks of light marred her vision. She'd never been so desperate to come in her life, until she finally understood the darkness in sex, the ultimate, encompassing need to do anything for the orgasm being held from her.

"You're so wet. So hot. You're coming apart right underneath me, little one. Your responses are perfect. Ask me again."

"Stone, please let me come!"

"Yes, baby, now, against my mouth, give it all to me." Curling his finger, he plunged inside her tight channel while his tongue increased the pressure on her clit, licking harder and harder and then—

She screamed. She cried. She yelled. The orgasm hit her like a train wreck, squeezing every muscle in her body with an agony of pleasure, all she could do was shake beneath him and surrender. He never stopped, his tongue and teeth nibbling and licking her right up to another orgasm, letting her free-fall in space.

Arilyn fell back into the mattress, giving herself over to him. She watched from heavy-lidded eyes as he donned a condom, paused before her dripping center, and began to fill her inch by slow inch.

Her body reawoke. The delicious friction and pressure as he invaded and took over her body was too much. She flung her head back and forth against the pillow, moaning, not even sure if she was fighting him or urging him closer. His fingers entwined with hers, holding her hands trapped against each side of her head, not stopping until he was buried balls-deep within her. Arilyn blinked up at his face: teeth clenched, sweat dripping from his brow, his gaze pinning her as helplessly as his body.

"Too big," she gasped. "Can't."

"You can. Fuck, you're so tight, little one." He moved an inch, going even deeper, until she felt split apart. Slowly he rocked back and forth as she opened up further, every muscle in her body squeezing him. "You fit perfectly. Holy shit, you're coming again, Arilyn, I can feel it. Let go, baby, give it to me."

"Too much—I can't—oh!" And then he pulled back out and slammed inside of her so fast and so deep and so hard, she climaxed again, surrendering to the brutal, aching pleasure that almost bordered on pain.

She rode out the climax, whimpering deep in her throat, and hung on as he pounded inside her body with all the rough violence and lust she craved, until he shouted her name, giving her his orgasm, never pausing until there was nothing left of either of them.

Somehow, he managed to roll over so he wasn't crushing her. He spooned against her, his arms slipping around her stomach, keeping her close, his lips buried in the crook of her neck. Surrounded by his warmth and delicious smell, she relaxed completely in his embrace.

"What did you do to me?" he whispered in her ear.

She managed to rouse herself enough to answer his question with one of her own. "What did *you* do to *me*?"

Arilyn knew they spoke of something bigger than the sex, but she couldn't wrap her mind around it. She did the only thing left.

She lost consciousness.

STONE STARED INTO THE darkness, listening to her steady breathing.

Well, wasn't he completely screwed? In a good way. And in a very, very bad way.

He knew exactly what he expected from fucking Arilyn Meadows. Oh, definitely orgasms. Pleasure. Some ups and downs, since they were so different and annoyed the crap out of each other. A few laughs. Then a clean pathway back to the single life, with a clear conscience.

Now?

Not so much.

Stone tried to figure it out. What had happened? Yes, she called to him on a level he'd never experienced before. The physical connection overwhelmed him, but when he slid deep inside her body, felt her core clenching him with those silky muscles, he wasn't just thinking about her sweet pussy. No, instead he became entranced by the open vulnerability in her grass-green eyes. The way her mouth opened in a breathy gasp, and that look of wonder on her face when he surged inside her, making him feel like Spider-Man and Superman and fucking Thor all rolled up into one holy mix of hotness. The sting of her nails digging into his shoulders, and the way her body fit perfectly to his, like they belonged together. But the worst? Oh, God, the worst part of all scared the living bejesus out of him.

It was the feeling of peace and homecoming when they were connected. As if they were meant for each other.

Stone closed his eyes and tried to take those deep yoga breaths she had taught him. He fought the need to run for the exit and never return. This mix of emotions was brand-new and more threatening than the Headless Horseman on Halloween. He was in it for the sex, Stone reminded himself. It had been a long time. Of course, she looked at him like he was a hero. She'd been stuck with a dickhead for five long years and she was hungry for connection. By morning, they'd both be over the strange feelings.

That had to be it. Right?

The alternative was not allowed.

He tried to ease into sleep for a well-needed nap,

but even though he'd just had the best climax of his life, he wanted her again. She stirred, mumbling into the pillow, and the scent of musky sex and coconut body lotion flooded his nostrils. Her body was magnificent, but even more so was her pride and grace in the way she carried herself. As if she realized on her own that she was enough. That kind of confidence was sexy as hell, and he couldn't wait to have more of her.

Stone stroked her creamy white skin, tracing the scattering of freckles in a sensual game of connect the dots. His thumb traveled up to the sweet curve of her breast, over her nipple, which stiffened up to meet him, practically begging for his tongue.

Stone didn't fight it. Leaning over, he sighed and tongued her nipple, nibbling, until she woke with a moan spilling from her lips. He smiled and didn't lose his pace. She rolled over and offered herself up to him with an open surrender that made him grow back to rock-hard status. Twining her fingers behind his neck, she arched up, asking for more.

He moved slower this time, being more thorough as he tasted every inch of her. The sensitive curve of her hip, behind her knee, the part where neck met shoulder. As if she knew this time was different, she didn't push the pace but met him stroke for stroke. Her hands fisted him and rubbed up and down his dick in slow, silky movements that had precum spilling onto her fingers. She rubbed the tip, and kept her grip strong and tight, bringing him right to the edge in a matter of moments.

They fell back into each other like a poem in which each stanza eased into the next. The stroke of her hand, the slide of her tongue, the warmth of her breath, the lilting sound of his name on her lips. It was as if they'd spent an eternity waiting for each other rather than engaging in one night of carnal sex. Stone fought hard, but when she climbed on top of him and took him deep inside, he almost sighed. The heat grew to blistering proportions, yet she rode him at a slow, intense pace, building up to the rhythm that would allow them both to shatter together.

She cried out. Her body arched, thrusting her small breasts high in the air, red hair streaming down her back. He watched every precious moment, taking it in, and then she collapsed forward onto his chest with him still inside her.

Stone's second orgasm was even more intense than the first, as if the Fates mocked his plan and were having a joke at both of their expenses. This was the crap they spoke of in chick flick movies and Jane Austen novels. The garbage they spewed when sex and lust mixed with love and commitment. He didn't believe in any of it; yet, as his balls tightened up and he exploded, releasing his seed, a possessive ferociousness claimed him, driving him to take her again and remind her she belonged to him.

Mine, his mind screamed. *She's mine.*

Shut up. This is about sex.

The voice fell quiet. Panting, trying to gather his sanity, he fell back to the bed with her still cuddled against his chest. Time ticked by. They lay quietly in the dark. He waited for her to ask him her endless questions that he couldn't answer.

But she didn't speak.

And once again, her breathing deepened and she slept.

Stone lay awake for a long time, wondering what he was going to do.

sixteen

"STONE! WAKE UP!"

"Five more minutes," he groaned, rolling away. His body was shaken harder than a bad eighties Polaroid picture, causing him to open one eye. Where was he? Oh, Arilyn's place. After sex. Great sex. Hell, the best sex he had ever had in his entire life, including when he lost his virginity to Sally Poole in the tenth grade. And that had been epic.

She squinted those incredible green eyes and moved closer. Poked him as if he were a dead body she was trying to investigate. He held back a laugh. Damned if she wasn't as cute in the morning as when he got her all riled. Her hair was a tangled mess, her eye makeup was smeared, and a crease from the sheets ran across her right cheek.

"Stone! You have to go!"

His other eye winked open. Huh? His gaze dropped to where her peach-tinted nipples peeked from over the covers. Had they really fallen into slumber after only two times? He needed to make up for his lack of planning. The emotion stuff actually threw him off his game, but he'd get back to the main goal of wringing as much pleasure from her as possible and—what? "Wait. Are you throwing me out?"

She gave an impatient huff and climbed out of the

bed. The morning light spilled through the window and bounced off her skin. She was gorgeous. She seemed frantic to find something she had lost, opened up a closet, and muttered to herself as she finally tugged something out and wrapped it around her. The silky black robe clung to her skin the way he wanted to. He lost the vision of her bare ass and mourned. "You have to go! I completely forgot that Pinky is at your house, and she'll be scared in a new environment, and you need to feed her and change the water and the poor thing hasn't been walked." She nibbled at her lower lip, ginger brows snapped in a frown, and took out a pair of striped socks. Hopping on one leg, she donned the socks while he enjoyed the bobbing up and down of her breasts. "Are you listening to me? You need to get home to Pinky."

"I heard you." Only the first day of being a dog owner and he hated it. Why the hell would anyone want to leave a warm bed and a gorgeous half-naked woman to take care of a *dog*? Were people truly nuts? He sat up and gave her his best come-hither smile. "Half an hour more won't make a difference to Pinky. But it will to me." His dick screamed with happiness as she seemed to struggle with the temptation.

Then she belted her robe tighter. "After you take care of Pinky."

"I live across town!" he bellowed. "You're seriously kicking me out this early? Pinky won't care. Hell, she probably pooped in the house anyway; I'll deal with it later."

The familiar stubborn lines of her face told him a battle was about to be launched. "Pinky needs structure and routine. She needs to trust you. Leaving her alone with no care will only enforce what the old owners did to her. I'm sorry, Stone, but fostering is a full-time job and it's important. You have to take it seriously."

He glared at her, still aroused, and now mightily pissed off. "I didn't volunteer for this shit," he reminded her. "You forced me, remember? You can't call me out on not doing a job right that I never wanted in the first place!"

She pressed her lips together. "Semantics. Now, get dressed, take care of Pinky, and we'll see where that leaves us later."

Forget this! Now, she wasn't gonna get any because he was mad. He got out of bed buck naked and stabbed a finger at her. "Fine. I'll go and take care of the rat fink. But next time you want a bit of morning sex, you'll . . . you'll . . ."

"Yes?" she prodded, her eyes filled with amusement.

"You'll be denied!"

He ignored her quiet laughter, stomped to the bathroom, and slammed the door. He dressed in his suit again, totally flaunting the whole man-whore walk-of-confidence vibe, and made his way into the kitchen. This time Robert didn't come flying at him but looked up from his food bowl with an eager look on his face. Stone smothered a groan. The dog would be with Arilyn for two weeks, so he should try to make friends so he wasn't scared shitless. Hunkering down, trying not to wince, he held out his hand. "Here, boy. Ugh, Robert. Good boy."

The dog couldn't wag his tail, but his ear pricked. He dragged himself away from his precious food bowl, moving slowly, as if he knew Stone was nervous. Finally, he got close enough to push his wet nose into Stone's palm, nuzzling.

Huh. Kinda cute.

As if he realized he'd gotten through round one, he moved an inch closer and rubbed his head against his hand, giving him a quick lick. Stone's muscles relaxed, and a sense of comfort flowed through him. Reaching out with the other hand in careful motions, Stone stroked his body, eliciting a rumble of happiness and another lick.

Arilyn laughed. "I knew it wouldn't take you long to be friends. There hasn't been a person Robert hasn't won over."

Stone looked up. With her shapely bare legs peeking out from under the silk, her socks pulled up to mid-calf, he longed to take her in his arms and kiss her senseless. Drag her back to bed for the entire day, until they both couldn't walk normally. Instead, he tried to hold on to his grouchiness at being thrown out.

"Can I have any coffee before I go?"

"Sure, I have a pot here. Black?"

"Yes."

She fixed him a mug, and with one last pat, Stone stood and took a grateful sip of the hot brew.

Then choked.

"What the hell is this?" he asked. "This isn't coffee!"

She cocked her head with confusion. "Yes, it is. Organic beans specially roasted."

He stared at the mug in horror. "Is this decaffeinated?" he whispered.

"Of course. Caffeine is bad for you, Stone. Once you get used to it, you'll never notice the difference."

He threw the cup in the sink, trying to hold on to his temper. God help him, they'd break up right now if they didn't straighten this out. "Like I didn't notice you took away my meat and replaced it with frozen soy? No. Arilyn, I need real coffee. Black. With lots of caffeine. I don't care if it's not good for you, I can't function without it."

She stuck up her chin in that stubborn way of hers. "Caffeine is an addiction like smoking."

"I'm not a saint. I'm grateful I haven't fallen off the wagon with the smoking, but if you take away my coffee, I'll be institutionalized. This is not a gray area. It's make-or-break time."

He stared at her, the battle waging between them, and finally, she relaxed, her lips curving in a small smile. "Okay."

"Okay?"

"Yes. I'll go to the store and get real coffee for you."

He studied her with suspicion. "Why did you give in so easy?"

She laughed that half giggle he already adored. "Because this is important to you. Stone, I know many of my choices seem weird to you. And I respect yours, too. I just don't want you stressed or sick or unhappy. That's all."

That's all. Yet it was more than he'd ever had before. Imagine a woman caring about him on such a level, beyond sex or a few laughs. The possibility dangled in front of him like a huge, juicy carrot, but he was no vegetarian and he knew the real deal. So Stone ignored it.

"Thanks. I better go." He turned to take off, but she called out his name. "Yeah?"

"Aren't you going to kiss me good-bye?"

Her honest question did him in. He took two big steps, picked her up, and kissed her thoroughly, senselessly, and with a deep satisfaction. He slid her back down to the ground, loving the wonderment and desire on her face as she looked at him.

"I'll come back."

She smiled. "Good."

He walked out with a lighter step, and a lighter heart.

STONE STARED AT THE dog. Frustration nipped at his nerves, along with something else. An emotion that bothered the shit out of him.

Guilt.

"I didn't leave you for long," he explained. Yes, he'd discovered a small yellow puddle by the door, but he didn't know what to expect with the house training. Arilyn had brought him an endless amount of supplies, from food, to toys, to treats, and even a pink doggy bed that looked ridiculous in his masculine house. At least he had a yard to offer, and since he lived a bit outside town, there weren't many neighbors.

Thank God, he hadn't invested in the carpeting, since he had a feeling Pinky would take a while to get her bladder on schedule. He'd walked her outside, and she'd done fine. He'd changed her water and given her food, which she'd actually eaten a bit of. But now she just sat in front of him, staring at him like she expected something.

"What is it you want?"

The catatonic distance had eased from her eyes, but she was still dead quiet, never barked, and seemed to slip in and out of that place in her head she lived in during the time of her abuse. Stone wasn't a dog whisperer, so he figured he'd just keep doing what he was doing and eventually give her to someone who could actually help.

Arilyn.

He glanced at his watch. After he showered, changed, and had some real bacon, real coffee, and real butter with toast, he felt energized. Figured he'd go back to her place and spend the next few hours before his shift.

"Listen, I gotta go back to Arilyn's. I'll swing by and take you out before I have to get to work though."

Pinky gazed back at him with sad eyes.

Fuck. "I'm not a dog person," he explained. "I'm glad you seem a bit better, but I'm not sure what you want. I can't bring you over there because she has a dog." Stone had seen Pinky turn into a shaking, growling lunatic when she got too close to another dog. Robert would give her a heart attack by his size alone. He strolled over, turned on the television, and clicked on Animal Planet. "See, you can watch TV. I'll keep a few lights on. You'll have a nice, relaxing day."

More staring. She never even blinked, just kept her serious gaze locked on his. Why wouldn't she grow hair? Those white tufts on top of her head made her look like a damn gremlin, and who knew skin could be a light brown color? When she opened her mouth to eat, her teeth poked out, looking razor sharp, but the overbite was just plain weird. It was as if her teeth weren't aligned with her mouth so her jaw jutted out. Most dogs he'd seen looked more normal. She was a little thing, too. But the sores had healed. She'd always be ugly as sin, but at least she would be healthy. And safe.

"Okay, so have a good day." Stone grabbed his keys, wallet, and phone. Walked to the door. Opened it. "See ya."

He glanced back. She didn't budge, but a slight tremor shook her body. As if by being left alone again, she'd be damaged somehow. Ridiculous. He was being an ass. He was leaving.

Stone shut the door and headed toward his car. Son of a bitch. He was going to have more great sex, go to work, and deal with the rat fink later. No way was a dog going to cramp his style now. No way.

He drove away with a roar of the engine, refusing to look back.

"WHAT THE HELL IS that?"

Devine stood on the curb, gaping at Stone as if he'd just announced he'd gone gay. He shifted the weight under his arm and glared. "A dog. What do you think it is? Get in."

They were outside the police station, ready to do a drive-by check. The early afternoon had been perfect. Ideal. When he returned, Arilyn greeted him at the doorway with no clothes, proving she had a secret bad girl inside he'd managed to spring loose. They'd spent the rest of the morning in bed, exploring all the ways he could make her scream, and he'd barely had enough time to get back to Pinky before racing to work.

Another small puddle greeted him along with a suffering, mournful expression of doggy unhappiness. Stone took the dog out, redid her water-food routine, and ripped out a new squeaky toy. Pinky refused to touch it. Just sat in the middle of the room, refusing to budge but asking for something he couldn't seem to figure out.

"See, this is why I don't have a dog," he offered, buttoning up his uniform. "This is also why I got a divorce. I'm busy. I don't know how to make you happy. I have to go to work and bring home the money. Do you understand?" Stone finished dressing, grabbed his stuff, and paused at the door. "I gotta go. I'll be back in eight hours and we'll spend some time together. Okay?"

Nothing. Well, what the hell did he expect? He was talking to a damn dog.

Frustrated and pissed off, he opened the door.

Then heard it.

Whimpering.

Stone turned his head. Pinky had dropped her head in full grieving mode. Body shaking, little moans of distress emitted from her mouth. A shiver raced down his spine. No. Oh, God, this was worse than a woman crying. He rubbed his hands over his face and prayed for it to stop. How could she go from isolated silence to codependency so soon?

"Don't. I can't take you to work. I drive in a police car and you'd hate it."

Pinky lifted her head and whined again. Took a few steps toward the door, cocking her head as if asking the all-important question. *Can I go with you please?*

"Absolutely not. You'll be fine. Hang out, take a nap, chew on a bone. I'll be back later."

He shut the door. A few steps toward the car, he stopped cold, listening to the eerie, sad whine of the dog. Crying.

Fuck. Fuck, fuck, fuck.

He opened the door, grabbed the ridiculous pink collar and leash Arilyn had bought, and scooped Pinky up in his arms. The dog barely took up his whole hand, and immediately snuggled into the crook of his arm. Then Stone did the unthinkable, the impossible, and the insane.

He brought Pinky to work with him.

Devine was still staring in shock through the window at the dog sitting in the backseat. "That thing is a dog?" he asked in a high-pitched tone. "Are you kidding me? Trying to pull a practical joke? Is it real?"

Stone rolled his eyes. "Just get in the damn car, please, before the rest of the dingbats come out here. It's a Chihuahua."

Devine slid into the front seat, glancing back. "I know what a Chihuahua is, and that ain't one. Where's its fur?"

"Gone. Well, I called it Rat Fink, but Arilyn got pissed."

"Ah, now I get it! This is the one you tried to get me to take. You slept with her, and this is your punishment!"

"Shut up, Devine."

His partner belted out a laugh, shaking his head. "Thought you hated dogs."

"I do, but like I said, this one was abused, and the shelter was crowded, and she couldn't take the dog because it has issues."

"Issues, huh? You two are perfect for each other. What's the rat fink's name?"

"Pinky," he mumbled. He winced, waiting for the inevitable.

"You're fucking kidding me."

Damned if he didn't feel a flush stain his cheeks. So humiliating. "No."

"Her collar is actually pink. I told you she's a foo-foo dog!"

"She's tough. Arilyn named her, for God's sake, not me. And she's only mine temporarily."

"Why does it have to come with us? Dogs are left home all the time."

Stone made a right and headed into the neighborhood where they'd nabbed Pinky. "I know. I tried. She was shaking and crying, and I was afraid if I didn't take her, something bad would happen."

Devine laughed harder. "You are such a sucker. Dogs hate being alone, they all do it."

"I'm telling you, this is different. Look, it's only tonight. I'm begging you not to tell the guys or I'm gonna have to take shit for this stunt for the rest of my life. Then I'd have to transfer."

Devine wiped his eyes, looking happy over this complication. "Fine. But you owe me."

"Fine." They drove in silence for a while, scanning the quiet surroundings. Pinky was surprisingly well behaved. She sat perfectly still and stared out the window. Stone could use a little action tonight, but Verily seemed determined to keep the peace. "You find anything else out on that property I told you about?"

"Bluebird? Nah. Let's go check it out and see if anything's cooking. Night seems pretty dead."

"Yeah."

"So, how was the sex?"

Stone hesitated. Usually he enjoyed sharing details with Devine. They liked to rib each other, all in good fun. Sometimes compare. "Great."

"First time?"

He shifted in the seat. "Yep."

"Cool. Do it on the bed? Against the wall? Floor?"

He concentrated on his driving and made a left, heading toward the outskirts. "Normal stuff. You know."

Devine didn't answer. When Stone glanced over, his partner sported a shit-eating grin that was pure trouble. "Holy crap, it finally happened. You won't give me details because she's important."

Stone snorted. "That's ridiculous. Well, of course she's important; I don't sleep with women I don't like. Just don't feel like getting into it."

"Bullshit. You care about her, so you won't give me the down-and-dirty details." Devine shook his head in glee. "This is the best night ever. You got taken out by a dog and a woman in one shot."

"You're an asshole."

"Maybe. But I'm also right."

Stone refused to answer. After all, his friend was being ridiculous. Just because he couldn't stop thinking about her? Just because he felt addicted to her scent and taste and legs wrapped around his hips as he pumped inside her sweet body? No, it was the early flush of a new affair. A few more days, and the crazy need for each other would fade away.

He turned the car onto the dead-end street, but this time lights flickered around, and a variety of vehicles were lined up and down the street. A fire gave off smoke from the backyard. Stone's instincts flared. Oh, yeah, something was going on here, and it was time he figured it out. Catching Devine's excitement at some real action, his partner nodded and checked his gun.

"We got something, dude. Ready?"

Stone nodded, his cop radar going off in shrieks. "Let's do this. Pinky, stay here."

The dog perched on the seat, not blinking, and quietly watched him get out of the car and shut the door. She didn't whine or cry or move.

Pride shot through him. She might not be a drug-sniffing warrior, or have the genes of a shepherd or Lab, but something told him she'd be a good partner for the road. She was, after all, a survivor.

Stone quickly pushed the thought aside and followed Devine down the road.

THE BUST WAS EVERYTHING he'd wished for and more. Drugs. Dog fighting. And finally, some damn justice for not only Pinky but Arilyn. They ended up rescuing a bunch of other dogs and nailing a major drug dealer. Stone was buzzed for hours and reminded once again why being a cop was worth it.

He couldn't wait to tell Arilyn.

seventeen

ARILYN LOOKED AT the men before her. Dressed in shorts and tanks, they gazed at her a bit warily. She'd recruited them to the Tuck-N-Pack gym, where she occasionally taught a yoga class to help out the community. The private room she reserved was used for a hot yoga class, which incorporated steamy temperatures and a rousing ashtanga workout. She'd used it for many of her clients, including Kate's husband, Slade, back in the day, and found the technique a good tool in breaking down barriers, especially ones leading to anger.

Unfortunately, she was quite distracted today. If Arilyn admitted the truth, she'd been fighting for focus the moment Stone took her to bed. Even now, her gaze kept getting stuck on his powerful bare thighs dusted with dark hair, the way his tank showed off his corded arms, the wicked glint of satisfaction in his inky eyes when he looked at her. Like he knew what she was thinking. And wanting.

Because he did.

Five days. Only five days, and already she craved him like all the bad things she kept away from her body. Sugar, caffeine, chocolate, alcohol, all the wonderful, terrible items in life that made one happy in the moment and miserable later on. Sex with Stone had now topped any impulse and appetite she'd ever owned before. It was awful.

It was wonderful.

They couldn't keep their hands off each other. Between their work schedules, driving back and forth to care for Pinky, and the scattered visits with Poppy and her newly adopted dinner guest Mrs. Blackfire, they met when night fell, tumbling into bed with an endless yearning that never seemed to be satisfied.

Arilyn tried to ignore the faint warning in the back of her mind. She didn't want to fall in love with a man who intended to leave when the fun stopped. She tried to concentrate on the bruising pleasure he wracked from her body and told herself it would be enough. If only she hadn't learned to look past his gruff, crude, annoying exterior and see the real man underneath.

A man who her friends liked. A man who showed up to have dinner with her neighbor and Poppy with a smile on his face. A man who helped with a dog he didn't care for. A man who had told her in a casual way he'd made a drug bust at Bluebird and shut down a dogfighting ring in the process. He hadn't given up investigating the house, even though everyone else had. When Anthony called her, telling her that a variety of shelters and the Humane Society were stepping in to help with the dogs, she'd turned to Stone with tears in her eyes and thanked him.

He just shrugged and told her she could make it up to him in bed.

Arilyn took a deep, calming breath and refocused.

"I'm going to take you through a demanding yoga routine. It's commonly known as hot yoga, so we do the workout in a set temperature of one hundred degrees. I've placed water bottles by your side and checked with your respective physicians to be sure each of you is in proper health."

Luther spoke up. "How is this supposed to help with anger?"

"Funny, I was gonna ask the same thing," Stone drawled. "Sure this isn't just a way to punish us and get your kicks, Teach?"

She narrowed her gaze, but his dancing eyes told her he was deliberately baiting her for a show. She smiled at Luther and ignored her lover. "Hot yoga is a great way to break down both your body and mind. We've been studying barriers and mental blocks that keep anger suppressed. Any exercise is excellent, but this is particularly cleansing. You'll be uncomfortable, and when your mind fights, anger can take hold. The mat is a safe way to practice all the scary things in life, master them, and move on."

Luther nodded. "Thanks. I understand better now."

"As for you, Officer," she said, tone hardening, "do your best to keep up."

Eli snickered.

"Let's begin."

The routine was long, hard, and messy. She kept her attention on all three men, making sure they weren't experiencing any health issues or emotional blockages that sometimes radiated through such a cleansing process. She was surprised at the loosening of Stone's hamstrings and biceps during the transitions. Funny, it was almost as if he was doing something different. His body was more relaxed and limber than before. As she moved into Downward Dog, Stone tossed off his tank. The sight of his bare chest gleaming with sweat, muscles bunching as he moved, caused her to miss a step and almost fall on her ass.

By the end of the session, she was wet in many places.

They completed circle time and broke for the weekend. Luther and Eli chatted with her awhile as Stone helped stack the mats in the corner. He checked his phone and waited for them to leave. Finally, the room was empty.

Her heart pounded. Her skin prickled with awareness. He stalked her slowly, those lush lips twisted down in the familiar sensual sneer that made her hot. "Slade warned me about your tendency to torture men with hot yoga. You enjoyed that, didn't you?" he asked.

She took in his hard, sweaty body and smiled with promise. "Slade is right. And yes, I did enjoy it."

"Payback's a bitch, little one. Everything you do to me in this room will be done to you later on. In private."

Her gaze deliberately raked him from head to toe. She dragged her tongue across her bottom lip as if imagining his taste. He growled low in his throat in warning.

"You're a lot of talk, Officer," she answered coolly. "Not much action."

Sexual tension squeezed between them. Arilyn tried to keep up her demeanor even though her core throbbed painfully and her nipples begged for release, hardening with anticipation. Excited to see what he'd do, she studied him in silence, the obvious challenge in the air sparking like an electrical current gone crazy.

"I'll be at your place by eight tonight. Then you'll get your action. And your lesson."

Disappointment cut through her. She craved his kiss, his touch, but as if he knew what she wanted, he dropped one eyelid in a wink and sauntered out the door. "What if I'm busy?" she called out.

"Don't be."

He shut the door. Arilyn tried not to sulk. He thought he could play sex games with her, huh? Well, wouldn't he be surprised when she countered with her own demands tonight.

Bring it.

STONE PUT HIS HAND out and shook his head. Hard. "No way. I already took you to work twice this week. Tonight I'm getting laid."

Pinky walked quietly across the floor and sat in front of the door, blocking his way.

"Oh, you think you're smart, huh? Well, guess what? If I did take you, you'd freak out because there's a pit bull over there. You'd probably go into convulsions and I'd have to turn right back around. You have to stay home, and I'm not giving up getting lucky just to watch football with you tonight."

Pinky sighed.

How had this happened? How had a half-catatonic dog suddenly become a manipulative, mushy, demanding pet? Sure, he'd spent a lot of time at the shelter talking to her. Sure, he'd given her a quiet, safe home to heal again, and finally let her sleep in his damn bed. Sure, he took her with him almost everywhere because he couldn't stand the idea of her crying. But this? Messing up his sex life?

Not gonna happen.

"Move out of the way. I bought you a new bone—it's the chewy kind, 'cause I know you hate the hard stuff. Probably because you still have baby teeth." Pinky stared. "For real, you are definitely not a man's type of dog. If the guys at the station other than Devine caught sight of you, I'd be fucked. And not in a good way. Not like I'm getting tonight."

Pinky cocked her ear.

Stone grabbed his coat and stomped over. "Go sleep. I left the TV on, and I'll be over at the crack of dawn again to take you out." The accidents were hardly happening anymore so somehow, the dog had been trained. Stone tried not to think that the dog had had a good life before she was dognapped or lost to the scum in the world. Hated to imagine she'd once had a family and children to love, and that she was still struggling to process it.

He grasped the doorknob and made a mistake.

His gaze met hers. In those brown puppy eyes, staring from beneath tufts of crazy hair, above her rat nose and strangely proportioned face, he saw it.

Adoration.

She looked at him with pure love, making low sounds of need in her throat, only wanting to be near him. And just like that, the big bad wolf fucking retired to become the wimpy grandma who liked cookies.

"Ah, crap. Fine. But I swear to God, if you give me problems, I'm gonna lose it."

She wriggled with joy, knowing she'd won, and he scooped her up into his arms.

ARILYN OPENED THE DOOR. Wearing a sexy black camisole, stretchy pants, and bare feet, she was both comfortable yet a bit naughty. She always preferred cotton to lace anyway, and Stone seemed to agree. Ready to jump into his arms and throw him off his game, she dropped her voice to a seductive whisper. "Why, Officer, are you coming to arrest—oh!" She blinked. He filled her doorway, dressed in his usual jeans, a faded blue-and-green-checked flannel shirt, and a fierce frown. His midnight-black hair slid over his brow in tousled disarray, setting off the intensity of his narrowed dark eyes. Waves of irritated male energy beat from his aura. Tucked under his muscled arm, peering out from beneath the cuff of his shirt, was Pinky.

"Look, I'll leave her in the car if she can't deal with Robert. The little rat fink was freaking out about me leaving again, so I broke. I told you this would be a disaster, Arilyn. I don't know why you were thinking I could take care of a dog."

And that's when it happened.

The great sex turned into more. Arilyn looked at this massive, pissed-off male cradling the tiny Chihuahua, with her pink collar and soft brown eyes that had come back to life, and did the dumbest thing in the whole wide world.

She tumbled into love right then and right there with Stone Petty.

He loved Pinky. Oh, yeah, he fought it and hated

the idea, but he loved her so much, he didn't want to leave her alone. That was just the type of man he was. He didn't fall gracefully or willingly, but when he did, Arilyn knew he belonged to you for life. God, how she wanted him to belong to her like that.

What had she done?

Swallowing past the lump in her throat, she fought for composure, swearing to bottle up the tide of crazy emotions to deal with later. Smiling through the sting of tears, she reached out and took Pinky from him, murmuring soothing nonsense to her. She shook slightly in her arms, looking back to Stone with an imploring look. "Don't be silly, I'm glad you brought her. The worst-case scenario: she can stay in the bedroom. But let's see how she does meeting Robert." She turned at the sound of front paws skittering over the wood floors and kept Pinky safely tucked in her arms. "Here's my good boy. Robert, we have a special guest tonight. Her name is Pinky, and she's been hurt. But she's a fighter like you."

Robert's tongue lolled out in excitement, but he stayed quietly in front of her, waiting for the go-ahead.

"She's scared, especially of pit bulls, so we need to show her how to trust again. Just like Stone did."

Robert looked up at Stone as if giving him a doggy high five.

"I want you to stay. I know you're happy for some company, but don't move. Understood?"

Robert dropped his head to his front paws and stilled.

"Damn, he's smart," Stone muttered. "Good boy."

Arilyn smiled and slowly knelt. Pinky began to

shake with mini convulsions, a high-pitched whining beginning from her throat and growing into a panicked howl. Arilyn settled her on her lap, her hands stroking her small body, and allowed her to get used to Robert's presence. The howling went on for a while, but Arilyn never moved, and neither did Robert. As if he understood how important it was to remain completely still, Robert barely breathed, keeping his submissive posture.

Finally, the howling stopped. Pinky stared at Robert, who didn't make a move to attack her, and calmed.

Stone let out a breath. "My ears won't recover."

Arilyn kept soothing the dog and whispering low nonsense. "It's the only thing she had left, I think. Her voice. They're going to be okay together, but I think we'll keep Pinky separate for a while. Build up her level of safety. Can you take Robert to his bed and give him a dog treat? His purple bunny squeaker should be there, too. Tell him to stay."

Stone followed her instructions, and Pinky's body finally relaxed as Robert trotted off.

Arilyn pressed a kiss to her tiny head. "You did so good. You were very brave. Now, I have an extra dog bed so I'll set you up where you'll feel safe."

They fixed up the separate spaces and finally both dogs were happily settled. Stone went to the refrigerator and pulled out an IPA. "I'm sorry, Arilyn. I shouldn't have brought her. Do you want wine?"

"Yes, please." She let him fix both drinks and leaned over the counter. "I'm glad you brought her, Stone. She's doing so much better. Because of you, she gets to have a real life."

"Well, it's only a week left. I guess I can handle one more week."

She didn't answer, just sipped her wine. His voice held a tinge of regret, and Arilyn knew he wouldn't give her up. But he didn't realize it yet. He needed to figure it out on his own. "How was work?" she asked.

He tipped the bottle back and drank. Wiped his mouth. "Fine. We found a stolen car, which was so fucking exciting I thought Devine was gonna have a heart attack." She laughed. "Anyway, ended up being a kid dared by his friends, but for a while it was like being back in the Bronx, having a car chase."

She traced the rim of the wineglass with her finger. "Do you miss the Bronx?" she asked. "I mean, I know it was tough, but you got used to being challenged all the time. You nabbed real criminals, made a difference. Would you ever want to go back?"

He scratched his head. "Hell, no. Sure, it fed my ego a bit. I was always *on*, the rush of adrenaline kept pushing me for more. I worked around the clock, needing the hit like the junkies I busted. But I like Verily. I like what it represents. I have a real life here I wouldn't want to give up."

Happiness flooded her. She kept her head down so he wouldn't catch how much his words meant to her. "I'm glad."

"Are you?" He studied her thoughtfully and placed his beer down. "Why?"

She shifted her weight. "Because you're good for this town."

"Anything else?"

"Because I want you to be safe and like where you live."

"Hmm. I think there's more here you're not telling me." Her breath got trapped in her chest and she fought for oxygen. "There's a selfish reason you want me to stay."

She opened her mouth to answer, gave a squeak, and tried again. "Nope. Just want you to be happy."

His eyes held amusement. Slowly, he opened the freezer, took a cup, and began filling it with ice. "I think you like torturing me. Forcing me to exercise in a hundred-degree room while I watch you parade around half-naked. Tempting me with your gorgeous body on display, flaunting what I couldn't taste and touch, while you called me 'Officer' in that snotty tone."

Her skin heated. She watched as he took the half cup of ice and set it on the counter. "I didn't think you liked beer with ice."

"I don't. I have another use for this. You'll see in a minute." She looked at the cup. Worry creased her brow. There was something almost threatening about his tone of voice. "You were hot in that room with me, weren't you, Arilyn?"

"Yes. That was the point. Pumping the temperature helps release the toxins. I bet you felt amazing afterward."

"After a cold shower, I did. Will you take off your clothes for me?"

She stared at him. A shiver of trepidation raced down her spine. "Am I going to be naked again while you're dressed?"

"Yes."

"Why?"

He smiled. "Because it turns you on."

He was right. The secret, shocking exhibitionist in her had been let loose. Maybe it was the way he devoured her with his gaze. He never let her doubt what she did to him, giving him pleasure, and that made the whole encounter more exciting. And the naughtiness with him fully dressed, using his authority to command her to do things, totally wrecked her head. In a good way.

She placed her wineglass down and backed up. Arilyn had already planned to take charge with his seduction tonight, so this went with her goal perfectly. Slowly, she took off her clothes, running her fingers lightly over her skin in a caress, causing a groan to rip from his lips as she stroked her belly and thighs before shedding her entire outfit and underwear. By the time she was done with him, he wouldn't know how to speak English anymore. That would teach him she wasn't a woman who always bowed to direction. His hot gaze probed every inch of her body, lingering on her hard nipples, her tummy, her pussy.

His voice came out hoarse. "Every time I look at you I die a little. I brought a little present with me. Wanna see?"

She nodded, so aroused already she'd be lucky to know English herself. He reached in his back pocket and drew out two strips of red silk.

His ties.

Arilyn tamped down a moan. He watched her carefully and then, grabbing the cup of ice, began to close the distance. "I want to tie you up, Arilyn. Do things to you. Very bad things. Will you let me?

She meant to say yes but ended up releasing a husky moan.

"I'll take that as permission. Come with me." He led her into the bedroom and shut the door. Studying her queen-size bed, he ran a hand over the teak headboard as if assessing its potential as a sexual weapon of torture. "Hmm, posts too far apart. I'll have to improvise. Lie on the bed, little one."

Heart beating madly, anticipation tangling with a hot arousal that singed her nerve endings, she climbed on the bed, lying quietly, and he gently clasped her hands and raised them over her head. "I'm going to tie your wrists together. Keep them in that position. I don't want your arms too stretched by the headboard so I'll have to trust you'll keep your arms still. Just like you trust me to take care of you."

He situated her on the bed, checking the fit of the bright red tie and pulling her legs down the mattress a bit. "Perfect. I may never recover from this. You're so fucking beautiful."

A half laugh escaped her lips. "I may never recover from letting you do this."

He leaned over, his mouth inches from her. "I'd never hurt you, little one. You're too precious." He kissed her and she melted, surrendering to everything he wanted from her. When he broke away, a fierce tenderness gleamed from his eyes. "Let's play."

Stone took the other red tie and dangled the edge over her breast. With teasing, deliberate motions, he dragged the silky edge of the fabric over every inch of her body. She shivered at the gentle caress, the slight tickle over her hard nipples, the length of her arms, the sensitive skin of her belly. Down her legs, over her knee, and round her toes. He took his time, watching her face with an intensity that made liquid warmth trickle between her thighs.

"You like this," he murmured. "The feeling of being bound for my eyes, for anything I want to do. The excitement of not knowing what happens next." Her body prickled with awareness, until every stroke of the tie ramped up her arousal and sensation. He parted her legs wider and ran the fabric over her swollen pussy until a long whimper broke from her lips. "So wet and ready for me." He tossed the tie onto the floor. Flashed a wolfish grin. "Are you feeling a bit hot?"

Hot? She was burning alive, desperate for him to touch her where it mattered. Frustration nipped her nerve endings, stripping away the layers of civility until there was only the man before her and what he could give her. "Yes."

"Then let's cool you down, shall we?"

He took the cup from the nightstand and shook it. The rattle of ice echoed in the air.

"Wh-What are you going to do with that?"

He lifted a brow. "Whatever I want."

And then she knew what her punishment was going to be.

Her eyes widened. He stripped off his clothes. Laid a condom on the edge of the bed. Then, taking his time, drawing out the tension, he lifted an ice cube and sat on the edge of the bed. Studied her body as if deciding where to touch her first. Arilyn stiffened, waiting for the first slide of ice against her skin, and then he pressed the cube to the curve of her neck.

Wet. Icy. She shivered, and he ran the ice down to the valley of her breasts, tracing circles round and round them. She gasped at the sensation. Her nipples hardened, lengthening, begging for contact as he moved closer to the center. Arching up, silently begging, he finally slid the melting cube over her right nipple.

Oh, God.

The sharp burn of cold numbed her nipple. Arilyn hissed out a breath, shaking her head to ward off the feeling, and then he lowered his mouth and sucked on her nipple.

She gasped. The delicious wet, the heat of his tongue, the slight scrape of his teeth, all combined to fire her senses off like an explosion. He moved to the other breast, repeating the motions, and Arilyn tugged at her bound wrists, crazed to touch him and move and make him stop and make him continue.

"Ah, you like that. Let's see what else you like."

"Stone."

"I love your sweet body. I love the sounds you make in your throat, and the way you say my name." Rivulets of water trickled down her tummy and slid lower. He kissed his way down, lapping up the liquid. "I love the way you explode in my arms and give me everything you got." He grabbed another ice cube and traced patterns over her stomach, dipping into her navel and licking. "Spread your legs, little one. Wider. Yes, like that, beautiful. So swollen and wet. Now be a good girl and don't move."

Her thighs shook. He ran the ice over her inner thighs, tracing the line of pubic hair, moving closer to his goal. Her clit throbbed for attention, and she was so ready, she knew she'd come if he just gave her enough pressure.

He didn't. He teased her mercilessly, allowing the cube to melt around her channel but not close enough. He licked, he bit. She twisted, she moaned.

"Please, Stone. I can't take any more."

"Not done with you yet if you're still able to talk."

And with that, he pushed the ice cube inside of her.

Arilyn shot up, a keening whine echoing in the air. The freezing chill met with blistering heat, setting off mini convulsions of pure arousal and need. He moved the melting cube in a slow rhythm. At the same time, the second cube was pressed against her throbbing clit.

She cried out his name and jerked.

The brutal pain/pleasure ramped up her arousal until she hung on the edge of a cliff, desperate to be pushed over. Then Stone replaced the cube with his hot, wet tongue, licking the swollen nub. Once. Twice.

She came hard, tears stinging her eyes at the intensity of pleasure. Instead of softening, he sucked more violently, his fingers replacing the ice and thrusting again and again into her pussy, curving just perfectly to hit the magic G-spot and setting off another chain of orgasms.

Tears leaked from her eyes. Beyond anything she had ever experienced, she began to shake, calling his name as the only anchor she had left in a world that had just shattered away.

"Fucking magnificent," his voice growled. He surged up, over, and inside in one perfect thrust. "Fucking *mine*."

The raw possession swallowed her whole, the punishing, greedy strokes of him driving into her body over and over, the dirty whispers in her ear as he claimed her.

Arilyn broke free, taking all of him, and felt the next climax gobble her up whole. He shouted her name, his hands gripping hers, his dark eyes drilling into her soul until they both came together, and fell into each other's arms.

Mine.

The word echoed like a mantra repeatedly as he gently untied her, rubbed her wrists, and pulled her close.

Mine.

Yours, she whispered to herself. Then closed her eyes.

"WHY DID YOU STAY with him for so long?"

The dark was good for sharing secrets. With his arms wrapped around her, snuggled under the covers, his mouth against her ear, nothing seemed off-limits.

"I thought I loved him," she said simply. "He had this way of making me feel like the most important person in the world. The way he focused on me. Listened. Shared with what I believed was pure emotion. He seemed so honest and real. He was also my yoga teacher, so he introduced me to a spiritual practice that changed my life."

"Was that the first time he cheated?"

She sighed and pressed a kiss to his palm. "No. It was the third. Each time, he explained that the others didn't mean anything to him. Cliché, I know, but he made me actually believe it. He used to say men weren't made for monogamy, that he was fighting his own nature, but he'd keep fighting because we were soul mates."

"Damn. He was good."

She laughed. "Yeah, he was good. It was also easier to continue because we were a secret. Think about it. Nothing really invaded the intimacy he claimed we had. No bickering parents, or in-laws, or coworkers. No friends or public events. It was just me and him on an island together."

They lay quietly for a while, both sifting through her answer. "Do you still love him?"

Arilyn rolled over to face him. Stroking his beloved face, the rough, carved features, the silky scratch of his goatee, she shook her head. "No, Stone. I don't love him anymore." *I love you,* she ached to say. But it was too soon. He wasn't ready, and Arilyn wondered if he ever would be. Still, she'd tell him one day, because he deserved to know.

"Good."

She smiled. "What about you? Do you still think of your ex-wife?"

"Sometimes. But not because I miss Ellen or still love her. I think over where it really went wrong, which I think was straight from the beginning. I don't think I was ever made for a long-term relationship. Once I accepted it, I seemed to do better by not expecting something from myself I can't give."

Her heart broke a little. Why couldn't he see it? He was meant for a family and love. He was loyal and protective and deserved so much. "You're wrong," she finally said. "If you believe that, you're just like my ex."

He drew back a little. "Don't ever compare me to him."

"He didn't believe he was capable of being monogamous. By allowing himself to believe such bullshit, he made himself into what he wanted. Ellen cheated on you, yes, but it wasn't your work that drove her to it or your selfishness. It was both of you not wanting to work, or communicate, or fix the tears." She blinked, refusing to get sloppy and emotional. "It's the coward's way out."

"I'm being honest, not a coward," he shot back. "Don't get any ideas about who I could be, little one. I'll only disappoint you."

Her heart couldn't take it. Anger replaced the pain, and she grabbed his cheeks, forcing him to deal with her. "How do you know?" she shot back. "You buried your head in the sand after your divorce and locked yourself in a world of limitations that don't exist. Bullshit you can't be in a healthy, committed relationship. Bullshit your work and cynicism will ruin everything. Bullshit to all of it, Stone Petty, because you're just lying to yourself for one big fat reason. It's easy. And safe."

"That's two."

"Asshole."

"Shut up." The frustration twisted, until he pushed her back on the pillow and took her mouth in a deep, thorough kiss. She dug her nails deep into his naked shoulders, eliciting a grunt of pain, and nipped at his lip, aggressively giving back to the kiss until his hips pinned hers and he was surging again between her thighs, already half-erect.

He broke the kiss, panting, staring at her with a mad gleam of lust and something more. Something deep that gave her pause and hope. "We have this," he said fiercely. "It's real, and brave, and good. Can't that be enough?"

Arilyn arched for more of him. He slid deeper, and the pleasure gripped her mercilessly. "For now," she gasped out. "Fuck me, Stone."

He muttered a vicious curse, took her mouth, and fucked her long and hard. Arilyn clung and shattered around him, refusing to deal with the dawn of day and her love for a man who didn't believe in it.

Afterward, sated, wrecked, lying in his arms, she finally heard him speak.

"I'm taking you to the movies tomorrow night."

She roused herself enough to wonder if the sex had killed his brain cells. "Huh?"

"The movies. You know, a date. Dinner, too. Okay?"

Her throat tightened. "Okay," she whispered. She knew it was his way of showing her what she meant to him. His gift, and a reminder he wasn't her ex, and refused to keep her locked up in his bedroom because it made things less messy. A complete contradiction to the mind-blowing sex they'd just engaged in.

"But none of those chick flicks. I hate them. Something with guns. Okay?"

She thanked the dark for masking the tears that stung her eyes.

"Okay."

Arilyn smiled and cuddled close. She'd take what she could. It was enough. For now.

eighteen

"I'M IN TROUBLE, Kennedy."

Her friend arched a brow and studied her from the doorway. Arilyn had just finished a counseling session in the purple room and couldn't focus. Every thought and action kept going back to Stone and their incredible night together. Maybe if she talked it over with her friend she'd be able to work out the tangled emotions wrecking her system.

"What type of trouble?"

Arilyn sighed. "Man trouble."

"The worst kind. Wait here." Kennedy disappeared, and then came back with her cell phone. "Hang tight."

"What are you doing?"

"FaceTiming with Kate."

"No! She's on her honeymoon! Oh my God, do not call and bother her!"

"Too late. It's connecting. Hey, babe, how's the sun, sand, and sex?"

Arilyn squeezed her eyes shut.

Kate's voice drifted from the phone. "Fabulous. Is something wrong? Is Robert okay? Kinnections?"

"Take a chill pill, things are fine. Except we have a crisis with Arilyn, and since she never comes to us with boy trouble, I knew you'd be pissed if I didn't bring you into the conference call."

"Damn right. Turn me around so I can see her."

Caught between laughter and a groan, Arilyn opened her eyes. "Hi, Kate. I'm sorry about this."

Her friend looked tan, well rested, and deliriously happy. She was in a black bikini and floppy-brimmed hat, and held a cocktail with a purple paper umbrella sticking out of it. "Don't be sorry. I've been dying to have this convo with you for a long time. Thank God you dumped Yoga Man. Now, tell us all the details."

Kennedy squeezed into the circle so they could all see each other.

Arilyn decided to go with the unvarnished truth. "I'm in love with Stone Petty."

Kate gaped. Kennedy gasped. Silence settled over the room for a few moments.

"Damn, girlfriend, you didn't even give us a warm-up. Hard-core," Kennedy said.

Kate squealed. "I'm so happy for you! This is the best news ever! Isn't it? Wait a minute, why don't you look happy?"

"Are we ever happy when we realize we've fallen for a man?" Kennedy quipped. "Most of them are not as smart as us and fight it to the end."

"Except Nate," Kate said. "He said you were worse than any man."

Kennedy beamed. "Well, I gotta make him work for it, don't I?"

"Guys, I don't know what to do. When we started this thing, we agreed it would be about sex. Then we moved it a bit into companionship, and you convinced me to invite him to the wedding."

"Which went famously well, I thought," Kate said. "He was a big hit. Slade loved him."

"So did Nate."

"I know, but now he did something terrible and ruined the whole affair thing."

"What?" Kate demanded.

"He fostered Pinky for me. And fell in love with her. And he hates dogs, because he got bit by a pit bull years ago, but he took in Pinky as a favor and now he carries her around with him because he refuses to leave her alone, and he has this great big heart, and he wrung, like, a million orgasms from me that night with the ice, and I fell in love with him. And if I tell him, he'll run and refuse to look back, because he doesn't think he can be in a relationship because of all these excuses he believes are true."

Kennedy let out a breath. "Dudette, this is crazy. How many orgasms? Did you like the ice?"

"Focus!" Kate snapped. "We can't talk about the sex now."

"Sorry. Umm, okay, most men run at the idea of the word *love* being thrown around. Maybe he needs some time to get used to the idea."

"You think?" Arilyn murmured. "He's been divorced so he's bitter, and he says he's a workaholic, and I know we're opposites, but there's something about us that just fits."

"Slade was divorced," Kate said. "We had a lot of ups and downs, but eventually he came to realize just because it didn't work with his ex doesn't mean it never works at all."

"I think he's using excuses to keep him from admitting the truth," Arilyn said softly. "I know it's only been a little while, but I swear he has all these emotions inside to give. There's a connection between us. The way he looks at me, touches me. He just hates talking about feelings."

Kennedy rolled her eyes. "Men like to work out their emotions in bed. It's the simpler way of communicating. I think he calls for a bit of patience. Cops are bristly, hard-core cases."

Kate chimed in. "I agree. Give him some time to discover it on his own."

"So I shouldn't tell him I fell in love with him?"

"No!" they both said together.

"At least, not yet," Kate clarified. "Slade freaked out. Kennedy did the same. So did Wolfe when Gen finally confessed her love. We don't want you to go through the same thing. If you give him a bit more space, he'll figure out he's madly in love with you and you'll get your happy ever after."

"Probably," Kennedy said.

"Definitely," Kate said.

Arilyn sighed. Her friends were right. She'd gone from refusing to spend time with him, to liking, to passion, to love. How could the poor man keep up? The knowledge of her feelings ran deep and true. This was no transitional or recovery period. Stone Petty was the man she was meant for, and the last one on earth she'd ever look for.

Fate was a tricky bitch.

"Okay. We'll finish up the course, and I'll keep my revelation to myself. See how it goes. Thanks, guys."

"No problem. I'll be home soon, but keep me updated with texts," Kate said.

"I will. Love you."

The phone clicked off and Kate's image disappeared. Kennedy patted her shoulder. "I know this is hard, A. But just remember: men are limited. We need to work with them in order to catch them up to speed. Now, I want to hear all about the ice."

Arilyn laughed. Then told her.

ONE WEEK LATER, STONE wondered what was happening.

His life was usually easy. Mapped out. He worked every spare moment, slept, played pool, worked out, and went drinking with the guys. Sure, there were dates and some sleepovers in the middle, but mostly his freedom was key, and he relished the open road, even taking the bits of loneliness in stride.

Now, things had . . . changed.

He got into the habit of bringing Pinky to Arilyn's house after work. After the first sleepover night, Pinky stopped howling every time Robert got close. The second night, Arilyn put their food bowls and beds closer together, still keeping a safe distance but forcing Pinky to see Robert in her space. The third night, they ate side by side without communicating. Almost as if Robert knew Pinky was delicate and needed to move things on her own. Oh, they watched each other, and sometimes Robert looked over with pleading need and adoration, wanting to play with a friend, but he kept chill. Stone fell hard for the pit bull, with his smarts and gentle soul. He even learned how to hook up his scooter and helped Arilyn take care of him when Patrick couldn't get over there in the afternoon.

Arilyn and Stone's relationship had also changed. What began as annoyance and attraction and then melded into hot sex and passion had now morphed into more. Affection. Tenderness. Comfort. Stone didn't know when it had transitioned or at what moment he realized that he was enjoying having dinner, going to the movies, or hanging with her and the dogs just as much as being in bed.

Well, almost as much.

He never experienced such intense liking before. Sure, he enjoyed women and took them out on dates, but when he was alone, he never really missed them unless he had a hard-on. Never thought about them during the course of the day. Maybe because Arilyn was wrapped up with him in the anger management course, he'd gotten used to seeing her on a daily basis. That had to be it. Because the alternative was impossible. He didn't lose control of his boxed-up mess of emotional crap, because it never worked out. Being honest was the best he could give.

Though something had happened between them the night he tied her up. Rollicking passion, yes. Numerous orgasms, definitely. But a bond had been strengthened, a connection that had always simmered between them but now seemed fused together permanently. She made him ache all over, inside and out, and drove him to claim her in bed endlessly in the drive to get rid of the madness. So far, no good.

Maybe once anger management was over, things would calm.

He'd work an extra shift. Pick up a little OT, gain some distance, and remind himself about real life. It would be good for both of them.

Stone pulled up to her house and glanced at his companion. The sore spots had now fully healed. Her new pink collar glittered with fake bling, which embarrassed the hell out of him, but since it was a present from Arilyn and Pinky seemed to like it, he hadn't ripped it off. Yet. Hell, he'd almost bought a spiked leather collar at the pet store, but it reminded him too much of a BDSM relationship. So the pink stayed.

Her bat ears stood straight up with pale pink centers, and she panted with what he now knew was excitement. Her jaw jutted out with the excitement, exposing tiny sharp teeth. Those chocolate-brown eyes stared at him with sheer adoration, making him shake his head. "Come on, you little rat fink. Let's go see Robert." He scratched her head affectionately and pulled her into the crook of his arm.

He didn't knock. When he came for dinner, she left the door open, and already the scents and sounds of the small bungalow drifted from inside. He walked in.

Arilyn stood in the kitchen, surrounded by pots and pans. She wore a stained apron that encouraged him to KISS THE CHEF. Feet bare, hair twisted up, clad in yoga pants, she grabbed her glass of wine and sipped while the sounds of a singer belting out lyrics not in English filled the air. Robert lay near the edge of the kitchen, purple bunny squeaker tucked firmly between his paws, head lifted as he waited for scraps to drop. Mrs. Blackfire and Patrick sat at the pine table with crackers and what looked like hummus, arguing over old movies and who were the greatest actor and actress of all time.

"There's just no way you can't pick Bogie," Patrick stated. "He was a man's man and a great romantic lead. No one touched him."

Mrs. Blackfire snorted with disgust. "He mumbled and talked weird. Also not what you'd call handsome. Sorry, the real winner is Newman. Mr. Blue Eyes himself. He was a much better actor. Arilyn, do you have Ritz? These wheat things are a bit too crunchy."

"Sorry, Mrs. Blackfire, Poppy needs to watch his salt intake, along with getting more fiber. How about the rosemary and garlic toast bits I made?"

"Yes, they're better. Well, hello, Officer Stone. Were you called out to the bingo hall? Marilyn said there's a thief who's stealing the petty cash. Did you catch her?"

Stone nodded a greeting, clapped Patrick's shoulder, and eased into the kitchen. "Wasn't a theft, Mrs. Blackfire. Mr. Olsen is beginning to forget things, so he moved the cash and didn't tell anyone. We found it. Crisis averted."

"Oh. Well, I'd keep an eye on him. I always knew he looked suspicious. He's even wearing an eye patch now!"

"He had cataract surgery." He stopped in front of Arilyn. "Hi."

She smiled and his heart stuttered. Damn undependable organ. "Hi." He kissed her properly, his hands skating over her slim hips. "Need help?"

She laughed, rising up on her toes, and kissed him again. "Not your kind."

"Hey, I helped the last time."

"You thought the Brussels sprouts were broccoli."

"They look the same."

"Trust me, you're a better help out there. Keep an eye on Poppy and make sure he's not sneaking slugs of beer. I cut him off."

"Mmm. 'Kay." They stared at each other for a few moments. Funny, he'd never experienced that sensation of having the world melt away, but he couldn't give a crap if a crime happened right in front of him. Stone seemed unable to move from the spell of those green eyes. Her delicious clean scent rose to his nostrils like heaven. "Whatcha making?"

"Pasta with creamy cauliflower sauce. I saw it on Thug Kitchen. I promise you'll like this one."

His lip twitched. It was a fifty-fifty shot. Some of her recipes he was actually getting used to. Other times she finally took pity on him and gave him something he recognized. Still, he left with his belly full, feeling pampered and cared for in a way he had never experienced.

Patrick spoke up. "With real sausage. She promised."

He raised his brow. "Seriously?"

She shook her head but grinned. "Yes. I went to the organic butcher. I bend if you bend."

"Sweet." He opened the refrigerator, grabbed an IPA, and took a pull. Reaching into the right top cabinet, he took down four bowls and lined up the silverware. "Mrs. Blackfire, I saw your driveway is starting to crack. It'll never make the winter. Do you have someone you trust to do it?"

"The last company did a terrible job, but they won't come back to fix it. I called several times."

Stone frowned as he set the table. "Is it that place on the edge of town with the dirty red truck parked in front?"

"Yes! I can't get them to make good on the work, even though I paid for a guarantee."

"I'll take care of it. I know some people over there."

"Thank you." It came out soft and grudgingly, but Stone had been making great strides in cracking Mrs. Blackfire's hard shell. The more he got to know her, he realized it was all a farce. She had no one in her life, and because she was so abrasive, people didn't stay around long enough to get to know her. Arilyn set out the portions, with a vase of happy yellow flowers, and poured water in all the glasses. "Of course, you can really help if you convince your girlfriend to chop down that tree for the winter. When the snow piles up, it's going to fall."

Patrick shook his head. "Joan, I promise you, it won't fall."

"You don't know that, Patrick! It's leaning much more to the right!"

Stone spoke up. "How about I personally trim that bigger branch back?"

"Great idea," Patrick said. "A compromise."

Mrs. Blackfire glanced back and forth, then sighed. "Fine. I can compromise."

"Done. Hey, how about—"

"Stone." His name shot out in the room like a cannon ball. He turned to Arilyn, worried, and saw her staring at something behind the counter. Her face reflected a bit of shock mixed with something close to joy. "Come over here. Slowly."

He took a few steps toward her and followed her gaze.

Pinky was sprawled out on Robert's back, her small head resting on his, nestled in the soft spot between his ears. Her eyes were half-closed in ecstasy.

Robert didn't move, his chin comfortably resting on the ground, a look of pleasure planted on his face, a half doggy grin widening his mouth.

And in that moment, something broke inside Stone's chest.

A gooey mess of junk poured out, making his damn eyes sting and a tightness squeeze his heart. Damned if that wasn't a sight to see. The two survivors, together, happy, and safe. A rush of emotion fought for dominance. He engaged in the fight of his life to keep it together.

"Cool. Guess they hooked up."

Arilyn jumped into his arms and hugged him tight. "I knew you could do it," she whispered. The warning in his head bolted to the danger zone, but she felt so good in his arms, so warm and solid and real, he ignored the flashing red lights for a while.

"No, *you* did it."

Patrick gave a booming laugh. "You both did it. Now sit your butts down and let's test out this Thug Kitchen recipe. They're a bit badass, so this may work."

Grinning like idiots, they sat at the table and ate.

And things were good.

Hours later, temporarily sated, holding her naked body close, Stone surrendered to his need for more. Once again, in the dark, in the quiet, it was safe. Morning would arrive soon enough, and he'd bury himself in work, gain a bit of distance. "Tell me about your mom."

She snuggled against him, as comfortably as Pinky did with Robert, and spoke. "Mom was amazing. Full of spit and vinegar, as Poppy would say. She did everything bigger than life—whether it be partying, eating, drinking, smoking, having fun. She liked the extremes. She wanted a bunch more children, but then they diagnosed her with the cancer, and she battled it for a year." Arilyn dragged in a breath. Stone stroked her hair, waiting. "In the end, I watched her die a little bit more every day. The cancer ate her alive until there was nothing left of the mother I knew. Dad couldn't handle it. He'd always been in her shadow and adored her more than the average husband. He kind of doted on her. After she passed, he lost something—the drive to go on. I thought I'd be enough, but I wasn't. Poppy was the one who found him. Swallowed pills. Left me a good-bye note."

Stone squeezed her tighter, the horror of losing both parents so quickly washing over him. "I'm sorry, little one. I can't even imagine how you got through it."

"I didn't for a while. Poppy thought he'd lose me, too. I guess I could've decided to go off the deep end or turn my life around. I chose the latter. A friend got me to go to a stress management workshop that incorporated yoga techniques. At the end, some of the poison I'd kept inside began to release. That's when I knew I had to commit to a different path. I thought if I worked on myself really hard, I'd find a way not to just survive but to live. The deeper I got, the more I loved it. Yoga and meditation and the karmic path felt right for me. Like I finally found a place of peace." She gave a half laugh empty of humor. "Sorry for the drama. I know you didn't have a picnic for a past either."

"Stop. Don't apologize for something real, something that made you fight. You know how many people I see day after day that just disintegrate—either with drugs or some other vice to kill the pain? You took the hard way. You're stronger than most men I know."

She relaxed a bit in his hold. "Poppy helped. That's why I want to be here for him. I told him I'd find another place and he could live with me, but he insisted he wants to stay at the center."

"He seems to be settling better. I think as long as he can go to Ray's for pool and see you regularly, he'll be okay."

"Me, too. I can't believe he's a bit sweet on Mrs. Blackfire. You know he mentioned Thanksgiving to her? Wants the three of us to be together. Who would've thought I'd be serving tofu turkey to the Wicked Witch of Verily?"

He chuckled. "Miracles happen. Since dating you, I haven't eaten a Big Mac."

"Thank God." She ruffled his hair and grinned. "What do you usually do for the holiday?"

He shrugged. "Work. Give the other guys with families a chance to be home."

"Well, it's an open invite to come here. Even after your shift, I'll keep your tofu hot."

The sudden realization they were now talking holidays after a cozy meal with her grandfather and neighbor hit him hard. Panic stirred. What was he doing? Things were moving way too fast; he needed to slow everything down. For God's sake, he now had a dog, had promised to fix Mrs. Blackfire's driveway, and had become well-known at the senior center. What was happening to him?

He grimaced. “Tofu will never touch my mouth. You’ll need to up your game.”

Her green eyes sparkled with mischief. “Consider it upped.” With one graceful movement, she rolled over to straddle him. Strawberry hair tumbling down her shoulders, hard peach nipples peeking through the strands, she arched, cupping her breasts, and he was hard again and ready to go. “How’s this?”

He had no spit but managed to mutter, “If I’m stuck with tofu, you better give me more.”

She dropped her voice to a husky, naughty growl. “Oh, I intend to.”

Lowering her head, she dropped kisses over his chest, moving down his body, until she cupped his throbbing erection in her soft hands and began to work him. Stone gritted his teeth and hung on. Her mouth opened over him, sucking him deep, her tongue running up and down the front and sides with an expert precision that almost made him weep like a girl.

After endless minutes of sweet torture, she pushed him to the edge, until he exploded in her mouth, his hips jerking as the brutal release of his orgasm crashed through him, pulling him deep into the pit. The last conscious thought echoing over and over in his head as he came was:

Mine.

Then he didn’t think anymore.

nineteen

STONE SAT IN the squad car. Fingers gripping the wheel, he stared at the door leading to the station and tried desperately not to panic.

"I can't do this. I've got a pile of paperwork that'll ground me in there all day, plus a double shift. You may have won over Devine, but those guys in there are hard-core, mean-ass brutes who'll eat you alive. And me. I'd have to transfer, and I just got used to Verily. I'm not fucking doing this."

No answer.

"Just because you don't piss me off in the car doesn't mean you can handle the station. And no, you can't stay with Robert, because you're getting way too attached to him. We need to learn to survive on our own. Not be needy for happiness or shit like that. We need to distance ourselves from both of them. Right?"

Still nothing. He glanced in the mirror.

She sat in her usual position in the backseat, body trembling with excitement. The damn rat fink now held Devine in the palm of her dainty paw, but she'd never make it with the others. His partner now admitted her coolness and even started sneaking her treats. Ridiculous.

Pinky and Robert had grown so close over the past few days that it was like watching the beginning of a love relationship in first bloom. They cuddled, lay on each other, shared food from one bowl, and played. How Pinky went from being catatonic and terrified of other animals to a charming hussy, he had no clue. But when she pulled the same shit and tried to block the door this morning, whimpering in disappointment at his departure for work, he decided not to rely on Arilyn and Robert and to bring her with him instead.

He was an ass.

"Fine. Let's get this over with. Not a word. And be cool. Do you understand me?"

He got out of the car, picked her up, and walked inside. After today, he might need to transfer. He'd need to make sure the guys understood it was a temporary situation and he was doing this to get laid. It was the only way to preserve his dignity.

Muttering a greeting to Jessica, the dispatcher, he pushed his way toward his desk, which was a mess of candy bar wrappers, stacks of paperwork, and the empty pack of Marlboros he still needed to smell on occasion. He hung his jacket over the back of his chair and placed Pinky down by the desk. He wished Devine were there to back him up, but he was coming in late from a dentist appointment.

"Stay quiet," he ordered. "You're so small, maybe no one will notice you. Got it?"

Pinky seemed to nod. She circled twice, then plopped down on the floor, looking content.

"What the hell is that?"

The booming voice came out of nowhere. Stone clenched his jaw and turned to meet Chief Dick. He pointed at Pinky, an expression of horror on his face. Yeah. This was not good.

"Uh, a dog, sir."

"I know it's a damn dog, Petty. What is the thing doing at your desk?"

Of course, his booming voice brought the crew over to investigate. Dunn and McCoy appeared, eyes bugging out as they stared, then burst into laughter. Why the hell were they there? He figured they'd be off duty by now.

"It's wearing a pink sweater!"

"Are those diamonds on its collar?"

"Why does it look like a rat?"

"It's the Taco Bell dog, but not."

Pinky raised her head, sensing the attention. Her little body began to shake as if she sensed she was being bullied.

"Cut the shit," Stone bellowed. "You're scaring her." His boss and coworkers stared at him as if he'd announced he was going to begin dancing at Lucky Cheng's. "Listen up. I'm dogsitting, her name is Pinky, and she's been through a lot of shit, so give her a break. Some jerks used her for bait, so she was torn up and abused. If you want to be a bunch of assholes, go ahead, but don't do it near her or me. She won't bother anyone, and if she acts up, I'll take her home. Okay?"

He waited for the jibes, jokes, and general insults. Instead, Chief Dick rolled his eyes. "Whatever. One bark and she's outta here." He dropped more papers on the desk. "Get to work."

"Yes, sir."

Dunn and McCoy snickered. "Did you go shopping for her, Petty? Going metrosexual on us, dude?"

He gritted his teeth and took it like a man. "Why

don't you go and sew a drag queen outfit, Make It Work Dunn?"

"Asshole. Hey, I saw you at the gym the other day. Was gonna have you spot me, but you were walking into some stretching class. What's up with that, Petty? You lose your balls, too?"

"You wish. I took the boxing class beforehand and left my water bottle. But you could use a few stretches, Timmy boy. Maybe bust out something better than missionary position for the ladies."

McCoy groaned in approval. Dunn gave him the finger and stalked off.

McCoy shook his head. "Rookie's gonna freak. He hates dogs." A glimmer lit his eyes. "Hey, can we put Rat Fink on his desk for when he comes in? That'll be a hoot."

Stone shrugged. "Sure, why the hell not."

McCoy wandered off, excited to make someone else's life a bit miserable, and Stone let out his breath. He glanced down at Pinky and winked. "We're good for now. Take a load off."

She collapsed back on the floor with a big doggy sigh and went to sleep.

IT WAS THE LAST day of anger management.

She was proud of what they had all accomplished together. One of her favorite things about the classes was getting to know people on such an intimate basis. The barriers were stripped; everyone got real and realized they weren't alone. Luther and Eli had blossomed over the session, and she felt that they would approach life differently. She had really helped.

Arilyn looked around the firehouse. Strange emotions pumped through her, and she took a moment to reconnect with her center.

Six weeks and her life had changed. Six weeks since Officer Stone Petty had trudged through the doors with a scowl and stole her heart. He challenged her, pushed her, surprised her, angered her, and gave her everything she'd always wanted from a man. But she'd learned a valuable lesson from Jacob. One had to be willing and present within the relationship or it was doomed. Already she sensed Stone backing away over the past few days, trying to find his lost footing.

She sensed he loved her. It was in his touch, the way he gazed at her, the way he buried himself deep in her body with satisfaction and tenderness. But if he fought his emotions and refused to believe they could have something permanent, she may need to make a hard decision.

Stone Petty showed her she deserved better.

Five years with Jacob had trained her to accept and be grateful for any crumbs. No more. She was whole, and good, and had a ton of love to give to someone. She wanted a man brave enough to leap with her and not blame his limitations on his inability to love or commit.

Arilyn sighed and paced the empty space. He'd changed over the past few days. Kennedy would have said he got spooked. He cited work to explain his sudden distance, defensively telling her that he needed to do double shifts for a while. His calls were brief and to the point. Already her body and heart ached for him, but he needed to find his way back to her on his own. If he even wanted to come back.

She was done chasing a man who didn't want her one hundred percent.

Stone had been right. She wasn't cut out for a one-night stand or short affair. She craved . . . everything.

There was one final counseling session to complete. Arilyn knew it would be her greatest challenge. She needed to approach the session as a therapist, not his lover. He held one final secret, and if he didn't admit and accept it, the wound would fester. She had sensed it from the beginning, but it hadn't been the right time to push.

Now it was.

A heavy sadness pressed upon her. She could lose him before they even had a fair shot. But it wasn't up to her anymore. The only thing she had left was to offer the truth. She loved him. He could fight it, accept it, or leave. Either way, she had to try, because that was her karma and path.

Arilyn dragged in a breath and got ready for class.

"HAVE I EVER TOLD you my fantasy? You're the star in that video by Van Halen, 'Hot for Teacher.' Short skirt, librarian glasses, hair pinned up."

She lifted a brow. "Wasn't she also half-naked and draped over a car?"

"No, that was a Whitesnake video. But that's a great visual. You on the hood of my Pontiac. I may never recover."

She decided to hold their final session at Kinnections. Stone sat across from her in the purple chair. Today he sported a charcoal Verily Police long-sleeved tee, jeans, and a Ray's Billiards ball cap perched sideways. One ankle was hooked over his knee. The chair barely held his big, muscled length, giving him that extra bolt of masculine roughness that always turned her on. He was looking deliciously scruffy and casual, and her fingers curled with the urge to touch him. She'd prepped herself for some snarky comments during the last class, but he'd been quiet, even slapping Luther and Eli on the shoulder and fist bumping in that male bonding tradition. They'd walked out together as usual and scheduled their last official counseling session for the books the next day. But things were a bit strained. When she told him Kate was picking up Robert in the morning, he used the excuse of meeting the guys at the billiards place later, then picking up another shift.

Oh, yeah. He was completely spooked.

Arilyn cleared her throat, looked down at her notes from the last session, and tried to get back to business. "I've never done this," she offered. "Counseled my lover. But I promise not to cross the line during the next hour if you do the same."

"I know another way we can spend this session," he growled. "And clothes are optional."

"Stone."

"Sorry." He slouched in the chair, looking resigned. "I'll be good. Pick away."

She took a few breaths, recentered, and began. "Let's talk about the incident that caused you to transfer. Another domestic abuse case."

His muscles stiffened. He began picking at a cuticle, a sure sign he was trying to distance himself. "Yep. Same type of thing. Asshole was beating up his wife. Things got out of control. My gun went off."

Her sweaty hand clutched the pen, but her voice

remained serene. She'd read through the description many times. Combined with his past and his record, Arilyn had a good idea he was hiding something. It was her job to poke the sore so it could bleed clean and heal. "Can you take me through all the details, please? You responded to the call with your partner."

His tone was flat as he recited from his mental list of canned answers. "We got the call. My partner and I arrived at the home. Heard screams from a child and a woman. Male shouts. A verbal threat he intended to kill her. We busted in the door and found the perp punching the woman at the bottom of the stairs. She was trying to crawl up to get away. My partner ran to get the child out of the line of immediate danger."

"And then what happened?"

He refused to look up. "Perp turned toward me and lurched forward. Went to reach in his pocket to pull out what looked like a weapon. I shot first."

Her throat tightened. She waited a moment to gather her thoughts. "But you didn't kill him."

"No, it was a shoulder shot. Internal affairs investigated and found me clean, with a validated threat to warrant the shot. Partner backed me up."

"Then why did you really transfer?"

He lifted his gaze. Dark eyes filled with ice stared back at her. "Because after I shot him, I lost it. My temper. My sanity. I beat the shit out of him and couldn't stop until my partner pulled me off. I was deemed volatile, so they suggested I go to a less intense territory. I picked Verily and here I am. Good enough?"

No. Oh, he'd been truthful. Stone didn't lie, but his omissions were the key. She wanted to go to him as his lover, press her head against his chest, and tell him it was okay. But Arilyn stayed frozen in the chair, knowing she had to finish what she had started and keep her role neutral. It was the only way.

"Why do you think that particular incident incited such rage?"

He let out an aggravated breath. "Oh, let's see. Maybe because I watched my father beat the hell out of my mother? I watched a similar situation unfold and reacted. Come on. It's textbook. You can do better than that."

"Yes, I can." She studied him, and the way he held himself stiff, as if warding off an attack. "I agree with your theory. It is textbook, and you've admitted it, tried to fix your limitations, and move on. I admire you for that, Stone. But there's something you haven't told me yet. Haven't told anyone, I think."

He glared. "Look, I gave you everything I got. If that's not enough blood for you to play with, excuse me while I go tap another vein."

"Who else were you trying to protect when your father pushed your mother down the stairs?"

He jerked as if she'd shot him. Raw, ugly emotions crossed over his features, dragging him to a dark place Arilyn knew she couldn't follow him. She could only try to get him back.

"No one."

"I don't believe you."

"Fuck this." He scraped back the chair and got to his feet. "I think this session is officially over. I've done what you wanted, and I deserve for you to sign those goddamn forms so I can get back to work and my real life."

She tried not to flinch at the open anger pouring from him in choppy waves. "This is your real life," she said calmly. "There's a bigger trigger going on, and until we find it, you're not going to be able to get past it."

"The only other trigger is in your imagination. Now that you taught me to breathe properly, I should be fine." He yanked his cap down low over his eyes. "I'm outta here. Do what you want."

"Stone?"

"What?"

"I'll be home if you want to talk."

He didn't answer. The door slammed behind him, and Arilyn sank into the chair, wondering if she'd pushed too hard. Wondering if she had lost him forever.

WHO THE HELL DID she think she was?

Rage pumped through his muscles. At first, the end of the anger counseling sessions caused a strange mix of confusion. Sure, he wanted it the hell over with, but he'd become used to seeing her every day.

He'd pulled back these past few days. Worked extra. Met the guys for a few rounds of billiards. What scared him the most?

He missed her. And Patrick. And that damn wicked witch neighbor he was beginning to like. He missed her cooking, and the general chaos, and the way she pulled him in tight at night, her body completely surrendering to every dark, dirty thing he wanted to do to her and with her.

He waited for her to whine, or complain about him

not coming over. He readied himself to battle for his freedom and guys' night out. But she never said a word. Just supported him in whatever decision he made, said she'd miss him, and let him go.

The woman frustrated the hell out of him.

But this? This was too much. Poking around in his head again under the guise of therapist. If she wanted to know about his past, all she had to do was ask. He'd never hidden anything from her, even the shit he preferred to keep locked up nice and tight.

Who else were you protecting?

A shiver bumped through him. Screw it. He was gonna meet the guys, have a few beers, and go home. He'd take an early shift in the morning and keep his head straight. Then maybe he'd call her to sort out what the hell they were doing.

Stone played pool. He looked for Patrick, who wasn't there, and settled in with his coworkers. They bashed each other in good fun, drank, and had a decent time. He ignored the clawing emptiness in his gut and decided he was hungry. When they pushed a plate of fried shit over to him, he thought he heard her voice whispering in his ear to please eat something grilled, since it was a lot healthier.

He lost it.

"I gotta go." He stood, said his good-byes, and headed out. The November air was chilly and brisk, but he zipped up his jacket and decided the walk would be good for him to clear his head. With each step closer to her house, the anger built. He hadn't asked for a permanent relationship with a woman who'd drive him crazy. He liked to keep things simple, but she didn't know what simple was. He needed to confront her tonight and remind her that their relationship was about sex. *Just* sex.

He also needed to give Pinky back.

Kate had returned. Robert was to go home, and that would leave Arilyn available to take Pinky. Hell, he'd warned her it was temporary anyway, and Pinky would do better there. Much better than carting her around to the station and in the squad car. Better than sneaking her hamburgers and allowing her to sleep in bed with him as if she were a person.

Better than him.

The light shone brightly on Arilyn's front porch. He walked up the path, noting her top step needed repairing and the bungalow could use a fresh coat of paint. The screen in the window was still torn. He meant to replace it last week before the winter kicked in. Stone knocked on the door.

When she opened it, he lost his breath.

God, she was beautiful. She'd changed into a cotton nightgown with little pink roses on them. Old-fashioned. But delicate lace edged a low scoop neckline, emphasizing smooth white skin and a hint of cleavage. The fabric clung to her so he could clearly see the outline of her lithe body. Her hair was loose and wild, falling to her hips. Feet bare. Face scrubbed of makeup. She stared at him for a few moments. Then smiled.

Stone tightened his stomach muscles as if he had taken a hard punch to the gut. Had he ever met another woman who stopped his heart cold and filled him up with emotion? Just being around her made him damn happy. Her smile gave everything she was and asked for nothing in return.

The weight on his chest pressed harder, until he wasn't able to pant, let alone breathe.

Arilyn reached out, took his hand, and pulled him inside.

"Did you have fun playing pool?"

He studied her in moody silence. His head felt like it was cracking open, and she was trying to be polite. "What the hell are we doing, Arilyn?"

She dropped his hand and took a step back. He cursed when he saw the hurt flash in those meadow-green eyes, but he was too far gone. "Don't you know yet?" she said softly. "I do."

He rubbed his scalp and began to pace. "Actually, I know what the plan was. Have great sex. Date. A few laughs. But lately it's been more than that. I'm feeling pressure and I don't know if this is working out."

He waited for her thoughtful response and her need for a dialogue. Instead, she grabbed his arm, yanked at him, and got in his face.

"Don't give me those lame excuses because you got spooked!" she shot back. "The only pressure you're feeling right now is from yourself. I didn't ask for this, either, buddy, but here it is, and I'm going to deal with it!"

He sneered and leaned in. "I knew you'd start spinning cozy fantasies about us. How many times do I have to tell you I'm no good for the long term?"

"Bullshit." She shoved at his chest in pure fury. "So you're divorced? Big deal. So you're a cop? Big deal. So you like to go shoot pool with the guys every Friday night? Oooh, so scary! I didn't put any pressure on you, and I don't intend to. But I'm not going to pussyfoot around the big bad cop and not be honest about my feelings. I've done that enough with my ex."

"Don't compare me to him again!" he yelled. "He's a son of a bitch who never deserved you!"

"Neither do you if you keep acting like an ass!"

"I know!"

They fell silent, panting, the energy building and raging around them. The sexual connection crackled like a live wire, and then he was pulling her against his chest and his lips slammed down over hers and he was drowning.

He ripped down her bodice and shoved her gown up to her waist. She moaned in the back of her throat, clawing at his jeans, her mouth opening wide to the thrust of his tongue. Stone tore off her panties, yanked her leg up, and drove his fingers deep into her core.

She cried out. He lowered his forehead to hers while his fingers sunk into wet, burning heat. He curled his middle finger just the way she liked it until he hit the sweet spot and she shuddered violently. "I gotta have you now," he gritted out, frantically searching for the condom he always kept in his pocket.

"Quickly," she urged. Another shudder caught her and a rush of liquid coated his hand. She fumbled, then her hand closed around his erection, stroking, guiding him to the sweetness between her thighs. "I can't wait."

In two seconds, he donned the condom, lifted her leg higher, and buried himself deep inside.

Mine.

Everything in him shifted, falling into place, giving him a sense of rightness at the same time his body practically wept with the need to claim her. He couldn't be gentle or slow, but she matched him thrust for thrust, her short nails digging into his shoulders, her back slammed against the wall, moans being ripped from her throat as she bit into his bottom lip and hung on.

He fucked her, possessed her, and fell in love with her in that moment.

Then he came.

Her cries in his ear told him she was right there with him, and they fell into each other with no safety net, her body shaking as he pulled her tight and held her. Whispered in her ear. Stroked her hair.

Surrendered.

"I love you."

Her voice drifted up, over, and around him. Simplicity and truth and elegance in those three little words. Stone held her tight, but his throat closed up and there was nothing to say.

"I know you don't like it. Maybe you don't even believe me. I know it's fast and complicated and messes up a great affair. I'm not even asking for the words back. But I love you. Every part, good and bad. I love your big heart, and your crankiness, and your loyalty. I love your work ethic, and the way you deal with the world, and the way you look at me. I just love you."

Half-naked, still inside her, her musky arousal rose to his nostrils like the sweetest of perfumes. Stone closed his eyes and spoke.

"The night my father pushed my mother down the stairs, I found out she was pregnant. It was supposed to be a surprise. She hit the fifteen-week mark, and when I got home from school, she took me aside and told me I'd have a brother or sister."

He paused in the shattering silence. Then continued. "I was so happy. Things had been good for a while, and I thought my father would change once he heard. I was so lonely that I fantasized about having a sibling to take care of. To talk to at night. I imagined we'd be close, and it would be us against the world. I swore that day I'd protect the baby. But that didn't happen. Instead, he came home drunk that night and went at my mom with a baseball bat. Said she was keeping secrets from him and thought she was having an affair. She told him about the pregnancy, but he didn't believe her. Too late anyway. I tried to stop him, but she fell and broke her neck and lost the baby and I didn't have anyone anymore."

Something eased in his chest as the words spilled forth. Her arms held him tight, and he buried his lips in her hair, and it wasn't as bad as he had thought it would be. No one had ever known about that part. And he'd decided if it was his own secret, the pain and guilt would just go away. He couldn't protect his mother or the unborn baby. He couldn't protect anyone.

"That night in the Bronx," Arilyn said. "When you shot that man, and beat him up. The wife was pregnant, wasn't she?"

"Yeah. Five months. The baby was okay, though. She got lucky."

They stayed together for a while, not speaking. He'd never experienced comfort without sex, and he allowed himself to surrender to the embrace and the woman he was in love with.

"I'm so sorry, Stone. Thank you for telling me."

He thought about where they could go from here. Still, there was no way it would work. He was a stubborn SOB, a lifelong bachelor, and had no desire to set up a future with children and dogs and a white picket fence. It would be good for a while. Real good. But then he'd work one too many late nights, go back to eating shitty food, lose his temper, and begin disappointing her. The spiral would begin.

"Come to bed with me."

The invitation was more than physical. It was an askance of the next step for them both.

Stone pulled back and stared at her beautiful face. Stroked her swollen lips. Cupped her cheeks. Kissed her again.

"I can't, Arilyn. I can't do this."

Pain and grief flickered in those green eyes. "You can. You're choosing not to try."

"I'm choosing not to disappoint you. It's better this way. You're better off without me."

She pushed him away and he let her. He got himself together, disposed of the condom, and when he came back, she was frozen in place, her arms wrapped around her chest, squeezing tight, as if desperate for warmth. Something broke inside of him and Stone realized he'd never be whole again. Still, he didn't reach for her.

He believed he was doing the right thing. Better now than later. Better now before it was too much for both of them.

He stopped at the door. "I'll bring Pinky over in the morning."

Her words were cold and deliberate. "Don't. I'm

asking you to keep her longer, Stone. You don't have to be there for me. I've learned I'm strong and can heal. But Pinky needs to believe in something, and for now, that's you. If you let her go, you'll break her heart. And she may not heal from that."

His eyes burned as he reached for the knob. "I'll think about it."

He left.

I LOST HIM."

Tears streamed from her eyes, and a horrible hiccupping sob kept escaping her lips. She'd officially lost it. No breathing or meditation or calm reflection for her. She was falling apart in a wreck of emotion, and thank God, her only audience was her best friends.

After Stone left, she spent the rest of the night in a numb state, trying to accept that she'd lost the battle. She got dressed for work the next morning, followed her strict routine, and managed to keep it together for the first few hours at Kinnections. Then when Kate and Kennedy popped their heads into her office to ask about Stone, she completely broke down.

"Oh, sweetie!" Kate took her in a tight embrace. "Kennedy will hurt him for you."

"Hell, yes I will. What happened? Oh my God, did he cheat? Get nasty? Lie?"

Arilyn gulped and dashed away her tears. "N-N-No. I told him I loved him, and he couldn't handle it, so he left."

Kennedy groaned. "I told you not to confess it yet! The son of a bitch got spooked!"

"Stop yelling at her," Kate said. "She did the right thing telling him the truth. Arilyn can't handle deception well. Maybe he'll come back?"

Arilyn hiccupped again. “No. He’s not coming back. He even wanted to give back Pinky. I hate him!”

“We do, too.”

Arilyn shook her head. “No, I really love him. Ugh, he was supposed to be my transitional. How did this happen? I didn’t even like him at first.”

“He used sex to blind you to his deficiencies,” Kennedy said. “It’s like men get a training session in how to do that and not put down a toilet seat.”

“I hate crying! I’m so pissed, I want to do something crazy.”

Kennedy jumped up from the couch. “I’ll call Gen. We’ll dress up, go out, get trashed, and torture men.”

Arilyn gave a half laugh when Kate nodded frantically. “Yes, that’s good. Let’s do it.”

“It’s three o’clock,” Arilyn pointed out. “It’s a workday.”

“Not anymore!” Kate announced. “We’re closing up for the day and heading out. I’ll come with you to your place, and we’ll all meet at Mugs. Deal?”

“Done,” Kennedy said.

“I don’t think solving problems with alcohol is a good idea,” Arilyn said weakly.

Kennedy rolled her eyes. “Darlin’, it’s the only thing we have left. Get your ass in gear. We’re drinking.”

This time Arilyn didn’t protest, just followed them out.

“DUDE. WHAT’S UP WITH you?”

Stone maneuvered the car through the packed streets of Verily. People were out in droves to shop before the holidays rolled in, and the stores were taking full advantage. The town pulled out all the stops to draw crowds. Even now, the streetlamps were strung with cheerful white lights, and shop windows competed with displays of food, clothing, or art to draw in pedestrians. Dogs and their owners lined up at the Barking Dog Bakery for treats, and people strolled sipping espresso, holding large bags, and giving in to the draw of the upstate river town that charmed with an innate grace and character.

Stone grunted. He spotted Pinky in the rearview mirror, staring out the window at the other dogs with perfect manners. After that first day at the station, he'd brought her in twice more, and suddenly his coworkers were getting all weird. Even Chief Dick said it was okay to bring her in every day as long as she behaved. As if Pinky realized she was the new police mascot, her confidence spiked and she now preened for them all. Dunn began feeding her the damn Munchkins from Dunkin', and McCoy bought her a frickin' squeaky toy. Even the rookie stopped complaining and threatening him with the Board of Health. In a matter of a week, his hard-core cop buddies who'd once made fun of her now took turns visiting his desk to hang.

It annoyed the crap out of him.

But Pinky was getting much better. Probably good enough to find a permanent home. He kept delaying the day he would give her back to Arilyn but decided it needed to be done sooner than later. Pinky needed a real family. Not a bunch of workaholic, donut-eating cops.

Devine kept talking. "You're a real asshole plus a

bore. When McCoy rigged your computer mouse not to work, you freaked so bad, I thought you were gonna beat the crap out of him. When you're not surly, you're moping around, making me miserable. Hey, should we stop at the Barking Dog for her? She likes those sugar cookies."

Stone shot him a glare and kept his eyes on the road. "No, she's eating too much sugar lately. Sorry if I'm not your Mr. Charming, but I hate the holidays. They're full of expectations and promise that never get fulfilled."

"Did you graduate from Harvard psychology, man? What's up with that mumbo jumbo?"

"Forget it."

"I thought you'd be happy. You're the one who broke it off with her, right? You had some good sex, got your freedom back, a cool dog. What more do you want?"

Arilyn Meadows. He missed her more than smoking. He missed her body, her smile, her laugh. He missed her makeshift family and the anger management sessions. There was this big-ass void in his gut and his life that he couldn't understand or get past.

He'd never been in love before. His marriage with Ellen had been a pale ghost of the real thing, which he knew now. The short affairs before had just been lust. Now that he'd experienced the real thing, he was ruined.

"Nothing."

"Son of a bitch." The softly spoken curse jarred his ears. Devine let out a hearty laugh. "You fell in love with her! Why the hell did you break it off?"

"Shut up."

"Hell, no, I'm not shutting up. What's up with you, dude? If she made you happy, why didn't you just be with her?"

He gritted his teeth so hard, he thought shards would snap out of his mouth. "We're not good together for the long haul," he said tightly. "I only did it sooner to spare both of us heartache."

"Yeah, how's that working out for you?"

"Fuck you."

"No, fuck you! You finally meet a decent woman who wants to put up with your crap, and you break up with her for the greater good? What about what you want for a change? What did you do so horrible in your past life that you don't deserve to be happy?"

Stone glared. "Look, my marriage was a mess. This job sucks you dry. I don't do long-term."

"You never did before because you didn't meet the right one," Devine pointed out.

"I don't want to talk about this anymore. Drop it. We got a double-parked vehicle in front of Xpressions. Go do something with your life rather than ride me and write up a damn ticket. The town needs money."

Stone pulled over. Devine studied him, shook his head hard, and muttered something foul. "Whatever, dude. It's your life."

"That's right. My life. My decision."

"It's an asshat decision. Ain't no guarantees for anyone."

Devine climbed out of the car, pulled out his pad, and began to run the plate. Stone stared out the windshield, his mind turning over his friend's words.

LATER THAT NIGHT, HE made his decision.

It didn't take him long to pack up the belongings. A dog bed, some food, her favorite chew toys. She was already wearing the sweater and collar. The fuchsia bling-encrusted leash should be illegal, but it was the perfect length and size, so he kept it.

Pinky raced to the door, sitting quietly, body shaking with excitement. A sick nausea hit his stomach. Damn. He hoped he wasn't getting a virus. Stone forced a smile he didn't feel and knelt down to her level.

"Look, this is going to be for the best. You're gonna be with a real family. Kids, parents who love and take care of you. No one is ever gonna hurt you again, I swear to God. And I'll never forget you."

As if sensing something hidden, Pinky frowned, then trotted close to lick his cheek.

Stone cleared his throat and picked her up. "Let's do this."

By the time he reached her porch, his nausea had gotten worse, until he felt as if he could vomit right there in her bushes. He pushed down the feeling and waited.

She opened the door.

He jerked back. God, why did it feel even worse? Wasn't time supposed to make things better and more in perspective? He drank in her appearance, from her usual yoga pants and T-shirt to her hair scooped in a ponytail. The scents of dinner cooking drifted outside the door. Music came from the background, and he caught Patrick's booming voice as he talked to Mrs. Blackfire.

Panic struck him. He took a few steps back in retreat, not knowing if he could go through with it.

"You really want to do this, Stone?" she asked.

Those beautiful green eyes were devoid of her usual vibrancy. They stared back at him with a flat coldness that stripped away his sanity.

"I'm sorry," he managed to choke out. "I just think it's for the best. She's getting better with other dogs, and I know she'll do well with you. You can get her a real home."

Her gaze narrowed in disgust. "She already has a real home. With you. She loves you."

His stomach roiled. Stone tried to speak, but nothing came out. Bile blocked his throat.

Finally, she released a small, disappointed sigh, shaking her head. "Sorry. I forgot. You don't do love." Arilyn reached out and took a quivering Pinky firmly into her arms. "Come on, baby. Robert's not here, but maybe we'll take a walk to Kate's so you can see him. I promise we'll be okay."

Feeling like he'd been slapped, Stone quietly handed over the equipment. Stepped back.

Pinky seemed to catch the vibe and wiggled in Arilyn's grasp. A low whimper broke from her throat as she swiveled her small ratlike head to gaze imploringly at him.

Please. Don't leave me. I love you.

As if the dog had shouted the words, the sickness rose up and strangled him in a death grip. He turned quickly, trying to take in air, needing to escape, needing to rip off the Band-Aid before he took them both back and damn the consequences.

"Thank you," he muttered. Then, like the coward

he truly was, Stone turned and disappeared, the echo of Pinky's whines ripping at his ears.

A WEEK LATER, STONE nursed an IPA at Ray's Billiards. The guys were playing a rowdy game of pool behind him, and the normal dialogue consisting of insults, ribbing, and cursing filled the air. It was familiar. Nice. Of course, they were still pissed at him for giving up Pinky, which was so ridiculous he didn't even know how to defend himself. Dunn still wasn't talking to him. Whatever. He'd done his best.

Still, nothing seemed able to thaw the nugget of ice that had lodged inside his body and refused to go away. Not even his constant mantra that he'd made the right decisions.

Damn, he was tired. Since their breakup, Stone did everything that always previously satisfied him. Lots of drinking and pool and hanging with the guys. He'd gone through the McDonald's drive-through every day. Worked extra shifts, covering for most of the guys until he had a fat OT check deposited in his account. Things had picked up around the holidays, offering him a big drug bust, so for days he'd achieved a contact high from all the weed kept in the evidence locker. Hell, even his house was relaxing. The bed to himself, the television as loud as usual, no dog hair or ridiculous pink items scattered about.

Things were great.

He took another sip of beer.

Yeah, he was falling apart. And he didn't know what to do anymore.

A shadow fell across the bar. He glanced over and

took in Patrick's thoughtful expression. Since the breakup, he hadn't heard a peep from him and figured he was avoiding Ray's to keep from punching him in the face. Stone ached for anything to pierce past the numbness.

"Wanna take a shot at me?" he mumbled. "I won't budge."

Patrick raised his hand in greeting to Ray and ordered a Guinness. "Nope."

"I mean it. Let's see what you got, old-timer." Stone slid off the bar stool and faced Arilyn's grandfather. "I deserve it. Punch me."

Patrick laughed and shook his head. "Damn right you deserve it. But no punch is necessary. One look at you gave me all the revenge I ever needed. You look like shit."

"Flatterer."

God, he needed help.

Patrick sipped his beer and remained silent for a while. "Gonna play a round?"

"Nah." Stone waited for him to bring up Arilyn, but the man seemed happy drinking and pondering life. "How are things?"

"Good. The center put on some comedy show. Ended up being pretty decent. They made fun of the old people instead of pussyfooting around stuff. Even Emma laughed, and she's like a corpse."

"And Mrs. Blackfire?"

"She's joining us for Thanksgiving. Finally gave up on the Tree of Spite and promised me she wouldn't give Arilyn crap anymore."

"Great." He waited. Still nothing. "Anything else."

"Nope. What about you? Still taking extra shifts?"

"How is she?"

This time Patrick raised his brow. Gave him a hard stare. Stone took it all, lifting his chin and open to receiving any blistering insult he deserved. He was such a fuckup. He was the one who had broken up with her, yet he was desperate just to hear her name. Sometimes he said it aloud in his empty house. He'd called her damn cell phone from a blocked number, hoping to get her voice mail.

"Surviving," Patrick answered. "She misses you but is pushing forward. Arilyn is a survivor. She'll make it without you just fine."

He muttered a curse under his breath. Took another large gulp of beer. "Yeah. I know. Better this way."

"Actually, no. It's not better. That's just in your screwed-up head. Funny thing is, I get it. I've been there."

"What do you mean?"

Patrick pushed a hand through his silver mane and stared at the wall. Seeing something no one else could. "The damn war. When I got back from Nam I was all sorts of messed up. I watched my buddies explode before me. Kids die. The stench and the heat and the feeling I'd never get out of there alive. War takes something human from you, and it's difficult to get it back. Arilyn's grandmother was the one who had to deal with it all. When things got serious, and I realized I loved her, I did terrible things. I hurt her bad in the name of protection. Told her over and over she was better off with someone whole, someone who could give her what she wanted."

Every muscle tensed, waiting for the rest of the story. "What happened?" he asked.

Patrick gave a sigh. "I sent her away. But she just kept coming back. It was the damnedest thing. She just took that crap I dealt her and showed up on a regular basis. She knew I loved her, and she decided to stay in it for the long haul. It could've ended up differently, but thank God, something finally broke and I realized I was being an idiot. I'd gone through war. Seen the worst. Why couldn't I also experience the best? Why deny myself a gift of a woman who loved me and my crap?"

He emitted a humorless laugh. "Men are different from women. We put these obstacles and expectations on ourselves, thinking we need to protect and always win the war. Sometimes you just don't. Shit happens. Crime, divorce, and abuse. But I had a choice to try to do my best with the woman I loved. Yeah, I made tons of mistakes. But we were married for thirty-three years before I lost her. Worth it? Hell, yes."

Stone stared at the man across from him, who had the gleam of misty memories in his green eyes, so like his granddaughter's. "You know what, Stone? Sometimes it's not as complicated as you think. If you love her, then just love her. Do your best. Why don't you deserve something great, too? Because Arilyn really doesn't need much from you except for you to try, and be there, and love her back. How's that for expectations?"

The deep freeze that had taken root for over a week suddenly shifted. A sliver of the ice moved, melted, and suddenly the breath that hadn't been there before eased back into his lungs. His heart beat a bit faster. Well, damn. What a concept. How was that for some enlightened Buddha shit?

Just love her back.

He already did. Yeah, it wasn't gonna change his crap, but he had that part covered already.

He loved Arilyn Meadows. Heart and soul. And he loved that damn rat fink dog so much, if he didn't get her back, he was gonna lose it.

As if knowing his emotions were about to implode, Patrick patted him on the back. "Got it?"

Stone shook his head. "Yeah. I got it."

"Good."

"You need a ride back to the center, Patrick? I have to make a call."

"No, go ahead. I'm gonna play a round. Devine will give me a ride."

"Thanks."

Stone fumbled for his phone and headed out the door. The cold air whipped at his face, clearing his head, and without thinking, going on pure impulse, he dialed her number.

One ring. Two. Three.

"Hello?"

"It's me. No, don't hang up!"

The silence spoke volumes. Her usual musical voice was flat. "What do you want?"

"I want Pinky back."

The endless words he ached to tell her backed up in his throat until only that one sentence spilled out. Maybe she'd understand what he meant. Pinky was the symbol of everything he wanted but never thought he deserved.

"You want Pinky back. Why?"

"I made a big mistake, Arilyn. Huge. Colossal. I'm coming over to pick her up and talk to you."

"You're drunk, aren't you?"

"No! No, just a bit—not really. I had a few beers. But I'm not drunk."

A small sigh puffed over the phone. "I get it, Stone, I really do. But I can't do this. You get drunk, you feel lonely, you think you can handle it. I've been here before. You miss Pinky's company and the way she adored everything about you, with no concept of asking for anything back except your attention. Trust me, in the morning it'll all come flooding back, and you'll back away again. I lived this dance, and I'm done. I'm sorry. Maybe you were right after all, and we're better off apart. Including Pinky."

His heart now exploded and his body went into junkie-in-need-of-a-fix mode. Sweat poured from his skin, panic settled in his gut, and he couldn't seem to catch his breath. "No, please listen to me; it's different than you think. Just let me come over and explain it."

"No! I won't open the door, Stone. You need to go back to the bar and your friends and your life. You'll thank me tomorrow."

"But Pinky— "

"Pinky's gone," she whispered.

No. No, no, no, no. "What do you mean?"

"Anthony is sending her to another shelter to work with a behaviorist. He's an expert in abused animals and thinks they can get her a family. I'm fostering three new dogs who come in a few days. It was the right decision."

"You gave her away?"

An arctic blast exploded into the phone. "No. *You* gave her away, remember? Please don't call me again."

The phone clicked.

Stone stared at his cell phone. This couldn't be happening. How had he experienced the biggest revelation of his life, yet she wasn't ready to listen to him? Pinky wasn't meant to be with another family or a behaviorist who didn't understand she only liked hamburgers and slept on the right side and preferred peanut butter chewy bones.

Pinky was meant to be with him.

In the middle of a full-fledged panic attack, he closed his eyes and did the only thing possible before completely losing it.

He breathed.

In and out. Feeling the air seep and fill up his lungs with everything good and positive. Then release all the bad toxins and thoughts out into the universe. His body calmed. His mind cleared. And an odd peace settled over him, showing him the only road he had left to take.

ARILYN FINISHED HER MEDITATION and slowly opened her eyes. The screens were down since Lenny and Mike had left, but she'd need to erect them again when her new charges came later that day. She usually enjoyed the hushed quiet that filled the bungalow, but lately it beat with an undercurrent of loneliness she seemed unable to fight.

God, she missed Stone.

Anger hit her full force when she thought of his phone call. Stupid drunken musings. She was well versed in those from Jacob. Jacob, who'd have too many cocktails and get weepy. Who promised to change and begged her forgiveness, only to go back to exactly how things were. The crazy thing? She knew Stone loved her. Yet he'd not only walked away from her without a backward glance, but he'd also walked away from Pinky. The last week with the Chihuahua had been heartbreaking. She waited at the door for Stone to enter, a frozen statue who believed her master would reappear. Arilyn had taken her to Kate's every day to spend time with Robert, who seemed to be the only one to calm her. With genuine love and affection, he'd nudge her with his giant nose, flop down, and allow her to crawl over on his back.

Kate had mentioned adopting her, but Arilyn believed the new behaviorist and a clean slate would give Pinky what she needed.

Trying to swallow past the tightness in her throat, she rolled to her feet, blew out her incense sticks, and strode to the kitchen. It would be a long day at Kinnections, and then she needed to go pick up her new dogs. Ever since opening up more to her friends and her grandfather, she felt better able to cope. Oh, it hurt so bad, sometimes she just lay there clutching her chest. Then it eased, and she reminded herself of all she had to give. She had a full life, and she would have the love she dreamed of. This time, it would be with someone who'd give it all back to her.

The sharp knock on the door interrupted her mental cheerleading. She peeked through the curtain and opened the door. "Hi, Mrs. Blackfire. Everything okay?"

"Yes. Do you have a minute to talk?"

Arilyn frowned. "Sure. I'll make you some tea; I have to leave for work soon."

The walker clicked over the floors and her neighbor settled in her favorite chair by the pine table. “None of that crazy stuff, please. Good old Lipton. Why does it smell like drugs in here?”

Arilyn grinned. “It’s incense. Helps to connect the body-mind center through the sense of smell.”

“Smells like marijuana to me. Where are the dogs?”

“They don’t come till later. Poppy’s coming for dinner tomorrow.”

“Good, I’ll bring dessert this time. I’m baking some Irish soda bread. Your grandfather has an affinity for it, though he eats too much.”

“Sounds perfect.” She handed her the cup of hot tea and sat down. “What did you want to talk about?”

“Officer Stone Petty. You love him, right?”

She almost dropped the cup. “Umm. Umm. Well, ummm—”

“Yes or no will do, missy.”

“Yes. But it won’t work. He got spooked and took off. It’s over.”

“Bah,” Mrs. Blackfire spit out. “He’ll be back. They always come back. Usually drunk.”

This time the cup clattered to the table, spilling tea. “Oh my God, how did you know that?”

“Because I was young once. Before I lost my husband in the war, we played a bit of a chess game ourselves. He didn’t want to settle so young. I wanted to get married. We broke up once. He had too many whiskeys and ended up at my front door, begging my forgiveness.”

“What did you do?” she asked, fascinated.

“Made him suffer a bit and then took him back.

Sometimes you need to be the better one. We have no choice."

Arilyn's shoulders slumped. "I don't know. He gave up Pinky. I don't know if I trust him not to spook again. I just don't think I can do it."

"If you love him, you have to make a decision to give him a second chance. If you think he's the one, you have to take a leap. But first, torture him. It's only fair." She finished her tea in a few unladylike gulps and stood. "I better let you go. I'll see you tomorrow."

She grabbed her walker and headed out.

"Mrs. Blackfire?"

"Yes?"

Arilyn smiled. "Thank you."

Her neighbor scowled. "Just make sure you keep that tree trimmed. It's already leaning way too much to the right."

The door slammed behind her.

twenty-one

I'M HERE TO pick up Pinky."

Anthony stared at him. Blinked. Stone had come in full uniform, because he wasn't fucking around anymore. He laid a sweaty palm over his gun holster and held his gaze with a steely determination.

"Pinky? Didn't Arilyn tell you? We're sending her to Jim, who's our new behaviorist. He'll be working with her from his home, and then a permanent home will be found for her."

Stone lay both palms flat on the desk and leaned in. "I don't think you understand, Anthony. Pinky already has a home. With me. I want her back."

Was that a small smile on the man's face or a flash of light? The director turned away so quickly he wasn't sure. He perused a shelf, pulled out a manila folder, and glanced through his notes. "I know you got attached to her, Officer Petty. But she needs a proper home. Arilyn explained you gave her up because you couldn't handle the responsibility of a dog, so we won't be able to give her back to you. Happens too many times. The owner decides it's too hard to take care of a dog, gives them up, misses them for a while, and wants them back. A few weeks go by and we find ourselves with the dog back in our shelter and a heartbroken animal we need to rehabilitate."

"I understand," he said calmly. "I do. I was an asshole, and I was confused. About a lot of things. But I'm ready to commit to being Pinky's owner on a full-time basis. I'll sign whatever you want. Give you money."

Anthony frowned and cocked his hip. "It's not about the money. Never was. It's about commitment. Now, why don't you think about it some more, and if you still want a dog, I'll find you one that will fit your lifestyle better. Maybe a German shepherd."

"I don't want a shepherd," he said through gritted teeth. "I want my Chihuahua back with her stupid pink collar and sweater and bat ears and rat face. I love her, okay?"

Stone saw the softening of the director's features, but he still didn't budge. "And I appreciate that. But you were the one who told me your shifts are endless and there's no one to take care of her. Not a good match."

"Oh, for God's sake, man, give me a break. I take her to work with me."

Anthony coughed. "You what?"

"Yeah, I take her. She likes the station and the squad car."

Anthony crossed his arms in front of his chest and looked doubtful. "Why am I finding that a bit hard to believe?"

"Ah, fuck. Give me a minute." Stone grabbed his cell and punched in the number. "Devine? Yeah, is McCoy there? Dunn? I need you down at the Animals Alive shelter. Don't give me this shit, I said I need you now or I'm not going to get Pinky back. We need to prove she's allowed at the station and in my squad car, and the director doesn't believe me. No, just take the police cars, 'cause I need you quick. I don't care! I'll take the heat with Dick! Get your asses over here now."

He clicked off. Anthony's mouth gaped open.

"They'll be here in five." He stabbed his finger in the air. "And once they give you the proof you want, I want my damn dog back."

ARILYN SCROLLED THROUGH ENDLESS pages of data and held back a sigh. She wasn't feeling her usual mojo, and all the numbers and matches and characteristics were giving her a headache.

Ah, heck, she had to admit the real reason.

She just didn't feel like matching anyone today. She was feeling a bit small, embittered, and whiny. The toddler voice beat through her head in an unending rhythm.

When is it my damn turn?

She sighed. Time to get it together. Maybe she'd cheer up once the dogs came. New fur babies were always a nice distraction, and their sweetness filled her up and gave her hope.

Her phone buzzed. "Umm, Arilyn? Can you come out here for a moment?"

She tried not to be bitchy, but she so did not want to meet with a client today. "Is it important? If it's a client, could you take care of it for me?"

A pause. "Not this one, babe. Better come quick."

She blew out a breath. "Fine. Be right there." Arilyn took a moment to breathe deep, in and out, find her center, and touch the calm. No reason to take out her bad day on someone who deserved her best. Trying to find the old spring in her step, she strolled out of her office, down the hall, and into the main reception area.

Then stopped short.

Stone Petty stood in the waiting room. There were two other clients there, staring at him curiously. In full uniform, looking badass and sexy as hell, he held Pinky.

Clad in her pink sweater and bling collar, the dog looked as if she had found her nirvana. The look of complete love and trust filled her eyes and her body, and emanated in waves of endless energy.

Pinky had forgiven him.

Her fingers flew to her mouth and pressed against her lips. "Wh-What are you doing?" she asked.

"I got her back." Those inky eyes were fierce, seething with raw emotion in a twist of lust, need, and determination. His muscles seemed locked and loaded, as if ready to explode in a rush and take her with him for the ride. The heat in her belly uncurled and spread through her veins like wildfire until she could only tremble, helpless under his gaze and the promise she so wanted to believe in.

"I fucked up. I won't again."

The room was eerily silent. Kate held her breath beside her. The two clients leaned forward, as if desperate to hear his next words. The slow patter of footsteps stopping in the hallway alerted her to Kennedy's presence. Nothing mattered but the man in front of her holding his dog.

"How . . . how do I know?"

"You don't. Look, I'm no poet, and I suck at these big endings and declarations like in a sappy romance novel, but I love you. I love you, body and mind and soul, and I love this rat fink dog more than I can ever say in just words. So I'll show you every damn day instead. I want to be in this with you. I know we're gonna fight, and you'll piss me off, and I'll piss you off, but I think we were meant to be together the moment I first laid eyes on you and decided I didn't like you."

A choked sob of half laughter escaped her lips.

"See, I told you I suck at this. I want to be happy, and you're the one who makes me happy. Happier than I've ever been in my whole sorry life. So, that's it. All of it. I love you, and I want you to take my sad ass back. What do ya say?"

Her eyes stung. It was the worst, best, most romantic speech she'd ever heard in her life. Better than Browning or Keats or Nicholas Sparks. Better than . . . everything.

"I say yes."

He closed the distance in three strides, shifted Pinky to the side, and kissed her. Long and deep and sweet, it was a kiss that promised a future and a life full of mess. Exactly the way she wanted it.

"I love you, too," she whispered against his mouth.

Pinky barked.

Suddenly, there was a loud clapping, and the two

clients stood up, one brushing away tears, and Kate choked up and stumbled over to them for a group hug. Kennedy patted her shoulder and shook her head.

"This is going to get us so many new clients," she whispered in her ear.

And then together, they all laughed.

And things were very, very good.

epilogue

"I HAVE TO SAY, that was one of the most romantic declarations of love I have ever heard," Kate said, refilling her drink.

Kennedy nodded. "Damn straight. Right in the league of my golf course declaration."

"And my matching leather recliners," Kate added.

"Don't forget Wolfe's announcement to my whole family," Gen said.

Arilyn giggled. "They were all epic. And well deserved."

Kennedy raised her martini glass. "Cheers. It's been a long road for each of us, but we did it together."

"There were a lot of bumps in that road, but we never lost sight of the goal," Kate said.

Arilyn sighed with pure pleasure. "What should we drink to?"

"Boys who are worthy of us?" Genevieve asked.

Kennedy rolled her eyes. "Silly girl, haven't you learned yet? We drink to us. Friendship. Female power. Earth Mother!"

"Yes!" they all shouted together. Glasses clinked, green liquid sloshed over the table, and Arilyn stretched out her feet on the braided rug, completely content. Her three best girlfriends had called for a night of celebration with pizza and apple martinis back at the bungalow. So far they were on their way to solidly tipsy and getting emotionally sloppy.

Ah, Stone was in for a surprise when he returned home. Sometimes drunk sex was so much damn fun.

"Speaking of Earth Mother, did we get rid of that love spell book?" Genevieve asked. "Did we ever decide if it worked or was just a scam?"

Arilyn hiccupped. "Scam."

Kate's eyes widened. "Wait a minute. Let's do a roll call. My list was all Slade. Kennedy said hers was Nate."

Gen spoke up. "I thought mine was my ex, but when I read it over, I realized all the qualities I wrote down were Wolfe. So that's three. Arilyn?"

She blinked, pleasantly buzzed, and thought over her list. After they had completed the love spell a year ago, right here in Gen's bungalow, they burned each of their lists in the fire. They were supposed to slip the second copy under their mattresses. Something about the power of unconscious sleep to make your soul mate appear. After she moved, she remembered finding the list and shoving it in one of her notebooks, thinking the whole idea had been a waste. After all, Jacob had cheated on her for the third time. She'd thought he was her soul mate.

But he wasn't. Stone Petty was.

"Huh. Wait a minute. I took the list and put it in one of my journals. I didn't think it worked. Let me get it." She found her journal on the small bookshelf, plucked out the plain piece of ledger paper, and carried it back to the table.

"What does it say?" Gen asked breathlessly.

Arilyn scanned the contents. Did it again. And again.

No. Way.

"You're killing us here, dudette. What's on the list? Did it work?" Kennedy asked.

Arilyn bit her lower lip. "I don't believe this. My list. These aren't Jacob's qualities at all. They're Stone's."

"Can you read it aloud?" Kate asked.

Arilyn cleared her throat. "Okay, here we go. A man who challenges me. A man who makes me laugh. A man I find sexy and dominating in bed." She fought a blush at Kennedy's cheer and went on. "A man who makes me feel alive. A man who's loyal. A man who won't cheat. A man who loves me with a desperation that doesn't make sense. A man who gives me all of him. A man who wants to share all of my life, including friends and family. A man who loves dogs. That's it."

"Definitely not Yoga Man. Girlfriend, that is Stone Petty. The love spell does work," Kennedy stated.

They looked at each other, unsure of how to process it. Gen finally spoke up. "I still have the book, you know."

Kate shivered. "When I touch it, I get an electrical shock. It's spooky."

"But powerful," Kennedy pointed out. "Ladies, we have stumbled upon the greatest gift a woman could find. A way to find our true soul mates."

Arilyn leaned against the aqua chair and pondered. "There is something about harnessing the power of our thoughts, wants, and needs to the universe. Maybe a combination of fire and writing and being with each other made the difference."

"Wow, between Kate's touch and *The Book of Spells*, we can make Kinnections the most famous place on earth!" Kennedy squealed.

Kate laughed. "Hold on, tiger. We are not going public with my witchlike abilities or the book. This stays between us. It's sacred."

"And we can use it for good," Arilyn said. "Is there someone else who needs it?"

They thought for a few minutes before Gen spoke up. "Izzy. She's changed. Can you imagine what meeting the right guy can do for her?"

"But she has to do the spell," Kate said. "That's a leap of faith. You have to want it."

Gen nodded. "I'll talk to her. Who knows? It's worth a shot."

"Good. In the meantime, Gen, you keep it safe, and we'll see what happens. Anything is possible," Kate said.

"Especially with us," Kennedy said.

Arilyn looked around the circle. "I love you guys."

"Back atcha, sweets," Kennedy said. Kate and Gen sniffed, overemotional from too many apple martinis, and they all squeezed together for a group hug.

Arilyn realized once again how finding love can change a person's life. Funny thing is, even before Stone, her life had already been blessed.

By true friendship.

acknowledgments

AH, SO MANY people to thank.

First off, a huge thanks to the Town of Montgomery Police Department, who welcomed me into the station when I came to ask a bunch of ridiculous questions and treated me with both respect and warmth. A huge shout-out to Officer Jason Meehan, who let me ride in his cool car for an official "ride along" and let me pepper him with what-if scenarios so I could create a truthful environment for Officer Stone Petty and his coworkers. Any mistakes I made are mine and mine alone. They are truly an exceptional team and I thank each and every one of them for keeping us safe.

Thanks to my editor, Lauren McKenna, who wanted me to write a cop story and refused to settle for anything less than perfection. It's a joy working with you. Thanks also to my agent, Kevan Lyon, for all the advice along the way.

Thanks to my local shelter, Pets Alive, who gave me my beloved Lester, and rescued the real pit bull Robert—who you can find living happily with his own Facebook page, Rockin' Robert, at www.facebook.com/RobertPetsAlive. Pets Alive works tirelessly to make sure all animals have a fair chance at love and a safe home. They inspired me to create another canine survivor in Pinky.

A shout-out to the Probst Posse, who help me with all of my books and are a great support system on this writing journey. You guys seriously rock.

Thank you to all my writing friends who keep me laughing and writing. I wish I could name them all here but there are just too many and you know who you are. You make every writing conference the absolute best!

If you enjoy the Searching For series, please tell your friends. Leave reviews. Help spread the word. I'd love to give a few more characters their happy ever afters. Don't forget that the original *Book of Spells* is available as an ebook for only $0.99 and includes an exclusive short story featuring Alexa and Nick from *The Marriage Bargain.*

Finally, as always, to my readers. Thank you for your emails, posts, tweets, and shout-outs. Thank you for your belief in me and my stories. Thank you for reading them and allowing me to write full-time, fulfilling the lifelong dream I've had since I was six years old. I love you all.